AN ACT OF PEACE

Klaus-Pierre is the love-child of a young Frenchwoman and a married German officer serving with the forces occupying Paris. His father is killed before he is born and his mother is rejected by her family of resistance workers, so Klaus-Pierre is sent to live with a maiden aunt in Provence, until his father's family learns of his existence and takes him to Germany. As he grows up he tries to make his own 'Act of Peace' with his French relatives. The result is a horrifying confrontation between the two families when they meet by accident in Provence.

AN ACT OF PEACE

AN ACT OF PEACE

by

Ann Widdecombe

Magna Large Print Books
Long Preston, North Yorkshire,
BD23 4ND, England.

3133619

British Library Cataloguing in Publication Data.

Widdecombe, Ann
 An act of peace.

 A catalogue record of this book is
 available from the British Library

 ISBN   978-0-7505-2710-1

First published in Great Britain in 2005 by Weidenfeld & Nicolson

Published in Large Print 2007 by arrangement with
Orion Publishing Group

Magna Large Print is an imprint of Library Magna Books Ltd.

Printed and bound in Great Britain by
T.J. (International) Ltd., Cornwall, PL28 8RW

For those who taught me at La Sainte Union Convent, Bath, especially Sister Mary Evangelista, Sister Bernard Xavier and Rosamond Rhymes, with gratitude and affection.

Author's note

In the 1950s I was growing up in Britain but Klaus-Pierre was growing up in West Germany and I have had to draw heavily on the recollections of others for a picture of life there at that time. In particular I am deeply indebted to Peter Meier and Hannelore Bartle for their memories of childhood in Northern Germany and to Ute Sampson for her family photos of that period. I am also much indebted to Hugh Williams for inviting me to Caux and describing its fascinating history. Any errors or anachronisms are entirely my own.

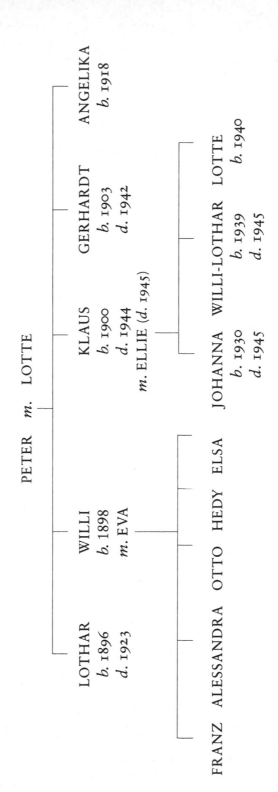

A simplified version of the von Ströbel Family Tree which Klaus-Pierre saw in the Library.

PETER   *m.*   LOTTE

LOTHAR
b. 1896
d. 1923

WILLI
b. 1898
m. EVA

KLAUS
b. 1900
d. 1944
m. ELLIE (*d.* 1945)

GERHARDT
b. 1903
d. 1942

ANGELIKA
b. 1918

FRANZ   ALESSANDRA   OTTO   HEDY   ELSA

JOHANNA
b. 1930
d. 1945

WILLI-LOTHAR
b. 1939
d. 1945

LOTTE
b. 1940

prologue

Berlin 1989

As I watch the young demonstrating in the streets I think of Paris in 1968, but then we were angry while the sounds which reach us now are those of rejoicing. Yesterday the last restrictions were lifted and people are pouring through the wall, families separated for more than a quarter of a century are embracing and not a single shot is fired.

Ernst has a piece of the wall; a small knob of concrete – unremarkable, symbolic, a remnant of a shattered, cruel regime. We stare at it with all the reverence men once showed the moon rock.

'Not another planet,' Kurt observes when I voice the thought, 'but another era. We watched that wall being built, your mother and I, and we grew so used to it that few thought it would fall in our lifetime.'

'We are witnessing the end of communism,' muses Ernst. 'The end of the cold war. Surely there can be no need for an arms race now? It's peace.'

'Peace,' repeats my mother, Catherine. Her tone is flat, sad even, and Ernst looks at her in surprise. His gaze travels to me and then to Kurt, and his puzzlement grows.

'None of you looks very pleased. I said it's peace. Is peace no longer a good thing?'

Kurt smiles. 'Peace is always good, Ernst, but it brings its own problems. A new enemy always rises upon the demise of the old.'

Ernst keeps his expression respectful enough but impatience tinges his tone when he says he supposes so and if nobody has any objection he will rejoin Willi-Klaus and their friends in the street and by the way would anyone like another bit of the wall?

Kurt laughs as Ernst leaves us. 'We spoiled it for him. They are so excited out there.'

We are all excited in here too. It was just the sudden use of the word *peace* which sent all our thoughts in the same direction, causing that momentary gloom so baffling to Ernst.

Peace. I look at the crippled Kurt, my step-father, for whom peace meant repatriation as a disabled prisoner of war straight into the oppression of Soviet occupation, a last-minute escape from East Berlin in the final wave of refugees before the wall went up, coming to terms with life as one of the war limbless in a country that had been all but destroyed and for whose inhabitants few could bring themselves to care.

He guesses my thoughts and glances at my mother whom peace had cast into a hell of hatred and isolation. I too look at her. She is still beautiful, an older, statelier version of the Catherine Dessin who should have been the toast of Paris, if my stepfather is to be believed. Instead, scorned as a Nazi's whore, disowned by those on whose love she relied, she had fled to the homeland of the enemy. *'I was happy during the war,'* she had once told me with conscienceless, shocking truth.

14

As for me, I had been three months old when the Second World War ended and I spent the first three decades of my life coming to terms with the peace. I look out at the dancing, celebrating, chanting crowds and see a woman weeping with emotion, two young girls hugging each other in ecstasy.

My mother comes to stand beside me. 'Thank God it's over,' she whispers.

I expect she said that when the war ended before she found out her ordeal was just beginning, before latent hatred turned into overt persecution, before I was old enough to want friends and playmates.

Our eyes meet and I know that she too is remembering. We look out together at the scene of euphoria below us and see only a house and garden in a small village near Aix-en-Provence.

one

Hatred in France

My start in life was unpromising. I was the illegitimate result of a wartime liaison between a senior and married German officer serving with the forces occupying Paris and a young, naïve French girl, whom he seduced when she was scarcely out of her convent school. My father was killed in an Allied strafing attack during the retreat from Paris and I was five before his family learned of my existence.

My maternal grandparents – patriots and resistance workers – disowned their daughter so completely that, estranged from both them and her siblings, she remained in Provence with the maiden aunt who had agreed to hide her as the Germans fled France and the tide of vengeance, at last undammed, swept across the country, destroying traitors, collaborators and those who had the bad taste to love the invader.

My grandfather, Pierre Dessin, an erstwhile professor of the Sorbonne, would have been quite willing to watch his erring, nineteen-year-old daughter suffer for her generous-hearted folly and, had he prevailed, Catherine Dessin would have been dragged through a jeering, spitting crowd with her head shaved, but his bitterness was thwarted by my father who, in the dying weeks of the Occupation, made sure my mother was many miles away, safe and hidden in the small Provençal village, where the woman I called Aunt Marie, a second cousin of my grandfather, taught infants and played the organ in church.

My earliest memories are of Aunt Marie's garden, of wide green lawns, rockeries and shrubberies, and a lily pond beside which I never seemed to stand alone but always with my hand firmly clasped in my mother's. Later I crouched beside its gently rippling water and sailed a boat, formed from the base of a matchbox, in the centre of which was glued an upright match from which fluttered a small piece of brightly coloured cloth. Later still I floated a yellow and red wooden battleship, its mast secured to my hand by string, lest it should float to the centre of the pond and tempt me to lean too far over to retrieve it.

In the middle of the large lawn was a sundial on which our cat, Macfidget, would often climb to doze. On summer evenings I would wave goodnight to him before my mother drew the curtains of my bedroom window and we prayed to my guardian angel to keep me safe during the night. This puzzled me because it was not the nights I feared but the days, especially the days when we left the haven of the garden and went Outside the Gate.

Outside the Gate was a foreign country full of hostile natives whom I feared so terribly that I would hide behind my mother if one approached, especially if it was a child native, for the children were spiteful and threatening while the grown-ups were merely cold and unfriendly. There were two, a brother and sister, who would always put out their tongues at me before crying, 'German brat! German brat!' and a third, a boy twice my size, who never failed to yell 'Nazi!' whenever he saw me.

Once, when I saw tears in my mother's eyes and was looking at her in ill-defined consternation, Aunt Marie crossed the road to remonstrate with his parents but their only reaction was a shrug. I could have told her that protest was useless, that Outside the Gate rudeness and bullying and tormenting were legitimate as long as I was the victim, that here the adults regarded me not as a small being to protect but as one who had no real right to be in their midst. I could have told her all that and more if I had known how to turn instinct into thought and thought into words.

I hated going Outside the Gate and most of our excursions beyond the garden were preceded by noisy scenes of weeping and pleading, my only means of communicating my dread. I sensed that Aunt Marie might have let me stay in my sanctuary but my mother was insistent. 'We cannot hide him away for ever,' was her oft-repeated refrain.

'Well, change his name,' Aunt Marie would retort.

My name is Klaus-Pierre but Aunt Marie as often as not called me Little Aeneas and my mother called me Klausi, especially when we spoke in our secret language which Aunt Marie could not understand. Outside the Gate they spoke like Aunt Marie and I had never met anyone who spoke our special, secret tongue, in which somehow Klaus seemed so much easier to say than Pierre.

Sometimes my mother held me to her, murmuring, *'Mein liebchen, liebchen Klausi.'* Even before I had any real notion of grammar I knew this phrase to be a nonsense, a piece of silliness unique to our small household, in much the same way that I knew lambs were not called woollies and Macfidget did not understand what I said to him when I ran my fingers through his smoky fur as he lay, purring, on the sundial.

I was called Klaus-Pierre after my father, General Klaus von Ströbel, and my grandfather, Pierre Dessin. It was to be many years before I understood the unintended cruelty of that decision. I did, however, learn very early that announcing my name was guaranteed to provoke hatred and derision, or at the very least a cold withdrawal.

'Why does Aunt Marie call me Aeneas?' I asked my mother, wondering if it might be more acceptable Outside the Gate.

'Because once there was a beautiful queen called Dido and a very brave man called Aeneas fell in love with her, but eventually he had to go away, far away across the sea and, when he had gone, Dido cried and cried and wished he had left her a baby Aeneas. You see, your daddy was also a brave man from far away, but when he went back he left me a baby: you. So I am luckier than Dido. I have my little Aeneas.'

'Were you a beautiful queen?'

My mother smiled, not with her usual amused indulgence but with wistfulness, her eyes briefly focused on a scene played long ago. 'Not a queen, no, but I was beautiful. That is why your daddy fell in love with me.'

'Will he come back to see us?'

'No. He is in heaven.'

'Why?'

'Because Jesus wanted him.'

I thought it decidedly selfish of Jesus to take my father away and I added a prayer to my usual quota, petitioning each night for my father's return, until my mother overheard me one evening and urged me never to do so again because my father was happy in heaven and we would all be together one day. I would, she promised me, understand when I was older.

It seemed there were many things which I could do when I was older. I would go to school and know a great deal about everything. I could stay up late and eat what I liked. I could own a dog and take it for walks and no words would be too hard to read, no sums too difficult to add up. I could also go Outside the Gate alone.

I had no ambition to go Outside the Gate at all, but I had seen grown-ups coming and going through it and, almost always, they were alone. Perhaps then, when I was a man and peered on the child natives from a great height, it would be safe to venture through. Occasionally children came through the Gate with some visiting grown-up, and I came to realise that when this happened they did not hurl abuse at me or sneer, but nor did they play, and when I rushed up to them my mother or Aunt Marie always called me away. I would edge backwards, watched curiously by the child and with relief by the adult.

This even happened on the occasion when Mathilde brought her children, Hélène and René. Mathilde came once a week to do the washing and, although I was used to watching my mother work in the house or garden, I somehow sensed that the work Mathilde did was different, that hers was a lowlier status, that when my mother scraped vegetables and cooked and washed up she did it for herself and Aunt Marie, that such things were a normal part of being a grown-up, that everybody did them in their own homes, but that Mathilde must do them for others and at the whim and behest of others. I do not think I ever saw Mathilde receive her pay but, even so, I knew she was an employee and that I was ranked with the employer, though I knew neither word.

By the same subconscious process of reasoning I thought Hélène and René were my inferiors, that they would no more dare to insult me than would Mathilde my mother or Aunt Marie. They must have been two or three years older, and when my mother shooed us all out into the garden and told us to play outside because she wanted to wash the kitchen floor, I was half frenzied with excitement and, my fears forgotten, I ran about wildly before wandering up to them to see what we would play.

'We can't play with you,' sniffed Hélène in disgust. 'You're much too little.'

I knew she wanted to say I was the German brat but did not dare.

'Mummy said you have to play with me.'

René was more subtle. 'We can play fighting the Germans. You can be the Boche and I'll be the Maquis. Hélène can be the nurse.'

I may have lacked the skills to analyse what was being proposed but my instinct told me that this was not play, that it was personal, that it was a means of legitimising Inside the Gate what went on Outside. I shook my head.

'Baby,' sneered Hélène, but her contempt turned to alarm when tears squeezed from my eyes. She glanced towards the house.

René rescued her. 'Let's play catch. We'll run and you can try and catch us.'

They sprinted away across the lawn and dived into the shrubberies. At first I raced after them enthusiastically but then they disappeared and, when I had hunted in vain, I knew I would not find them until it was time for them to go. I did not mind being outwitted but I could not bear being so hated and I collapsed on the ground, wailing loudly, until my mother came out and scooped me up, muttering words of comfort. I kicked and struggled until she put me down, holding my face between her hands, trying to force me to look at her.

I pulled my head back, away from her, and sent a scream into the air which seemed to travel to the very heavens. Far above me a rook flew and I yearned for its freedom, for its easy ability to escape the bonds of earth by wheeling and flapping through the skies. So intensely did I envy it that I could almost have put the thought into my three-year-old vocabulary.

Hélène and René never came again and, after a while, nor did Mathilde.

However safe I was Inside the Gate, I could still hear the children and, though I feared them and would always flee if one walked by, I was lonely and unhappy. My mother and Aunt Marie were kind but they could not fulfil the role of playmates. Sometimes I tried, cautious and afraid, to see what was happening Outside the Gate, peering through the bushes which divided our garden from the road. At first I was easily spotted and the cry of 'German brat!' soon brought my mother from the house, but in time I learned to hide more effectively and spent hours staring at small girls with skipping ropes and boys kicking footballs. I learned the principle of tag without ever having played it, I knew who owned which tricycle and I followed the adventures of the Germans and the French as children acted out scenes from the war and made up their own stories. In these games everyone wanted to be French and the Germans always lost.

Once an arrow flew over the gate and landed on the gravel path. I left my hiding place to retrieve it, looking at its bright red point, its pale green tail. A child came up to the gate and called out to me that it was his and I must return it to him. I shook my head and held the arrow behind my back.

'Oh, come on. I'll tell your mother if you don't.'

Again I shook my head, aware that for once I had power over those strange beings Outside the Gate, that I had something they wanted. Other children had begun to gather and all were clamouring for me to hand over the toy. One had paint on his face and feathers in a band around his head.

'It's the German brat,' said one of the older girls in disgust. 'What a little thief.'

I began to back away, suddenly frightened, uncertain if those Outside the Gate could invade my own territory, wanting to call out for my mother, knowing I faced a chorus of scorn if I did so. For a few seconds I hesitated, then I threw the arrow on the ground and ran towards the house, pursued by cries of 'Nazi' and 'Coward'.

Aunt Marie appeared in the doorway. 'What are you doing?' Her voice was sharp with displeasure and, for a moment, I wondered what wrong I had done, but her gaze was on something behind me and, turning, I saw that the child with the Indian feathers had come onto our path and was at that moment bending to retrieve the arrow. I kept behind Aunt Marie as she advanced on the trespasser with angry purpose.

'What is your name?'

'Louis,' he mumbled, and I was aware that there was silence in the strange country which was Outside the Gate.

'Louis what?'

'Louis Lenoir.'

'Well, Louis Lenoir, next time you need to retrieve something from this garden I suggest you ring the bell and ask if you may do so. Hasn't your mother told you that it's bad manners to wander about in other people's gardens without their permission?'

He crept away and joined the now silent group Outside the Gate, leaving me triumphant, gloating, secure. My enemies had no power in my own territory. I could walk up to the very gate with impunity, could defy them, snatch their toys even, and as long as I stayed in our garden they would be unable to exact any revenge. The thought gave me only fleeting comfort: I wanted friends, not defeated foes.

Then, miraculously, friends arrived. I was in the garden, building mud castles from the wet earth, when my mother called out that she was going indoors to speak to Aunt Marie. All day I had listened to the sounds of children playing next door, their noise seeming very near. Instinctively I knew these children were not from the village. I recognised none of their voices; there had never in the past been any child in the neighbouring garden and, above all, they too had a secret language, different from that which I spoke with my mother. I heard them talking and knew the way they spoke would be as incomprehensible to the village children as it was to me. They seemed to switch between this funny language and French quite happily, often in the same conversation. I knew one of the children must be very young because, although I heard the others speak to her with exaggerated simplicity, I did not hear anything but babble in reply.

It was impossible to penetrate the thick hedge which separated the two gardens so I ran to the gate and peered up and down the road, but there was no sign of the hostile natives. I tried unsuccessfully to reach the catch and pull the gate open, before starting to climb over. When I stood on the third bar I became aware that I was very far from the ground but I climbed on, terrified when I found myself at the top, but still drawn by the sound of voices. On the other side I ran, knowing I was now in enemy territory and that it would be a hard, slow business to return to safety.

The children next door saw me as I was climbing their gate and the boy ran down the path to meet me. I hesitated but he was grinning, so I completed my descent into his garden.

'*Diable!*' he said in tones of admiration and at once I was reassured because I knew it was a bad word which only grown-ups were allowed to say.

'That was a hard climb for a baby.'

I protested that I was not a baby and he laughed. 'I'm Nick. What's your name?'

'Klaus-Pierre.'

'I'm glad you're a boy. I'm fed up playing with girls.'

'So am I,' I said loftily, conscious that I was lying but wanting very much to be part of his world.

'Let's play pilots and bomb the girls.' He flung

his arms out wide and began to run about, imitating the noise of an aeroplane, occasionally running up to his sisters crying, 'Whoosh, bang, got you!' causing them to squeal with delight.

'My dad flies planes. He bombed the Germans. What does your father do?'

I was on the verge of trumping the boast, of announcing that my father had been a general, which I knew to be very important, when concepts began to join up in my head so suddenly that there was an almost audible click. The *German* brat. The *Germans* always lost in the childish games I watched being played Outside the Gates. My dad bombed the *Germans*. We must not speak *German* to Aunt Marie because she does not understand. Your father was a general in the *German* army. Why do you have to say Klaus in so emphatic a *German* accent – you must surely see it makes it worse for him here? *German* brat! *German* brat! *German* brat!

The voices of Nick, my mother, Aunt Marie and the children Outside the Gate ran through my head and, amidst their din, I arrived at some kind of childish understanding before becoming aware that Nick was looking at me curiously.

'My father's dead. He was killed in the war.'

'Oh, sorry. But we won.'

Did we? Was I part of 'we'? In that moment I understood what my mother had always told me but which, until that instant of revelation, had been of no more importance than what I ate for lunch. I was both German and French. What she had not said was that I was therefore neither one nor the other, that I had no identity, that I

26

belonged nowhere.

I could not then have articulated any of this but I knew it all nonetheless, so much so that even now I can see the innocent expression on Nick's face when he asked me what my father did. Nevertheless, the period immediately following this incident was a happy one. I heard my mother and Aunt Marie calling me but I was much too engrossed with my new companions to answer and, by the time they had worked out where I was, I was firm friends with Nick, Alice and one-year-old Julienne who amused me with her determination to be part of a much older group. Wherever we ran she crawled after us at high speed. When we were still she hauled herself up by grasping the nearest convenient object and stood there, watching us, clutching on to the support with all her puny might. I had never before had anyone younger or weaker than myself to look after and I adored her.

Nick, whom I found with surprise to be only a few months older than me despite being taller and sturdier, had a shiny new tricycle and his father, speaking to me in funny French, was teaching me to ride it when my mother and Aunt Marie arrived, anxious and wondering.

There followed two months of play and laughter, punctuated by only the occasional quarrel, quickly made up. My new neighbours came to tea and I was sick, less from the unusual amount of cake than from sheer excitement. Eventually the others were joined by more friends. I remember Marcel, who had bright ginger hair, and the very Louis Lenoir whom Aunt Marie had rebuked so sternly. I was teased much less but I still knew the chill of disapproval.

Nick's grandmother disapproved, and when I played next door I hated going inside. Nick's father had taken me under his wing and talked to me as if we were man to man while his mother spoiled me, but her own mother had never acknowledged me in all the time I had lived in the house next to hers and she was not inclined to do so now. I suppose they must have argued about it and Nick's parents had won. Louis Lenoir's elder sister, who always came to collect him when it was time for us to disperse, would invariably make a point of talking warmly to all the other children before turning to me with brief, dutiful, reluctant formality. I was afraid of her, and if my elders had not insisted that I say goodbye to each child and wave him off I should have hidden as soon as I saw her approaching the house.

I learned too that my acceptability was confined to my own house and to Nick's, that I still could not join the other children in their gardens or in the small village play area with its swings and slide without incurring abuse or teasing so hostile that it amounted to bullying. Nick stoutly defended me on these occasions and once Alice fought an older girl, pulling her hair and slapping her in furious indignation. Invariably we would go back home and tell Nick's parents who would comfort me while his grandmother sat tight-lipped, her expression saying more clearly than words: 'I told you so.'

Nick's father, Mr Dyer, was an English airman who had married Marie-Louise Lecompte before the war and taken her to live in Britain. As a result, she had not seen her mother for nine years and the family was now making an extended visit of two months following Mr Dyer's demobilisation. Other members of the family came to see them and occasionally Nick and Alice stayed with us to make room for visiting relations.

Through these gatherings I came to understand that most children lived with a mother and a father, not with a mother and an aunt. I had always known this from the stories my mother or Aunt Marie read to me but the idea had meant little to me until now. Once, when the children next door had been taken to Paris for a week to see relatives and I was again lonely, I climbed onto a chair and stared at the photograph of my father which stood on the chest of drawers in my mother's bedroom. Somewhere in the back of my infant mind was a sense of unfairness, a vague resentment that my father had died, the beginning of a belief that it was his fault he had done so, a small seed of blame.

I told my mother I wanted to have two sisters and that one must be like Alice and one like Julienne and, when that demand had been gently batted away, I asked why I could not have a granny, although I was by no means sure I wanted one if she was like Nick's. I had, however, seen pictures of grannies in my story books and knew that, in general, they had buns of grey hair and looked kindly over the tops of spectacles as they sat by fires, knitting, with cats on their laps. I had an idea that this was the norm and Nick's elegant, cold grandmother was the exception, especially as even she spoiled her grandchildren and cooed over Julienne.

Aunt Marie threw a worried glance at my mother. 'So now it begins,' she muttered.

My mother told me I did have a granny but that she lived far, far away in Paris and when I protested that Nick, Alice and Julienne had gone there she told me we were too poor to do so. I accepted the explanation with a grumble but without disbelief.

Before the Dyers went back to England, Alice had a fifth birthday and Madame Lecompte gave her a party to which a dozen or so children were invited. Post-war austerity and scarcity meant that on these occasions everyone helped with the food, and the smell of Aunt Marie's baking drifted up the stairs to my room the night before the event. I lay in bed, happily expectant, too excited to sleep, untroubled by a future in which my friends were about to disappear, oblivious to the consequences, knowing they were leaving the following week and yet convinced my world would continue as it then was.

During the party I found myself arguing with Louis Lenoir that my boat was bigger than his boat and so fierce did the battle become that I decided to go home and get my precious red and yellow battleship, which by then had become faded and chipped but was still magnificent to my adoring eyes. I found it by the pond but, as I was about to return next door, I remembered something I wanted to ask my mother and, the large glass door at the back of the house being open, I ran inside, impatient to put my question.

From the kitchen I could hear Aunt Marie's voice. At first I noticed nothing unusual, but, as I crossed the living room into the hall, something in her tone caused me first to hesitate and then to stop altogether. I had never before heard her arguing with my mother and indeed I vaguely thought that grown-ups did not argue.

'...hell for him when those children leave. It will all start again. You must get him away from here. Make peace with your father, call the poor little thing Pierre instead of that silly name you gave him and speak to him in French instead of German.'

'No. He is Klaus's son. I will not teach him to disown his father.'

'He will do that of his own accord once he is old enough to understand and realises what his father did to you. Bloody Klaus von Ströbel!'

My mother was crying as I crept away. I could make little, if any, sense of what I had heard but I was conscious of unease and an ill-defined fear. Grown-ups should not quarrel and cry – that surely was the lot of children – and nor should they dislike each other if they belonged to the same family, yet the one strong impression I had received from that incomprehensible exchange was that Aunt Marie did not like my father. A few minutes later I had all but forgotten the incident, as Louis and I placed our boats side by side and I gave a yell of triumph.

I remembered again when the party was over and I was playing with Alice while the adults cleared up the debris. Mrs Dyer was upstairs putting Julienne to bed and Nick was helping his

31

father to stack the outside toys in the shed. The only grown-up in the room was Madame Lecompte to whom I rarely dared to speak unless addressed first, but now my question seemed suddenly too urgent to wait.

'What does bloodyklausvastrudel mean?'

I backed away as her voice rose in outrage asking me how I dared to swear in her house, in front of Alice and after they had all been so kind to me. I did not even know what swearing meant but I was sent home in disgrace nonetheless, howling with bewilderment, my feelings hurt and my heart bursting with indignation and misery.

At home they could not calm me for an hour but when my mother finally made sense of the situation, Aunt Marie went next door to apologise, to explain that I had heard the word from her, that I did not know what it meant. She came back looking uncharacteristically angry.

'The Dyers said it would have been funny if Klaus-Pierre had not been so upset. I think they are horribly embarrassed by the whole thing but Madame is immoveable and it is her house.'

I later found that her words meant I could not go next door again and, for the few remaining days of their visit, Nick and Alice came to our house when we wanted to be together. When the day of their departure arrived I stood at our gate and waved, as Madame Lecompte stood at hers. She did not once look in our direction but I was relieved rather than regretful, disliking and fearing her.

'I wonder what it will be like now?' said Aunt Marie as we went indoors, but the words seemed insignificant, the type of comment grown-ups often made, and I did not invest them with any ominous importance.

Innocently I waited for Marcel and Louis to turn up on my doorstep again but they did not do so and nor did any of the other children with whom I had played over the last two months. When my mother took me to the small recreation area, those already there seemed to melt away but it was a while before first the teasing and then the bullying returned. When the wretched chanting began again, I shouted back, tears flowing, but soon learned to run and hide because it was easier and my tormentors gave up their persecution more quickly than when I gave battle.

Occasionally the adults intervened and I sensed greater kindness from the grown-up world and from time to time in older children but among my own age group I was an outcast, the rejection more painful than before because I had all but forgotten it and, with the easy adaptability of childhood, had assumed my recent status would last for ever.

My mother began to talk about moving somewhere else, with more determination than before, and especially before I should be old enough to go to school, a prospect which had held neither wonder nor terror for me because I had no concept of what school entailed. Alice was due to start school on return to England, but that was the only context in which it had entered our conversation. Now repeated anxious references to that time, still years ahead, when I must daily learn and play with a whole class of children my own age, did nothing to enlighten me but much to alarm.

Towards the end of 1948, when memories of its happy spring had all but disappeared, we ourselves had a visitor to stay. An old schoolfriend of my mother, whom she called Bette and I Mademoiselle, arrived from Paris. My mother had told me she was my godmother who sent me cards on my birthday and, because Aunt Marie was also my godmother, I was vaguely surprised to find our guest young, fashionable and with a forceful personality. Her impatience with my mother created an impression much less vague, especially when I realised that Aunt Marie agreed with this Bette lady more often than with my mother.

Naturally I thought my mother sure to be right and I became very uncertain in the presence of her friend, except when she took me into the village because it was soon apparent that the hostile natives were afraid of her. In an early encounter with a jeering boy some three years older than myself she marched into the school to complain to the headmaster, after which I suffered somewhat less, the bullies keeping a wary lookout for her appearance on the scene, but the respite lasted no longer than her visit.

Bette often referred to Paris and once I asked her if she knew my granny. I had accepted without question my mother's explanation that we were too poor to travel there but had never forgotten that I had a granny in this far away place. Bette's 'yes' was half-formed before she caught my mother's warning look. I sensed her wariness and knew immediately that this was one of those cases where the grown-ups had secrets I

34

was not allowed to share. Usually I forgot about such moments but this one lingered in my mind, shrouding my grandmother with a dark mystery, and I was no longer able to picture her looking benignly over spectacles as she sat by the fire with a cat on her lap.

Yet I still yearned to go to Paris and, a few months after my fourth birthday, in the June of 1949, my wish was at last granted. My great-grandfather died and my mother decided we should both go to the funeral. I sensed that Aunt Marie was less enthusiastic, but I was too excited to give her attitude much attention and even more so when I learned I would not only see my granny but also my great-granny and some uncles and aunts.

'You will like your Uncle Edouard,' my mother said before going on to warn me that my great-granny would still be very sad about the death and might be too upset to be friendly and that my grandfather, her own papa, was so strict that sometimes he did not speak to children at all.

It was a wretchedly inadequate preparation for the reception awaiting me in Paris. Whatever hatred I had encountered in Provence had been from outside my home and family and it never occurred to me that such an ugly force could disfigure my life from any connection of my mother's. I still divided the world into home and Outside the Gate and could not think of grannies or aunties as having any characteristics similar to the hostile natives.

Even now I cannot blame my mother. She thought that my age would be my protection, that even if her relatives could feel no affection for me they were all responsible adults who would not seek deliberately to wound a child. If she could place no hope in their forgiveness she believed that she could place confidence in their reason. Anyway I was still only four years of age and she could hardly explain that I was the product of her illicit relationship with a married enemy, that she had been called a traitor and disowned by those among whom she now proposed to take me, that she had not a single friend in Paris beyond Bette and a priest, that she had defied and shamed her family for years, that people could despise those whose parents had no marriage certificate and could feel ill-will throughout their lives towards those who gave comfort to their persecutors.

Nor could she explain in any terms which I might understand that my single biggest crime was to be a German in France now that peace had broken out, that though I was called Dessin most of those who bore the same name would regard me as a von Ströbel but that no von Ströbel had ever heard of me.

Ignorant of it all, I spent the long train journey to Paris jumping up and down with excitement, telling the strangers who shared our carriage that I was going to see Granny. Ignorant also, they beamed at me and told me that I was a lucky boy and would have a wonderful time.

two

Love in Germany

'Klausi, please try to understand.'

My mother held me by the shoulders and looked at me with pleading eyes. She had crouched down to my level and was peering directly in my face from a distance of inches. It was the posture she always adopted when she wanted my earnest attention.

'My grandfather has gone to heaven and everyone is missing him. People are going to be very sad at this funeral and if you keep on jumping up and down like this you will simply make them all annoyed and they will think you are rude and naughty. I want Granny to believe you are a good little boy so that you can come to Paris again.'

I heard the implied threat and was briefly sobered but the nearer we drew to the church the more difficult I found it to be still and quiet. I had a granny and a great-granny and uncles and aunts just like all the other children. They would be certain to spoil me and give me treats because that was what grannies and aunties did. Nick said so, and indeed every time he had met a relative he had a toy, game or outing to prove his point. Even if they were too poor to do any of that they would love me and want to cuddle me.

My mother had told me that today I must

speak only French, that I must not, absolutely must not, speak in our secret language, which I now knew to be called German and in reality not to be secret at all. They spoke it in Germany where my father had lived. She had said that it would be unkind not to speak in French because other people would not understand and would feel left out, but some instinct told me this was not the real reason and I almost succeeded in translating that feeling into a clear thought, which hovered just out of reach and would have told me that if I spoke German people would not like me because nobody liked a German.

My mother reminded me now, with urgency, and I nodded, impatient to arrive, yearning to be embraced by Granny, the language in which we would enthusiastically greet each other seeming but a trivial consideration. As soon as we entered the church gate, I looked along the path to the steps on which was assembled a party of black-clad mourners. At once my mother slowed her steps and I sensed uncertainty, perhaps alarm. I looked up at her and saw her staring at the group.

I tugged impatiently at her restraining hand, pointing with my free one at an older woman on the left of the small cluster. 'Who's that?'

'Your granny. Don't point. It's rude.'

I gave one immense pull and broke away from her, running along the path as fast as I could lest she catch up with me and once more imprison me in her grasp.

'Granny!' I shouted. 'Granny!'

Her reply was given in a gentle tone but it was final, admitting no contradiction. 'No, sorry, I am not your granny.'

My mother had made a mistake. I turned and ran back down the path calling to her. 'That's not Granny. Which one's Granny? Hurry, we must find Granny.'

She had come to a halt halfway along the path and both she and Aunt Marie were staring at the group on the church steps. My mother's expression was blank but Aunt Marie's was outraged. I joined them, still pleading for help with finding Granny, but something in their faces, in their stillness, caused me to be suddenly quiet. I turned to look back at the lady who was not Granny and for a few seconds we looked at each other. Beside her was a man with an angry face and beside him a boy of about twelve, who looked impassively on the scene, and two young women looking embarrassed but unfriendly.

Miserably I understood. This *was* Granny, as my mother had said, and these were my uncles and aunts, and that very old lady just behind them was Great-Granny and they did not like me or want to know me because half of me was German. I might have cried had I not been so frightened, for what disturbed me more than my own rejection was their expression as their eyes moved from me to my mother, a collective grimace of scorn and shame.

We sat at the back of the church and, at the graveside, stood away from the family mourners. I looked about me, more from boredom than from curiosity, and noticed covert glances from people who stood with their heads bowed. My mother stood straight, head up, staring at nothing. For a few seconds I looked up at her and then I too lifted up my head and squared my shoulders, trying to copy her expression, as I absorbed my first lesson in pride.

I heard only one exchange between our small group and theirs. As we left, Aunt Marie waited for the man with the angry face to disengage himself from the embrace of a weeping woman before saying in clear, ringing tones, which caused many a head to turn: 'For shame, Pierre Dessin. The child is only four.'

'And Martin was only twenty-two.'

Aunt Marie said something else but I could not hear what it was because my mother was towing me firmly towards the gate, looking neither to right nor left. As we passed through it, the priest caught up with us and asked to see my mother before she left Paris. He looked kindly at me and, despite my newfound pride, a tear squeezed from my eye and rolled sadly down my nose.

In the days which followed our return to Provence I sensed anger in my mother and something akin to despair in Aunt Marie. The words Cahors and Versailles were frequently mentioned and long telephone conversations took place. I began to understand that we might move house and live with some relatives of Aunt Marie in these places, but we were still in the same house a year later.

It was about this time that the Letters started coming. The first one was very large and thick. I know this because my mother showed it to me and told me it was from my godmother Bette, who I knew had gone to live in Germany with her new husband, who was something called a dippy-bat.

'Diplomat. This is a very important letter and Mummy must read it very carefully. Do you think you can listen to the wireless all on your own today?'

I nodded and she switched on my daily programme. I might have forgotten the incident altogether but for the fact that the Letter appeared everywhere. Aunt Marie read it at supper and I often saw my mother re-reading it in the days which followed. She was tense and, after a few more days, I realised another Letter was expected.

When it eventually arrived, Aunt Marie kept me away from my mother while she read it, for some strange reason glancing worriedly at the ceiling as she gave me supper and then at the landing when she was bathing me. From my mother's room came absolute silence and Aunt Marie fidgeted with anxiety as she read to me and settled me for the night. When I asked when Mummy would say goodnight, she gently shushed me and told me my mother had a most important Letter.

Letters were clearly very serious matters and I began to stare at the post with respect and wonder, thinking that any of the missives which Aunt Marie laid on the hall table might cause my mother to disappear to her room for hours on end.

Years later I was to learn that Bette had encountered an old friend of my father's in Berlin, a junior officer from the days of the Occupation. He had been keeping a letter which my father had been writing to my mother when he died and this was the one which had caused Aunt Marie so

41

much anxiety on my mother's account for it was stained with the dried blood of his terrible injuries. Bette's previous letter had been to tell my mother of its existence.

My father's friend was called Kurt Kleist and Bette told him that Catherine Dessin had had a child from the affair, that both he and she had been disowned and were living with a distant relative in Provence, that I, the child, was being visited with the sins of my father and was hated and bullied. Kurt wrote at once to my father's family but, uncertain how such news would be received, he did not confide this to Bette.

I suppose my mother might have made an attempt to contact the von Ströbels herself but for the obvious problem of my father's widow and their children. Now Kurt told Bette that she had died, along with two of their children, in the Dresden bombing, that only the baby had survived, having been left behind on account of a minor ailment when the others travelled to Dresden to be with the widow's mother who was dying.

Of course, I knew none of this at the time, but after the Letters came the Lady. I had been playing outside and, the day being hot and dry, had come into the house for some shade and a cold drink. I was on my way out again when there was a knock on the front door and I stood on tiptoe to open it. A lady stood on the doorstep and I stared back at her with wonder. She was tall and smart and a bit younger than Aunt Marie but I noticed none of those characteristics. What caused me to stare was that she looked so pleased to see me.

'You must be Klaus-Pierre? I am your Aunt Angelika.'

I had an aunty who was pleased to see me. She had spoken to me in French but I knew that her natural language was the one I spoke to my mother and it was in that tongue that I replied, watching the delight in her face as I did so. Afterwards my mother had asked me how I had known she was German but I was unable to offer any explanation. Perhaps it was the way she herself spoke French, confidently but with an accent that was not the same as the accent Nick's father had. Perhaps. All I could say then and all I can say now is that I *knew*.

Aunt Angelika stayed some days and I wept when she left.

That night my mother bathed me and put me to bed as usual but instead of reading to me she began to tell me a story, *my* story. Once upon a time there had been a beautiful lady living in Paris with her mummy and daddy and brothers and sisters who were very clever. This lady was called Catherine and her grandparents also lived in the same house. Grandmère was very strict but Grandpère was kind and loved her dearly. They were all very happy but then a war broke out and her older brother went away to fight. Her other brother was only a baby, just walking.

The war was between the Germans and the French. At first the Germans were winning and they marched into Paris and stayed there many years. One of them, Klaus, was brave and handsome and he fell in love with Catherine but they didn't have time to get married because the

Germans started to lose the war and he was sent away. Meanwhile Catherine's family was so cross that she had loved an enemy that she too had to leave Paris but she had a very kind aunty who hid her until the war was over.

Klaus died before the war ended but Catherine had a little baby to remind her of him. At first she was very happy living in the country with her aunty and the dear little baby but people still hated the Germans and were very cruel to the child as he grew up. Then one day another beautiful lady appeared. She was Klaus's sister, Angelika, and she told Catherine not to be unhappy because the little child had a big family in Germany: a dear old granny and an uncle, aunty, cousins and a half-sister. The half-sister was called Lotte and Klaus was her father too because once, long ago, Klaus had married and had three children, but his wife and two of the children had died in the war so poor little Lotte was an orphan.

Then Catherine took the child and went to Germany to live in a big house with this large family and they were all happy ever after.

Thus was the tale of shame, betrayal, adultery, illegitimacy, hatred and estrangement presented for my infant consumption. I believed it un-critically and, largely oblivious to the doubt and impending separation from Aunt Marie which sobered the adults, I talked non-stop about Germany and the big house and big family. Even Aunt Marie lost patience and told me to hush. I was encouraged to play outside where I poured my happiness into the uncomprehending ears of Macfidget.

'You're coming too,' I told him but he remained resolutely asleep on the sundial, unmoved by the news and the wonderful future opening before us.

I made the mistake of telling the natives. There were two playing Outside the Gate and they stopped to stare at me before calling abuse. This now happened only occasionally rather than constantly, but today it did not matter because I knew I was to escape their persecution. I made a rude face and announced triumphantly that I was going to Germany to live in a big house. Throughout the weeks which elapsed before we finally left the cries pursued me whenever one of my tormentors spotted me: 'Goodbye. Good riddance.'

This time adults did protest and I saw one girl receive a sharp smack on the bottom as she stood chanting Outside the Gate, unaware of her approaching mother. The flames of hatred were waning but I felt not the slightest regret or sentimental tug when the hour of our departure arrived. Aunt Marie hugged me tightly and, embarrassed, I wriggled away.

A large car, driven by a uniformed chauffeur, drew up at our gate and Aunt Marie asked, in tones of wonder, who had lost the war. Children, then returning from school, stared and I knew that in their gaze was envy and something akin to respect. I, Klaus-Pierre Dessin, their despised victim, was making a grand, triumphal exit as I headed into a fairy-tale future.

'How on earth did they manage that? The petrol...' Aunt Marie's words trailed off into soundless awe.

'Angelika could manage anything.'

'Herr *General* von Ströbel,' muttered Aunt Marie, and I sensed displeasure.

'I shouldn't think that has anything to do with it,' my mother snapped. 'Bette says even the grandest Germans are slogging away at menial tasks just to feed their families. I suspect this is merely a gesture to show those awful kids that Klaus-Pierre might have been worth knowing after all.'

I saw tears in my mother's eyes as she got in to the car beside me and for the first time I understood fully that I would not see Aunt Marie again for a long time and that I would miss her. I knelt up on the seat and waved through the back window until she was out of sight. In the days and weeks to come I was often to pretend that she was still with us and I would hold imaginary conversations with her.

As we drove along, people stopped to stare at the car and I waved enthusiastically. My departure from that small village is etched in my mind with the expressions of those who watched us go. Most grown-ups looked amazed, some grinned ruefully and waved back to me, others were outraged at such a display. An older boy who had once called me a Nazi bastard looked on in disbelief but then his resentment gave way, visibly and dramatically, to amused defeat and he called out, 'Good luck, German brat!'

Two of my tormentors ran beside the car to see how long they could keep up with it. The next door neighbour, who had not spoken a word to me since I was shamefully ejected from her hearth for unintentional profanity, turned a stony face towards me as we glided past her outside the butcher's shop; an old man lifted his stick in a friendly gesture of farewell; a dog barked as if to menace the car; the occupants of an ancient Citroën stared so hard that their vehicle swerved violently and a nearby pedestrian called out in alarm.

In Aix-en-Provence itself we attracted a few curious glances and it was a shock when we arrived at the station and had to leave the car behind. A porter helped us with our six or so cases and Macfidget's carrier and installed us in a first-class carriage on the train. Here there were more glances, of mixed surprise and disapproval, as if others in the same compartment would have disputed our right to be there. Indeed, as long as there was other space to occupy, travellers avoided us, deterred by the profusion of cases, yowling cat and voluble small boy.

It is only in hindsight that I see that journey in terms of its changing landscape, from the quaint hilltops of Provence through vineyard country, then the mountains and forests of Germany, only in that same retrospect that I can understand the tortuous route we took to avoid changing in Paris because my mother had sworn an oath never to return there. At the time I was aware only of alternating sleep and boredom and, in my waking moments, of irritation at the continued vocal protests of Macfidget.

I remember a young couple who briefly sat with us and talked to me, the strange sensation of believing that we were moving while my mother tried to convince me that we were still stationary and it was the other train which was moving, the glimpses of passengers on passing trains. I recall vividly my mother's harassed efforts to move our luggage when we changed trains, the night in a small hotel when Macfidget wailed and scratched at the door for so long that the guests in the next room banged angrily on the wall.

I suppose I must have noticed that people calling to each other on platforms were suddenly doing so in German rather than French but what I actually remember was my mother's response when I came drowsily out of sleep and asked, for what must have seemed to her like the millionth time, how much longer we must travel.

'You must not speak in French now. I do not want to hear French again.'

Now I can understand well enough the doubts which must have assailed her. She told me in later years that her worst moment on that journey was when she heard, for the first time since 1944, male voices calling to each other in German and the memories of the Occupation came flooding into her consciousness, memories of persecution, bullying, intimidation, executions. For an instant she wanted to turn back but then she remembered a very different persecution and instead held to the course she had taken, emphasising the decision by telling me to speak henceforth only in German.

I had known for weeks that I was going to spend the rest of my childhood in a house full of other children but when Uncle Willi met us at the station and introduced two small girls as Lotte and Elsa, I at once hid behind my mother, briefly convinced I was meeting hostile natives. They took

48

pity on me, coaxing instead of sneering, and by the time the grown-ups were loading the car we were chatting away merrily and our conversation as we drove through the countryside of northern Germany gave me the first of many surprises.

Baffled, I endured the hilarity and mimicking with which Lotte and Elsa greeted my German pronunciation. My mother, of course, would have always spoken German with a French accent and, not having heard the language for six years, had no opportunity to improve her linguistic performance, no chance to fine-tune her mastery of the tongue. Taught by her, I spoke as she did and assumed everyone whose native language was German did the same. Perhaps my mother was equally unaware of the inadequacy of my command of the language for certainly she never warned me that the Germans I was about to meet might have difficulty in understanding me. At first I was disconcerted, then curious, then determined that I would speak German as convincingly as my cousin and half-sister.

Macfidget kept up his noisy protests and the girls told him to be quiet, trying to peer into his carrier, endeavouring to coax him into silence with reassurances about what he would find at his journey's end. I told them it was no use and, in the end, they gave up with puzzled expressions.

When we at last arrived, the house looked huge, causing me to feel less impressed than intimidated. A tall, elderly woman appeared on the doorstep and I asked my mother who it was.

'Your granny.'

Something stirred in me, something faintly

reminiscent of hurt and rejection, but even as I hesitated, she held out her arms and I flew into them and into a new era.

I remember little of that first evening. I suppose I must have eaten, must have talked, must have met other members of the family, but I was too tired to concentrate on anything and my mother carried me to bed, where I fell into a sound sleep before I had any chance to notice that the bed was not my usual one, that the room was strange, that my possessions were not yet around me. Later I was briefly aware of the landing light as my mother looked in on me, but my eyelids were heavy and, when I next woke, daylight filled the room.

I sat up and then immediately retreated once more under the bedclothes, as the cold air chilled me. With the blankets pulled up to my chin, I looked round the room curiously. The ceilings were higher than in my old home and the curtains were longer and duller. I stared at them with a fleeting nostalgia for the bright yellow bears and blue dogs which had decorated my curtains in France. The floorboards were very dark and an assortment of worn rugs lay scattered across them. At the foot of my bed was my large brown teddy bear, Alphonse, with his torn red jumper. Other than yesterday's clothes on a chair, he was the only familiar thing in the room.

I braved the cold to grab the bear and pushed him under the bedclothes beside me. I became aware that I needed the lavatory and realised that I had no notion where it was. The cold made me reluctant to explore and for a while longer I stayed under the bedclothes, but the necessity was too great and I was compelled to venture out into the corridor. I reached the door, jumping from rug to rug to keep my toes warm, and looked cautiously round it. At once a large black dog appeared at the head of the stairs and, with a bark of greeting, ran towards me. Unused to any animal but Macfidget, I yelled in terror and darted back into the room.

'Hermann! Leave Klaus-Pierre alone!' I did not recognise the voice but presently a tall young man pushed open the door, said 'Hallo, I'm your cousin Franz,' and, summing up the situation accurately, took me along the corridor to the bathroom. When I emerged there was no sign of either dog or cousin and I ran back to my bedroom at full pelt, lest the large, black, bounding shape should again appear.

Elsa was sitting on my bed. I stood just inside the door hesitating, knowing that last night she had been my friend, remembering that then there had been adults about and wondering whether she might now metamorphose into a hostile native. She looked back at me curiously but I discerned no threat and decided it was safe to get back into bed.

'Aren't you going to get up?' asked Elsa with a suggestion of a disapproving sniff. 'I've waited ages. Granny said I was not to wake you because you had come all the way from the South of France, which is right down there.' She drew an imaginary map in the air and stabbed 'there' with her index finger.

I had no concept of geography but I agreed

with Granny that it was very far away, so far away that it had gone altogether.

'It's cold,' I protested.

'I wear two jerseys and this one has fleecy lining. I'm not cold.'

Elsa sprang up and drew back the curtains behind which was a window seat. I looked at the condensation on the panes with the clear sky beyond and shivered.

'Where's Mummy?' I asked.

'Baby! Get dressed, then you will be able to go and find her. Do hurry up. I won't look.' She turned her back and climbed up to kneel on the window seat.

I vaguely recalled that it was rude for other people to see you dress, although this rule did not apply when grown-ups were dressing you, and from time to time I glanced at her to make sure she was not looking. Eventually I joined Elsa on the window seat, still miserable with cold. I gazed out on the rolling woods and meadows. I could see a large expanse of water.

'That's a big pond.'

Elsa giggled. 'It's a lake, silly. Haven't you ever seen a lake?'

I shook my head. 'Is that the end of your garden?'

She followed my pointing finger to where a formal hedge divided shrubs and lawn from rough meadow and nodded.

'It's enormous.' For a moment awe made me silent, then I asked the question, fearing the answer, fearing my happiness might yet prove short-lived. 'Are there children Outside the Hedge?'

Elsa stared at me through uncomprehending eyes. 'Children? How could there be? No one lives in our fields or woods – no one proper anyway. Sometimes Old Joachim sets up his tent there but he doesn't have any children.'

'*Your* woods and fields? You said your garden ended *there*.'

'The garden does. Woods and fields aren't garden.'

I looked out at the expanse of trees and meadows, trying to grapple with an alien concept. 'So where does your everything end?'

Elsa pointed, squinting along the length of her finger. 'You see that wood over there – no, there, that's right – just beyond that. There's a road but you can't see it from here.'

I tried to absorb the implications. 'Are you very rich?'

'No. We used to be long ago but now we make do.'

'Where are the other children?'

'They're all at school. I should be too, but Daddy said I was to stay at home this week and look after you. Lotte is wild with jealousy. She thinks she should stay at home because she is half a sister and I am only a cousin.'

'No, I mean where do they live?'

'Oh, in the village, here and there, ages away. Why?'

'I don't like them.'

Elsa's eyes widened. 'You haven't met them. How do you know you don't like them?'

I shook my head, uncertain how to explain. Elsa went on looking at me with amazement before giving up the puzzle and turning to more pressing matters.

'Shall we play outside?'

'Won't it be cold?'

My cousin treated that with scorn. 'Baby! Anyway, you must have a coat. It'll be in there.'

I followed her gaze to the untidy heap of luggage which had been deposited near the bed. Together we began to pull out the cases and open them, searching for the red jerkin that my mother made me wear in cold weather. The bags were heavy and the trunk, which had been sent in advance, defied our efforts to open it. Scarlet and panting with exertion, Elsa gave up.

'I'll call Franz. He's nineteen.' She went out into the corridor, leaving the door wide open, and I heard her calling her brother. Finding the draught unbearable, I moved across the room to close the door but before I could do so Hermann bounded in and I shouted in terror.

Elsa came running back and, though she again called me a baby, tried to restrain the animal, which was licking my face, before Franz appeared and succeeded where she was failing. He made Hermann sit down and, assuring me that the dog wanted only to be friendly, tried to persuade me to pat its head. I refused, trembling and backing away, calling for my mother.

She did not come. Over the next few days it seemed always to be Aunt Angelika or Franz or my grandmother who materialised when an adult response was needed. My mother remained largely in her room.

'Mourning,' I heard Aunt Angelika reply briefly

when Franz asked where she was.

I knew what the word meant but could not understand how it could be applied to my mother. Mourning was what people did when someone died, but no one had died. I could not then have realised that my mother was, for the first time, in my father's house, among his family, surrounded by his possessions. His image looked at her from photographs and from the portrait on the wall by the stairs, reminding her of her loss. At last she was in an environment where Klaus von Ströbel was remembered with affection rather than hostility, where she could speak his name without embarrassment, where she saw his features each time she looked at Uncle Willi or Franz. My father had been dead for six years but only now could she come to terms with what had happened.

One day I saw her coming from the barn and I stopped what I was doing to run to her, Hermann, whom I no longer feared, barking beside me, Elsa calling after me in protest. She looked down at me and smiled, and in that smile I saw a serenity I had not encountered in her before. My mother had made peace with the past and its ghosts, but for me there was merely respite.

three

Respite

Elsa stared at the figure of my retreating mother with wondering awe.

'Did she really go in there?' Her gaze became fixed on the door of the barn. 'It's haunted.'

'You mean there's a ghost?'

Elsa nodded solemnly before looking around to make sure she was unobserved. 'Let's see if we can open the door. Otto says he's been in but I don't believe him.'

I knew Otto to be one of her brothers, older than Elsa but younger than Franz. I had not yet met him because he spent schooldays at Lübeck, which Elsa said was a large city, and came home on Saturday afternoons. I was looking forward to his return because Elsa talked about him constantly, making him sound daring and good fun.

We leant against the large wooden door and pushed, but it was too heavy for our puny efforts. Elsa tried to encourage Hermann to jump against it but he threw himself at us instead, excited rather than deterred by our voluble protests. Inevitably the commotion drew adult attention and Franz warned us to keep away from the barn.

'It's a bad place,' Maria told me as I sat on an old stool in the vegetable shed and watched her peeling potatoes with formidable speed. I had seen both my mother and Aunt Marie perform this simple household task but there was something different and curiously fascinating about the way Maria worked on the vegetables with her large, red, bony hands. I felt mildly repelled and that, together with the sepulchral tone in which she had just uttered her verdict on the barn, caused me to shudder, but the sensation was as much one of excitement as fear.

I had discovered Maria in my second week at Ströbelfields, as I now knew the family estate to be called. *Ströbelwiese*: the von Ströbel meadowland. Elsa had returned to school, but I was still too young and spent my days playing alone, left largely to my own devices with only occasional checks from the grown-ups as to what I might be doing. I ran with Hermann and was occasionally mounted on a small pony, which Uncle Willi wanted me to learn to ride but, because he was away teaching and the women always seemed busy, I made only limited progress. It was different at the weekends when Otto or Franz would take the pony out on a leading rein, and my skill and confidence increased.

At first I played mainly indoors, reassured by the sounds of voices from distant rooms, but it was bitterly cold so that even the weakest shaft of sun outside seemed to promise warmth and Hermann's company gave me the courage to venture out and explore. On one of these ventures I had heard noises from the vegetable shed, investigated and found an old woman scraping parsnips. Maria had given me a gap-toothed smile and I had sidled in.

From then on no day was complete without a visit to the vegetable shed to hear Maria's tales, although at first we had difficulty in understanding each other, her strong local accent confusing me and my French one frustrating my attempts to make my words clear. Through her I learned of the past glories of Ströbelfields, of days when my father and Uncle Willi were still boys, of how she and all her five sisters had been part of a huge staff, of fine carriages and cars and visits from relatives of the Kaiser. When she had first come to work here, she told me, there were four young boys 'livening the place up, always into mischief, except poor Master Gerhardt, of course, who was never any trouble. Then your Aunt Angelika came along but by then there was the war and nothing was ever the same again and then...'

I was no longer listening for I had suddenly remembered the barn. Otto had brushed aside our request to help us get in and the big black shape which stood close to the house on the kitchen side had once more become part of the background of our lives, half-forgotten, taken for granted, no longer the subject of active curiosity. Maria's reply that it was a bad place now drew it out of the shadows and threw it into stark relief.

'Why?'

'Things you mustn't know until you're older, Mr Nosy.'

Lotte shook her head when we asked her what Maria had meant and Elsa called her names for not telling, but my half-sister was adamant that we were far too young to share what she, at nearly ten, claimed to know. Quiet, earnest, dark-haired

58

little Lotte would not be drawn, despite Elsa's increasingly desperate attempts at cajolery, bribery and blackmail. She did not want Elsa's share of the Sunday cake and she did not care if Otto found out who had broken his bicycle pump and now, if we would excuse her, she had English verbs to master for a test tomorrow.

Elsa stamped in frustration. 'We could make that door open if we drove a car against it.'

'That's silly. We don't know how to drive the car.'

'Well, we could use one of the horses.'

'Horses pull not push.'

Elsa looked at me in surprise. 'You're quite clever for five years old. Uncle Klaus was supposed to have been very clever. You must get it from him.'

It did not occur to me to ask why I might not have got it from my mother. There was an indefinable suggestion in the way other grown-ups spoke to her that she was not quite one of them, that she was something halfway between child and adult. Everyone was kind and there was no overt condescension, but I somehow sensed that the von Ströbels regarded Franz more seriously than they did Catherine Dessin.

In the end it was no member of the family but Werner Pletz who told me why the barn had so dark a reputation. Werner was seven years old, a year younger than Elsa, and we played together every month when his family came to visit. He had a younger brother, Ernst, who was the same age as me and destined to become my best friend when we both started school on the same day, but in that first year at Ströbelfields it was Werner with whom I played.

In the old days, Maria told me, it had been a tradition for several families to meet for very grand lunches after church on Sundays. There might be twenty grown-ups around the table and a farm animal slaughtered especially for the occasion. The war had put an end to that but a more modest version of the tradition had been reinstated and two families visited us for Sunday lunch once a month. In those years immediately after the war they often brought their own contributions to the meal with them. The other families were the Pletzes and the von Forstners, and each came with four children but I remember playing only with Werner and Elsa.

Werner's father, Walter Pletz, seemed a grown-up version of Otto, with a strong sense of humour and a boisterous laugh. The contrast he offered to Uncle Willi puzzled and intrigued me for, with the brief exception of Nick's father, I had known no men until my arrival at Ströbelfields two months ago.

On the first occasion I met Werner, the Pletz family had arrived on horseback, having ridden five miles. Exhilarated by air and exercise, they were in high spirits and, while Frau Pletz and the children hurried inside to get warm, Walter began to tether the horses, assisted at first by Otto and then by Erich von Forstner, whose family had arrived by car some twenty minutes earlier. Overwhelmed by the presence of so many strangers and temporarily deserted by Elsa, I hid behind a mounting block. Presently Otto emerged from the stables and went indoors and I would have gone with him had I noticed him sooner. Instead I remained where I was listening to the voices from the stable.

'You never know what the von Ströbels will do next,' Walter was booming incredulously. 'You know they have even brought home the mistress?'

'Hush! Yes, I heard it from Willi himself. Plus child, I gather. Poor little devil.'

'Funny, I never thought of old Klaus as a libertine.'

'I can't say that I see him in that light now.' Erich von Forstner sounded uncertain and troubled, his seriousness throwing Walter's levity into relief.

'So what else do you call a man with a wife and kids who seduces a schoolgirl?'

'She was a bit older than that, I think.'

'Not much.' Walter Pletz laughed again and I heard the sound of a bolt being shot as he secured a horse. The two men came out and walked towards the house just as Elsa appeared at the door calling for me.

The meal was very formal and, used to the normal freedoms which Uncle Willi allowed within the family, I became uneasy and grateful for the banter of Walter Pletz and the whispered irreverences of Werner who sat beside me. After lunch the children were ushered outside to play and immediately broke up into groups to engage in familiar pursuits. Adrift, I trailed after Elsa, who had attached herself to Werner. We went down to the lake by which Otto had years ago constructed a den but which he was now too old to use. We crawled in through the bare branches of the

61

winter trees and huddled together in a space that was comfortably big enough for one but decidedly cramped for three.

'It's no good. We'll have to find somewhere bigger.' Werner began to wriggle out and I knew I had spoiled their fun.

'I wish we could go in the barn. It would be warm in there like it is when we play in yours.' Elsa was plucking bits of twig from the thick padded jacket Aunt Angelika made her wear whenever she was outdoors.

Werner stared at her with scandalised eyes. 'You can't go in *there*.'

We both looked back at him, a sudden suspicion dawning, the possibility of revelation dancing tantalisingly before us.

'Why not?' asked Elsa with forced innocence in her tone.

'It's haunted. There was once a murder there and it's also where your Uncle Gerhardt hanged himself. At night it's full of noises as the ghosts walk and wail.'

'How do you know?' Elsa was looking at him not with the gratification of enlightenment but with resentment that he knew more about events on her territory than she did. I sensed she wanted to deny what Werner had just told us but was too eager for further details to do so.

'Maria was telling Old Joachim one day when I was here and she didn't see me listening.'

Old Joachim was a tramp who occasionally slept in our woods and sought work on the farm. When he had earned enough money for his simple needs he disappeared for months on end. I had never seen him but Maria sometimes spoke of him and worried about where he slept in winter.

'Who was murdered?' demanded Elsa.

'A Jew who was hiding there.'

'What's a Jew?' I asked.

Elsa adopted her lofty 'I know more than you, but you are only five' tone. 'Well, Germans come from Germany and Chinamen from China and Jews from ... er...'

'Israel,' Werner rescued her. 'I'll tell you everything I heard if you swear not to say how you know.'

Elsa immediately swore a great oath on the head of Hermann and, not to be outdone, I swore one on the life of Macfidget. We sat down on the remains of a trunk from a fallen tree and Werner began his tale.

'It was ages and ages ago, when Hitler was in power. Do you know who Hitler was, Klaus-Pierre? He was a wicked ruler who cast a spell on Germany and made everyone be very unkind to Jews. Well, there was a Jew who used to teach at the village school where your father teaches, Elsa, and he ran away because he was so frightened and he hid in your barn, but no one knew except his wife who used to bring him food at night. Then one night everyone in your house was woken up by dogs barking and there were policemen in the yard. Your father, Klaus-Pierre, didn't live there then and there was only Elsa's father and your Uncle Gerhardt, who of course didn't really count, to protect the women and children. Maria was a live-in maid in those days and she told Old Joachim that she wanted to hide but was shamed by your grandmother, who followed your Uncle Willi into the yard and asked what was going on and how dared they walk all over your grounds without asking.

'Anyway they didn't take any notice but opened up the barn and sent the dogs in. Two of the policemen went in after them but the others wouldn't let anyone else in. Then there was loud shouting. Maria told Old Joachim it was the worst sound she ever heard and then' – here Werner paused dramatically – 'it all went very quiet. Maria said she didn't know what quiet was until that moment.'

Elsa held my shoulders in fear and excitement as we listened, our breathing seemingly suspended, eyes wide with the happy expectation of some fearful horror.

'Then a policeman dragged him out. He was dead. One of the dogs had torn his throat out.'

I screamed and clutched my throat, while Elsa bent double as if to be sick. Pleased with the effect he had produced, Werner fell silent while we gave vent to our horror and disgust.

'Ugh! Ugggghhhh!' screeched Elsa, and we hugged each other in the ecstasy of knowing a horrible grown-up thing.

'They took your father away for questioning, Elsa, and your mother was very frightened, but it was all right because he really had not known the Jew was in the barn. When you have got over what you have just heard,' went on Werner in his grandest grown-up tone, 'I will tell you about your Uncle Gerhardt.'

At once we assured him we were ready but he

played with us for a while, savouring his power, saying that I was only five and Elsa only a girl, and perhaps he should not tell us too much at once. He continued in this mode until Elsa reminded him she was eight, a year older than he was, and taunted him with the doubt that he knew anything further at all.

'All right. Here goes but I warn you now, it will give you nightmares and if you wake up screaming for your mummies like little babies you mustn't tell how you know. Swear.'

The oaths were energetically renewed.

'Your Uncle Gerhardt was your fathers' younger brother and he was a bit simple. You know.' Werner tapped his head and Elsa nodded impatiently, indicating that she already knew that particular piece of family history. I was not sure what he meant but I was unwilling to distract him so I nodded too but failed to fool Elsa who whispered, 'He was mad. He couldn't even talk.'

'But he was very kind and everyone loved him,' continued Werner. 'Well, after your fathers had gone off to the war, soldiers came and took him away and made him work in one of those camps where they tortured Jews.'

I imagined a group of tents but had little idea what 'tortured' meant.

'Of course, he was so kind and gentle he wouldn't do what they wanted, so they brought him back, and he was so upset he went out to the barn and hanged himself and your Aunt Angelika found him and screamed.'

We must have looked disappointed because Werner then began to elaborate on the two ghosts who haunted the barn. One had no throat and the other swung, groaning, from the rafters.

My limited comprehension protected me from any after-effects of either story, but Elsa was less fortunate. Long after the Pletzes and von Forstners had gone I found her in the yard, drawing sums in the light layer of snow. A shaft of light from the stables illuminated her calculations.

'See. It couldn't have been ages ago. Werner said it happened in the war and I was born in the war. I must have been in the house when Uncle Gerhardt died.' She looked at the barn and shuddered. 'We lived here because of Daddy's job and Mummy's illness. Uncle Klaus lived in his own house with Aunt Ellie, so Lotte would have been with them, but I was there.' Elsa pointed at the window of her bedroom, which overlooked the barn.

'The Jew may have been ages ago.'

She shook her head and pointed to the sums in the snow. 'Hitler came to power in 1933. We learned that at school. 1950 take away 1933 is seventeen. Franz is older than that and Otto is nearly that and they are only just not children. It wasn't ages ago. It was now take away a bit. And Werner said that man had a wife, just like my father had a wife, and so she must have been upset because you are upset when people die. I hate Werner. I wish he hadn't told us. I want that man to have his throat all right again. I hate the dogs. Hermann wouldn't do that to anyone. He would cry if you told him to.'

I looked at her in miserable incomprehension, knowing only that she was now upset by something we had both enjoyed when it was first given to us, baffled by the jumble of childishness and semi-adult glimpses of reality, seeing no significance in the timescale she found so upsetting. I was incapable of offering comfort and my confusion was complete when she burst into tears and ran inside.

Through the storms of nightmares, and the adult consternation which followed them, Elsa remained faithful to her promise to Werner Pletz and never revealed the source of the nightly disturbances. It was I who was the innocent cause of displeasure with the Pletzes and it was Walter not Werner whom I gave away.

The whole household was in a fever about the approach of Christmas, the grown-ups harassed, the children excited. Uncle Willi, Franz and Otto went off with axes to take a tree from the woods, and returned with one vastly bigger than Aunt Angelika had expected. My grandmother was amused and commented to my exasperated aunt that her offspring were all unpredictable. 'You just never know what the von Ströbels will do next.'

'No,' I piped up, recognising the words and wanting to join in. 'They've even brought home the mistress.'

There was a short silence during which the adult world seemed to freeze, Aunt Angelika pausing in the act of bending some tinsel into the shape of a star, my grandmother raising her head slightly as if listening for something, my mother staring at me aghast. Then everyone began to bustle again, talking brightly, ignoring my contribution to the conversation. I was not deceived and knew they had been disconcerted by what I had just said.

'Walter,' muttered Aunt Angelika to her mother. 'Who else?'

'I wonder what else he said?' replied my grandmother with a worried glance at me.

I hastened to satisfy her curiosity. 'He said my father was a libbybean.'

I watched them trying to work that out. My mother, used to my malapropisms, arrived at the right conclusion first. 'Libertine,' she said, the bitterness distorting her normal tone. 'Klaus of all people! A libertine!'

They told me libertine was a rude word and I must never say it, so I stored it in my memory alongside knickers and lavatory for future retrieval, but as I still said libbybean I found it had no effect other than to produce briefly baffled looks. The looks my mother thereafter bestowed on Walter Pletz were of a quite different nature and a vague but disturbing recollection kept tugging at my mind, but France now had all the distance of another planet and I could not place it.

Christmas was a time of carols around the piano, the table groaning with food, logs blazing on the hearth, presents and family games. On Christmas Eve I was sick with excitement and Uncle Willi took me into the library to 'calm down'. I had not been into the room often as it was used mainly by Uncle Willi, and my only previous reasons to enter it were when I had been sent to call him to a meal. The remains of a fire glowed in the grate and the room smelt of leather armchairs, Hermann and Uncle Willi's pipe. Through the door I could see the Christmas tree shimmering in the large, panelled hall.

Uncle Willi placed me gently in an armchair and told me he would be back in a few minutes, but when I woke the room was dark and Hermann was asleep by my feet. I dozed again and was carried, still sleeping, up to bed, by Otto. Later my mother came in and laid her hand on my forehead and under my ear, murmuring that I had no temperature and it must just be excitement. She crept out and when I next woke I thought it must be the middle of the night and that everyone was in bed, until I heard the music from the hall.

I pulled my woolly dressing-gown around me and pushed my feet into the fleecy lined new slippers which Granny had produced for Christmas, before creeping out on to the landing and looking down. They were all there and, crouching, I peered at them through the bannisters.

My grandmother, whom my mother, Aunt Angelika and Uncle Willi called Mutti and I Omi, was sitting in her usual armchair under the vast picture of her long-dead husband, Peter, who had died along with their eldest son, Lothar, in a flying accident a few years after the Great War. She was smiling at Elsa's efforts to sing descant to Otto's 'Silent Night'.

Franz was seated at the piano, earnestly concentrating on the music, his eyes serious behind the dark-rimmed spectacles. He had just spent a whole term at home recovering from scarlet fever, but was to return to his last year at school in Switzerland after Christmas before going to university in the autumn. He was very thin and a stranger might have attributed his physique to the disease, but Franz was always thin ('You would think we starved him as a child,' Uncle Willi would complain) and still is. Size apart, he was very like Uncle Willi in looks and I often heard the grown-ups comment that the von Ströbel features ran strong in the males of the clan.

Otto was the exception. At fifteen he was large-boned, sturdy and very fair, where the others tended to slimness and darkness. His eyes were a piercing blue and Aunt Angelika called him 'our perfect little Aryan', a joke I was only able to understand many years later. He had seemingly endless energy and ran everywhere, excelling in sport at school but also at academic lessons, having inherited the von Ströbel brains. He was good-natured and good fun and we all adored him.

My gaze travelled from him to Alessandra and I felt a small chill. She was seventeen and conscious of it, but it was not that which made me wary. In her I sensed a coldness and disapproval towards my mother which none of the others had ever shown. It was not overt and Alessandra was polite to my mother and formally kind to me – helping me up when I fell over, explaining if I did not understand something, helping me tie my shoe laces – but I knew there was no warmth there. Once I asked Otto why Alessandra did not like me and he hastily said she did, then modified his answer. 'She was very close to Aunt Ellie,' he explained before looking as if he wished he had not said the words. To me they meant nothing. I knew Ellie had been my father's wife and was Lotte's dead mother but, still innocent, I did not see why closeness between her and Alessandra should explain the latter's dislike of me or of my mother. Otto saw my incomprehension and seemed relieved.

Like Otto, Alessandra spent the week in Lübeck, where she went to school, and so I saw little of her. She was never much more than a shadowy figure in my life but it was a shadow I tried to avoid.

Hedy was Otto's twin but did not in the least resemble him, being more like her cousin Lotte, small and dark, but she alone showed little academic seriousness and, as I grew older, I asked her less often for help with homework than I did the others. She went to the same school as Alessandra in Lübeck.

Otto was now taking Franz's place at the piano and the quality of the music at once became more joyous as Otto played with great enthusiasm but little precision. Then, in the middle of a carol, when everyone was singing of gold and frankincense and myrrh, he broke suddenly, loudly, wickedly into Offenbach, missing notes in his zest for the rhythm, his hands travelling along the keys with vast speed.

Uncle Willi and Aunt Angelika laughed, but Elsa began to dance wildly, kicking her legs, swishing her skirt like a can-can girl. Alessandra and Aunt Angelika moved simultaneously to put an end to such an exhibition, and I heard Omi ask Hedy where Elsa could have learned such a dance.

The music went on, vibrant, noisy, intoxicating. I gripped the bannisters in excitement and Uncle

71

Willi suddenly looked up and noticed me. A few moments later my mother appeared and I was returned to bed. Although I was not then capable of making the analysis, what I had been watching was a group of gifted, healthy, utterly confident young Germans whose family had miraculously preserved an impressive proportion of its lands and possessions through two world wars and whose country was to stage a spectacular renaissance from the ruins. Franz's earnestness, Otto's wildness, Elsa's innocent exhibitionism were all indicators of the people they would become when they left Ströbelfields for the world, and in later years my mind would often re-run that Christmas Eve gathering of the von Ströbel clan.

For the present I was just glad to be among them, spoiled by Omi, teased by Otto, taught by Franz, played with by Elsa. Among them I was secure, warm even in the cold corridors, well even when ailing, loved even when quarrelling.

Among them. Yes, I was among them but I was not *of* them. Even here I was different. I was learning to write a name which was different from theirs: Dessin. Klaus-Pierre Dessin. I attended a different church, for my mother and I were Catholics whereas they were all Lutherans. I alone of all my generation at Ströbelfields had a mother, but as the seasons passed and Ströbelfields turned from white to green to brown and back to white, these differences seemed unimportant. I shared secrets in the vegetable shed with Maria, raced Elsa through the fields, learned that I could make cows afraid of me and how to find the eggs the roaming hens had laid. Indoors

I crayoned increasingly intelligible pictures and counted beads on Elsa's loftily discarded abacus. Omi read me stories and my mother stitched up my dilapidated bear.

France, the cries of 'German brat', the daily fear and the disapproval all seemed to belong to another century as I learned to expect only good from the world about me, an expectation reinforced when I found the barn door open one day and no ghosts inside. I learned to quarrel without assuming rejection would follow, to suffer defeat without giving up, to look those I met in the eye.

It did not occur to me that this might change, that there might yet be danger beyond our distant gate – not, that is, until I was old enough at last to go to school in that peace-torn corner of Europe and there met Wolfgang Mueller.

four

A Fear Returns

Uncle Willi had been teaching at the village school since the end of the First World War when the survival of Ströbelfields had been in serious doubt and he and his three brothers were faced with finding employment instead of leading the leisured lives of gentlemen which hitherto had seemed their destiny. The eldest brother, Lothar, had set up an aviation venture and their father, Peter, had joined him in the enterprise. The family, which, alone of those they knew, had lost none of their sons in the war, was devastated by the loss of both men in an aerobatic display some five years later. The youngest brother, Gerhardt, had been born mentally handicapped and spent his days pottering among the farm animals.

It was the lot of my father, Klaus von Ströbel, and Uncle Willi to keep the estate going but in those days mainly the duty of Uncle Willi, as my father, who had survived the slaughter of the trenches, had departed for university to read history and was developing an academic career at Heidelberg. At first Uncle Willi was inclined to give up teaching, but in so isolated an area there was a shortage of available substitutes and he was persuaded to remain for a further year. Three decades later he was still there, having been away from the school only for the duration of the Second World War.

Each day he drove his Volkswagen the six miles to the school. Some of my earliest memories of Ströbelfields are of waving to Elsa as she and Lotte sat in the back of the car, with Hermann running and barking beside the vehicle. He always seemed to give up at the same point, just past the lake, and stand watching till the car was out of sight, its exhaust fumes still lingering in the air. Then he would come racing back to me and I would marvel at how he would seem so small in the distance yet so large as he bounded the last few yards.

On the day that I too joined the morning exodus from Ströbelfields I was beside myself with excitement, talking volubly, bidding farewell to Hermann, gloating over my new satchel, the brightly coloured pencils within it and the cone of presents with which every German child started school. I felt a brief sadness when I thought of Maria because I realised that I would not be able to visit her in the vegetable shed until the holidays.

I recognised Ernst Pletz among the small group of new pupils and I suppose I must have met Wolfgang Mueller at about the same time but I have no real recollection of him during that first year. He was a name and a face, just one of many who were taught alongside me in a class spanning the age groups of the younger half of the school. He was a year older and already beginning to manifest the anger of the alienated.

I began to notice him only when he began to get into trouble. By then he must have been about nine but he was taught maths in the same group to which Ernst and I had been allocated because he could not keep up with his own age group. One day I covertly helped him with some long division and, though he presented the results as his own, he retaliated by deliberately jogging my arm as I wrote, causing my pencil to make a long mark across the page of neat numerals. He had taken no precautions against his action being observed and the teacher, a plain, harshly spoken woman who wore her grey hair coiled around her ears in the mode of a much earlier period, pulled him to the front of the class and made him recite multiplication tables.

At break he vented his anger by snatching my large, green marble, which I had won from Ernst the previous week. I shrugged because I was too afraid to hit back, but an older girl intervened, threatening to tell a teacher. It was a trivial incident but something stirred in my memory and the cold tentacles of the long-forgotten taunts reached out, touching me lightly, reminding me of their existence and their power.

A fortnight later my tormentor was in trouble again and sent to the headmaster for some offence, which I cannot now recall. His name was becoming synonymous with bad behaviour and each time he was punished he revenged himself on me. As I had never set out to hurt or upset him, this was painfully baffling to me – and perhaps also to him – but I had no idea what I should do. Ernst was afraid of him and told me to tell Uncle Willi, but I balked at using my position at Ströbelfields as a means of obtaining justice at school.

'Frenchie,' sneered Wolfgang as I passed him in the corridor.

'I'm not!' I yelled when he repeated the taunt in the playground.

'I'm not French, am I?' I protested indignantly to Elsa when we had arrived home and were on our way upstairs to change into old clothes.

'Only sort of,' she answered soothingly. 'Only half.'

I did not mind being French but I did mind being different and, still too young to be other than artless, I allowed Wolfgang to see that his taunts upset me, which naturally encouraged him to further cruelty. Whenever he saw me, the cry of 'Frenchie!' was certain to follow.

He lived in a small, dilapidated house on the edge of the Pletz grounds where his father made a living labouring for Walter and doing odd jobs for the village elderly. His mother was a thin, wan creature who was bullied by her husband and ignored by her sons.

Once, when I was playing with Ernst and we had ridden our bicycles past Wolfgang's house, I felt a sharp sting on my bare leg.

'Ouch!' I stopped to investigate, believing I had been the victim only of some passing insect. Three more stings followed before Ernst saw Wolfgang crouched behind a bush, expertly flicking elastic bands at my exposed flesh. On that occasion I fought him while Ernst alternately shouted encouragement and screamed for help.

When aid did arrive it was in the form of Elsa and Werner Pletz, but by then I was a pitiable sight – scratched, cut and bleeding with torn, muddy clothes. Elsa tried to comfort me while Werner gallantly fought Wolfgang, cheered on by Ernst, until the brawl was interrupted by the authoritative tones of a grown-up and Wolfgang's father pulled the combatants apart, demanding to know the cause of the fracas.

Werner was too out of breath to explain but Ernst was delighted to be able to contribute something more substantial than applauding the efforts of others and he gave an unsparing account of Wolfgang's misdeeds. With smug satisfaction I expected Herr Mueller to deliver a stern rebuke and order his son back home, such a course being the predictable reaction of any adult of my acquaintance, and I waited, smarting with pain but gleeful, for the reluctant apology I was sure my assailant would now be obliged to make to all of us.

I was utterly unprepared for the animal snarl of rage with which Wolfgang's father seized him, or for the dreadful beating that followed.

Werner and Ernst cried out in protest and Elsa, sobbing, actually tried to pull the man off, pleading with him to stop, but he brushed her aside with angry irritation, intent only on the blows he was landing on his son. In the end we grabbed our bicycles and fled. Casting a glance over my shoulder, I saw Mueller complete the punishment with a hefty kick. Only then did I realise that, in all the noisy scene, the one person who had uttered no sound was Wolfgang.

Werner told his father, who had come from the house to find out the cause of the commotion as we pedalled furiously along the drive, calling for adult help. His mouth tightened as he listened before saying that Werner and I must go and clean up.

Frau Pletz followed us to the bathroom and applied disinfectant to our cuts and grazes, pretending to be unmoved by our moans of agony as the lotion flowed into the wounds. 'That will teach you not to fight.'

She applied sticking plaster in abundance, causing Aunt Angelika and Uncle Willi to exclaim with alarm and amusement when Elsa and I were delivered to Ströbelfields in time for supper.

My mother coaxed a repetition of the tale from me, and my grandmother actually took Elsa on her knee, which seemed to me a terrible indignity for so big a girl but which appeared to comfort my unembarrassed cousin.

Later I lay in bed and waited for my mother to come and read a story but instead Uncle Willi appeared and, sitting on the edge of the bed, he began to talk to me gravely about Wolfgang Mueller. He was very poor and his father was bad-tempered with the effort of feeding and clothing a wife, two sons and a baby, especially as the wife was very weak and unable to help much. Christians must be kind and act like Good King Wenceslas, but sometimes it was more than just food or warmth which people wanted. They needed friends.

I imagined trailing through the snow to bring friendship to Wolfgang Mueller, encouraging Ernst, who in my fantasy played the role of the page. The throbbing reality of my injuries soon put an end to such notions.

'He doesn't want to be friends. I tell him the answers at school and let him copy my spellings but he just hits me at break. It's not fair.'

'Life isn't fair. You live in a big house with plenty of other children to play with and you are clever at school. He is poor and stupid and probably lonely too and he knows it, which is why he hits you in the playground. It might be better not to tell him all the answers for a little while.'

I did not entirely follow the logic of Uncle Willi's argument, but his insistence on friendship impressed me and, a few weeks later, when I had endured no torment from Wolfgang in the playground – mainly because he was engaged in persecuting someone else – I invited him to spend the following Sunday at Ströbelfields and he unexpectedly accepted.

At once I was uneasy, having thought my hospitality would be spurned and certain that I was doing my duty just by asking him. I wondered what Elsa would say but she was uninterested, having decided to spend the afternoon with Lotte learning from Hedy how to make a dress which flared from the waist. Werner and Ernst Pletz were also invited but they said they could not come, although now I suspect that their father would not let them mix in such unsuitable company.

Wolfgang and I played together, taking Hermann for a walk, sailing my old wooden boat on the lake, balancing on the trunk of a tree that Werner, Ernst and I had watched being felled a year ago. Then it had been exciting but the fate of that proud old oak had since disturbed me. I could remember it, the pride of the largest wood on the estate – huge, powerful, its branches stretching into the sky – and now only its rotting trunk remained, fallen, a plaything for the smallest creature which lived in the forest. Elsa had cried when it was laid low and I had jeered at her, but now I too was sorry for the tree.

'Do you mind being French?' Wolfgang asked curiously. 'My father says they are hopeless in France. We invaded them in the war and they just gave up.'

'But they won.'

'No, they didn't. They had to be rescued by the English. They eat frogs and snails. Do you eat frogs and snails?'

'Of course not,' I snapped.

For a while we talked, with delicious disgust, about the horror of eating frogs. I could not believe that anyone really did so and I made a mental note to ask my mother if it was true. Then there was a rustle in the undergrowth and a large black cat wandered into the clearing, regarding us with a haughty stare before disappearing once more into the brambly tangle.

'Is that yours?'

'It belongs to the farm.'

'Does it live in the barn?'

'No.'

'I bet it does. Farm cats always do. They catch the rats.'

'Ours don't. They are not allowed to. Nothing lives in the barn. We don't use it.'

'Why not?'

The barn's history was no longer a taboo subject and it was some time since I had been considered old enough to know about the Jew, although the manner of the murdered man's death was not specified by the grown-ups and, when I had asked Aunt Angelika if there were ghosts in the barn, she had smiled and said, 'The ghosts of Ströbelfields smile kindly on their successors.'

My mother had told me about Uncle Gerhardt's suicide. It was, she said, very sad but sometimes great good could come of great sorrow and my father had been so upset by his brother's death that he had spent the rest of the war helping Jews to escape the Nazis in Paris. It had been wonderfully brave of him and I must be proud of his memory. Some instinct warned me not to tell Wolfgang this part of the story and instead I related only the details of the Jew's death, feeling rewarded by his rapt attention and the amazement and awe in his eyes.

'I bet my father killed him,' Wolfgang's eyes sparkled. 'He used to be a policeman round here and they used to track people down with fierce dogs. He told me.'

I looked at him, appalled. 'But ... but, it was *murder.*'

'Don't be daft. Policemen can't murder. If a policeman chases you and you don't stop then it's not murder if he sets a dog on you. The Jew shouldn't have run away. It was against the law.'

I remembered how Werner had told Elsa and me the terrible story. Then, of course, we had been sickened merely by the physical aspect of the victim's sufferings, or at least I had. Thinking back now to the nightmares which plagued Elsa afterwards I realised that she had glimpsed some different dimension, some dim shape which now hovered just beyond my own comprehension but I knew it was there and it compelled me to argue with Wolfgang.

'Yes, but these were Hitler policemen. They were wicked.'

'My dad says people only say Hitler was wicked because he lost. While he was winning they didn't say that.'

The puzzle was too much for me but it left me with a vague wariness towards my new friend, stemming from a source far deeper than any simple fear that he would return to bullying me. That same wariness warned me not to repeat the conversation to any grown-up and, although I meant to tell Elsa when she had finished her boring dress-making, I somehow forgot.

After that I played occasionally with Wolfgang, but neither Ernst nor Werner ever seemed to join us and I soon realised this was not coincidence, that the Pletz children were not allowed to mix with the Mueller children. Evidently Uncle Willi's view of Wenceslas-style Christian charity was not shared by Ernst's parents, although I once saw Frau Mueller returning to her home with two baskets of produce which must have come from their farm.

Meanwhile Wolfgang found other victims to torture who often appealed to me for protection.

'He says he'll knock me into the middle of next week,' wept a terrified seven-year-old.

'He can't,' I soothed from the lofty eminence of my nine years. 'At least, only by metaphor.'

Aunt Angelika had explained the concept of metaphors to me the previous evening and I was pleased to be able to air my knowledge but the child looked back at me only with horror. 'But what if he's got a metaphor? I'm scared of metaphors.'

I asked Wolfgang why he must torment smaller boys.

'Because they're stupid,' was the uninformative reply.

The one child I never saw him bully was his younger brother, Horst, who must have been about four or five and towards whom Wolfgang was protective to the point of fussiness. My first venture inside the Mueller house, when a driving, freezing rain had forced us indoors, provided the reason: the entire family was united in fear of the father, whose notion of reprimand was to administer a sharp cuff and to whom real anger could mean vicious use of a strap. He was irritated to madness by the thin, pitiable wails of the chronically sick baby in her cot and faced the world in general with bitter hostility, refusing to forgive it for the defeat of Hitler whose rule had brought him power over his fellow men for the first time in his impoverished, disappointing life.

He struck his wife as readily as his children and, although I never saw him land a blow on the baby, he shook the cot until the wails turned from miserable complaint to screams of terror. No one dared to attempt any restraint and during these episodes the rest of the family cowered or fled outside. Once he threw Wolfgang against a wall so violently that, banging his head, he actually lost consciousness for a few seconds and seemed to reel rather than walk for hours afterwards.

I visited as little as possible and we played outside or at Ströbelfields. Soon he began to bring Horst with him and, although I found the child's presence an irritating inhibition when we wanted to engage in activities beyond his ability, I understood the reason too well to complain. It was with greater difficulty that I gradually came to understand also that Wolfgang longed to be old enough and strong enough to compete with his father rather than old enough to escape and rescue the family.

On one occasion Wolfgang wanted to retrieve something from his house but his father was in such a rage that he did not want to risk going inside and I was reluctantly prevailed upon to undertake the task, persuaded by my friend's insistence that Mueller never hit other people's children. As I fled, unobserved, I glimpsed the inside of the main bedroom and saw a swastika, a symbol I knew to be forbidden, hanging from a wall. I knew I must not tell Wolfgang what I had seen.

It was the tune which finally alerted Uncle Willi to the nature of the company I was keeping. I often heard Herr Mueller humming it when he was in one of his better moods, and was innocently doing so myself one afternoon when we were all in the yard at Ströbelfields cleaning tack. Maria used to grumble that it was not a task for gentlemen and that my grandfather had known a time when six grooms were employed to do such menial work, but this was a Saturday in the school holidays and she was not there to utter her usual strictures.

I was humming to myself as I plied saddle soap when I became aware that there was some change in the atmosphere around me. I looked up with casual curiosity to see Franz pausing in the act of unbuckling reins. I glanced from him to my mother, who was looking at me with widening eyes, water dripping unheeded from a cloth in her hand, and then to the rest of the family, who appeared frozen in a tableau in which all looked at me before turning as one to look at Uncle Willi.

The tune died as I faltered to a stop but somehow its notes seemed to hang in the air.

'Where did you hear that?' My uncle's voice was worried rather than angry.

'Herr Mueller's always singing it.'

'Does he sing words?'

'Only sometimes. He usually just hums. Why, what's the matter?'

'Klaus-Pierre, you must never sing that. It is a Nazi song.'

He left the matter there and soon we were once more talking and laughing, but not before I had heard my mother mutter, '"Horst Wessell"' by way of explanation to Otto, who was emerging from a stable with two saddles and who had caught only the end of the exchange. The words briefly puzzled me as I imagined they must refer to little Horst Mueller who must have 'wesselled', but then I realised there was no such verb and that what I had heard was the title of the song.

After that the excuses began. At first they were quite plausible. Wolfgang could not visit today because Otto planned to take Elsa and me riding. We had left too late to call on Wolfgang and must go straight to the Pletz house. I must begin to do some proper homework soon and that would mean playing less often after school. When I had not seen Wolfgang once throughout the entire holidays the truth began to dawn: Good King Wenceslas would no more trek through the snow to the Mueller household because my uncle had come to the same view as the Pletzes.

The withdrawal was not brutal and I still played with Wolfgang at school. He was not turned away when he arrived at Ströbelfields, panting and exhausted from a five-mile ride on his rusty bicycle, and my mother helped me choose a birthday present for him, but both he and I knew what was happening and it was not long before the bullying at school returned with a new ferocity.

'Frenchie! I've brought a frog for you.' He produced the slimy, dead creature from his mackintosh pocket and the girls screamed. 'I'll make you eat it,' he threatened, the glee springing into his eyes as I recoiled.

'Do you really eat frogs?' whispered Ernst, and that innocent question left me cold with isolation. I was different. Klaus-*Pierre Dessin*.

Then others began to join in.

'My father was murdered by a Frenchman,' one girl told me. 'It was before I was born, and he didn't even see me. All he was doing was helping an old lady pick up some shopping she had dropped and this man crept up and stabbed him.'

'My mother says the only thing the French are any good at is cooking and of course the other thing,' muttered another girl.

'What other thing?' I looked at her baffled and she assumed an air of knowledgeable superiority but must have understood as little as I did.

It was the same girl who delivered a much sharper barb. 'Your mother didn't marry your father. My mum told me.'

'So? There wasn't time before he died. It was sad.'

'It was stupid. Your mother could have gone to a home for bad girls.'

Wolfgang, however, understood only crude physical fear and successfully instilled it until I was driven to confide in Otto.

'Find something he is afraid of,' he advised. 'Everybody is afraid of something. For example, if this lad likes to be king of the playground he might fear being made to look a fool with everybody laughing at him. Supposing Fräulein spanked him in front of the class or he had to spend the morning standing in a corner or something like that? Remind him it can happen without actually threatening to tell tales.'

I shook my head. 'He's always in trouble and he just doesn't care.'

'Then perhaps the time has come to speak to Uncle Willi.'

I was cowardly enough to hope that he would do it for me even as I again shook my head and told him that the other children made life impossible for those who ran to the teachers with complaints. Instead he decided to intervene himself and took me, protesting, to see Wolfgang from whom he demanded a promise that there would be no further bullying.

Beside him Wolfgang suddenly seemed very small and insignificant, but I knew that he would retaliate as soon as he felt it safe to do so, that though he might be cowed in Otto's presence he would revert to brutality when he had only those of his own age with whom to deal and, obscurely, I believed that I was to blame, groping towards the realisation that I should have resisted the efforts of my elders to break off the friendship. Otto concluded by threatening that if there was any more bad behaviour he would come to the school in person and make my tormentor crawl on his hands and knees across the playground in front of all the girls. I could have told him that he was wasting both his time and his anger. Wolfgang would gladly have endured any retribution or humiliation for the simple pleasure of seeing the fear in my eyes, of jeering as a tear rolled down my nose, of sensing power as Ernst and I ran from him in abject fright.

Although I knew it would avail me nothing I still tried to brazen my way through our encounter the following day when the torture resumed.

'You weren't so big yesterday, were you?' I turned to address the group which had gathered round us: 'You should have seen him shivering and saying sorry to my cousin. He was crying and promising to be good and—'

I got no further as Wolfgang flung himself on me, the profanity rushing from him. 'Your cousin's a German. He's got a right to tell me off but you're just a little Frenchie. Frog! I can make you jump like a frog and crawl like a snail. Slimy Frenchie!'

This time his assault was so violent that I heard someone cry he was going to tell sir. I bit and screamed and kicked until suddenly my blows met with nothing and, looking up, I saw Wolfgang's contorted face becoming smaller and more distant as my uncle hauled him from me and held him above me. As I lay there looking up, I glimpsed a large black bird flapping high in the clouds and I sent a scream after it as once, spurned and scorned, I had cried my despair in Provence.

The other children crowded around me saying that Wolfgang would be beaten but I did not believe them. In an age when children were routinely subjected to such punishment it was unknown at Ströbelfields, where both my mother and Aunt Angelika regularly flailed their hands in the direction of our legs when Elsa and I were being particularly tiresome. I had long ago lost any expectation that such blows might land and knew the gestures to be warnings rather than evidence of intent.

Occasionally an exasperated Uncle Willi would promise to give me 'what my father once gave your Uncle Lothar,' but as Uncle Lothar had died in 1923 the threat seemed remote and unconnected with whatever misdemeanour had prompted it.

It did not occur to me that, although it was Uncle Willi who had rescued me from Wolfgang's attack, it would be the headmaster who would decide his fate until he arrived in our classroom clutching Wolfgang by the collar with one hand and carrying a cane in the other. We were told to put down our pencils, sit up straight and pay attention.

There was a tangible sense of shock as we nervously obeyed.

'Stand up all who have been bullied by this boy.'

Everyone remained still, perhaps afraid to arouse scorn by telling tales or perhaps suddenly afraid for Wolfgang. The head stared at me and I reluctantly stood up. The child who was afraid of metaphors did so next. It must have only been seconds but it felt like hours as, slowly, unhappily, children rose to their feet and stood, looking down at their desks to avoid meeting Wolfgang's contemptuous, threatening eye.

'Ten.' The head told us to remain standing until he had called our names and then began to apply the cane, calling out a name with each stroke. After the first three I realised that I was to be the last, that the final blow in that pain and humiliation would be delivered on my account.

'All bullies are cowards,' Otto had reassured me, but Wolfgang Mueller proved an exception to that rule. He did not utter a sound, although he did begin to struggle at the fifth blow, and I remembered how he was so often beaten at home, that he was always bruised and cut all over, and realised that what was happening to him now was happening to already torn flesh.

On the instant of the revelation I put my fists into my eyes and screamed, 'Stop!'

The head looked at me and I began to cry but he merely called out the next name. My desk seemed to fall away from me and, when I opened my eyes, I was lying in the sick bay and Fräulein was looking down at me with a kindliness I had never seen in her countenance before. Then Uncle Willi appeared and sat beside the bed, telling me that I would soon be all right but that I should lie still for a little while. I had fainted and hit my head on the desk behind me.

The memories rushed back. 'Did sir really give him ten?'

'No. You managed to bring the proceedings to a dramatic halt but it would have been no less than he deserved. Anyway, he will not be bullying any of you again. He is being expelled.'

Expelled. Sent home. Home to be beaten yet again by a furiously shamed Herr Mueller.

I began to cry again but this time my tears were accompanied by explanation. I told of the beatings, the swastika, the shaking of the baby's cot, the frightened wife, the way Wolfgang protected little Horst. I doubt if much of it was a surprise to them but the extent of it may have been.

91

Fräulein said it was very kind of me to pity Wolfgang after what he had done to me and Uncle Willi said I must not worry because Wolfgang would be taken away to a special place and looked after properly.

In the event the entire Mueller family left the district shortly after his expulsion and school once more became a secure and happy place in which I appeared to be accorded a new respect. By the time Elsa followed her brothers and sisters to school in Lübeck, my circle of friends was considerably enlarged and several made the long journey to Ströbelfields to play in the holidays.

I was not bullied again and shortly afterwards moved into the senior of the two classes, being taught by Uncle Willi. It was at that time that Elsa moved to the gymnasium in Lübeck and I became the only child at Ströbelfields during the week. Uncle Willi spent hours supplementing the education he dispensed at school and Omi, who had always spoiled me, thoroughly enjoyed having her youngest grandson so often in the house looking for adult company instead of outside playing with Elsa.

My grandmother was now nearly eighty and had reigned over Ströbelfields since the death of her husband more than thirty years ago. When I had first arrived she had often called me Willi-Lothar, which had puzzled me greatly until my mother explained that that had been the name of my father's son, my half-brother, who had died along with Lotte's other sibling in the Dresden bombing. When he died he was roughly the same age as I was when I arrived at Ströbelfields and, as we apparently looked very much alike, the adults occasionally confused our names, and Omi did so very frequently.

I still remembered my first night in the von Ströbel family and how Omi had been standing on the doorstep to greet me, arms wide, smiling broadly, light from the kitchen streaming around her. The scene is as vivid to me now as though it were yesterday, whenever I recall the moment when I moved from a hostile to a secure environment.

In the months after Wolfgang's departure I occasionally thought of him, sometimes vengefully and sometimes pityingly, but gradually he became a distant memory as do numb limbs before a fire. Ströbelfields wrapped me in its cocoon but I was growing up, acquiring knowledge, ceasing to believe everything I was told without question. The fairy tale of the handsome, brave soldier and the beautiful lady was beginning to seem less convincing, and I asked my mother questions which I knew worried her despite her breezy answers. I asked Aunt Angelika, who paused in some calculation as she did the weekly accounts and looked at me over the top of her reading glasses before distracting me with a question of her own.

It was Elsa who enlightened me, not because I asked her but because we quarrelled one winter afternoon in the Christmas holidays, and the beautiful fairy-tale of my birth became a story of ugliness and betrayal.

five

Truth

Elsa was nearly fourteen, clever, wilful, forceful, greeting every new experience with unfeigned enthusiasm, but she was alone. Otto and Hedy had left school and Lotte at sixteen suddenly seemed very grand and grown-up. She had inherited our father's brains and was outstripping even the rigorous education which the gymnasium could offer. Her particular strength lay in languages, as had our father's, and she had taken to speaking to me only in French in order to practise. She had been clamouring to be allowed to complete her education in France or England.

Uncle Willi had been less enthusiastic. He was keen enough for Lotte to follow in his brother's footsteps and knew that Klaus von Ströbel would have actively encouraged such a project, but Lotte, for all her academic prowess, was shy and retiring, reticent in company, keeping her own counsel, and he did not believe she would withstand the hostility of countries who had so recently been at war with Germany. In the end it had been agreed she would go to Switzerland where the family had both money and relatives.

The arrangement left Elsa without any young company in the house at Lübeck. It was owned by a couple called Schultz, who had had teenage children of their own when Uncle Willi first sent Franz there. The remoteness of Ströbelfields made a daily journey to the gymnasium imposs-ible and the Schultzes preferred to fill their house with young von Ströbels, Pletzes and von Forst-ners than with the refugees who had then been flocking into northern Germany by the million. Ernst and I would be the last to pass through their hands but we were still at the village school when Lotte left.

Elsa's isolation had been completed when Werner Pletz was also sent to boarding school, but in his case less for academic reasons than because he disobeyed the Schultzes' rules once too often. The difference between a girl of four-teen and a boy of eleven is greater than the years which separate them and while I looked forward to her homecomings she was beginning to find my company irksome and was particularly put out over that Christmas holiday when Lotte attached herself to Hedy rather than her.

She made little attempt to conceal her irritation when my mother called me, as I was pulling on my boots by the back door, wanting to know if I had done up my fur-lined jacket, which was warm but restricting, and reminding me not to use the green toboggan, which was dangerous and in need of repair.

'Baby,' grumbled Elsa. 'I suppose you still believe St Niklaus brings the presents.'

'All mothers fuss.'

'Do they? I wouldn't know. I haven't had one.'

'You've got Omi. She is like a mother to you.'

'She is my *grandmother*. Anyway these days she

is too busy spoiling you.'

I knew this to be true. Only that morning I had been allowed to scrape out the saucepan in which my mother had made custard, but when Elsa asked to share the treat Omi had called out sharply that such an activity was for children not for young ladies of fourteen. There was no intention on my grandmother's part to be unkind but she had the values of her generation and class, and expected more poise and formality from Elsa than was ever forthcoming.

'Well, at least you've got your father,' I consoled her. 'I never knew mine. He died before he could come back and marry mother.'

'Oh, don't be stupid. Uncle Klaus couldn't have married your mother.'

'He could. After the war. But he died.' I looked at her uneasily as I jerked out the fairy-tale, my confidence ebbing, and, as some dark shadow danced in a corner of my mind, I steeled myself for the loss of something precious, for the disintegration of diamond into dust.

'Yes, *after the war* he could have married your mother.'

I was disconcerted by her agreement and the emphasis she had given to *after the war*. I knew she had suddenly realised that she was on dangerous ground and was trying to climb to safety, but irritation still rankled and she could not resist a last taunt.

'When you are old enough I will show you our family tree – the one my father keeps in the library – and you will understand more than you can now.'

At once she looked alarmed, knowing she had gone too far and had hinted at a revelation her elders still considered taboo. I tried to take advantage of her fear but could not break down her belated discretion. We quarrelled several more times both that day and the succeeding one, until I crept into a stable to cry into the neck of Cicero, my beloved tan gelding to whom I had recently graduated from Caesar, my childhood pony. Uncle Willi had wanted to sell Caesar but I protested so bitterly that he relented and the beast now enjoyed a premature retirement, exercised only on the leading rein.

Otto found me there and prised the source of my misery from me.

'Girls!' He pulled a face of disgust. 'Just ignore her and look forward to Christmas.'

Both pieces of advice were good. I left Elsa alone and spent my time instead with Otto, who always seemed to need me for some task. As for looking forward to Christmas, I needed no encouragement. Subtly, almost imperceptibly, our Christmases had grown grander, and in 1956 we celebrated the festival on a scale that impressed even Maria, who had retired the previous year but came from the village to help when we had special need of it. Producers of our own food, we had not suffered as much as others from the grim post-war austerity, but the slow increase in availability of some imported goods and petrol, together with the gradual reappearance of luxury items, was felt as much at Ströbelfields as elsewhere.

Aunt Angelika was a shrewd manager and I cannot remember much extravagance. Leftover food was recycled as soup, soap ends were crushed into a jar, clothes and stockings were darned, but the grown-ups were learning to relax and to allow themselves to believe that Ströbelfields had once again miraculously survived a world upheaval, that the money held in Switzerland would not be seized, that if the life they had known before the First World War was just a distant memory, life after the Second World War might yet prove privileged and comfortable.

Certainly the extent to which we entertained our neighbours had expanded. As many as six families now came to Sunday lunch each month and a whole baron of beef would repose on the sideboard. During that Christmas of 1956 there was a huge party – the first since the war – in what Otto told me had once been a ballroom but which had been under dust sheets throughout my time in the house. Many guests stayed overnight and everywhere I looked fires burned in grates and Christmas decorations shimmered.

I observed it all with wonder but my favourite times were when the family was alone and Otto played carols while the rest of us sang. I watched the scene with a more discerning eye than when, as a child of five, I had peered through the bannisters and stared at my newly acquired family. I had begun to appreciate that each was a person with particular characteristics.

Aunt Angelika was strong and self-willed, a spinster by choice not chance, a grown-up and more controlled version of headstrong little Elsa. Uncle Willi was kindly, responsible and very much in charge, but he was now only a few years from retirement and the thick, dark, von Ströbel hair, which I saw in photographs of him and my father – and in the living reality of Lotte and me – had turned thinner and silver. Omi must have been frailer than when I first knew her but to me she had not changed at all and neither had my mother, whom I loved uncritically and was as yet incapable of seeing as anything other than above reproach.

Franz also seemed unchanging. Tall, thin, serious and kind, he was now a lawyer, practising in the town of Cloppenburg and visiting frequently at weekends. For a few months in the early part of that year he brought home with him a girl about two years his junior, who was called Emmi, but now he came alone. Alessandra was spending her first Christmas away from home, having become engaged the previous year to Hans-Jurgen von Heinzburg, an ambitious young diplomat whom she had met at university. I was obscurely glad that she came so rarely to Ströbelfields as I sensed her disapproval of my mother had not diminished with time. Otto and Hedy were at Heidelberg University, he reading medicine and she law. Otto came noisily home each holiday, but Hedy too was courting and did not always come with him.

On the day following the party Elsa and I quarrelled yet again and she said she could not waste any more time on me but would spend the morning skating on the lake.

'It's not safe,' I told her, conscious of malice and satisfaction in spoiling her fun. 'Uncle Willi says the ice is not yet thick enough.'

'Nonsense. That was last week. I know when it's safe.'

I did not skate well and rarely joined the others on the ice, although I was content to watch. We were not allowed to skate alone and Elsa and I were not supposed to be on the frozen lake at all without an older person present. Undeterred, she fetched her skates from her room and carried them unobserved through the house, ignoring my feeble protest, walking down to the lake with her head held high, pretending to be unaware that I was trailing miserably behind her. I made no further attempt to reason with her, hoping that she would be caught and punished.

Elsa skated well and confidently, and my resentment was soon replaced by envy and admiration. She circled and twirled, jumping, balancing on first one leg and then the other. As she danced on the ice her bad temper seemed to melt away and her eyes sparkled with pleasure. After a while, Hermann came to watch, flopping down beside me. I patted his ageing head, remembering how once he would have bounded onto the ice, causing Lotte and Elsa to squeal that he would knock them over.

The ice cracked with a sound like a pistol shot, startling Hermann who began to bark. There was an exclamation of fear from Elsa and then she disappeared into the freezing water beneath.

Alarmed, I began to move towards the hole, treading gingerly, afraid not so much of the ice giving way as of falling down on its hard surface. Elsa's head appeared and she screamed at me to go back and hold out my scarf to her. I might have done so had she not added the words 'silly little fool'.

'I'll get help,' I told her and ran towards the

house, yelling for Uncle Willi. It was a fair distance to cover but all I thought about was that Elsa would now get into trouble and it would serve her right. She would be told off and banned from skating for the rest of the holiday. I had no fear for her, the last image she had presented to me being of irritation and scorn rather than shock.

Franz was the first to hear my shouts and came running towards me but I was by then so out of breath that it was a few seconds before I could explain what had happened. He told me to run into the house and tell the others, then turned and raced for the lake, looking not angry as I had expected but terror-struck. Soon everyone was shouting and running, leaving only Omi indoors, who forbade me to return to the lake. I sensed panic behind the command and began to understand that Elsa could be in real danger.

It must have been a quarter of an hour before Otto came panting back to announce that Elsa was all right, but it felt like much longer. Omi said she had telephoned for the doctor and then the kitchen was full of people and anxious enquiries as Uncle Willi came in with Elsa, wrapped in a blanket, blue with cold and shivering convulsively in his arms. Aunt Angelika followed them up to Elsa's room, clutching hot water bottles, in turn followed by Hedy with a steaming hot drink. I watched the procession with diminishing alarm and increasing curiosity, as the others stamped their feet to ease numb toes and talked of similar incidents in the long-ago past, most of which seemed to have culminated in mustard baths and nasty colds.

Presently Uncle Willi returned to announce that Aunt Angelika was coping. He was wheezing badly and gripped the rail of the kitchen range for support. His lungs had been affected decades ago in the freezing seas of Jutland, from which he had been plucked by the British who had then made him a prisoner of war. In cold weather he wore scarves around his throat and wrapped up like an invalid, but in his concern for his youngest child he had just rushed from the house in indoor clothes. Franz was looking at him with concern.

'It will be all right,' Otto assured him, understanding that his anxiety was greater than his physical discomfort. 'People have survived much longer immersions as you well know.'

'Yes, but I was a fit young naval officer and appropriately clothed when the order came to abandon ship.'

'They don't come much stronger or fitter than Elsa.' Lotte was handing round hot drinks and now she told Otto to fetch brandy and her uncle to sit down. We all stared at her, the quietest member of the family, as she took charge and I saw Uncle Willi and Franz exchange glances of surprise.

Where was my mother in all the drama? I looked round in time to see her accepting a steaming cup from Lotte and a vague unease stirred within me. Omi, Aunt Angelika and Hedy were all upstairs tending my cousin, Lotte was organising refreshments for the rescue party, Franz and Otto were discarding dripping wet jerseys and fussing slightly over Uncle Willi while my mother sat with Macfidget on her lap and watched everyone else.

The word *ineffectual* had recently been added to my vocabulary and I thought of it now. It left me feeling vaguely unhappy and somehow an outsider. The Dessins stood by while the von Ströbels rallied round each other.

'Well done, Klaus-Pierre.' Franz's words broke into my miserable thoughts and I saw that everyone was looking at me. 'If you had not run so fast to raise the alarm, Elsa could have frozen to death or drowned. You probably saved her life.'

At once I was the centre of attention with Otto clapping me cheerfully on the back and the others adding their own words of praise. I felt once more an insider, a part of their family, until my conscience reminded me that I'd been running to tell tales, that I had wanted Elsa to get into trouble.

'What's the matter?' Uncle Willi had not missed the change in my expression.

'I wasn't trying to save her life because I hadn't really realised how great the danger was. I was trying to get her into trouble.'

I expected their faces to fall, to be rebuked for so silly an attitude at my age, to see disappointment on every countenance. I was disconcerted, therefore, when gales of laughter shook the kitchen and my elders clutched each other in helpless mirth. They gasped uncontrollably, trying not to spill the coffee from their cups, and when the noise had subsided it immediately rose again.

Otto put an arm around my shoulder, seeing my bewilderment, but he was still shaking with laughter. 'Good things can come from bad, Klaus-Pierre. We may all thank God you quarrelled with Elsa.'

'Good things also come from good,' muttered Franz to Uncle Willi. 'We may thank God the boy was here at all.'

He had not meant his words to be overheard but they fell into a sudden silence and he looked disconcerted. Immediately everyone began to talk at once but not before I had seen the blush spread across my mother's face, causing me once more to feel ill at ease.

'May you always be as honest, Klaus-Pierre,' said Uncle Willi.

Pieces of the conversation re-ran themselves in my mind as I played alone the next day while Elsa recovered in bed. The doctor had prescribed forty-eight hours rest and warmth, but it was no surprise when my cousin developed a heavy cold and began to cough chestily. I resigned myself to spending the rest of the holiday without her, deciding to explore the winter whiteness of Ströbelfields on my own unless Otto called me to a task.

Sometimes, in childhood, knowledge and understanding creep up on one so that their arrival is scarcely noticed, and what was once misunderstood or mysterious is no longer so and this seems in no way remarkable. At other times fragments of information join together with an almost audible click, providing sudden enlightenment, causing surprise, excitement or simple comprehension. In neither of these ways did I come to confront my origins. Instead I began to grope my way through the maze of half-understood explanations and indiscretions, unhappily aware that at the centre of the puzzle was something I did not really wish to find.

We may thank God the boy was here at all. I did not belong at Ströbelfields. My being there was not in the natural order of things as it was for Uncle Willi's children and for Lotte. I was there because someone had taken pity on my plight, a plight I now struggled to understand. What was the difference between Lotte and me? We were both the children of Klaus von Ströbel after all.

Good can come from bad, Klaus-Pierre. I was now sure that I was a good thing that had come from bad, although certainly there was no suggestion of that in the context in which the words had been spoken.

She was very fond of Aunt Ellie. That had been the unguarded explanation for Alessandra's coldness towards my mother and me. It had made little sense to a five-year-old but to my eleven-year-old mind it now seemed obvious that my mother must have upset my father's wife in some way or wronged her.

Don't be silly. Uncle Klaus couldn't have married your mother. Why not? What had my mother told me? I recalled the tale well enough: my father had been far from home and had to go back before he could marry my mother. This seemed to tie in well enough with what Elsa had said when she had snapped that of course my father could have married my mother *after the war,* but it tied in with the words not the tone.

When you are older, I will show you our family tree, the one my father keeps in the library, and then you will understand more than you can now. Well, I could

105

read family trees well enough, having been taught by Uncle Willi himself, and if this was where the clue to it all lay I saw no need to wait until I was older or for Elsa to condescend to show me. I could go to the library when the grown-ups were not about and locate the tree for myself, even though I had no idea where it was kept.

Over the next few days I made several attempts but my search was fruitless until one morning when I was so absorbed in my hunt that I did not hear Uncle Willi enter. I opened and shut an empty drawer with impatience and then started with fright when his voice asked me what I was looking for. At once I lied and said that I had lost a ruler.

Uncle Willi went on looking at me and my eyes fell. *May you always be as honest, Klaus-Pierre.* Unwillingly I muttered that I was looking for the family tree.

'Why?'

'I want to know.'

He did not ask me what I wanted to know but, hesitating only fractionally, he walked over to a bookcase and took down a large Bible. From the front of it he extracted a sheet of paper and I repressed an instinct to run away as he unfolded the seemingly vast diagram and laid it on the table which stood in the centre of the room. As I moved to look down at it, he quietly shut the door and, going to the fireplace, took his pipe from the mantelpiece and began to fill it, watching me as I studied the document.

My name was not there. Lotte and Elsa and all the others were there, their births faithfully recorded but, according to this family tree, neither I nor my mother existed. I looked up and met Uncle Willi's eyes.

'Well?'

'I'm not there, but I wouldn't be, would I? I'm a Dessin and this is a von Ströbel family tree.'

'Do you know why you are called Dessin?'

'Because ladies only change their names when they marry and my mother couldn't marry my father.'

'Yes, that is right, of course, but do you know *why* your parents could not marry? Look again at the tree, Klaus-Pierre. Are there any dates there you recognise?'

I looked at my father's entry. He was the third son of Peter and Lotte von Ströbel. Of the five children, only he and Uncle Willi had married and had their own offspring. Lothar had died in 1923 and Gerhardt – the one who had hanged himself in the barn – in 1942 while Angelika remained single. My father had married Elizabeth Maria Alessandra Priller (Ellie) in 1929 and had three children – Johanna Elizabeth, Willi-Lothar Peter and, of course, Lotte, but I did not get as far as her entry, my eyes remaining fixed on the date of death of the two older ones: 13 February, 1945. My finger moved back to their mother's entry. Ellie had died on the same date, on the very day I was born, and six months after my father's own death.

Ellie had been alive when my father died. He had never been free to marry. She was alive right up to the day I was born. I looked up and met Uncle Willi's eyes.

'Were my father and his first wife divorced?'

He shook his head. 'No. She wasn't his first wife, Klaus-Pierre. She was his only wife.'

Walter Pletz's guffaw sounded again in my mind. *You never know what the von Ströbels will do next. You know they've even brought home the mistress?* What was that word I had struggled so hard to say? Libbybean. Libertine.

'Uncle Willi, what's a libertine?'

'Something your father was not. Put that right out of your mind. He fell genuinely in love with your mother and you are the result of that love, of a deep, serious, tender love. I want you always to remember that.'

'But isn't it wrong to have babies when you can't marry?'

'Yes. Your parents did wrong, but all human beings do bad things occasionally.'

'Am I a bastard?' I spoke in French, ignorant of the German equivalent.

'That is an ugly word.'

'It's what they called me in France.'

'I do not want to hear it in this house. You are the child of your parents' love.'

With that, for the time being, I had to be content. Uncle Willi then began to talk of other matters, about how babies came into existence and the changes in my body I might notice as I grew older and about what happened to girls of Elsa's age every month. If ever there was anything I did not understand I must ask him or Franz or Otto, but not other children who might pretend to know everything but in reality know nothing. I made only the haziest connection between this

108

conversation and the one that had immediately preceded it, my main feeling one of embarrassment and a fear that he might realise I already knew much of what he now so solemnly told me. I pushed from my mind any thought that my parents might have engaged in such undignified activity.

Two years later Uncle Willi once more shut the library door and supplemented the information he had already given me because I was due to go to the gymnasium in Lübeck and to live away from Ströbelfields during the week. This time he talked not about girls but about other boys, and again I refrained from telling him that Ernst Pletz had many months before whispered these things to me in tones of scandalised horror.

By then I had also added the words 'adultery' and 'illegitimate' to my lexicon, and the warmth and security of the fairy-tale had long since disappeared, leaving only truth in its wake.

six

Growing up

I had always expected 1958 to be a significant year in my personal annals. It was the year in which I wore long trousers and went to the gymnasium, began to learn Latin and to live with the Schultzes, made a host of new friends at school and played team games on its generous sports pitches; the year in which Uncle Willi at last retired from teaching and Alessandra, who had married her diplomat the previous year, presented him with his first grandson, who arrived complete with the dark hair and features of the von Ströbels; the year in which Hedy announced her engagement and my mother's childhood friend, Bette, came to spend a fortnight with us in the summer.

Bette made a fuss of Macfidget, who was now a prodigious age and spent most of his time asleep in front of the kitchen range, and I had to listen, yet again, to reminiscences of how she and my mother had found him in the looted apartment of a Jewish schoolfriend and had carried him away in a pillow case. My father had agreed to look after him but had returned him when my mother was leaving Paris to live in Provence. More surprisingly, Bette made a fuss of Alphonse, my even more aged teddy bear, which she had given to my mother also when she was leaving Paris.

'Actually, I think I lent him to you,' she said, and I was half afraid she would take him away even though it was a long while since I had played with him. The bear was one of my earliest memories and treasured accordingly.

Once, when I approached without either of them hearing me, I heard her tell my mother that she should get married. On another occasion I heard them arguing because my mother had rejected France so resolutely that she refused even to speak its language and insisted that, as Bette spoke fluent German, they should converse in that tongue instead. I formed a vague impression that Bette was impatient with my mother and wanted her to make some change to her life which I could not quite understand but it seemed almost as if Bette thought we should not be at Ströbelfields, which might have alarmed me if my mother had looked at all convinced.

I did not much like the idea of my mother marrying but as there was no suitor I pushed it to the back of my mind. I did, however, very much want to speak French because I excelled in the subject at school and wanted to impress my new teachers when I went to Lübeck the following term. As we walked down to the lake together I asked Bette about Paris and, after a nervous glance behind me, whether she saw my grand-parents there.

At once I sensed caution but she answered straightforwardly, telling me that she had known my mother's family when she lived in Paris but that she had lost touch long ago. Occasionally she saw my mother's sister, Annette, in the street when she visited her own parents and thought, there-fore, that she must live close by, but she could not remember seeing any other member of the family for years. I was still curious and persisted to a degree which I knew my mother would have resented.

Apparently somewhere in France, probably still in Paris, I had grandparents and an Uncle Edouard as well as two aunts, Annette and Jeanne. My grandfather was a clever man who had taught at the Sorbonne, which Bette told me was a famous French university. I replied that my father had also been clever and taught at Heidelberg, which was a famous German university, and she laughed, telling me that she knew both of Heidelberg and of my father's brilliance. Then I asked her if she knew my father when he was a general and if she thought he was handsome and brave.

'Probably the most good-looking man I ever saw,' she said, 'but don't tell my husband I said so, and yes, he was undeniably brave, but he should not have been in Paris and I did not know him well.'

This time I had the discretion to press no further, sensing disapproval towards my father, and the same instinct prevented my recounting the conversation to my mother, but after Bette had gone I found my thoughts sometimes wandering to Paris and I wondered whether any of my relatives there remembered me or my mother. I had, of course, seen them briefly at my great-grandfather's funeral, from which wretched incident I could recall no one but the grandmother who had rejected me, a lady with dark hair and cold, unmoving features.

There were two other events in 1958 which were to have a huge impact on my life, changing its course, determining the future, but which passed by unremarked at the time.

The first took place in another country, in Austria, where, four years earlier, the Obernkirchen Children's Choir had had a very unlikely and world-wide hit with its song 'The Happy Wanderer'. It was now enjoying a major revival and for weeks the strains of 'fol de ree-ee, fol de raa-aa', could be heard as people in shops, the streets, bus queues and workplaces hummed, whistled and sang the lively strains. The song again became a favourite in elementary school music lessons and a must for end-of-term concerts.

'Fol de raa-ha-ha-ha-ha-haaaa,' sang Gunther the farmhand as he forked a heap of muck in the yard.

'I raise my hat to all I meet and they wave back to me,' trilled my mother as she sewed yet another nametag on to yet another school shirt.

'Oh, may I go a-wandering until the day I die,' roared Otto, thumping the piano keys with verve.

More surprisingly still, Walter Pletz led the entire company in song when he next came to Sunday lunch. I could never remember singing at the table before but Uncle Willi joined in as enthusiastically as everyone else.

'They've all gone mad,' whispered Ernst in amazed disgust. Aunt Angelika bought a bear for Alessandra's child and solemnly dressed it as a happy wanderer. It was thrown from the pram during a family visit to Ströbelfields and not noticed until they had left. Uncle Willi picked it up and left it on the kitchen table, and that was the last I saw of it for a long time.

The second event which was to shape my destiny occurred one summer Sunday when my mother had too severe a cold to take me to mass and Franz, who was visiting for a few days, offered to drive me there. My mother responded with relief and I with resignation, my brief hope of escaping church defeated.

From the beginning of my time at Ströbelfields our attendance at mass had caused a problem. The rest of the family went to a Lutheran service in the village but the nearest Catholic church was fifteen miles away and the difficulties in obtaining petrol made a weekly visit impossible, so we went once a month, my mother driving the ancient Volkswagen while the rest of the family crammed into the Horsch, the children sitting on each other's laps in the back seat. Indeed, when petrol became more available, the greatest relief to the others was being able to go to church in a convoy of the two cars.

On the Sundays when we did not go to mass my mother cooked lunch and kept me employed in a series of assorted tasks to help her, over which I never failed to grumble, and as soon as I heard the approach of the Horsch I would rush outside, hoping one of the others would take my place and that my absence would no longer be noticed. In this at thirteen I differed little from when I was six.

In those days, long before the second Vatican council and the ecumenical movement, Catholics and Protestants had little understanding of or patience with each other's religion and, from the outset, I had sensed not merely difference but disapproval. Although no one ever said so, I knew that the von Ströbels would prefer me to be Lutheran and that my mother regarded their Protestantism as the one regrettable feature of the household.

My first communion had presented a problem as I could not attend the classes of preparation, but eventually Uncle Willi heard of a monk who had come to live with his family in the village for six months while he recuperated from tuberculosis and, two years after others in my age group, I was given the necessary instruction. My mother's eyes were bright with tears as she took photographs with Aunt Angelika's childhood camera, but I hated the entire ceremony as I stood with a row of little girls dressed in white and two younger boys, feeling a fool, too old and out of place.

Now we went to church nearly every week but Omi was no longer strong enough to do so and we took it in turns to stay with her on Sunday mornings and cook the lunch. On that Sunday morning it had fallen to Aunt Angelika's lot to remain behind. My mother made a half-hearted offer to help her but was so obviously ill that it was Omi who looked after *her* rather than she Omi. I sensed that Uncle Willi would have preferred Franz to accompany the rest of them to the village service but it chanced to be a day when we had guests and he probably reasoned that Aunt Angelika would have her hands full, with her mother and mine needing attention, and would not welcome the addition of my noise and energy.

When we arrived at the church it was raining hard and Franz initially said he would stay in the car, but after the mass I saw him standing at the back of the church. It was only later that I could appreciate how alien the church, bright with candles and fragranced with incense, must have seemed to him. He was unusually quiet on the way back, occasionally asking questions about the church, the services and the priest, but otherwise content for me to prattle on until we arrived at Ströbelfields and I jumped from the car to greet Ernst.

'...but still blasphemous and idolatrous...' Uncle Willi's words drifted from the library, where the men were gathered after the meal, reaching me as I raced upstairs to find some item which I needed. 'They sacrifice Christ all over again as if that might augment what He did at Calvary, and they pray to graven images.'

'They think you can buy time off purgatory with money...' The conversation and Walter Pletz's contribution faded into inaudibility as I reached the landing, and by the time I was on my way down again they were talking about something else.

My mother had often told me that the most momentous events in our lives can stem from very small, unremarkable ones.

'Once I was with a group of other girls in Paris and we decided to defy the curfew – only very briefly, of course. We thought it would all be over quickly and were giggling and being pretty silly as we climbed out of the window. Now I know that, when I stood on that sill and had doubts about jumping down and really doing what we had so glibly talked about and egged each other on to do, I was about to change the course of my life because we were caught and that was how I met your father. Indeed, you are only here because I *did* jump rather than do what I should have done and gone to bed.'

Now I too look back in wonder. If my mother had not caught a cold, if it had not been at its worst that Sunday, if Franz had not been at home to take me to mass, if when we had got there it had not been raining, what would the course of my own life have been? Perhaps it would not have been so different. Perhaps Franz would have come into contact with Catholicism in some other way...

Ströbelfields was changing, as the older children visited less frequently, and I too began to look outwards, sometimes spending weekends and parts of holidays with boys from school. From these visits I learned that most German families lived very different lives from my own.

Since my earliest excursions beyond the family estate, I had been aware of the widespread devastation the war had left in its wake. Everywhere there were ruins and rubble and large signs proclaiming buildings too dangerous to enter. Amidst the destruction children played, often running to look at our car, which was a rare sight. Once I saw a lorry delivering coal to the hospital shed some of its load and, within seconds, both children and grown-ups had flung themselves on the bounty so unexpectedly rolling in the road, fighting over individual lumps as if they were made of gold, racing from the scene triumphantly, clutching the coals tightly, fearing to be robbed. At Ströbelfields we had but to go into the woods when we needed fuel for our fires.

In the houses of my friends I was offered turnips, potato and bread sprinkled with sugar. All of them had at least one stranger living with them and I learned of the millions of refugees who had flocked into Germany after the war – Germans expelled from territory their country no longer owned or where they were no longer tolerated – adding themselves to a population which was itself hungry and homeless. Uncle Willi told me that once there had been refugees at Ströbelfields but that they had drifted away because there was no work there and they wanted to rebuild their shattered lives.

My friends both at the village school and at Lübeck wore *lederhosen*, leather shorts, which were durable but always scuffed and scratched. The girls darned and re-darned their clothes. For entertainment we listened to crackling radio sets. I was particularly fond of a detective series called *Gestatten, Mein Name ist Cox*. Some of my friends read comics, and I followed the exploits of Nick Knatterton and Mickey Mouse. For ten *pfennigs* we could go to the cinema and watch cowboy films. Maria Schell, Hans Harber, Hildegard Knef and Heinz Rühmann, the film stars of those years would, for two hours, transport us from our war-torn corner of hell into a world of excitement and daring. As we grew older we listened to Manuela and Peter Alexander singing on the radio but I cannot recall a single gramophone outside Ströbelfields other than the one at the Schultz house in Lübeck.

I saw adults steal from children and elderly men scrabble in the street for a discarded cigarette end and I watched women scavenging gingerly in the rubble, afraid of unexploded bombs.

By the time I started school in Lübeck there was visible improvement, with most of the rubble cleared away, more goods in the shops and the occasional car parked in the streets. By the time I left school the early signs of what was to become a galloping prosperity were well in evidence.

I was academically competent, top only in French but near the top in most subjects, enthusiastic rather than technically excellent at sport and a passable actor in school productions. I disappointed Uncle Willi by demonstrating a woeful lack of any musical talent but somewhat compensated for the failure by proving a forceful and fluent debater.

'You must get it from your mother,' he observed when I won a cup. 'Your father apparently once admired her rhetoric.'

My mother smiled modestly but then went on to lament my decision to spend the first part of the Easter break with Fritz and Jurgen, two brothers, who for a short while had also lived with the Schultzes while their mother underwent a serious but successful operation.

'I see so little of you, Klaus-Pierre.'

I understood. When I was away in Lübeck my mother had no family of her own and, indeed, none of my cousins to look after. Omi, to whom she had always been close, was in failing health, while Uncle Willi had been preoccupied with the estate since his retirement and was closely assisted by Aunt Angelika.

It was Aunt Angelika who answered my mother now. 'Easter is a long way off. We are together for Christmas and he must have his freedom, Catherine. He has his own way to make in life.'

I knew, as surely as if she had told me, that my mother was worried about exactly that; that she was foreseeing a time when my returns to Ströbelfields would be as sporadic as were those now of Franz, Alessandra, Otto and Hedy. Perhaps she felt that her moral claim to be under Uncle Willi's roof would die with my own departure and that she would feel obliged to leave too.

I was growing at a rapid rate and could now look upon the photograph in my mother's room at eye level with Klaus von Ströbel. When I had first arrived at Ströbelfields I had had to stand on tiptoe, resting my hands against the tall chest of drawers, in order to see the likeness of my father, taken in his uniform, and in which he always seemed to be smiling in my direction. As the years passed I had pressed my palms against higher drawers until, one day, I found myself able to rest my hands on the top. Now I merely stood and stared at the photo. There were, of course, many other photographs of my father in the house: family photographs, one showing Lotte as a babe in arms held by Ellie while my father and other half-siblings smiled at the camera.

Sometimes when I looked at that family group I thought of how the children had died, wondering if the bomb had dissolved them instantly or if they had felt pain as well as fear. In most of these photographs my father was in civilian clothes but there was one of him in the uniform of a First World War soldier, which stood next to a picture of his elder brother, Lothar, who wore flying clothes and goggles, posed by an aeroplane. Uncle Willi had once told me it was called a Fokker Triplane.

When I was younger I had liked the photograph in my mother's room best because it showed my father was important, smart and commanding in his general's uniform, but lately I liked it because

I understood that this was how he had looked when he fell in love with my mother, when, together, they had done the thing which had produced me. This was the man I would have known had he lived.

Once, when I was so absorbed in my study that I had not heard the door open, I was startled by my mother's voice.

'He was a marvellous man. I do so wish you had known him.'

That day I had sat in class revising English verbs while the Protestants learned scripture but the words of the lesson drifted into my consciousness: *Thou shalt not commit adultery.* A man must be faithful to his wife and she to him. I could not associate my mother with wickedness but Pastor Steiner had been clear enough in his teaching that there were no exceptions to the law Moses had brought down from Sinai.

It was a puzzle that could wait, fading from my mind when I heard Elsa calling me to say the car was ready for the trip to the village to do the last-minute pieces of Christmas shopping, lingering only in an occasional, small, cold knot somewhere in my stomach, which I knew one day would reach my heart.

Arguments were rare at Ströbelfields. The older children had been through too much to be distracted by petty irritations, but Lotte, Elsa and I had known no war, no loss of loved ones which we were capable of remembering. The pain had been absorbed by others while we were too young to understand or, in my case, not even born. The gradual easing of post-war restrictions allowed us to live less deprived childhoods than my older cousins and, lacking tragedy to inform our sense of proportion or grief to draw us close, we were more prone to fall out over trivia.

Lotte changed that. She returned from Switzerland that Christmas to announce that she wished to abandon her studies in favour of marriage. Uncle Willi flatly refused to contemplate such a possibility when she was only eighteen. It did not help that her choice was Rudi Pletz, Walter's eldest son. His father, also considering the proposal preposterous, given Lotte's youth and the eight-year difference in their ages, spent hours in urgent conference with our uncle while the rest of us endured the plaint of Lotte's mutiny.

Only Omi was on Lotte's side.

'Mutti, it is not like it was in your day. Women go to university now,' argued Aunt Angelika. 'Lotte is clever. She should make the most of herself and marry later on.'

'But she does not want to. I married your father at nineteen.'

'Yes, but Lotte is a very young eighteen. Klaus would have had a fit. You know how keen he was on education. Please don't encourage her.'

'I know my own mind best,' raged Lotte.

'I thought that at your age,' observed my mother and there was a sudden silence, which not even Lotte knew how to break.

When the Pletzes came to lunch with us at New Year, Rudi tactfully stayed at home. Werner and Ernst said their father had argued with their elder brother throughout the holiday, frequently reducing their mother to tears. Ernst thought Rudi mad to be in love, as girls were all soppy and useless, but Werner was quieter on the subject and I knew he understood something which eluded Ernst and me. After a while he went and sought out Hedy, on whom he had a crush, which caused her no emotion greater than slightly irritated amusement.

The Pletzes departed at six and it was only then that Lotte was missed, everyone having assumed she was with someone else or perhaps sulking in her room. Cicero was missing from the stables and Uncle Willi and Walter exchanged resigned glances. She returned at eight, having spent the time since lunch with Rudi.

'You are not my father.' The words were spoken quietly but I saw the hurt on Uncle Willi's face as he turned from her. 'You don't understand. You come from the last century.'

I knew that never again would those words be a familiar, comfortable family joke. Uncle Willi had been born in 1898, two years before my father's birth at the turn of the century. Whenever he expressed displeasure with fashionable trends or surprise at modern developments, one of his children would tease him by telling him that he had been born in the wrong century. Never before had I heard it flung at him in insult and I stared at Lotte aghast.

I was almost glad when the end of the holidays returned me to school and the Schultzes' care. A fortnight later my mother told me in a letter that Lotte had returned to Switzerland, having been persuaded by Rudi himself that she must complete her schooling as originally planned, after which they would become engaged. More importantly she told me to prepare for bad news: Macfidget had died peacefully in his sleep, curled up on the end of her bed. I cried miserably into Frau Schultz's cardigan-clad bosom, noting the scent of lavender and cheap powder and wishing she instead smelled like my mother.

I thought of Macfidget dozing on the sundial in Provence, the house and garden enlarged in my memory to twice their real size; of him lying next to Hermann by the fire at Ströbelfields; of his purr late at night when he had chosen my bed in preference to my mother's. She must have been engaged in very different recollections, perhaps recalling my father's hands as he stroked the smoky fur or the large feline eyes which peered at her from under the chair in my father's office or my father's smile as he coaxed the animal into confidence. Macfidget had been the one continuous link with Klaus von Ströbel, a living being they had shared and loved.

Hardly had I absorbed this news when it was followed by that of Hermann's death. The dog had trotted off on his usual teatime wander and not returned. Uncle Willi had tracked his prints through the snow and found the body by the lake. It looked as if Hermann had dropped in mid-stride. I thought of how frightened I had been of him when I had arrived at Ströbelfields and of how much pleasure he had given me since, running beside our bicycles when Werner and I went exploring, stealing the odd piece of food from an outraged Maria, pleading with large, hopeful eyes when I smuggled biscuits into my bedroom.

'At least it is not a human being,' said Herr

124

Schultz unhelpfully.

'They'll get you another dog,' was Ernst's clumsy attempt at comfort and I found myself wanting Franz or Otto, sure that they would understand.

When I went home one Saturday afternoon it was to find both of them at Ströbelfields. Franz had arrived to tell an incredulous Uncle Willi that he was converting to Catholicism, having persuaded Otto to accompany him for moral support. Their father made no attempt to deter Franz but equally did not conceal his disquiet that the heir to Ströbelfields was departing from the Lutheran tradition which had been the family's religion for generations. Later I saw him give my mother's back an unguarded glare and knew that he blamed her for contaminating his elder son with Papism.

I had little understanding of the fuss, having always accepted Catholicism as synonymous with divine truth, and was enthusiastic merely at having Franz and Otto at home to ride and talk with, lamenting that tennis would not be possible for another couple of months. By the time that season had arrived the household was in a ferment with plans for Hedy's wedding. I watched the preparations with all the detachment of a fourteen-year-old, preoccupied neither with taffeta nor bridesmaids but with television.

The Schultzes had recently obtained one and I had become sufficiently engrossed with some of the regular programmes to resent being deprived of them during the school holidays. A small number of aerials testified to the existence of television in Lübeck, although none of my friends yet had sets in their homes, but Uncle Willi had remained obdurate about 'not needing' one, having abandoned his previous objection that we were too remote to obtain a good picture when Walter Pletz finally capitulated to the demands of Werner and Ernst and the reception proved both adequate and consistent.

'It is a most unnecessary apparatus,' resisted Uncle Willi.

'At your age you should be outside in God's fresh air, not goggling at some silly little screen indoors,' remonstrated Aunt Angelika.

'I don't lack fresh air,' I protested with indignant truth. From the moment I had arrived at Ströbel-fields I had spent the majority of my leisure hours outside. My classmates, who had grown up in Lübeck and post-war stringency, were thin and pale, while I had the health, strength and complexion of a teenager who had spent his childhood on horses, bicycles and toboggans in the fresh air whatever the weather. The estate produced our food and we had never been lacking in anything which might be home grown or fished from a river. I was the second tallest in the class and by far the healthiest.

Only Elsa took my side on the issue. 'There are some very good educational programmes,' she told Uncle Willi with an innocent face.

'There is also some pretty good nonsense. I do not remember Klaus-Pierre talking about the educational programmes he has seen at the Schultzes.'

'Omi is getting too frail to do much these days. A television could give her hours of entertainment.' I spoke with a grin to acknowledge my guile but Uncle Willi looked thoughtful and Elsa raised her thumbs at me behind his back.

The set was installed that September but Uncle Willi would not have it in the living room. The dust sheets were removed from a small room which had formerly been known as 'the old servants' room', which was now decorated and supplied with chairs, but access was strictly regulated.

Ströbelfields was full of such nooks and crannies, and there were several rooms which I had seen in use only for Alessandra's and Hedy's weddings, but when we raised our glasses to welcome 1960, Aunt Angelika said, 'I think the lean years are over. We should open up the house again.'

'And the barn,' said Uncle Willi quietly.

'Especially the barn.' We all looked at Omi, surprised by the emphasis in her tone. 'We cannot forever be haunted by the past. Germany is looking to the future and so should we. I should like us to open up the barn before I die.'

I thought back to my early years at Ströbelfields, remembering Elsa's nightmares when Werner had told us the grisly history of the barn. I saw again, in my memory, my mother walking from it a few days after we had arrived, her face shriven, some great weight rolled away. I was excited, repelled, apprehensive and I rebuked myself for a superstitious fool. Was it not many years since I had seen the door open and told myself I need never fear it again?

Two days later the farmhands began clearing the barn. I went in with Uncle Willi and followed his glance towards the rafters, knowing that that was where Uncle Gerhardt had hanged himself. I knew more of the story now.

Uncle Gerhardt had been seriously mentally handicapped from birth. A happy and peaceful child, he pottered around among the farm animals, apparently very skilled in calming them and sensing their needs. He had never been to school and the remoteness of the location meant that, with a bit of help from a kindly doctor, the family had managed to protect him from Hitler's infamous programme of killing the disabled. His existence and age were well enough documented, however, and eventually he was called up and sent as a guard to Dachau.

Alerted by Omi, my father had come back from Paris to find some way of rescuing his brother. Uncle Willi had made similar arrangements and so the entire clan was gathered at Ströbelfields for the Christmas of 1942. Uncle Willi told me that they had little idea what they could do, but a few days before they arrived home Uncle Gerhardt was suddenly brought back, without any explanation. In the middle of one night he woke his brothers and told them through mime, because he could not speak, what went on at Dachau.

'It was a terrible pantomime,' Uncle Willi had told me. 'It didn't leave us any room for doubt as to the atrocities he had seen and it left your father so devastated that he went back to Paris and began helping Jews to escape. God knows how he got away with it. His adjutant, Kurt Kleist, said he took the most the most incredible risks.'

Uncle Gerhardt had hanged himself that very night and been found by Aunt Angelika who was then a young woman in her twenties.

'The biggest mystery of all is one that remains to this day: why did they send him back? I am fairly certain who betrayed him in the first place. It must have been Mueller – you remember his son, Wolfgang, who used to bully you and half the class? He was revelling in his petty position of power at the time and enjoyed exerting it over people he had previously thought of as superior, but none of us have ever worked out who made sure Gerhardt came back to us instead of just perishing at Dachau as his condition warranted under that vile regime. Neither Klaus nor I knew anyone at that camp but someone, somewhere, helped us and probably took a chance in doing so.'

It was not the question which lingered with me. Mine was much simpler but one I could not ask. At the end of 1942 the adults of Ströbelfields had known how Jews were tortured in the concentration camps and appeared to have done nothing about it, with the exception of my father who had put his life on the line in Paris, where he helped the persecuted. I had grown up with an indefinable suggestion which seemed to hang in the very air of Ströbelfields that my father was somehow morally inferior to Uncle Willi. Of course, his only lapse from grace had been his affair with my mother but it was a very large and baffling one, whereas Uncle Willi was a good family man who had brought up his brother's children as well as his own.

Naturally no one would have dreamed of saying any of this but I knew they thought it and I longed to challenge the complacency, to cry, 'so what did you do, then?' Had I been younger I would have done so but by the time I was deemed old enough to know what had happened I was old enough also to know what I could not ask. So now I looked up at the rafters and said nothing.

We were emerging from the barn when Elsa called out that a car was coming along the drive.

Uncle Willi began to brush straw from his disreputable old clothes as he watched its progress. 'It's Hans,' he murmured in tones of surprise, and I prepared to meet the headmaster of my elementary school.

While Aunt Angelika bustled about producing coffee, the head explained that one of his teachers was in hospital for four weeks and none of the usual temporary help was available for a week after the start of term. Could Uncle Willi assist for just that week?

My uncle put up a half-hearted resistance, saying that he was retired and that the estate needed him, that with Franz and Otto living miles away and his long-serving farm manager working only part-time following a temporary but severe illness, he simply had no time. We could all see he wanted to return and be among the children again and Aunt Angelika snorted that she had managed the estate during the war and all through his teaching years and she did not see why anyone should consider her incapable now.

The vacancy was with the younger class and over the next couple of days Uncle Willi devoted a great deal of energy to wondering how he was to teach them when all his work had previously been with the older age group. It was my mother who noticed the Wanderer Bear which Alessandra's child had left behind a year before and which had been put on top of the dresser and largely forgotten.

'Make up a story about the Wanderer Bear,' she suggested. 'You could talk about the countryside and all the things the bear might have seen, teaching them the names of trees and plants and how farming works.'

'Then he could wander off to a city,' suggested Aunt Angelika.

'He could set them an example of good manners too,' offered Omi. 'Remember he raises his hat to all he meets.'

'He could go abroad for geography lessons,' I suggested.

'And back through time for history,' put in Elsa. 'He could raise his hat and all the ladies would curtsey and the gentlemen make old-fashioned bows.'

Uncle Willi propped the Wanderer Bear against a lectern in the library and began to draw him to illustrate his lessons. Every so often one of us would put a head round the library door with a new suggestion. Meanwhile we tried to remember the words of the song and the strains of 'fol-de-ree-ee, fol-de-raa-aa' were once again heard in the yard of Ströbelfields.

By the time I was sitting my end-of-term exams in the summer of that year, with the sun streaming through the windows on to my desk, Uncle Willi had a contract with a publisher for three Wanderer Bear books and, when I was in that same hall, penning my Christmas examinations, with snow falling steadily outside, the first book, which had been rushed into publication, was already well on the way to being a worldwide sensation and Willi von Ströbel to becoming a household name.

It was a heady, exciting time, yet now it seems but a prelude to the year which was to come, a last period of calm before my small boat entered the storm-tossed ocean of life and death and separation from Ströbelfields.

seven

Stepfather

The original Wanderer Bear was at Ströbelfields no more, having been borrowed for a display by a museum and booked for several similar engagements thereafter, but imitations lay everywhere. The design had been mass-produced to coincide with the production of the first book and had been among the most popular toys purchased that Christmas. A quantity of complimentary ones had been sent to their inventor and promptly despatched to an orphanage in Cloppenburg, but two had been retained for Alessandra's children and one for Hedy's baby, which was due in the late spring.

The children had also received bears from friends who might not have realised that Alessandra and Hedy were daughters of Willi von Ströbel, and about six bears were now strewn throughout the house. I fell over one at the bottom of the stairs on the morning of New Year's Eve in 1961 and stubbed my toe on the opposite wall. The sounds of my displeasure brought Lotte from the kitchen.

'Such words at your age! I'm surprised you know them.'

I tried to grin but my foot was horribly painful and I hoped I had not broken the toe.

'You could try an ice pack if you really must be so feeble. Meanwhile how about taking up Omi's coffee?'

'OK but give me a second or so. Are you here today?'

'Yes. Rudi is coming over. I will go there tomorrow.'

I took the cup and saucer from her, noticing again the sapphire on the third finger of her left hand. She was to marry in the summer and Uncle Willi, reassured by the test of time, seemed happy enough that he had done his duty by his brother's daughter and willing to commit her to the Pletzes' care. Walter Pletz, being likewise reconciled to the arrangement, was full of plans.

On the first floor I knocked gently at Omi's door and pushed it open. As I approached the bed I noticed her stillness. Normally she would turn and smile and bid me good morning. I was by the bed itself and putting down the coffee when she at last spoke without looking at me.

'Where is my husband, Hannie? Has he gone out?'

A chill entered my stomach. 'You have been dreaming, Omi. It is I, Klaus-Pierre.'

'Come where I can see you.'

I bent over her and looked down into confused eyes.

'Lothar! Where is your father?'

'I'll get him.' I fled to find Uncle Willi and cannoned into Alessandra.

She looked at me with more than her customary disapproval and it was with some satisfaction that I saw her face change as I blurted out my explanation. She ran along the corridor to Omi's room and I ran to Uncle Willi's.

Over the next few hours Omi called Willi by my father's name and me by Willi-Lothar's. By lunchtime we were all gathered around her bed, having left the room only for the duration of the doctor's visit. Alessandra's children were becoming fractious and she asked me to take them downstairs. I looked at her in indignation, wanting to protest that I had as much right to stay by Omi's bed as she had, indeed more because she had left Ströbelfields years ago and I still remained, seeing Omi each day.

'Let Hans-Jurgen go, Alessandra.' Uncle Willi did not take his eyes from his mother as he spoke.

Alessandra's husband drew briefly closer to her as if unwilling to leave her in a time of need, then he turned and, treading softly, left the room, holding the baby in the crook of one arm and the toddler with his other hand. I avoided Alessandra's eyes, looking straight at Omi who stared unseeingly into the middle distance. Presently she turned her head and smiled at Uncle Willi and Aunt Angelika, but she said no more until the room was beginning to darken and I was wondering whether it might be disrespectful to suggest a light.

'He should never have done it to Ellie.' The words were quiet, sad and very clear and they were my grandmother's last. She died twenty minutes later.

I passed a sleepless night between tears and memories, especially memories, the images dancing before my eyes as if they were real. I saw a small child coming in from the snow weeping with the pain of numb fingers and Omi soaking them in hot water, coaxing the life back into them, talking nonsense about how Hermann might need his paws soaked too; the same child a year or so older running in, drenched by rain, and Omi wrapping a tea towel around dripping wet hair, grumbling that God had given us mackintoshes for a purpose; a thirteen-year-old dropping his suitcase by the door, calling out to his grandmother that he had come first in Latin; the fifteen-year-old I now was whispering to her that girls were soppy.

Say your prayers, Klaus-Pierre. Wash your face, Klaus-Pierre. Are you going to help your mother, Klaus-Pierre? Your laces are undone, Klaus-Pierre.

I grinned into the darkness. 'Thanks, Omi,' I whispered.

The priest said we should not attend anything as heretical as a Lutheran funeral but we went anyway and I do not think he cared at all. Walter Pletz was there, looking as glum and serious as I had ever seen him. The normally cool, independent, vigorous Aunt Angelika looked crumpled, almost wizened. Franz was puffy-eyed and, with something like shock, I realised I had never seen a grown-up man cry before. When I found I too was crying I felt obscurely embarrassed.

I prayed for Omi in the words I had been taught, words I had heard regularly in church each week but which until now had no practical urgency for me. *Let perpetual light shine upon her, may she rest in peace, Amen.* I tried to imagine the elderly Omi bathed in perpetual light but all I could think of was a crumbling body deep in the earth. That was where Macfidget and Hermann had gone and I knew I was yet to be convinced that it would be different for Omi. For a moment I was so startled by the thought that grief was briefly suspended, while I marvelled at the revelation that I was not, despite my now weekly Mass attendance, much of a believer.

I defended my faith vigorously enough when I felt it under attack from Lutherans at school but it now occurred to me that if no one else had thought Catholicism so odd then I would in turn have thought about it very little. The reflection was soon lost as I became absorbed in thoughts of Omi, wondering what my life might have been if she had not been willing to include me in her family at Ströbelfields, remembering the persecution I had endured in Provence. Others must have been shunned and scorned, for I could not have been the only child of a liaison between the occupied and their oppressors. Did such children, now teenagers, still suffer?

Whatever their fate, I had been happy and still was. I prayed more earnestly that Omi might be in some land of angels, harps and perpetual light, clad in a long white nightgown, floating gently, cushioned by cloud.

'Peter has waited a long time for her,' Aunt Angelika said to Uncle Willi the next day and I tried to repress the thought that my grandfather was no more than bones, instead concentrating on a picture of him together with my father and uncles, lurking behind Saint Peter as Omi arrived through heaven's gate. I smiled, and Alessandra gave me an appalled glance.

Over the past few days Ströbelfields had filled with relatives, many of whom I had never seen before. I tried to ignore the covert curiosity with which most looked at me and the shadows of disapproval which I could not help but detect in the way they looked at my mother. *Klaus-Pierre Dessin*. My father's shame and betrayal was enshrined in my very name.

I knew, from unguarded comments I had heard in childhood, that Uncle Willi would have been willing enough for me to take his name, but my mother, who had renounced any connection with France and her family, was perversely insistent that I should remain a Dessin. As we sat behind the rest of the family, the *legitimate* family, at the funeral I wondered if it would have made any difference, if a change of name would have been armour against censure.

The death of my grandmother left a huge gap in companionship at Ströbelfields, especially now that my uncle spent a great deal of time away promoting the Wanderer Bear or closeted in his library at home writing its latest adventures. Shortly after my sixteenth birthday he proposed that I should leave the gymnasium after my

Mittlere Reife that summer and complete my education in another country. My mother strenuously resisted, pleading that it was too soon for Germans to be accepted, that I would encounter prejudice and hatred, and that I had led too sheltered a life to cope with it.

'He is called Dessin,' pointed out Aunt Angelika. 'He would find things perfectly all right in Switzerland. Neither Lotte nor Elsa had a problem.'

'I wasn't thinking of Switzerland,' said Uncle Willi quietly. 'I was thinking of England.'

I felt nothing but excitement throughout the voluble and weeping protest which flowed from my mother. England! Then excitement was succeeded by sharp doubt. I was top in Latin and Greek, bilingual in French and German, but an indifferent student in English. I regularly came ninth or tenth in the subject and when I was younger had dreaded the words 'let's speak English all day', which were prone to spill from my cousins as they approached examinations.

My father had specialised in Scottish history and had travelled extensively in Britain between the wars. Indeed, during the rise of Hitler, he had been teaching at Oxford. Ironically my French grandfather was also an English scholar, being a professor of the subject at the Sorbonne. It was not an enthusiasm I had inherited.

'His father would have wanted it.' Uncle Willi's words interrupted my thoughts. 'He believed that only by growing up together can men understand each other and live at peace. He wanted his children to be raised among other nations. He was always saying so and he was particularly fond of England.'

'The British killed him.' My mother looked at me and, realising that I was about to be persuaded, gave way to fresh agitation and tears.

I sensed rather than heard Uncle Willi sigh. 'It was war. We were all busy killing each other and Klaus hated it as much as I did. Now it is peace and we must try to ensure it stays that way.'

'Then I will go too. I will live in England while Klaus-Pierre is at school there and he need not board.'

Uncle Willi shook his head. 'Klaus-Pierre needs to spread his wings. He must go to England and live as the English, staying with other boys in the holidays, coming back here for Christmas and the summer.'

He spoke with gentle finality. My mother was an adult who could have lived where she chose, just as she could have insisted on following me to Britain, but I knew she would not do so. I understood her well enough now to be convinced that had the von Ströbels not intervened we would still have been living on my aunt's charity in Provence, my persecution lamented but endured. It would be when I was a man and could earn our keep that she would move from Ströbelfields and it would have to be at my insistence.

The thought made me feel grown-up enough to tell Uncle Willi that he had already done more than enough for us and perhaps I should leave school and earn. He responded with hurt bewilderment, causing me to feel guilty and clumsy but also obscurely reassured.

Perhaps it was in an endeavour to placate my mother that he decided I should be sent to a Catholic school and brought into daily rather than weekly contact with my faith. Eventually he told me I would be going to Ampleforth, a name we all found impossible to pronounce, and that he had traced an old friend of my father's who had invited me to spend a weekend at his house.

Certainly it was in an endeavour to placate my mother that he at last agreed to bring home my father's remains from their grave in France and re-inter them in the family row in the village churchyard. My mother had always wanted this to happen but the von Ströbels had resisted, saying that soldiers were buried where they fell and a war grave was an honourable memorial. The administrative procedures took a very long while and were far from complete when I left for England.

The plan was for my mother and Uncle Willi to accompany me and we would all spend a week in Yorkshire, obtaining my uniform and visiting the school before term started, but a few days before our departure a problem arose with a contract for Wanderer Bear and Franz was hastily pressed into taking my uncle's place. Given the inconvenience it caused him, my cousin seemed unaccountably enthusiastic.

My examination results in *Mittlere Reife* were excellent and I was to study Latin, Greek and Ancient History at what the British called A level. I soon added French to the collection of subjects, as I realised it was, for me, an easy option which would guarantee a top grade. Perhaps also I was already preparing to encounter hostility and wanted to stress my Frenchness.

Before we departed Uncle Willi invited me into the library and shut the door. As on those other occasions he wanted to make sure I knew the facts of life but this time the facts in question were those of British life. A lot of the people I would meet would have lost relatives in the war and would still harbour resentment against a country which had not once but twice brought conflict to the world. Furthermore, Germany was beginning to emerge as a force in the new Europe and there were many who regarded her rebirth with great suspicion and certainly with caution.

Hitler had been not merely an enemy of Britain but of civilisation and the evil of the concentration camps was still very fresh in people's memories. I was going to a Catholic school but I would inevitably meet Jews at some stage, perhaps those who had fled to England and whose loved ones had died in Belsen and its like. I must cope with dignity and remember Uncle Gerhardt and also what my father had done to help Jews in Paris.

Above all, the English were the most enormous snobs and illegitimacy was a serious stigma. I might find I was unwelcome in some of my friends' houses for that reason alone. Any who found out the whole story would regard my mother as a traitor as well as a floozy. I must therefore be discreet. Fortunately the British were very reserved and did not think it good form to ask too many personal questions. The headmaster, a Benedictine monk, of course had been fully informed but shared Uncle Willi's view of living at peace and it had been a relief to my uncle when he had accepted me.

'The English class system is a funny business. My brother never fully understood it,' mused Uncle Willi. It was not an encouraging conversation and it would not have taken a great deal to persuade me that my mother was right and that I should consider myself settled in Germany with Ströbelfields at the heart of my existence, but world events had overtaken us and by the time Uncle Willi and I were having that conversation in the library my own anxieties seemed very small beer.

My uncle and mother had recently returned from spending most of August in Berlin where tensions between the Soviet East and our own West Germany had erupted into a political volcano pouring forth the molten lava of thousands of refugees fleeing to the West. All around us was talk of another war and Aunt Angelika and I watched news bulletin after news bulletin, eager for news, jumping each time the telephone rang.

There were few family concerns. My father's wife's family had come from Dresden but only a younger brother had survived and there had been hardly any contact with him since the war, perhaps, I now reflected, because of the presence of my mother and myself. He had sent Lotte a modest wedding present but had not appeared at the ceremony itself. A distant von Ströbel cousin had been taken prisoner by the Russians but had been released in one of the last batches to be freed some years ago and now resided in Switzerland with his closer relatives.

Friends were a different matter. Uncle Willi

knew of several in the Eastern sector and my mother was well nigh beside herself about the fate of Kurt Kleist and had insisted they go to Berlin to try to find him. Uncle Willi had agreed and abandoned both business and Ströbelfields in his haste to help.

Kurt Kleist, having been my father's adjutant when they were serving with the forces occupying Paris, had been privy to his affair with my mother from its inception. It was he who had alerted the von Ströbels to my existence after running into Bette after the war and my mother had often talked about the debt we owed him. Apart from my mother, none of us had ever met him, although Uncle Willi had a dim recollection of seeing a young fair-haired officer in my father's outer office when he had visited him in Paris. Kurt had been terribly injured in the same strafing attack which had killed my father and had lost one leg altogether and the other below the knee.

I remember seeing on that old crackling television set the first pictures of the Berlin Wall, but more graphic still were the descriptions of eyewitnesses and news commentators which poured from the wireless. Walter Pletz forecast war while I wondered what all those people who had successfully fled would do, trying to imagine myself simply leaving everything I owned and arriving in a strange place with nothing but the items I had been able to carry. I wondered what happened to pets. Were they abandoned along with everything else? Were rabbits, mice and hamsters simply released from their cages to take their chance or did their owners kill them rather than leave them to an uncertain fate?

How much worse to abandon a human! The elderly, crippled and sick would stay behind while their families fled, or perhaps their relatives would refuse to go, deciding to face the worst together. Probably in such cases families split, with some adults taking the children to safety while others stayed with the ill and ageing. Would it have been Aunt Angelika or Uncle Willi who would have stayed with Omi? Many a family was to be rent asunder by that cruel wall which now divided a nation.

After a week of suspense Uncle Willi phoned to say that Kurt Kleist was in West Berlin, having been carried there in a blanket by two strangers. He sounded shocked, his voice a monotone. 'A day later and he wouldn't have made it. We're bringing him to Ströbelfields for a while but God knows when. It's total chaos and getting out of Berlin won't be easy.'

I pictured the former capital, a small island in the East, a tiny smudge of green in a red sea of Soviet occupation in my school atlas. I remembered stories of the Berlin airlift and wondered if the Russians would try to claim the whole city.

Walter Pletz shook his head. 'Things are very different now with the nuclear threat. But I shall still be glad to see Willi and your mother back again.'

They returned towards the end of August. I ran out to greet my mother but her manner was strangely absent, her usual animation returning only when she introduced me to Kurt Kleist. He looked up at me from the wheelchair and I shook

144

his hand, aware that my mother was watching the encounter with something akin to anxiety and Uncle Willi with curiosity.

I saw a man some eight years older than my mother, with fair hair turning grey and dark-blue eyes. Considering his appalling war injuries and the years of deprivation under the Russians, he looked remarkably young and cheerful.

'Klaus-Pierre,' he smiled. 'I should have known you anywhere. You are the image of your father. He was a remarkable man.'

Who left behind a remarkable mess. I was sure the thought passed through the minds of everyone present.

'I gather you are off to school in England?'

'Yes. Next week.'

During the next few days my mood alternated between excitement and fear, and when Franz arrived I felt as uncertain as the small boy who had cowered behind him, afraid of a large black dog. On the day before my departure I wandered through the woods and fields, remembering how I had played with Werner on the logs, chatted away to Maria in the vegetable shed and raced Hermann to the lake. I thought of Elsa, the companion of my childhood, perched on the hay bales, her grass-stained legs dangling as Hermann jumped up, pawing the stack, trying to reach her feet. I remembered how Otto would chase us when we had been tiresome and we had run from him, squealing in mock fear.

A memory of a small boy, uncertain, afraid of other children, clutching his cone of gifts, danced across my brain, calling to me, pulling me back to

Ströbelfields, begging me not to leave. I shook my head and banished the memory, staring instead at the lake. I could see the boundaries of the water, the grass at the far side in which a distant cow now wandered, but I could not see the boundaries of my new life, the one which would be made away from Uncle Willi, Aunt Angelika and my mother.

Once I had carelessly dropped the long string, which had been attached to my toy ship, and the bright yellow structure had floated away from me, tossed on the ripples of the wind whipped lake. Distraught, I ran to the house, panting, bereft, and Franz had come down to the lake with me, by which time my precious toy was almost invisible. He had got out a real boat and paddled to the rescue.

I vowed that I should not be buffeted about on life's waters, needing rescue. I should instead be a proud ship, with a tall mast, purposeful and handsome, sailing back into harbour with the spoils of success. At the thought, I stood straighter and squared my shoulders, before laughing at my absurdity.

Uncle Willi rang next morning to wish me luck. He spoke of a large American contract but his voice held fatigue rather than triumph.

'Look after him,' I urged Aunt Angelika, and she looked at me in surprise.

Lotte, together with Rudi, Werner, Ernst and their parents came to wave me off. They gave me a transistor radio and I wondered how to fit it in to my luggage, eventually deciding to carry it separately. My trunk had been sent on ahead weeks earlier and my mother regularly wondered if it had arrived safely.

As we drove along the winding road which took us through the estate we passed Caesar grazing in a field and Franz slowed the car while I shouted a farewell from the car window. At the station Aunt Angelika slid into the driving seat and turned the car back towards Ströbelfields, while I repressed a sudden terrified desire to run after it and abandon my great adventure.

My mother also gazed wistfully at the retreating vehicle and I knew that she too wanted to be returning, for I had noticed, with shock and premonition, the fondness of her leave-taking from Kurt Kleist. I had never thought much about her future other than having formed some vague notion that when I left Ströbelfields she would no longer have any reason to be there and that we would have to make alternative arrangements, but it would be some years yet before my education was complete and certainly I had no detailed plan.

Now I realised that she was still only thirty-six, which, though it seemed old to me, was still young enough to marry again, and that she was still a remarkably beautiful woman. Kleist was a link to my dead father and the time she had been with him, as well as being the indirect cause of our arrival at Ströbelfields.

Stepfather. At once I was indignant not on my own behalf but on Uncle Willi's. He had been my father in all but name and no one else must ever take his place. The train pulled in with a hiss of steam and doors began banging, forcing my thoughts back to the present. As we travelled my mother recalled that other long train journey we had made together when we fled Provence and hatred. I looked out of the window at the late summer sky and saw a large black bird flapping, made small by distance.

Then it had all been rubble, she recalled, as she stared in wonder at new buildings and commented, awestruck, on Germany's rebirth. I recalled Uncle Willi's warning that not everyone was enthusiastic at his country's renaissance and on the sea crossing to England I found it out for myself.

The crossing was calm enough but I found that I was not a good sailor and spent a great deal of the journey standing at the rail, peering down at the sea, and wondering if I was going to be sick. Certainly I had not the stomach to join the others when they went below to eat.

It was not cold on deck and the girl who presently joined me by the rail was clad in a light summer dress. Her hair was dressed in the bouffant style then so fashionable and her stiletto heels must have been three inches high. She was heavily made up and, used to the wild tomboy that was Elsa, I felt mildly repulsed.

She asked me if I was all right and I said yes, I had been feeling a little sick but was now quite well. I realised I had passed my first test of spoken English outside a classroom and felt disproportionately pleased. Her name was June and when our talk faltered to a temporary silence she seemed to want to stay with me, looking earnestly down at the foam beneath us but, I was sure, not for the same reason as I did.

Some conversation drifted along the deck from where two men stood with their backs to the sea, looking up at the ship's funnel and the wheeling gulls.

'Makes you wonder who won the bloody war. They're doing better than we are, that's for sure. Cocky too. It'll all end in another shenanigan. Should have crushed them into the ground when we had the chance. Damned Krauts!'

June threw me a look of startled embarrassment while I tried and failed to look nonchalant.

That night I dreamed of my great-grandfather's funeral for the first time in many years, seeing that black-clad group with white, stony faces, hard with hatred and rejection. Then into the dream floated June and, although I never saw her again, she was to haunt my dreams on many a night, causing me to wake with an excitement I only half-understood.

We stayed in a small guest house, which seemed perpetually to smell of steak pie and chips, and I was glad to exchange it for the air and space of Ampleforth. Franz appeared even more enthusiastic and spent most of his time there talking to the monks and attending Mass each day while my mother and I occupied ourselves with practical details of uniform and text books. One evening he told us between mouthfuls of watery vegetables that he had met a wonderful, truly holy monk called Basil Hume.

I understood what was happening and remembered the conversation I had overheard in the library at Ströbelfields. Franz's Catholicism was

149

deepening and the rest of the family would despise it. My mother appeared oblivious to the mental and spiritual processes through which my cousin was struggling and I suspected she was more concerned with what Kurt Kleist might be thinking or doing at that moment. *Stepfather*.

The next day they returned to Germany. I stood amidst the cars and other boys, identically clad, icy with loneliness, shivery with apprehension, as I waved them off.

'Dessin!'

All my life I had been Klaus-Pierre but now I was known only by my surname. I turned and saw a boy of my own age.

'Knightley. New men this way.'

I followed miserably, trying to understand the snatches of excited conversation I could hear around me, no longer feeling like a tall-masted ship but rather a little jolly boat which had strayed into the main shipping lines.

'Dessin? But that's not a French accent, is it? You sound German.'

'Do you play rugger, Dessin?'

'Dessin? I'm Bland. I was told to look out for you. Apparently my old man knew your old man. They met in the Great War.'

I had been expecting to meet him but the name took me by surprise. The decision to choose Ampleforth over several other Catholic schools had been made by Uncle Willi after he had tracked down an old English friend of my father's and had found, to his delight, that his son was in his last year at the school. He had told me the friend's name was Harry Bullchester and his son was called George, so naturally I was expecting a George Bullchester. Uncle Willi either forgot to explain the oddness of aristocratic nomenclature in Britain or he understood it as little as I did. When I found out that Bland had an older brother who had passed through Ampleforth some years earlier and was called Hugh Sandiscome my confusion was complete.

'It's easy, old chap,' Charles Emmett told me as I pulled on my boots in preparation for my introduction to rugby. 'Bland's father is an earl – the Earl of Bullchester – and Hugh, being the eldest son is a viscount – the Viscount Sandiscome – but poor old George is just plain the Honourable George Bland. Must be awful being a younger son in those families, knowing that however ghastly your big brother is he is going to get it all: title, money, land, seat in the Lords. Meanwhile you visit mater in the Dower House and envy it all from afar. Not that Hugh is ghastly, of course. George adores him.'

I understood about a quarter of Emmett's ramblings but mastered rugby with ease. I wished I had Otto's strength and speed, but I put up a creditable performance and sensed that somehow my prowess on the field at once made me less of an outsider in a way in which my sharp performance in classics and easy French did not.

I had been at the school two weeks, and was beginning to think the venture a success when I overheard two younger boys talking.

'That Hun's pretty good, isn't he?'

'Yep. Wouldn't mind being able to tackle like that. He almost flies.'

'They say he never played until he came here.'

They moved away along the corridor while I stood stock-still absorbing the insult. *Hun.* Barbarian. Savage.

'Oh, they wouldn't have meant it like that, old chap,' Emmett reassured me. 'It's a term of affection, like Fatty or Titch.'

The English are mad but I quite like them. I was sitting in the common room writing the mandatory Sunday letter home, describing the strange customs of the place, seeing in my mind the family at Ströbelfields, imagining my mother reading the letter aloud to Uncle Willi and Aunt Angelika. And to Kurt Kleist.

'Isn't that German? I thought you said you were writing to your mother.' Jack Marshall broke into my thoughts.

'Really, Marshall, you can't look at chaps' letters!' Emmett sounded outraged.

'I wasn't. I can't read German, anyway, but I just got a glimpse and it looks German, not French.'

'It is. My mother and I speak only in German.'

Curiosity pulsated through the short silence which followed and I glanced around the room. There were only four of us present and all were friends.

'My mother will not allow me to speak French and ironically the only times I spoke it at home were to my German relatives, apart from odd moments when I just forgot. You see, my mother is very bitter because of the way her family treated her and she has rejected France altogether.'

Emmett shifted uncomfortably as if such personal revelations were what he would doubtless

152

have described as bad form, but Marshall looked intrigued.

'Which language do you think in?' he asked.

I thought. 'German.'

A week before half-term the news I had been subconsciously expecting arrived. My mother was to marry Kurt Kleist. Her letter filled six pages and I detected anxiety beneath the joy, as if she feared my reaction. Kurt himself wrote a briefer but equally affectionate note. I was resentful, glad, hurt and happy, until eventually a single reflection brought the swirl of emotion to a sudden halt. My mother would be Catherine Dessin for only a little longer before becoming Catherine Kleist. Frau Kleist. Her transition from French to German would be complete and I alone would still be a Dessin. *Dessin*. She hated the very name but had insisted I kept it.

'Dessin!' Brother Francis called my wandering attention back to Cicero's denunciation of Verres, but my thoughts could not stay in Ancient Rome for more than a few seconds.

Klaus-Pierre Dessin. Klaus-Pierre von Ströbel. Klaus-Pierre Kleist. Which was I?

Brother Francis gave up the unequal struggle and set me extra translation instead.

eight

A Half-Term Holiday

I had been invited to spend half-term with George Bland. I would have preferred to have accepted a similar invitation from Jack Marshall, feeling greatly at ease with both him and Charles Emmett while hardly knowing Bland at all, but I knew my family expected me to visit my father's old friend and I felt duty-bound to do so, reflecting that I need only go once and thereafter could spend half-term with whom I pleased.

The family seat was in Leicestershire and Bland spent most of the train journey describing his family. I would meet three brothers and two sisters, his parents, grandmother and maiden aunt.

He had not thought it necessary to mention the large staff he took for granted nor did anyone else seem to notice my miserable confusion when dealing with the chauffeur, butler, housekeeper and vast array of valets and maids. In Germany I had led a privileged existence but nothing had prepared me for opulence on this scale. For the first time I understood what life at Ströbelfields might once have been and could better fathom the sentiment which people like Maria felt for days long gone, although I knew I was glad they were past, preferring the informality of Ströbelfields.

I did not know how to speak to servants, was too

shy to ring a bell and felt disconcerted at the way shoes and clothes disappeared from my room to return in an immaculate state. On the first evening I left my case on my bed, intending to unpack it later, and returned to find no case but all my clothes hung in the wardrobe and my personal effects arranged on tallboy and dressing table.

When we rode the horses were brought out, saddled and bridled, and on our return were taken from us as soon as our feet touched the ground. Guests came and went, treating the place as their own, confident, at ease, enjoying the Bullchester hospitality, the young with rowdy enthusiasm and their elders with quieter courtesy. Instinct told me that this family would have seen many a scandal in its time but that manners would prohibit any reference to my odd background and that almost certainly George's sisters would have been told nothing about it.

If you do not admit to ignorance then you will never learn. It had been one of Uncle Willi's favourite maxims, one I had heard almost daily at home and in his class at school. When I found myself alone with Harry Bullchester I admitted I was well beyond my depth.

'For instance, I do not know how to address you. Should it be My Lord or Your Lordship?'

He smiled. 'Neither. They are very formal. Lord Bullchester will do or just plain sir as you would call any other of your elders. But your own family are landed aristocrats, are they not? Your father was always quite at ease here.'

'I suppose my father must have grown up in circumstances fairly similar to this but since then

155

we have been ruined by two wars. We were luckier than most in that we hung on to a lot of our land and saved a certain amount of the wealth as well but now it is all just space. We have a big house but some of it is never used and we run it ourselves with minimal help. We all muck in on the farm during the busy season and we eat healthily but not richly. Omi used to sit in her rocking chair and darn our clothes.'

George's grandmother sat on the sofa and asked the servants for sherry. The words were unspoken but I knew that the thought had occurred to both of us and I was embarrassed, believing that he might take my comments as complaint when I had intended only explanation. Instead he looked at me and smiled with a tinge of sadness.

'You have been very happy there, haven't you?'

'Very. None of them could have done more. Uncle Willi has been a saint.'

'I met him once. I was going to visit Ströbel-fields with your father but we never got beyond Berlin. It was Kristallnacht and I came home the next day. Willi had brought a school party there and a few days earlier we all met up for a meal and a show. I remember how much he looked like your father. They seemed very close despite Klaus's having been away in Britain for so long.'

'What was he like?' The words were out before I could consider their wisdom and I saw the wariness enter Lord Bullchester's eyes.

'He was a fine man, brave beyond the norm, and a very distinguished academic. Did you ever hear how we met?'

I knew the story well, having been told it by

Uncle Willi before we left Germany, but I managed to raise my eyebrows in polite enquiry, knowing that he was trying to turn the conversation and that if I made any attempt to press him further he would close it down altogether.

'It was right at the end of the Great War and it was a miracle that either of us had got that far because we were in the trenches and men were dying by the million. I had been in the army anyway – I was the younger son and if my brother had not been killed in action I suppose I would have served my commission and then entered Parliament – so I was in it from day one. Your father had been fighting for much less long but had seen some pretty tough action.

'We all knew the end was near and most of us were just trying to stay alive. The worst injury I had received up to then had been a scalded foot when some fool of a cook dropped a pan of hot water. Then, one day, I was suddenly coming round from unconsciousness with blood everywhere. The pain was appalling but it was a clean wound in the shoulder and when I had managed to work that out I was almost grateful because I knew my war was over. If that makes me a coward I can only plead in mitigation that my next thought was for my men but none answered my shouts so I returned to thinking about my own survival. I realised I was on the edge of a shell hole and I crawled into it. At least, I tried to but rolled most of the way and passed out at the bottom from sheer pain.

'When I next came round there was a silhouette in front of me – a still dark figure against a blood-red sunset. I recognized the uniform and saw the dark outline of the gun pointing straight at me. All I could think was that it was just such bloody bad luck on my mother. My older brother had died at Ypres, my younger on the Somme and now me too, when it was nearly all over.

'I tried to brazen it out, telling him in German that he was a long way behind his men who were fleeing as hard as they could go. He was unprovoked and answered me in English.

'"You are hurt. If you surrender, I can do something with that wound."

'I told him I supposed I had no choice. I did not know where my gun was and even if I did I could not use it. He pointed to the top of the crater and told me my weapon was probably up there. As he was doing some elementary first aid I asked him if it was he who had shot me but he shook his head and pointed to a shape crumpled up on the other side of the hole. "I was looking after him, when you rolled down."

'"Is he dead?" I asked.

'"Yes."

'He made a pretty good job of stopping the flow of blood and patching up my shoulder. The light was going but all the time he was working on me my eyes were fixed on his Pour le Merite, the Blue Max, they called it. It was almost dark when he finished and then he introduced himself by name and rank and I gave him mine in return. I couldn't get much sleep because of the pain, so we spent the night talking about our families, the futility of war and what we would do afterwards.

'In the morning, I urged him to reverse the

situation and surrender to me, as it was obvious the German forces were in full retreat and he was unlikely to be able to rejoin them but he refused, picked up his gun, adjusted the bayonet, said, "Bloody awful things, bayonets. Might as well be savages with spears", and climbed out of the shell hole.

'I was picked up later on that day and taken back on a stretcher. The day after that it was all over. I often wondered if he survived and then, fourteen years later, I met him at Oxford where he was an academic and my youngest brother was President of the Union. He looked vaguely familiar but I could not immediately remember where I had seen him. As our eyes met, he too looked briefly puzzled, then his brow cleared and he came towards me smiling. "How's the shoulder?" he said.

'Thus began a friendship which lasted till the next war. I wrote to Ströbelfields afterwards and received a reply from his sister, telling me that he was dead, along with his wife and two of his children. He hated war, Klaus-Pierre, and deserved a better fate. Still, he spent his time in Paris well. Willi said in his letter that he took huge risks helping Jews. They wouldn't have given him a medal for that but I bet it took greater courage than the exploits which earned him the Blue Max.'

I saw the colour enter his face as he realised what he had said. *He spent his time in Paris well.* My father had used his time in Paris to seduce a teenager and leave her with his illegitimate child.

This time he did not dodge the issue. 'Men do strange things, sometimes, things that make them wonder if they know themselves. Your father was a good family man and I cannot explain what happened and probably nor could he.'

I could not think of any reply and was saved by George bursting in to demand that I join a croquet game. We played all afternoon till a procession of servants brought trays of tea and muffins on to the lawn. I looked at the copper-leaved trees surrounding us and wondered that it was still warm enough to eat outside.

'It won't last.' Arabella Bland read my thoughts.

I turned to look at her. She was a year younger than me, small, dark, freckled, playful towards her elders, full of energy and fun, a contrast to her elder sister who was quiet and sensible and often very dull company. Elsa and Lotte, I thought. It was easy to imagine Arabella coming to grief and Margery primly rescuing her. The younger girl reminded me of hayfields and rippling breezes, the older of musty libraries and lavender-scented cardigans.

I smiled. 'Then we must make the most of it.'

'Let's take Marmaduke for a walk.' Arabella jumped up from the rug, which a thoughtful servant had spread beneath the cedar, presumably out of habit, as the sun was too weak for us to need shade.

'Oh, do let the poor boy finish his tea,' protested her mother, but I was already on my feet.

'It might take a while,' advised Arabella. 'It will be chilly later, so why don't you get your coat while I find Marmaduke's lead? Anybody else for a walk?'

I was obscurely pleased that the only response

from the others was a collective groan. They would sit on the lawn a little longer and then wander inside to enjoy hot baths before changing for dinner. Guests were expected that night and I knew I must spend the evening making polite conversation to strangers, probably middle-aged women, whose talk was a mixture of gossip, racing and Mr Macmillan's housing policies. There was, of course, an immense amount of interest in the Berlin Wall and I was wearying of answering the same questions each time a new guest arrived.

Arabella ran ahead of me and Marmaduke, her West Highland terrier, unleashed and running free, barked with excitement. The October leaves were crunchy under our feet and already the light was fading, the moon pale but discernible as it waited for the darkness which would restore its dominance. In the distance sheep bleated and some piece of farm machinery ceased the dull drone which had formed the background to the afternoon's croquet.

'Is it like this in Germany now?' Arabella perched on the top of a gate, one hand resting lightly on the post. Marmaduke shot underneath the lowest bar and ran round in circles, still barking.

I thought of Ströbelfields, of Otto and Uncle Willi dragging in the logs for the winter fires, but Otto had long since left and my uncle would soon be too old for such labour. Kurt Kleist could hardly help. Perhaps the proceeds of the Wanderer Bear would soon ensure the availability of more paid help.

'It's much, much colder – at least it is in

Northern Germany where we live. This is my first English autumn.'

'I prefer the spring. Everything just springs: bluebells, crocuses, snowdrops, daffodils, little lambs. Last year I looked after a sock lamb in the Easter holidays. I cried when it went to market. Marmaduke was so jealous of it. Poor old Mint Sauce.'

'Who?'

'Mint Sauce. The lamb I was telling you about.'

I struggled with the British sense of humour and gave up, failing to reconcile the tears with the name, while Arabella twisted round, swung her legs over the other side of the gate and jumped down. I climbed over after her.

'I'll race you to that stream,' she cried, and sped away, pursued by Marmaduke. I ran at a condescending pace, manners requiring that she win, until I saw that she was increasing the distance between us at a phenomenal rate. Then I raced, panting, to keep up with her. I collapsed, gasping for breath, at the stream and looked at her in awe.

'You really do run, don't you? You should be in the Olympics.'

To my surprise she looked wistful. 'I should like to try. At Roedean they tell me I should run for the county at the very least, but Daddy won't hear of it. He says it's just not done for people like us but that's nonsense. School, of course, is different. I can win as many cups as I like there.'

I could make no sense of it. *The English class system is a funny business. My brother never fully understood it.* Uncle Willi's words rang in my brain and I grinned.

'I don't think it's funny.' Arabella sounded uncharacteristically cross. 'Grandma says everything is changing and that one day there won't be any aristocracy but that it will all be gradual, not a revolution like there was in France. She also says women will be equal to men but I can't see it. I mean, there are some things only men can do, aren't there? I wish I could be ordinary and run for the county and get a job.'

I looked at her, startled. 'A job? Why should you not get a job?'

'Oh, I'll do good works and things like that, of course, but I meant I should like to have a proper job, instead of just waiting to marry. I shall come out at eighteen and if I am lucky I'll persuade Daddy to let me go to Oxford but after that...'

I was filled with a wild desire to rescue her from the straitjacket of the lunatic British social system, to run away with her and hide her until she was twenty-one and able to organise her own life.

'If I were married to you, you would have whatever job you pleased.'

She stared, puzzled, and then laughed. 'It would be a bit late then. If I were actually married I wouldn't want a job any more, would I?'

I groped in my confused mind for an appropriate response, for a means of explaining that life must surely be more flexible than she seemed to think, but when it came it sounded rude. 'In Germany we live in nineteen sixty-one.'

Arabella pondered that for a while. 'Of course you lost a war but Daddy says you've done pretty well out of it. When did rationing end?'

'Rationing? I can't remember any rationing. I

163

think Aunt Angelika once told me there was rationing immediately after the war but it was over before I left France. Anyway you cannot ration what you do not have and there was precious little in Germany.'

'I remember rationing, or at any rate the end of it. One of the gardeners bought some sweets for Margery and me. Smarties or something. I must have been about five. What did you mean about leaving France? Did you live in France?'

I regretted my indiscretion but Arabella was too busy drawing her own conclusions.

'Of course! With a name like Dessin you must be French, even though you speak with a German accent. I suppose your father was in the forces occupying Germany after the war and that was how he met your mother?'

I wondered how many others had assumed this to be the case. It would explain my name, although if anyone were to think about it hard enough it was hopelessly incompatible with my age. I had been born, not conceived, in 1945 and several months before the end of the war. I hesitated, torn between truth and diplomacy, certain that Lady Bullchester would not want her daughter contaminated by acquaintance with the sordid history of Catherine Dessin and Klaus von Ströbel, yet reluctant to deceive Arabella.

I think I might have told her the truth but at that moment Marmaduke began yelping and, with an exclamation of distress, Arabella flew to find him. I too followed the sound of pain and fear, anxious on the girl's account rather than the dog's. We found him tangled in thorn and were both bleeding by the time he was released. Arabella's tweed skirt was in a sorry state and my slacks were fairly shredded. We inspected the terrier, which whimpered as we pulled thorns from its fur.

'I think he's all right,' said Arabella at last. 'I'll carry him for a bit. Thanks for helping.'

I stood up from where we had been crouching over Marmaduke, surveying the damage to my trousers and the torn flesh of my hands. The pain was petty but niggling and I wanted to be back at the house.

'Oh, dear,' muttered Arabella. 'It's raining.'

'Only very lightly. Let's hurry.'

A few minutes later the rain was pouring on us in earnest and jagged streaks of lightning flashed through the sky. To me it was just a nuisance, an added discomfort, so it was with surprise that I heard Arabella give a small moan.

'I hate lightning and Marmaduke hates thunder and we've miles to go.'

'Less than half a mile, I think. Close your eyes and you won't see the lightning.'

'I shan't see where I am going either.'

'Just hold my arm and walk steadily.'

I took the dog from her and she clung to me as we walked home, she with her head bent and her eyes closed, the dog cowering against me, I straining to see the path through the darkness. It was a slow business and at first I set about it with impatience but gradually I became so wet that the rain seemed to matter less and the girl on my arm to become a pleasant weight instead of a politely borne burden. In some strange way I was almost sorry when the house came in sight.

Arabella half-opened her eyes to see it but it was illuminated by the yellow lightning and she retreated behind closed lids, holding me tighter. The comparison with Elsa had been wrong, I realised. Nothing ever made my cousin afraid.

When we came to the steps in front of the house Marmaduke wriggled from my grasp and raced up to the door, which was shortly opened by the pale-faced under butler. I guided Arabella in and told her it was safe to open her eyes. She gasped with relief and planted an enthusiastic kiss on my cheek before running upstairs. It was I who described Marmaduke's plight to Lord Bullchester and helped him to inspect the animal's injuries.

'We have the vet out tomorrow anyway to look at one of the horses,' he said. 'I don't think this is any great emergency so unless you want to catch pneumonia you had better go up and have a hot bath. I'll tell Hawkins to bring you up a brandy. Needless to say I am very grateful for the way you looked after my daughter. It seems to be the lot of the von Ströbels to rescue the Blands.'

'Arabella knows me only as Dessin. She has alighted upon an explanation of my French name and German accent, which means my father was French and my mother German.'

He shook his head in amazement but offered no comment.

Later as I poured the brandy, untouched, down the sink and stared into the bathroom mirror I thought of Arabella's kiss and of her weight on my arm.

Descending to the drawing room an hour later, I was confronted with the usual array of guests, among whom Hawkins circulated with the drinks.

'Ah! Klaus-Pierre! Diana, meet a friend of George's. Lady Abingdon le Willows. This young man has just rescued Arabella from the storm. And Marmaduke too.'

It was a dreadful name to pronounce so I did not try to repeat it as I shook hands, nor did I try to say Hebblethwaite or to refer much to Ampleforth, as my connection to George was explained to the next guest. Lady Bullchester propelled me forward with proprietorial determination until, exhausted, I was being introduced to a Mrs Judy Margolis. She took one look at me and patted the spare place on the couch beside her.

I sank down gratefully and accepted a bitter lemon from Hawkins's tray.

Mrs Margolis peered at it over her sherry. 'Laetitia is a good sort but she does have a tendency to wear her guests out. I am Judy. You, I think she said, are Pierre and go to school with George?'

'Yes, but he is a year above me.'

'So how do you know him?'

'I don't really. My father was friendly with Lord Bullchester.'

'I see. Who is your father?'

'He is dead.'

'I'm sorry, but, if you'll forgive my saying so, you do not sound like a Pierre. That accent is German not French.'

'I am Klaus-Pierre Dessin. I am half-German and half-French.'

'And Monsieur Dessin did what?'

'He was a professor of English at the Sorbonne,' I replied with accuracy if not with truth. It seemed unnecessary to point out that Monsieur Dessin was my grandfather. She had made the same assumption as Arabella and I saw no reason to disabuse her.

'Hence your good English, I suppose.'

I could not assent without compounding my deceit, so I smiled and rose. Half an hour later I was disconcerted to find myself next to her at dinner. Throughout the first course I surveyed her covertly while she talked to the guest on her other side. She was a large woman, heavy-jowled, with bags under her eyes and bright red lipstick. I had not met a Mr Margolis but I wondered what he had found attractive in her.

Over the roast beef and Yorkshire pudding – a combination which to this day I find extraordinary – she turned to me and asked what I wanted to do with my life.

'I haven't yet decided. I think I shall study Classics at university. That is as far ahead as I can see.'

'You mean you will read Greats at Oxford? Even if you do not mean that you should say so.'

I returned her smile, wondering if she was laughing at the world of England which I still struggled to understand.

'Tell me about Adenauer,' she said suddenly. 'Can he really go on for ever?'

I had stammered my way through three or four sentences of commentary on German politics before she interrupted me without good manners but with considerable insistence.

'None of that is really important. What matters

is that he brought Germany to terms with Hitler.'

The name dropped into one of those silences which sometimes fall in the most voluble of parties. Suddenly everyone appeared to be looking in our direction and then conversation broke out once more but with an undercurrent of determination, as if the diners were straining to hear what we said beneath their own chatter.

'I think it was almost certainly Schoenberner rather than Adenauer who made us face up to Hitler, but that is different from coming to terms with the past. How do any of us do that? My uncle was mentally defective and they sent him to work at Dachau. He was driven mad by the horror of it and killed himself in our barn. My father defied the regime and almost lived to tell the tale. Others just kept their heads down and survived or died in battle. My Uncle Willi, who brought me up, was one of those.'

'Your father defied the regime? The professor at the Sorbonne?' She spoke the words almost playfully.

'My grandfather, Pierre Dessin, was the professor at the Sorbonne. My father was General Klaus von Ströbel of the German army. I am called Dessin because he died before he could marry my mother. I do not suppose Lord and Lady Bullchester want Arabella and Margery to hear such things.'

'Really? Arabella tells me she is studying *King Lear* at Roedean. Does that mean anything to you?'

Baffled, I shook my head. 'I know it is a play by Shakespeare—'

'Which contains the immortal line, *"now, gods, stand up for bastards!"* so I expect Arabella knows more than Laetitia or Harry may think. As for Margery, a little shock might do her good.'

I met her eyes and laughed. She was teasing me and I was enjoying it, albeit that much of her jesting was at my own expense. I thought that, perhaps, after all, Mr Margolis had shown good judgement.

'Why on earth were you talking to the Margoyle about Hitler?' demanded George when all the guests had gone. 'Don't you know she's Jewish?'

'It's pretty obvious, but of course I didn't mention Hitler. She did.' I tried not to sound defensive but recognised that I had been acting that way all evening, first trying to cover up my German origins and then rehearsing the anti-Nazi history of my family. 'Why do you call her the Margoyle?'

'It's a play on gargoyle, chump. She looks hideous. Surely you noticed? There's a gorilla in London zoo which always reminds me of her. Old Margolis must have been as blind as a bat.'

I had never heard the word gargoyle and resolved to look it up, nor had I heard the English talk of gorillas before, but that at least was an easy enough translation to make, the word being identical in German. I appreciated neither used in the context of Mrs Margolis and thought that the fabled English politeness was decidedly superficial.

'You don't like her?'

'Like her? I worship her. We all do. You won't find a better sort anywhere in the globe. Hugh fell in love with her daughter a couple of years

170

ago but of course it wouldn't do. I could have got away with it but not the son and heir. He was heartbroken, poor chap.'

George made no mention of the girl's emotional state but it seemed to me that the son and heir to the Bullchester title must be fairly spineless. My mother had defied every last convention for love and I felt a rush of respect for her wrong-headed courage.

'What were you all fighting for?' I heard the aggression in my own tone and saw the answering surprise in George's eyes.

'What?'

'What was the war all about? In Germany Jews were classified as sub-humans and here apparently they are fine unless you want to marry one.'

'You've got it wrong, old boy. It would have been just as difficult if Hugh had fallen in love with a non-Catholic. We're an old recusant family.'

I shrugged, remembering the conversation between Uncle Willi and Walter Pletz when it had become clear that Franz was toying with Catholicism.

'Anyway it seems a bit much to compare Pa with that Eichmann bastard.'

I had made no such comparison but the indignation on her daughter's account entered me with a new strength when I came down on the last day of the holiday and found Judy Margolis in the drawing room, chatting to George. Despite his disparaging comments, they appeared friendly enough and she kissed him with all the affection of a favourite aunt when he rose to go.

'All packed?' she asked as I approached.

171

'Yes, we catch the two o'clock train.'

'I hope the rest of term goes well for you. It is a pleasure to have met you.'

The words contained a suggestion of dismissal, as if she did not expect us to meet again. Although I knew it to be unreasonable I was hurt but I returned her smile. She held out her hand to me and, without thinking, I clicked my heels and bowed. At home it was a natural enough gesture in formal situations but here it seemed wildly out of place, possibly absurd, and in these particular circumstances an unfortunate reminder of my Germanic origins. To cover my confusion I raised her hand to my lips and as I did so her sleeve fell back.

I froze, staring at the number on her arm. Then I straightened from my bow and we looked each other in the eyes as I slowly released her hand.

'Auschwitz,' she said.

'Come on, old boy,' shouted George as I backed uncertainly away from her.

'I think you said your uncle worked in one of the camps?'

'Dachau.' The word was a strangled whisper.

'My cousins died in Dachau. I wonder if they ever met.'

The implication was unmistakable, and my horror dissolved into anger as I remembered the photographs of that innocent, unfocused gaze and thought of the gentle idiot torn from home and immersed in horror. Omi had cried when she told me the story, and Uncle Willi never failed to look grim at the mention of Uncle Gerhardt's name. I wanted to call her a bitch, and an ugly

172

one at that, and I wanted to grovel at her feet for the sins of my father's generation.

I was sixteen, a stranger in a land of peculiar manners and incomprehensible priorities, confronted with a situation which a man twice my age would have found impossible. I remember with pride, therefore, the way in which I said, with as much dignity as I could muster, that I was sorry she and her family had suffered so horribly, that I hoped my generation would build a very different world, but that George was obviously becoming agitated out by the car and that it was time for me to go.

She gave me a friendly rather than formal smile and I think I heard her call, 'Good luck' as I joined George and his father for the journey to the station. Lord Bullchester gave me a sharp glance but said nothing as the car began to wend its way along the drive. I hoped I should not be invited again. There was nobody there I would miss.

As we reached the large iron gate and the chauffeur got out to open it, Arabella appeared, returning home with Marmaduke. She picked him up and waved to us as we drove past and I made a single exception to the conclusion I had just reached.

We caught the train with a minute to spare.

'What on earth were you yapping to the Margoyle about?' demanded an aggrieved George. 'It was long enough for a lover's farewell.'

I gave him a non-committal reply, wondering what he would say if he knew that I was considering the competing claims to attraction of his

173

sister and a middle-aged Jewish woman. Oddly it was Arabella who seemed the more elusive, made remote by purity and innocence, the princess in a fairy-tale. Yet they all lived in fairy land, I thought when I recalled the servanted splendour and the quaint conventions. Surely it could not last? Surely rude reality must intrude and destroy? I wondered how any of them would have coped with the brutal fate meted out to Judy Margolis. Her daughter must have been a baby when the family was herded into the camps but somehow her mother had ensured her survival.

George was speaking and I dragged my attention back to him. He was talking of the army for which he was destined after Cambridge. An hour before we were due at York one of his contemporaries entered our compartment and he scarcely spoke another word to me. I made my own way back to school.

nine

A Salute to the Dead

Ströbelfields itself felt unreal when I returned there for the Christmas holiday. In the fourteen weeks I had been away the Wanderer Bear money had been put to its first visible effect in the house. Until now Uncle Willi had insisted on using our unexpected wealth to modernise the farm, husband the woods and bring the cottages

174

on the estate into the twentieth century. When I had left he was talking about repointing and rewiring the house, but now Aunt Angelika and my mother prepared our meals in a fitted kitchen of the latest design and I wallowed in a modern bath. Above all, Ströbelfields was warm.

I had shivered my way through my first months at Ströbelfields, gradually becoming accustomed to the climate of a northern German house with only log fires to heat it. In winter I would run between rooms rather than feel the draught of the chilly corridors. When I was a child I had often got dressed in bed before leaving its comforting warmth. None of my cousins seemed to suffer and Elsa would laugh whenever I complained of numb toes and call me a baby, to which I would retort that when I was a baby I had lived in a dear little house in Provence which was always cosy, that being my mother's daily explanation when I cried with cold.

Now we had central heating and the *whoompf* of the boiler as it burst into life made me start, as once the whirring of the grandfather clock had done when I had first stood close to it as it prepared to chime. Elsa had laughed at that too.

Yet these changes were small compared to that which had occurred in my mother. The long, lustrous, fair hair which I had thought like something out of a fairy-tale when we lived in France, and which had been piled on top of her head in the fashion of the early sixties when I had left for England, had been cut and permed. She looked older and somehow more confident, more of a woman, less of the lost girl whom fate blew hither and thither at its will. I had an obscure notion that she might even hold her own with the sheer force which was Aunt Angelika or calm Otto in one of his wilder moments.

Otto himself was there and beneath the usual booming energy I detected a mild discontent, a weary resignation to something unpalatable. I wondered if he had been in love and rejected.

'Oh, it's much worse, little cousin.' His smile had an uncharacteristic edge of sarcasm. 'Your mother didn't write?'

'I had a letter about three weeks ago.'

'That would explain your happy ignorance. It must have been about then that Franz told Father he wanted to enter a monastery. Apparently he came back from Ampleforth finally convinced of a vocation, of which he had been aware for some time. I have rarely seen Father so cut up but Franz is thirty and must lead his own life, and it appears that that life will be wifeless and childless and penniless.'

'Surely that degree of faith–'

'Oh, yes. He is entering a teaching order, thank God, not a silent one, and will spend his life in good works and praying for the rest of us. No one is going to say that is not admirable.'

'Why are you so angry?'

Otto smiled. 'I don't mean to be, but Franz's withdrawal from the world has knocked my life off course too. I was going to be a doctor, get married, have children and bring them to visit Granddad at Ströbelfields.'

I stared, my puzzlement absolute. 'So what's to stop you?'

'Ströbelfields, that's what. *Ströbelwiese*. Our damned meadowland. The family home. The von Ströbel estates. The carefully accumulated legacy of my ancestors. Generations of them. As the eldest son Franz would have inherited Ströbelfields in due course but Uncle Willi is increasingly tied up in the Wanderer Bear and is, anyway, getting on, so a few weeks back he suggested to Franz that he should begin to take over the running of the estate, leaving him free to consolidate the business which is bringing in so much money. That brought things to a head for Franz, who proceeded to drop his bombshell. So Ströbelfields is now mine – or it will be one day – and I must give up medicine and the delights of the city and live here, in the wilds, to learn estate management. To hell with estate management.'

'Surely Aunt Angelika can manage the estate for a few more years? After all, when Uncle Willi was teaching she did most of it. For that matter, surely we could now afford a manager? Why do it ourselves at all?'

'I think my father is worried about the longer term. We survived two world wars, the refugee influx and the land tax, but that makes us the exception which proves the rule. There are precious few of these big estates left now and he probably thinks that he can teach me ways and means which might elude even the shrewdest steward. You remember the von Forstners who used to come here when you were a child? Well, they have gone down even though their estate was vastly older than ours.'

I suppressed the revolutionary thought that

perhaps none of it mattered, that future generations might view Ströbelfields as an albatross around their necks.

'Of course, it's only for a couple of years while I learn the ropes. Then I can go back to being a doctor. I just wish it hadn't happened now. I wish Franz had taken a bit longer to renounce all his worldly goods.'

'Will he be here for Christmas?'

'Yes, his last here probably. He is going through quite an inquisition and won't be admitted for a while. Anyway, enough about Ströbelfields. How was England?'

I found myself describing not Ampleforth but my half-term at Lord Bullchester's. 'It can't last. It's like something out of Blandings Castle,' I concluded.

'Blandings Castle?' Otto looked bewildered. 'Is that another English stately home?'

I laughed and explained, but in that one innocent question my cousin had told me that I had become immersed in quite another culture, that my path and those of the others were diverging. Otto's future was firmly rooted in Ströbelfields. Mine would unfold elsewhere. His next words shocked me into the reality of that thought.

'Where do you suppose your mother will live when she marries Kurt?'

I stared at him, mentally denying what I had heard. I had assumed that Ströbelfields would be my home until I completed university and went forth into the world, but if my mother were to leave then I must too.

Otto read my thoughts. 'Of course, it will be

178

difficult for Kurt. I mean, he can't walk and it might be ambitious to try to be independent so soon. Perhaps they will stay here for a bit.'

I knew he was trying to comfort me but I felt as if I were adrift in a fog, unable to see my destination, unsure even of which direction it was in, straining my eyes for a dim light somewhere. The uncertainty made me resentful of any small gesture of affection between Kurt Kleist and my mother and, although I hated myself for it, it also made me unreceptive to my future stepfather's efforts to know me better.

The only positive outcome of my conversation with Otto was that I consciously set out to enjoy Christmas to the full, convinced that next year I would be in some other house for the festive season. I was disappointed that there were no children present as Alessandra was in Japan, where her husband was posted, and Hedy had gone with her family to her in-laws. Rudi and Lotte, now heavily pregnant, divided their time between us and the Pletzes, so that my companion was Elsa, who was already back from Switzerland when I arrived.

I tapped on her door and, when she had called, 'Come in,' I found myself in a bedroom icy with the winter cold, the windows open, the curtains billowing.

'This central heating is ghastly, isn't it?' she demanded in the same breath as saying, 'Hello! Good term?'

'I like it but you can turn off the radiator. England is pretty good.'

'I have done but I wanted some immediate cool. Switzerland is also good – my skiing is improving by the minute. Uncle Willi has already received your report from school and rest assured it is tediously brilliant. It has been handed round and everyone has reeled with amazement. I shall push you in the lake.'

'In England they would say "rot". My French scored ninety-six percent, which is hardly surprising. It's a lazy option and the Virgil happened to be the text I had done the previous year for *Mittlere Reife* so my Latin mark was the best too.'

'Rot,' murmured Elsa. 'I quite like that word. Is it swearing?'

'No, bad luck. Try rounding the o a bit more and don't bite off the t.'

'And now you're good at English too. You used to be quite hopeless. Don't show off too much or my father will decide I should go to England as well and I want to stay in Switzerland.'

I looked at her. She was in her last year of school and already arguing with Uncle Willi, who wanted her to go to university in Italy or England.

'Is it just the skiing? Or should I be asking what his name is?'

She laughed but would not be drawn. I might have been hurt by her reserve had I not guessed it to be because she was herself uncertain of the young man and unwilling to tempt fate by naming him. For much the same reason I said nothing to any of them about Arabella and hid her letters at the back of my sock drawer, albeit that they contained nothing more compromising than news of Roedean and Marmaduke.

My mother spent the first two days of the

holiday plying me with questions but I sensed her attention was elsewhere and, at first, I assumed that she was preoccupied by Kurt. I once walked into the kitchen and found her rubbing his hair with a towel, laughing at his protests. I tried to creep out without being seen but as I closed the door she called my name. Resentful of their closeness and its threat of turning my life upside down, I pretended not to hear, knowing I would hurt her and not caring.

Soon I learned that there was another reason for my mother's wandering thoughts. The formalities had been completed and my father's remains were to be brought home from France in the first week of the new year, Uncle Willi's final plea to my mother to reconsider the matter having failed. They were to be re-interred in the row of family graves which occupied a prominent place in the village churchyard.

When the day came my mother stood weeping, clutching Kurt's hand, while the pastor performed a simple service in the presence of a congregation which filled the church, despite Uncle Willi's attempts to keep the event as quiet as possible. Later a group of us returned to the grave to pay silent respect, unobserved by villagers and estate workers. I was a reluctant participant but would not upset my mother by refusing to go.

We stood for a while in the biting cold. From inside the church came the notes of 'Jesu, Joy of Man's Desiring' as someone practised on the organ, the tune swelling and dying as we turned to go. Suddenly Uncle Willi, Kurt and Walter Pletz, their faces grim with loss, simultaneously saluted, their hands touching their heads and falling again in perfect unison. It should have looked ridiculous but did not, and I walked back with them in silence, wondering about the man who, dead for more than seventeen years, should inspire such a tribute, despite the vague but discernible disapproval which often accompanied the mention of his name.

I stole a glance at Lotte and guessed she was similarly confused. Although she was my half-sister, I had never much distinguished her from my cousins. Indeed, Elsa felt far more like a sibling to me than Lotte, but now, as we left our father's grave, I was conscious that she was his daughter and that, although I had always taken her good will for granted, she had more reason than Alessandra to resent my mother and me. She could not remember her own mother well, but even the most tenuous of recollection must be precious in the circumstances, and I wondered that she had not felt more indignation on Ellie's account.

I moved to Lotte's side and began to slow my pace. As if by agreement, we lagged behind the others. I mentioned the salute.

'They worship him,' said Lotte. 'I don't. I would like to but I can't. I look at the photos of him holding me and I wonder what my mother would have said if she had known what was going on. Oh, I know he was brave and rescued Jews but what is that worth when he could have broken my mother's heart?'

'Do you remember him?'

Lotte shook her head. 'No. Not at all. I was a

182

babe in arms when he went off to France. He came back at the end of nineteen forty-two for some long leave but I was only two and after that we never saw him again. I remember Johanna, my elder sister, screaming and crying when the news came of his death but it meant nothing to me.'

'Do you remember your mother?'

'Yes. She used to sing to me as she was drying me after my bath and put daisies in an egg cup by my bed. She would say how good they were to have closed themselves up for the night and that I must also go to sleep, but that, when I woke, the daisies would be open and I must remember to say good morning.'

'Do you hate me?'

Lotte looked at me through incredulous eyes, 'Don't be daft! I love you to pieces.'

I hesitated, trying to find the right response. Before I could do so my half-sister tucked her arm in mine.

'I didn't really understand what had happened when you turned up. They didn't tell such things to children then. My older cousins knew, of course, but Elsa was also kept in the dark. No one ever really did tell us, now I come to think of it. In the end it just became obvious to us but, by then, I was used to your being about the place and was quite fond of you, with your funny little ways. I couldn't suddenly resent you.'

'What about my mother?'

'Oh, I did go through a phase of bitterly resenting her. Uncle Willi told me I should pity her because she had been so young and innocent when it all happened, but that seemed to make

183

what my father did even worse. Yet, when I said that to Uncle Willi, he just went on about how brave our father had been in France. I didn't know what to think and I honestly believe that marrying Rudi was one way of escaping it all. I adore him, but I would have been less ready to defy them if I hadn't felt so let down. I know that makes me a bitch because none of them could have done more for me, especially Uncle Willi.'

I squeezed her arm. 'I can't believe that we haven't talked about this before.'

'You were not old enough,' she responded grandly and, had she not been so pregnant, I would have pretended to strangle her, as I so often did when we played as children. The remark had lightened the atmosphere and, when I saw Rudi detach himself from the others and walk back towards us, I smiled to reassure him that all was well.

Long after I returned to Ampleforth I would see their salute in my dreams as once in my nightmares I had been revisited by the images of my mother's family, clad in black, turning their white, grieving faces from me when I ran to claim them as my own. But when I lay on my back on the rugger field, my knees drawn up in pain, hot arrows shafting my sprained ankle, and watched a black crow flap its way across the sky I found myself smiling at its impotence, knowing that the old images had lost their power to hurt.

'Bad luck,' sympathised Matron as she bound the damaged limb. 'There'll be no more sports for you this term.'

Unable to understand the English obsession with sport when I had first arrived, I now felt deprived. Worse still, I seemed condemned to hobble my way through the Easter holidays at Charles Emmett's house, which was a Victorian redbrick villa with four bedrooms, situated in a row of similar houses in a sleepy Warwickshire town. Jack Marshall also came to visit and I had my first experience of an English country pub. We drank beer, in my case worriedly, knowing we were breaking the law, the others seemingly unbothered, but when Jack offered me a cigarette I shook my head. We knew little enough then about the dangers of nicotine – some even disputed its being addictive – but I hated the taste of smoke and its smell when stale. I had smoked a single cigarette as a rite of passage when I was fourteen and had not succumbed to one since.

Charles and Jack began a *sotto voce* commentary on some of the women in the pub while I thought of Arabella, who no longer wrote to me. I did not want to visit the Bland household again but sometimes, when a picture of George's sister, hair blowing, face glowing with exercise, rose in my memory, I fantasised about doing so. An English rose, I thought, and despised the pub women of my companions' conversation.

At the end of the first week it poured with rain and we took refuge in a cinema. I cannot remember what the film was, only my intense embarrassment when the girl next to me, a stranger, put her hand on my thigh. From somewhere came the image of June, the girl of that brief meeting on the boat to England. I shuffled, wondering if I should say no, thank you, or physically put her hand back in her own lap. I did neither but sat through the rest of the film enduring her unwanted attention, glad that she attempted no further intimacy. When the lights came on she rose and tucked her arm in that of a man on her other side as they walked out. I made the mistake of describing the incident to Charles and Jack, who teased me without pity as I hobbled beside them to the bus stop.

Charles had an elder brother, Alastair, who passed his driving test during the holiday and we spent hours squashed in the so-called back seat of his Austin-Healey sports car as he drove around country lanes at dangerous speed. I held on and prayed and watched with amazement as the others cheered, urging Alastair to even greater risks. Until that holiday I had not thought of myself as especially staid or retiring but now, as I climbed out of the car and regarded with unfeigned gratitude the feel of terra firma beneath my feet, I wondered if I had more in common with Franz than Otto.

By the time rugby had given way to the tennis season, my ankle was back to normal and I played with vigour, finding a place in the school team almost immediately. Free from the pressure of public exams that summer, I rejoiced in away matches with Stonyhurst in the neighbouring county and once we even travelled to Somerset to play Downside, a venture which took two days of travelling in addition to the day's tennis.

My performance in the school exams that summer persuaded the brothers that I should sit the entrance exams for Oxford and Cambridge, and their only question was whether I should do so that autumn or return for a third year in the sixth form as was then common amongst the academically inclined. I knew the bigger question was whether Uncle Willi would let me continue my studies in England or whether he would expect me to complete my education in Germany or, more likely, in another country.

Greater even than that was my doubt as to whether I should expect him to see me through university at all. Surely that responsibility would no longer be his if we all left Ströbelfields when my mother married Kurt in late July? I confided my dilemma to Brother Francis, who in turn sought the advice of the head, who made an international phone call.

'I would have preferred you to go the Sorbonne but that is out of the question as far as your mother is concerned,' observed Uncle Willi when I returned home for the summer. 'I admit I would still like you to round things off in Italy because your father was very fond of that country, but you are Klaus-Pierre Dessin, not Klaus von Ströbel, and you must make your own decisions. Apparently you are likely to get four A levels and to take three of the subjects to scholarship level. The head called that "really rather good" which I divined to be an English understatement.'

I grinned and briefly embraced him. Neither of us mentioned the issue of who should pay, but he did refer obliquely to my doubts by saying that my mother and Kurt would be renting a small cottage on the estate, which he was converting for wheelchair use as a wedding present. Kurt was earning money translating German into Russian, having been obliged to learn the language during his time in the East. He was also doing a small amount of tuition, by correspondence, and advising my uncle's business about Eastern markets, such as there were.

He had shown more resourcefulness and independence in the space of a year than my mother had in the twelve years she had been in Germany, and a reluctant surge of respect softened my hostility.

The cottage had two bedrooms, Uncle Willi told me, so of course I could go with them, but my room would be kept for me at Ströbelfields and I must continue to treat it as home, especially if I needed the library for my academic work or space to accommodate friends. I knew then that the von Ströbels would miss me as much as I them and that I was being urged to divide my time between two homes.

Something of that thought must have stayed with me when the practical arrangements for the move were being discussed. My mother and Kurt were to honeymoon at Travemünde, a small town by the sea where the sailing was especially good and small boats abounded. Kurt said he could sit down and pull ropes, could swim using only his arms and that he would not be deflected by my mother's anxiety. They would return in mid-August. I pointed out that that would give me only a fortnight in the new house and that it might be better to sort out their move first and for me to follow them when I returned for Christmas.

My mother's mouth tightened and I saw Kurt

looking at me. He was the first to speak. 'You will never get all that stuff in the tiny room in the cottage. You will have to leave quite a lot here, if Willi and Angelika can stand it.'

My mother flashed him an angry look but I smiled gratefully.

'Anyway, if you wait until Christmas it will give us time to decorate it. You must tell us what colours you would like.'

My mother looked slightly more mollified but when I returned at Christmas with my first Beatles record and a passion for Radio Luxembourg, she looked embarrassed. She believed she was expecting a child and the second bedroom would have to be a nursery. There was no room for a cot in the main bedroom because Kurt needed circulation space for his wheelchair and all those rails when he struggled along on his false leg. Indeed, even after Uncle Willi's generous conversions, there was precious little room at all. There was an upstairs wheelchair as well as Kurt's usual one and a rudimentary lift between the two floors which erupted onto the landing. The bathroom was downstairs and the kitchen cramped.

I never moved in, and when the child turned into twins and a third was expected almost immediately I knew they would soon move out.

They moved back to Ströbelfields at the end of 1963. It had been the year in which Britain had been rocked by the Profumo affair, Germany by the end of Adenauer's chancellorship and the world by the assassination of President Kennedy. For me the main events had been winning a scholarship to Corpus Christi, Oxford and having my first major row with Uncle Willi – over the length of my hair.

Uncle Willi had converted the barn, which gave my mother and stepfather a huge amount of space. They lived downstairs and, over the next few years, the upstairs area was to be taken over by their children.

'I suppose she feels she has not a lot of time left,' Aunt Angelika had remarked to Elsa when the third child was announced. 'But women can have children well into their forties.'

More worrying was the observation she had made to Uncle Willi when the twins were named Catherine and Klaus: 'A haunted marriage.' I had not been supposed to hear the words but had passed by at the moment of their being uttered. *A haunted marriage.* A memory of three men saluting rose unbidden in my mind.

I remembered the supposed haunting of the barn and how Aunt Angelika had reassured me: *'The ghosts of Ströbelfields smile kindly on their successors.'*

I looked at the photograph of my father and walked over to the grand piano to take it from its place. 'Go away,' I said to it. 'Leave them alone. Haven't you done damage enough?' It was a childish action and I was glad nobody had witnessed it. Klaus and Catherine. My mother had chosen those names because she had not let go of the past and I felt a fleeting sympathy for Kurt. *Klaus and Catherine.* That combination of names must have hurt him in Paris when he hungered after my mother and hid it because my father was his superior officer. Now that distant suffering was enshrined in the names of his children. I wondered that he had agreed until I remembered the salute. He too had been under my father's spell.

I did not live in the barn, retaining my old room, but I spent much of my day there, helping to sort out the new accommodation, often baby-sitting while my mother went to the village, marvelling at the twins as they took their first steps and began to explore the world about them. They were my half-sister and half-brother, but somehow seemed as unrelated to me as Lotte had among my cousins.

1964 yawned before me as I had returned to Ampleforth in the autumn of 1963 to sit the exam for Oxford, but already had too good a collection of A levels to need to do a full third year in the sixth form. I was free until I went to Corpus Christi in October and had formed a vague desire to travel away the intervening months.

Charles Emmett was doing the full year but Jack Marshall was also free and had contacts in America. I considered joining him but when I put the idea to Uncle Willi he was not enthusiastic. I already spoke English and would be better employed in getting a job in Spain or Italy where I could learn the language. I irritably retorted that I already spoke three modern languages with native fluency, was about to study two ancient ones in depth and surely that was enough. He smiled as he conceded the point but said that as indeed I had such varied experience of the West why not spend my time somewhere completely different, such as Africa?

For a while I toyed with this idea. In England they had talked a great deal about Voluntary Service Overseas, although largely in the context of experience after university, and I decided to investigate German equivalents, but before I had made much more than preliminary enquiries I changed my mind about travelling and decided instead to earn some money of my own. Uncle Willi tried to persuade me that I was giving up an opportunity that might not come again but told me that if I insisted on spending my time in this way I should go off and earn in another country.

Even that I rejected, reasoning that I would probably have to take a job as a waiter. Instead I spent the months in Bonn in tourist information where my linguistic skills were much prized and in my time off offered myself as an unofficial guide to British and French tourists who wanted to see the city. I took the cheapest lodgings I could find and saved like a miser but it was an expensive city and I swallowed my pride when Uncle Willi continued my allowance.

I returned exhausted in the August of 1964, protesting that I had not even the energy to take a holiday, and irritated my mother and Aunt Angelika by doing little more than staying late in bed in the mornings and idling away the afternoons. Otto observed my collapse with amusement but eventually enticed me to help him with the horses and my vigour slowly returned.

I had been sufficiently immersed in my first experiment at independence to have taken less interest than I should in the world about me but I had been keenly aware of the developments in

Berlin. The wall had been completed in the first week of January and the East German regime had no compunction about shooting any of its citizens who tried to scale it. America had passed the Civil Rights Bill giving full equality to black Americans and had become embroiled in the tangle that was Vietnam while in the USSR Mr Khrushchev had resigned in a bad temper.

It seemed an odd background for an anti-German hysteria, with its roots in old conflicts, to take centre stage but it arose nonetheless as NATO divided over an American proposal to create a multi-national nuclear force. Germany was unwisely enthusiastic about the idea and both France and the Scandinavian members of the alliance revolted against the idea of 'a German finger on the nuclear button'. The controversy raged and an American satirist composed a poem which fanned the flames of fear, referring to the Bundeswehr as the Wehrmacht.

'They might look at what's going on in Berlin,' said Uncle Willi morosely. 'Then they might see where the new enemy is.'

'Trust France to take that silly line.' My mother's voice was full of contempt and I knew it was not just for the present argument.

The commotion had demonstrated deep fissures in the reconciliation process which was supposedly taking Europe forward, away from its past. My mother's puny battle with her family suddenly seemed less trivial when replicated by national governments. Walter Pletz derided the entire episode as a joke but Kurt shook his head over it and said it was time another generation took over.

'Eventually that will be Klaus-Pierre's generation,' responded Uncle Willi. 'It is time he went to France.'

My mother met the suggestion with a storm of protest and Uncle Willi, shrugging, desisted and kept the peace.

ten

Caux

'The only good German is a dead one.'

I toyed with the idea of putting aside my book and introducing myself to the man opposite. He was stout, greasy-haired and unshaven, making an odd contrast to the slight, pretty redhead who was his daughter. She must have been about seventeen or eighteen and had just finished telling her father a story about a friend who wanted to marry a young man from Germany but whose parents were refusing permission. Clearly her father's sympathies were with the parents.

I glanced at the girl and then returned to Herodotus. The door of the compartment was opened from the corridor, admitting a gust of cold air and the ticket inspector. I scrabbled in my pocket and produced the small piece of card. He hardly looked at it before clipping it, his attention already absorbed by the guilty nonchalance of the man and girl. Amused, I saw the man try to look surprised when the inspector said, 'This ticket is for Didcot, sir.'

'Didcot! We asked for two to Oxford, didn't we, love?'

The girl nodded.

'Well, they must have made a mistake,' smiled the inspector. 'That'll be another three and six, please, sir.'

'Each,' he added as the man handed over the coins with an expression of outraged innocence.

'My daughter paid for a ticket to Oxford. She has no more money left.'

'Then I am afraid I must take her name and address.'

'Why? Look here, she's already paid, I tell you. We haven't got any more money.'

I looked over the top of Herodotus and saw the girl struggling not to cry. Repressing a sigh, I proffered a half crown and a shilling to the inspector.

'Oh, you mustn't.' She might have at least tried not to sound so half-hearted.

'Thanks, mate,' said the man when the inspector had gone.

'Eet vass ein pleasure. Zees ve do in Germany. I hope ze Fräulein vass not too upset.' I hurriedly re-engrossed myself in my Loeb classical text lest I should burst into laughter, uncertain whether my mirth was inspired more by the man's stupefied expression or by my own exaggerated accent.

It made a good tale at dinner that night and the burst of hilarity which followed caused the dons to peer at us from High Table with amused curiosity. Later, as I was finishing an essay on Pliny, there was a tap at my door and the student from the room above looked in with diffident determination. I knew him only slightly, a physics student in his third year, clever, shy but with an amazing acting talent which had not gone unnoticed by Olivier himself when he had visited, unheralded, a student production at the Playhouse. His name was Guy Roper.

I offered coffee but he shook his head, sat on the edge of the only armchair in the room and cleared his throat several times. I sat with my back to my desk, afraid that if I so much as glanced at Pliny, Guy would think he was disturbing me and depart with nervous courtesy.

'I hope you don't mind but I couldn't help overhearing your story about the people on the train. I was wondering, do you, er, get a lot of that?'

'Prejudice, you mean? Yes, sometimes, but at least I'm not black so I don't think I'll complain too loudly.'

It was November 1965, and Ian Smith had declared UDI in Rhodesia. The morality of empire, apartheid in South Africa and the treatment of black people in general were the issues uppermost in British conversation at that time and furiously debated by students in particular. I looked at Guy, wondering what the purpose of his visit might be, as the haunting strains of 'Yesterday' drifted across the quad.

'Have you ever heard of Caux?'

I made a brief search of my memory. 'No, I don't think so. Who is Coe?'

'I mean the place. On Lake Geneva.'

'Perhaps vaguely. Why?'

'Moral Re-armament has set up a centre there. It aims to bring nations together. They have conferences which include German and French people, for example, and sometimes do very specific ones which bring together Germans and victims of Hitler.'

An image of Judy Margolis floated into my mind. I had not thought about her for a long time and the four years which had passed since our meeting now gave me a different perspective. That buffoon George had called her the Margoyle but I knew now that the deep lines that marred her face had been etched by suffering. Almost certainly it was her husband, not her cousins, who had died in Dachau, but she had been too kind to say so, taking pity on my youth. Nevertheless I did not relish another conversation with a survivor of the camps, even had I found the prospect of a Moral Re-armament conference remotely congenial.

Guy read my mind with sharp accuracy. 'Don't be put off by the title. These really are great international conferences. A friend roped me into one last year and I was glad I went. Then I heard you speak in that debate at the Union and I thought how you were just the sort who could give a superb lecture.'

I remembered the speech. Tariq Ali had been president and it was the first time I had participated in a debate. I had waxed eloquent on social inequalities and large council estates while hoping no one there knew the sort of estate I came from and my connection to the booming capitalist enterprise of Wanderer Bear. It had no possible relevance to the kind of conference which Guy had described so I could conclude only that he had decided I was an eloquent speaker.

'Surely, these days it must all be Africans, not Germans? That's where the problem is now, unless you have persuaded a member of the Politburo to meet a prisoner from the Lubyanka.'

Guy smiled. 'Not yet, but please give it some thought. You could do a splendid talk on your life experiences.'

'What on earth do you know about my life experiences?'

'I know that you have a French name, come from Germany and went to Ampleforth.'

I felt obscurely relieved and was as surprised as he when I said without heat but with every intention of shocking him: 'I am the illegitimate result of a union between a French teenager and a married German general. The French family rejected me and I was brought up in Germany by my father's family, who took in my mother as well, even though they had young children in the house, including my father's legitimate daughter. His wife and two other children had been killed in the Dresden bombing. Now, tell me, does that sound a tale for Moral Rearmament?'

'It sounds ideal.'

I gave up but I steadily refused to go to Caux and even when I was boarding a plane for Switzerland the following summer I still could not remember changing my mind. Guy had just won a first-class degree in physics and was very pleased with himself. I congratulated him gloomily, still uncertain as to how he had persuaded me to spend three days of my vacation in this fashion.

On my first evening I looked out of the large French windows at a magnificent vista of Lake Geneva and its surrounding mountains, and felt more reconciled to the project.

'That's France over there.' Guy pointed to the left.

France. I was looking at France for the first time since leaving it, at the country to which my mother had sworn she would never return, and to which she had always forbidden me to go. *France.*

'*Nazi, Nazi, German brat!*' For a moment the chanting was so vivid that I forgot it was only a memory and half-thought Guy must hear it too. Then the strains died away and a pale-faced woman in a black suit was saying, 'No, sorry, I am not your granny.' *France.*

'Are you all right?' Guy was looking at me with a worried face and I forced myself back to the present, but over the next few days I came back time and again to that view and looked always to the left. *France.* As the plane took off for Germany I stared down. *France.*

Guy's praises were ringing in my ears and I knew I had done well, but the conference had produced reactions in me which I found surprising, unable to understand why the sound of a group of girls speaking volubly in French, their voices pitched high with eager argument, should have caused that odd sensation in my stomach or why, when I had determined to try and find someone from Paris, I had moved away so quickly when Guy had introduced me to a middle-aged

Frenchman who came from that city.

I had given a highly successful lecture and my question-and-answer session must have been one of the best of the conference as I switched effortlessly between English, French and German according to the nationality of the questioner. Yet, although I had managed to keep my nerve steady and my answers thoughtful, I had been disconcerted by the probing nature of some of the interrogation – I could call it by no other name – which had ensued.

'Have you ever made any effort to contact your mother's family?'

I looked at the speaker, a young woman of perhaps nineteen or twenty, earnest, bespectacled, demure, sharp.

I was twenty-one and could hardly explain that I was afraid of upsetting my mother, given the eloquence and force with which I had just declaimed on the merits of reconciliation and international co-operation. I opted for truth and told an agog audience about my mother's vow, claiming that I felt I must respect it until I had come of age but I was now twenty-one and would have to consider the best way forward.

It had been a disingenuous answer for what I remembered was less a vow than a funeral and I was not in any hurry to meet the participants again. Yet the question haunted me. Nations were the sum of the individuals within them and a nation could not speak peace to another unless its members acknowledged the necessity. *A German finger on the nuclear button.* Pierre Dessin had probably used those very words. Unless challenged, unless confronted with a new generation, one that had not known Hitler, why should he not persist in his prejudice?

The next question had been a simple, factual one asking me about instances of prejudice with which I had met in England. I replied cautiously, not wanting to give an impression of grievance, trying to leaven my observations with humour, recounting hilariously the episode on the train when I had paid the rail fare of the bigot's daughter.

Did I consider myself European or German? I endeavoured to answer while my mind ran riot with the question: was I German or French? The law said French. My upbringing said German. *Klaus*-Pierre Dessin or Klaus-*Pierre Dessin?*

Was I proud or ashamed of my father? I replied I had never known him.

Then a man of about twenty-five – fair, athletic-looking, German – asked whether it was right that there should be any limit on the bringing of war crimes trials. I spoke eloquently of my Uncle Gerhardt and Dachau, told how the Eichmann trial had dominated my early years in England, spoke of the legal basis for Nuremberg, pointed to the trials, in West Germany, of the Auschwitz guards only the previous year and utterly avoided answering the question.

'You should have been a politician,' teased Guy.

'I went on like that because I did not know what I think and I was giving myself time to decide.'

'And?'

'I still don't know.'

I had spent my last hours at Caux looking again

towards France. Haunted, I thought, but the ghosts of France did not look kindly on me.

Arriving back in Germany, I confided the thought to Ernst Pletz, who was home for the summer.

'Ghosts are better confronted. You are twenty-one and can do as you please. Go to Paris and don't tell your mother, or perhaps you could visit your Aunt Marie in Provence. Frau Kleist can hardly object to that.'

'She can and she probably will, but I suppose that is the way to broach it. Not till after the party though.'

I had turned twenty-one in February 1966 and Uncle Willi had sent me a generous cheque which enabled me to have a large celebration at Oxford, but I had not been back to Ströbelfields since and my mother was insisting on a family party now as belated recognition of my majority. She was heavy with the pregnancy of her fourth child and radiant with the happiness of the new life she was carrying. I brushed aside her questions on Caux, not wanting to tarnish her joy.

To Uncle Willi and Otto I was much more forthcoming. Caux had been fun and successful and challenging, but it had turned my thoughts towards France. In my imagination I could see again the view of Lake Geneva from that large house in Caux and I found my head turning left although there was nothing more interesting in that direction than a pile of carrots on the kitchen table.

Eventually I forced myself to concentrate on my party. I pretended not to notice the whispering, which meant some surprise was being prepared, and instead began upon the guest list of school-friends from the village and from Lübeck and gave it to Aunt Angelika to add to the already lengthy one of von Ströbels and Pletzes. I asked both Charles Emmett and Jack Marshall along with friends from Oxford without any serious expectation that they would come but the surprise turned out to be the arrival of six guests from England, their fares paid for by Uncle Willi.

Every room in Ströbelfields was opened, together with the barn and my mother's old cottage. Sleeping bags were strewn in seemingly unlikely places and Walter Pletz accommodated some of my guests. It was a fine night and we danced most of it away to a South American steel band.

In the earlier part of the evening the children of my mother and of my cousins joined the celebrations before leaving unwillingly. In the latter part my elders retreated to bed.

I circulated with champagne, noting the healthy complexions and smart attire of people I had known as hungry and near-ragged children in Lübeck. I had not seen one or two of them since 1961 and I was eager for their news. Germany had changed in that time and so had their fortunes. *They are better off than the British.* The thought took me by surprise as I ruefully conceded that the complaint I had heard from so many English lips seemed to be true.

'What's funny?' The question came from a stocky, prosperous-looking man to whose family I had delivered gifts of meat and vegetables when I stayed with them in Lübeck. I could hardly share my thought with him and told him a joke instead. It was an English riddle which translated badly but it was all I could think of on the spur of the moment.

Most of them were still students, I thought with wonder, the German education system producing late graduates. I had not gone to Oxford for a year after leaving school and I had chosen a course which necessitated four years study instead of three. Had these been English contemporaries they would by now be working.

It was five in the morning before the party finally finished. I staggered across to the barn and towards my sleeping bag on the twins' floor. Charles and Jack had my room in the house. As I pushed open the bedroom door both Klaus and Catherine sat up simultaneously, although I had made no noise and had taken off my shoes.

'Did you like our present?' asked Klaus.

'It was very noisy,' reproved Catherine.

I wished only to sleep but sat on Catherine's bed for a while, not wanting to disappoint them.

'Who were all those funny people?' demanded Klaus.

'What funny people?'

'Those who spoke like this.' For a three-year-old it was a remarkable mimicry of the English accent which followed.

'Oh. They are from England.'

'Are they nice in England?'

'Some of them are. It's just like Germany. Some people are nice and some are not.'

'Is England far away?' asked Catherine.

That night it had seemed very far away. I had been more immersed in Ströbelfields, more cocooned by its security, more at one with its being than for a long while. Many of the people I had talked to that night had become almost strangers, so long had I been away, yet I had never felt more completely at home. Instead of a visitor twice a year I had been the host, a temporary owner of the house. I had been not a Dessin but a von Ströbel.

eleven

Pierre Dessin

I shut the window angrily as the sounds of yet another demonstration disrupted the concentration which I had been directing at Lucretius's *De Rerum Natura.* I was as angry as the protestors about the Vietnam war but finals were now only weeks away and I had wasted sufficient time in the past to generate despairing urgency now. There was one paper, however, in which I expected to distinguish myself and I had been toying for a while with adding a flourish which I knew would impress any examiner and possibly make the difference between a first- and second-class degree.

There was a document at the Sorbonne which was unavailable at the Bodleian, from which extracts were quoted either in French or in translation in many of the studies I had read of Cicero's *De Amicitia.* The academics concerned had drawn contradictory conclusions and I decided that I would go and examine the original document for myself. Lectures had now ceased so that we might give the time to revision and it occurred to me that if I spent a week closeted in a French boarding house, away from the distractions of friends, balls, punting and the pulsating fury of anti-war demonstrations, I might also get a lot of routine work done as well.

I obtained an exeat for a week's absence without difficulty and only the rough waters of the channel gave me any cause for regret as the ferry began its journey to Calais. I was conscious that my mother would disapprove strongly if she knew I was returning to France and to Paris of all places, but her vow could not bind me now I was an adult and I told myself that she need never know I had been. Indeed, with four children and a severely disabled husband to look after, I could not believe she would accord too much priority to the matter even if she did find out. For more than six years I had made my life away from Ströbelfields and my visit to France seemed somehow symbolic of my independence.

I did leave behind contact details with my college in case of an emergency from home but hoped nobody would have cause to make such an enquiry, so I was untroubled as I stood at the rail as I had on that first trip to England when I met June. It seemed I was still as prone to seasickness now as I was then and I looked miserably down into the water, knowing I would soon add to its contents.

In between episodes of nausea I glanced at my fellow sufferers. There was one now turning away from the rail, looking pale and queasy. Our eyes met and we exchanged comradely grins, which gradually froze as we recognised each other. The shock pulsed through me while I mentally denied his existence and waited for the illusion to fade. He came from the past and could not be part of the present, for merely by refusing to think of him for more than a decade I had all but convinced myself that he was little more than a bad dream. He no longer had any real substance in my mind.

'Dessin,' he acknowledged reluctantly.

'Mueller.' His uncertainty was reflected in my own voice as I returned the greeting.

As we hesitated, each wondering how to react, wanting a tactful exit but anxious to avoid rudeness, I studied his face. I could not have failed to recognise it even without the telltale mole near the left ear and the nose only slightly misshapen despite the severity of so many beatings. It had been thrust close to mine too often and too malevolently for me ever to forget its features. Yet it was somehow different, perhaps softer, the eyes calmer, the mouth kinder. The man who looked at me now, returning my scrutiny, possibly seeking signs of resentment, did not seem a bully but I was wary. I found myself looking at the sky but there were no black birds flying there, only pale gulls wheeling and swooping.

I brought my gaze back to his as he became the first to break the silence.

'I expect I'm the last man on earth you wanted to meet and I'll make myself scarce. But before I go, I'll just say sorry and thanks.'

'Thanks?'

'Yes, you've probably forgotten but when they started to beat me at school you fainted and stopped the whole proceedings. It was very decent of you in the circumstances.'

'Don't mention it.' My tone matched his wry note, but the ferry lurched suddenly and we both groaned. I remembered his father hammering him and how we had pedalled, shrieking, to Walter Pletz. I saw no reason to want to know him now but also no reason to hold a grudge against a damaged child.

'It was a long time ago. Forget it.'

He looked relieved and asked after Uncle Willi. I replied briefly but felt compelled to ask after his family.

'My father and mother are dead. So is Horst. My sister, whom you knew only as a baby, is healthy, beautiful and clever.'

My hostility, evaporated in horror. 'What happened to Horst?'

'My father killed him in one of his rages. He was shaking the baby's cot and Horst tried to stop him, but that only made him wilder. He threw Horst against a wall and knocked him out. He died a few days later from damage to the brain. I was there when they took my father away. He clung screaming to my mother, sobbing that he didn't want to go to prison and she, poor fool, tried to protect him, shouting at them to leave him alone, that she couldn't live without him, that he hadn't meant it. When I think how he treated her I couldn't believe it. I had never imagined a grown man could wail like that.'

I remembered how unnerving I had found the

tears of the grown-ups at Omi's funeral and wondered how I would have coped with the scene Wolfgang was describing now.

'Naturally he was found guilty and sent down, but he never served the sentence. He took his own life within a week. My mother did her best to struggle on but I was always in trouble and she had a breakdown. My sister was sent to an aunt but no relative would have me and I was despatched to a home and then another and then another.'

'I don't know what to say. Sorry sounds pathetic in the circumstances. Did your mother recover?'

'Yes. She died last year after a short illness. She had reclaimed my sister and they were reasonably happy. The aunt continued to keep an eye on them and helped with money, but she couldn't cope with me and nor could anyone else.'

'I wish I had flown,' I muttered as the ferry rolled again and Wolfgang turned back to grasp the rail.

'I would have flown if I could have afforded it.'

I waited, wanting to hear the end of his story, wondering how the spiteful, unhappy bully had become the man who now spoke in such quiet, measured tones.

'Some would say it was inevitable that I should turn to crime but I never did. My father's screams as he was taken to prison gave me a horror of the consequences. It was an irrational fear rather than a healthy respect for the law, but very potent and it is with me still. I do not think I shall ever so much as park a car in the wrong place.

'It was the only reason I did not truant from

school, having some notion that it was against the law, but I gave enough trouble to be constantly kicked out and left at the earliest opportunity. I began labouring on building sites, there still being plenty of them in Germany.'

I thought of the dereliction, the heaps of rubble, the grey ruins which everywhere had been a playground for children, a refuge for rats, a trap for the unwary with unexploded bombs. I remembered my first visit beyond the untouched lands of my father's family, the poverty, the leather shorts, the desperate scrabbling after a single lump of coal, the pinched faces of those who lived on a diet of turnip and potato, an old man eagerly picking up a discarded cigarette end.

I came back from the past to hear the story of my companion's redemption. A poorly erected piece of scaffolding had sent him plunging twenty feet and he woke in hospital with two broken legs and a kindly nurse, Helga, who was also young and attractive. He had no interest in books but the enforced inactivity left him with little choice but to read and to chat to his fellow patients.

'Something started to happen, the beginnings of a hankering after knowledge, which certainly never characterised my schooldays, an interest in other people and their stories, when only a few weeks earlier I would not have listened to them for five seconds. Helga was wonderful, bringing books from home, talking to me when the others had visitors and of course looking after my needs in all sorts of embarrassing ways.'

'The love of a good woman? The old story?'

He shook his head. 'I was in love with her all

right but she was in love with one of the doctors. No, it was a small child who was visiting his grandfather and behaving badly enough for the nurses to ask the mother to take him out. I asked him to help me draw a cat and he did. I think I suggested it largely out of boredom but I quite liked the way his face lit up and we must have drawn every beast in the animal kingdom by the time visiting hours were over. Of course, he took all the pictures away with him and next day his father arrived all agog, saying he was writing a children's book about a zoo and could I possibly illustrate it. I had nothing else to do and agreed. Everyone on the ward was excited about it and those who could walk kept wandering over to my bed to see what I was drawing next.'

He smiled. 'The book was never published but the publisher liked my illustrations and began giving me small commissions, so I convalesced surrounded by books and compliments from people who lived the sort of lives I thought could never be mine. I sought out my mother and sister and began to take some responsibility for them. Anyway that's enough about me. I'll leave you alone now.'

I found I did not wish in the least to be left alone with my seasickness and had in any case begun to like him. I asked him why he was going to France and he said he had been offered a job, in Frankfurt, as a commercial artist which he was to take up in July and he wanted to fit in some travelling so he had been seeing London, where he had run out of money. This had not worried him as he had a return ticket but he spent a couple of days as a pavement artist and on the second an old man had insisted on giving him twice what he had asked.

As he was settling to work on the third morning the same man appeared and asked him if he would consider coming to his house to draw his grand-daughter. It turned out to be a large house in a London square and the drawing turned into a painting, which took several days as the child would not sit still. Again he was given more than he asked and decided he had enough to take a ferry for France and live by his wits there for a few weeks. He intended seeing Paris, Versailles, Provence and more if he could sell his art there too.

'Of course, I'll try to keep my mouth shut until I've actually done the picture. I'm told they hate German accents even now and that I should claim to be Swiss. You presumably still speak French like a native?'

'Yes.'

I remembered him chanting, 'Frenchie! Frenchie!' and trying to make me eat a dead frog, and guessed from his suddenly heightened colour that his mind was similarly engaged. I tried to rescue him by telling him why I was bound for France. Beside me a man with a long beard and flowing hair was violently sick, gripping the rail, the beads around his neck swinging wildly as he leant forward.

'I shall never travel by sea again,' I gasped.

'Nor I, if I can help it,' murmured Wolfgang. 'Are you going to see the French side of your family?'

He was startled by the vehemence of my denial

and it became my turn to rehearse my life history, concluding, '...so I can't. My mother would never forgive me.'

'It is nineteen sixty-eight,' was all he said in reply but the words somehow seemed to imply a rebuke.

'They accused my mother of treachery.'

'We have been at peace for twenty-three years. Man cannot live in the past.'

I thought of Caux, of the pictures of the Queen visiting Germany and the headline 'The Crowning Reconciliation' which had been splashed across the British press, of Judy Margolis, of the Panzer unit which had visited Wales as part of a NATO exercise amid huge controversy, of the trial of Eichmann, of the seemingly endless war dramas on the BBC, of the protests on her wedding day which confronted Princess Beatrix of the Netherlands when she married Claus von Amsberg. The past was surely all around us.

The enemy was now the Soviet Union, with its vast nuclear arsenal and the Berlin Wall. I remembered lying in bed, wondering what sort of world I might wake up to during the height of the Cuban missile crisis. Western Europe faced the threat with unity but was it really at peace with itself? Could any number of treaties soften hearts eaten by grief and hate?

Wolfgang gave me a mischievous grin. 'Well, what about curiosity? Most people have some interest in their roots.'

'I met my roots once and that was enough.' I gave him an unvarnished account of the brutal rejection I had suffered at my great-grandfather's funeral and waited for his observation that it had taken place nineteen years ago, but instead he grimaced and made a none-too-subtle change of subject. At Calais we decided to wait before embarking on any more travelling and spent a couple of hours looking around until we were able to face a meal. I suggested a café but he shook his head, saying he could not afford it.

I tried to conceal my surprise, recognising that I had not encountered poverty for many years. I had seen enough of it when I was at school in Lübeck but at Ampleforth I met only those whose parents could afford such education. Certainly there were scholarship boys, but the distinction was hidden by uniform and a common routine. I knew students who were fiercely careful of their grants at Oxford but none who starved or shivered.

I asked him how he would eat and he said he would purchase bread at a local shop and that in his haversack he had a choice of meat pastes to spread on it. I at once offered to buy him a meal but he shook his head, so I said I would also purchase some food and we could eat it together, having a notion that if we bought different food and shared it his diet might be more palatable. He had no objection to that and we ate bread, cheese and fruit, rediscovering the appetites we had thought lost for ever on the sea.

It was evening when we arrived in Paris and I asked where he would be staying, to which he replied that he would 'find somewhere' but he needed little pressing when I invited him to share my room at the pension. I had deliberately chosen a twin rather than a single room because

I wanted to spread out my revision and I warned him that I would be both untidy and antisocial. If he thought it extravagant or odd to pay for an extra bed for the purpose of storing books on it he did not say so, and when we arrived he helped unpack my files and books with amused efficiency and also curiosity. I realised that neither Latin nor Greek would have featured in his haphazard education.

After a simple supper he picked up a German translation of Livy and lay on his bed to read it. When I looked up after a couple of hours' revision he asked me questions about Roman history and I tried to set the context for the volume he was reading. I felt nothing but admiration for the way he was getting his life in order and nothing but liking for him. I was therefore disconcerted when he disappeared shortly before midnight and did not return until the first hints of dawn. Yet when I left for the Sorbonne the following day he was once more immersed in Livy, seemingly untired from his nocturnal adventure.

At the library I presented my Bodleian card and a letter from my tutor and an hour later was poring over the document I had sought. It was written in archaic French and I struggled a little, but by four o'clock I had completed my task, smugly satisfied that I would impress the examiners. I decided to find a cup of coffee and walk a little before returning to the pension. After a day spent indoors I looked forward to a stroll through a May-scented Parisian park.

As I handed back the book and waited for the formalities to be completed I looked around and saw a noticeboard advertising various events and I wandered over to it in case there should be some classical lecture, imagining myself throwing a line or two into my examination papers about what Professor So-and-So had said when lecturing at the Sorbonne.

It was not, however, any advertisement for a lecture in the classics which caused the shock to enter me as I looked at the board or which caused my heart to give a great thud and a nervous shaking to begin in my stomach. I had been glancing down a short list under the title of 'Visiting Lecturers, May and June' when I read the words: 'M. Pierre Dessin, formerly Professor of English. The portrayal of the working class in nineteenth-century English literature.'

The notice went on to list my grandfather's academic distinctions during his years at the Sorbonne (1937 to 1960), his principal relevant publications and the international acclaim he had received. I noted the time and venue, knowing that I need not write them down, that they were burned into my brain, telling myself that wherever else I might be tomorrow I would not be at that lecture. I had no interest in the subject. I had no interest in the man who would elucidate it.

'Please don't go, Klaus-Pierre.' In my imagination my mother looked at me with alarmed, pleading eyes.

'Confront the ghosts. The path through the future lies often in the past,' countered the cheerful tones of Ernst.

'Do not hate, Klaus-Pierre. It can harm none but yourself.' Franz's gentle tones, which had

216

calmed many an argument between children at Ströbelfields, reached me now, although I was certain he had never used those words to me.

Then a stranger spoke, the words seemingly so real that I almost looked round to see where he was. 'Go, Klaus-Pierre. He is as much a part of you as I was.' I knew I heard the words in my brain alone, that I was re-creating what I believed my father might have said, but I felt a brief chill as if I had encountered a real ghost. He had never spoken to me before.

I felt the same chill the following morning when I stood at the back of a packed lecture hall, late because I had twice turned back.

He was tall with white but still thick hair and an authoritative, precise voice. I looked keenly at him but could see none of my mother's features. I tried to see those of Aunt Marie but her features had become blurred in my memory. Mesmerised, I went on staring, trying to remember him from the funeral, to imagine him remonstrating with my mother, to see him cradling her as a child.

It must have been ten minutes before I tried to make any sense of what he was saying and then I had but limited success. Dickens was a familiar name to me from my English education but I had not heard of George Gissing or George Moore. He was talking about some work called *Esther Walters*, no *Waters*, which dealt with illegitimacy among the poor. From his description it seemed not much had changed although we lived in an age which regarded itself as permissive. In Britain there was a Council for the Unmarried Mother and her Child. The agony aunts, Evelyn

Home and Marje Proops were always referring to it. I knew this because so many of the girls talked about the problem pages of the magazines they read with a detached superiority, which seemed at odds with their detailed knowledge of the contents.

Now my grandfather was talking about *The Nether World* and life in working-class London, now about Victorian orphanages, now reading extracts from the books he had mentioned in their original tongue. His English accent would have passed as native in Oxford academia. Only once did he falter and I looked at him in surprise as he was not saying anything very abstract or difficult at the time. His head was turned in my direction and for a few seconds I wondered if he was in pain, but the expression passed and he returned to his smooth exposition.

At the end he took questions from his large audience but only a few were academic. Many were political, and I guessed that the attendance resulted from a devotion to socialism, on the part of many students, which produced an interest in the conditions in which the oppressed classes lived. He answered all courteously and then said that he would be available for the rest of the day in a room borrowed from a fellow academic.

Again I did not bother to write down the details of the location. Again I promised myself I would not go. Again I went. Yet when I tapped on his door and heard him call, 'Come in', I had to repress a strong instinct to turn and hurry away. *Don't go in*, cried my mother. *Do*, said the entire cast of von Ströbels with whom I had grown up, and perhaps another whom I had never seen.

I pushed open the door diffidently enough but met his eyes as I sat down opposite him, a large oak desk between us. He waited and I realised I had given no thought to what I was going to say, that now I was facing the man who had cast off my mother and refused to acknowledge my existence, I was at a disadvantage because all I had thought about was whether I should have the courage to be here at all, not what I should do when the courage had been forthcoming.

It was true that I had often lived through this moment in my imagination. When I was younger I had a regular fantasy that one day I would trace his address, knock on his door and denounce him to his face. Younger still, I had dreamed of a chance meeting and a tearful reconciliation. Ernst had told me to confront my ghost but was I to exorcise it or walk with it? Had I come in peace or war?

He watched me quizzically. At last I said that I had been at his lecture that morning.

He still waited and I heard myself blurt out, 'I was interested to meet you because by coincidence my name too is Dessin.'

There was a short pause. Then he said, 'I am pleased you still bear the name of Dessin but I doubt very much if coincidence has anything to do with it', and my grandfather looked me straight in the eyes.

twelve

Two Photographs

I looked at him, amazed and helpless, recognising that I had lost control of the interview and that whether I had intended it to be an act of denunciation or an act of reconciliation it would be only what he decided.

He remained inscrutable and I could not tell whether he rejoiced in my discomfiture or not.

'It was not hard to work out,' he observed. 'You are the very image of your father and, of course, had I any doubts, your German accent would have confirmed it.'

I felt an onset of fresh surprise. French had been my first language in my early years and I had assumed that I spoke it as a native, that I spoke as my mother rather than as Uncle Willi, good though his French was. It did not occur to me that with my mother eschewing the language more or less completely I had heard it only from Germans for most of my life and must somehow have acquired an accent. I remembered how Elsa and Lotte had laughed at my German during that first car journey with them from the station to Ströbelfields and how disconcerted I had been to find I did not speak German as they did.

He read my thoughts. 'It is but a very faint accent. When I saw you in my lecture you were standing by the window and for a moment the way the light fell on you made you look older, made you look like ... him. Indeed for one mad, strange moment I thought it was he, come back from the grave. It almost made me forget what I was saying.' I remembered how he had faltered as he looked in my direction. 'Then I realised who you must be. I wondered if you would come.'

I could not produce any immediate response and regretted that I had not thought through the possible lines the conversation might take. I could not offer him my mother's regards and finally resorted to answering a question he had not asked.

'Your daughter is well.'

'I am glad,' he said in the formal tone of the uninterested.

'She is married and you have four more grand-children. It seemed a pity for you not to know that.'

'Did it seem so to you or to her?'

'To me.' It was clear I could not hurt his feelings by the answer.

He smiled slightly. 'Whom did she marry?'

'My father's adjutant. You may remember him. Kurt Kleist. They met again in nineteen sixty-one. It seems he was in love with her when they were in Paris. He was badly injured in the attack which killed my father and has only half a leg.'

If I had hoped to engage his sympathy I was destined to be disappointed. He tried to keep his expression neutral but I had seen the faint curl of his lip and I could read his thoughts as surely as if he had uttered them. *First a middle-aged married*

German general and now a useless cripple. Throwing herself away yet again, wasting her beauty, wasting her life. I tried not to let my hatred show in my eyes.

'He is a good man.' Even to my ears the tone was defensive.

'At least he must be a free one or they could not have married.'

'I realise that what my father did was wrong, but it cannot be undone and I at least had no say in the matter.'

'No. You blame your father?'

It was an odd question but before I could answer it my grandfather got up and turned his back to me, looking out of the window. His next words seemed drawn from the very depths of his being.

'You should blame him. He was old enough to know a great deal better but do not be too quick to assume that he made all the running. Your mother was determined to have him, although I do not believe that she had the faintest notion what that meant in the early days of that lunatic affair.'

I was silent, not trusting him, wondering if he wished to diminish my mother in my eyes. Eventually he turned and looked at me without resuming his seat.

'We always knew you might turn up one day, even if only out of curiosity but I am afraid the rift with your mother is too great to be healed. The Germans killed my son, yet she carried on with one of their generals quite regardless of how the rest of us might feel. She was a Catholic and knew he was married and did not care. She behaved like a slut and suffered not a moment's shame. She saw Jews taken away, her fellow Parisians starving and her siblings wretched, but nothing mattered to her except the indulgence of her own will. She was my daughter and she brought me nothing but misery.'

'She was young, silly and in love,' I countered in the lofty tones of one who has reached twenty-three.

I saw the amusement pass briefly across his eyes. 'Yes, she was in love and so was he. That seemed the greatest treachery of all. We could have borne it better had she been merely the dupe of his lust. His own family appear to have been quite saintly about it all and I am glad for your sake that it worked out that way.'

'May I meet my grandmother?'

'No. None of us wishes to take this any further.'

I wondered how he could know that and saw the unmistakable signs of the autocrat my mother had described.

'At least let me take a message from you to my mother.'

'I have none to send. Catherine made her bed and must lie on it. We are not going to busy ourselves smoothing out the sheets.'

I rose, angry, and uttered a short, ungracious farewell. He responded with dignified brevity and I walked away from him, out of the room and along the corridor, seething with fury, trying to repel the tears which felt so near. I wondered less that my mother should have been so resolute in cutting herself off from her family and instead marvelled that she should have lived amidst such cold brutality for so long.

Back at the pension there was no sign of Wolfgang and I found it difficult to settle to any work. Eventually I gave up the attempt and sat thinking about Pierre Dessin. *None of us wishes to take this any further.* I decided I would test that dismissal for myself but had no idea how to begin. I did not know where my mother had lived in Paris and could not remember where the church was where I had been so callously snubbed, but there was such a thing as a telephone directory and I went downstairs to the tiny reception desk to locate one. There was no sign of the owner and a cursory search behind the desk failed to produce any directory.

I quelled my rising temperature with a compromise. For now I would keep my sights on my exams but in the summer I would return and hunt down my mother's family, methodically, determinedly, and until each had rejected me I would not be deterred by Pierre Dessin. I was their grandson, their nephew, their cousin, and they should at least have to confront my existence. Surely one among them must be kind or secretly want to see my mother again?

Wolfgang returned in the evening, hungry, pouring an assortment of coins on the dressing table, the fruits of a day's drawing tourists outside various boulevard cafés. There was enough there for him to have a better meal than usual. We ate in a small, rather dingy bistro which served surprisingly good steak. He appeared to have an unerring instinct for places to eat which were both good and cheap.

He also had a keen eye for the foibles of his

fellow humans and I let him entertain me with stories of the day's clients, feeling my tension dissolve in laughter. My own account of the day would be a poor return, seeking not his amusement but his sympathy, and a vague guilt attended my opening before I saw that the tale held him in thrall. It occurred to me that, although I had given him a brief history of my family on the boat, he would until then have known little of my background. Everyone at school had known that I was half-French and I remembered the taunts from the girl who had somehow stumbled on the absence of a marriage between my parents, but we were then too young to understand the implications and he might not have even remembered that any complication existed at all.

So now I painted in the detail, telling him everything. I spoke of the different members of my mother's family and how each, apart from her grandfather, had rejected her; of my upbringing with Aunt Marie and the bullying I had suffered, even recalling how I had then divided the world between the safety inside our front gate and the terror beyond; I described how an old schoolfriend of my mother had a chance meeting with an army colleague of my father, resulting in the von Ströbels' learning of my existence when I was five years old and my subsequent rescue from Provence.

'As I told you on the boat,' I concluded, 'my mother rejected France as comprehensively as France had rejected us. She refused to speak any French from the moment we arrived at Ströbelfields and had apparently sworn a solemn oath never to return. She allowed me to go on calling her Maman rather than Mutti and, for some reason I have never understood, insisted that I retain my surname even though becoming a von Ströbel would have made things a bit easier for me but, beyond that, she simply refused to act as if there was a drop of French blood in either of us. But, damn it, you yourself pointed out that we've been at peace for twenty-three years and all I wanted was to let my grandfather know that his daughter was well, married and happy and had given him four perfectly legitimate, if German, grandchildren.'

Wolfgang looked at me and shook his head. 'No. You could have done that by letter. You wanted to find out what they were all like, to meet your own flesh and blood, and you hoped they would repent of past sins and love you. That might have been possible but you appear to have gone about it in the most extraordinary way. Not, of course, that it is any of my business.'

I stared at him. 'If I had written he would have refused to see me.'

'Yes, but if, instead of acting on the spur of the moment when you saw his name on the library noticeboard, you had thought it all out, he would have been the last not the first one you approached. You say he is arrogant, an autocrat and unforgiving, but that does not mean they all are, does it?'

I admitted the force of his argument. 'But it's now too late. He will warn everyone else and, short of hiring a private detective, there is nothing I can do on this trip. I don't know where any of them live and I haven't the time to find out. I am fairly certain Kurt would tell me my mother's old address unless he felt that was going behind her back and perhaps Bette or Aunt Marie would too. I could begin the search there but it is not the sort of information I can just ask for on the phone from my stepfather and I do not know the numbers of the others. It will have to wait.'

'Let me see what I can do. I'll start with the telephone directory tomorrow but you will have to buy my supper because I won't be able to draw tourists and play sleuth at the same time.'

'Find any of them and I will buy you a grand dinner on a *bateau mouche*.'

'It's a deal.'

The day's disappointment suddenly gave way to hope. Wolfgang was resourceful and seemed to be instantly at home in unfamiliar surroundings, but the next day we woke to a city in turmoil, as the student demonstrations, which had become almost part of the background noise to my life both in England and during my brief sojourn in France, suddenly erupted into a major and bloody confrontation with the police, providing the world's press with banner headlines and pictures of barricades in the streets.

We were so used to edging our way round columns waving banners and howling anti-war slogans that we realised too late that we were involved in something of an altogether different order of magnitude. By then we were too hemmed in to escape from it. I looked at Wolfgang and shrugged, irritated but not alarmed. Around us girls in jeans or mini-skirts chanted 'Ho Chi

Minh' and men waved placards, roaring protest. One was thrust into my hand and I glanced at it. It proclaimed 'Workers, cast off your chains'. A minute later it was taken again. I tried to look as if I was a part of the proceedings but, whereas Wolfgang might have passed muster with his shoulder-length hair and jeans, I presented a rather more sober appearance, having had my hair cut for an interview shortly before leaving England and wearing a dark blazer over casual trousers.

The crowd grew denser and more vocal and I began to feel uneasy. I could no longer see Wolfgang and I sensed activity ahead in which I did not want to become involved. Beside me an English voice shouted, 'No secret files', and I wondered what he was talking about. Someone else cried, 'There he is!' and, for a moment, somehow raised above the mass in front of me, I caught a glimpse of a wild, angry face from which a yelling mouth gaped amidst a flowing red beard. Danny Cohn-Bendit. A girl beside me stumbled and I held on to her while she regained her balance. She had long fair hair and stared at me from under lashes weighed down with mascara. Her lipstick was almost white and she was dressed in squares of black and white after the fashion promoted by Mary Quant. 'Death to the capitalist oppressors!' she screamed from a distance of inches.

'Hear! Hear!' I responded, Oxford Union style. She was looking surprised when a surge carried her away from me. For a moment there was a small space around me and I became conscious of something under my feet. I bent down and retrieved a peaked cap, of the kind worn by chauffeurs or bus conductors, presumably brought along to demonstrate solidarity with the working classes. I picked it up and looked around me, but no one seemed about to claim it, so I put it on my head. To my right an American was chanting a slogan in which I could identify only the word Vietnam. To my left was an entrance to a side street in which the proprietor of a café was urgently packing away chairs and tables. Relieved, I dodged out of the crowd and climbed on a chair in the forlorn hope that I might see Wolfgang. To my surprise I did. He saw me in the same moment in which I flung up an arm to attract his attention.

I jumped off the chair and began to help the café owner. He did not even thank me but hastened into his shop where he drew bolts across the door with an angry, frightened, clanging sound. It seemed an age before Wolfgang forced his way from the crowd.

'Let's go,' he panted, and we ran along the small side street. As we emerged we nearly collided with a group hastening to join the protest. The streets were becoming jammed with traffic and we walked back to the pension. Each time I showed any inclination to turn and watch, my companion hustled me on, but it was not until we turned into the Rue Louis Blanc and were in sight of the pension that I remembered his fear of the police and understood his terrified haste.

It would surely be an awesome sight if I could watch it from a safe distance, I told him when we lay panting on the narrow twin beds. What a pity I was not on the top of a tall building, I continued, wondering if it were visible from Notre

Dame. Instead I had to content myself with that evening's television news.

The pension was run by two elderly sisters, who were resolutely old-fashioned and dowdy in dress. It was therefore with surprise that we discovered they had a colour television at a time when many still contented themselves with black and white. On this we watched the day's events, the sound of the riots occasionally reaching us even above the commentary and the repeated 'mon dieu' of the sisters.

Twenty-four hours later Wolfgang and I pored over the pictures in *Paris Soir*. I had smuggled a bottle of wine into our room and we drank to equality and brotherhood while thanking God that we had escaped the comrades on the still unquiet streets. In one picture I spotted the girl in the black and white squares, her features distorted in hate. Then we both saw the two photographs at the same time and fell silent before I found myself shaking and Wolfgang putting his hand on my shoulder in shocked sympathy.

The photographs, side by side, took up half a page well into the paper where pictures and description had given place to commentary. Under a headline 'THE NEW OCCUPATION?' an article condemned the methods employed by the protesters, their bringing the city to a stand-still, the injuries to police, the lawlessness on the barricades and the propensity towards 'sit-ins' and 'occupations'. It expostulated that ordinary citizens were no more able to go about their lawful occasions without fear than they had between 1940 and 1944. On the opposite page an opposing article put the case for the protests and inveighed against the society which had been created by the so-called civilised world since 1945.

The author of the first article had chosen to illustrate his argument with two adjacent photographs. In the first a German officer stood outside a Parisian hotel with his arm flung up in the Nazi salute. It was not a portrait which was ever likely to be on display at Ströbelfields but I recognised my father at once. In the second I stood with my arm raised in an identical posture. Both photographs were in black and white and my chauffeur's cap at first sight bore a resemblance to my father's army cap although a closer look dispelled the illusion immediately. Both of us wore dark jackets, which again suggested a likeness that did not stand up to any further scrutiny, mine buttoning differently and bereft of shoulder straps and insignia.

It was the features which gave the spurious verisimilitude, my own slightly blurred by a shaft of sun, his by an age of inexact photography, and I remembered my grandfather's words: *'The way the light fell on you made you look older, made you look like ... him.'*

'My God,' I whispered.

There was no caption under the photos other than the dates but in the text the writer identified my father as Colonel, later General, Klaus von Ströbel. Naturally he failed to identify me but pointed out that I could almost be his son and was certainly his tyrannical heir.

'Thank heaven they won't see this at home.

231

They would never forgive me.'

'For being on the demo?'

'Dear God, no. For branding my father a Nazi.'

Wolfgang looked from the paper to me in puzzlement. 'But he was, wasn't he? They all were, and anyway, he's giving a pretty convincing Heil Hitler.'

I shook my head, still dumbfounded, but eventually roused myself to give Wolfgang yet another lesson in my family history, telling him about Uncle Gerhardt and my father's rescuing Jews in Paris.

'He hated Nazism and he hated war,' I finished. 'That photo would break my mother's heart. I wonder where the devil that damned journalist found it.'

'Oh, that's simple enough. Given the theme he is expounding, the first thing he would have done would have been to have compared yesterday's crop of press photos with some of the newspaper's archives and, one has to admit, he scored a bull's-eye. There was press everywhere and, to be blunt, no photographer worth his salt could have resisted taking a picture of you if he happened to spot you. With that jacket, trousers and haircut you looked like a time traveller from the nineteen thirties, anyway, but then to stand on a chair in that ridiculous cap!

'However, as you say, they won't see it at Ströbelfields but, although I don't want to make it any worse, I am sure you realise that all Paris *will* see it. I think we should postpone my investigations into your family tree. Pity. I was looking forward to that dinner *de gourmet* on a *bateau mouche.*'

232

I managed a smile. 'We can still have it. I can hardly believe my rotten luck.'

After that I could concentrate on my work only with the greatest difficulty. Wolfgang stayed resolutely in the pension but did not interfere and, with his usual facility for making an honest penny, or in this case an honest franc, spent his time drawing the sisters and then, at their insistence, their cat. He began to help them with the evening meal but after four days I was talking about cutting short my stay and returning to England a day early. Even had I not been intent on my work it was quite impossible to go anywhere in the centre of the city. Ten thousand workers had added themselves to the students and de Gaulle's own future was in severe doubt.

Wolfgang said he would return to Germany and we exchanged contact details, both wanting to meet again when I was over my exams and he had started his job. I told him I would be spending the summer, my last long vacation, at Ströbelfields. That evening we took our meal drifting down the Seine on a *bateau mouche* only to have it thoroughly spoiled by a demonstrator who had somehow concealed himself on board and emerged to harangue the diners as bastions of capitalist privilege, gorging themselves while their brothers lived in poverty and oppression.

A choleric-looking man in a dinner jacket decided to argue while his wife wept that it was their anniversary and the occasion was ruined. The boat made an unscheduled stop and was met by police to whom it must have signalled, whereupon the protestor jumped in the river to try to swim to freedom. Several customers left by the more conventional route and it was a depleted and very subdued company that continued its outing after the police had taken statements.

'This trip is jinxed,' I groaned when we were diverted by yet another road block as we travelled back to the pension by taxi. 'Surely nothing else can go wrong.'

'Famous last words,' said Wolfgang in English, and we both laughed.

It was a laugh I recalled with bitter irony in the middle of the following morning when a cable arrived from Uncle Willi: *'Come home immediately exams over.'*

'How did he know where to find you?'

'I left the details with my college.'

'It could be about something else.'

'No. He has sent this to Paris. He knows where I am and he has never written to me like that before. Clearly he doesn't want a row before I do my finals but he is letting me know that I am in trouble. Hell, they must have seen that picture, but how? They don't get *Paris Soir*, for heaven's sake. I would have staked my life on their never seeing it.'

'Wanderer Bear is an international business. There may have been some other article in that issue which someone thought they should see – something about the state of the markets with all the upheaval or maybe even some article on Wanderer Bear which we missed. We didn't read the commercial pages or indeed anything much which came after those photos.'

We had thrown the paper away and there was no means of putting Wolfgang's theory to the test. Presently my mood began to change from contrition to irritation and then to resentment.

'Uncle Willi must have known it was all an accident. The trouble is, they don't seem to know what to make of my father any more than I do. Sometimes they seem to have him on a pedestal – and what a bloody pedestal.' I described the spontaneous salute as we left my father's grave. 'At other times they are positively disapproving but whichever it is I always want to go the opposite way. When they adore I want to shout, "But look what he did to my mother and to me!" And when they are being politely censorious I want to ask them what they did in the war that was remotely morally comparable to my father's helping Jews. Obviously this photo has provoked a pedestal phase.'

'So you will say he was an adulterer?'

'I say worse. I say he seduced a teenager. I say he must have been a satyr even though my grand-father himself attached some of the blame to my mother. I say if he wanted to betray Ellie and the children then why not find someone older?'

'And the Jews?'

'We have only my mother's word that it was so dangerous. Of course, Kurt backs her up but what else is he to do? For that matter, how much would he have known? My mother admits she knew nothing at all until they were all leaving Paris. Who says he was so damn brave? Where's the proof?'

I was lying on my bed, my hands under my head, looking up at the ceiling. Wolfgang got up from his and drew first the blind and then the curtains, darkening the room.

'What on earth–?'

'Close your eyes and pretend for a moment to be your father, think of the streets we have walked along, think of them dark, think of them a quarter of a century ago, think of silence, think of night...'

At first I thought him mad and then closed my eyes to humour him, thinking a game might after all lighten the mood. I listened to the quiet voice and tried to enter into the spirit of it, striving conscientiously to re-create the scene.

Fear, fear that can paralyse. It seeps into my very soul as I walk along that narrow, empty, curfew-silenced road, the only sound the clicking tread of my boots, the only images those of my imagination, the wood bending as the swaying form of my brother's body moved in time with its dark shadow on the wall of the barn, his live, grunting, idiot's features distorted out of their normal gentle dream as he mimed the horrors he had seen in Dachau.

Fear, fear that does momentarily paralyse so that I stop and think about going back, back to the Kommandantur, back to safety, back to comradeship. *Juden. Juden.* The cry I had heard on Kristallnacht floats into my mind and the memory sends me forward again, unwilling, compelled.

I glance behind but it is not a curfew-defying knifeman I fear, nor any man in a uniform like my own. It is the plainclothes of the Gestapo, the darkness of the SS garb which I strain to see in the darkness. I am walking again. Forward. They can and will torture me before they shoot me. Let me know, dear God, please God, my Lord, my Christ, let me know before they catch me and I will shoot myself first. Then I can tell them nothing.

No, let them catch me and let them torture me and let my suffering be my redemption, my expiation for the uniform I wear, the devil's own clothing. Only do not let me fail under it. Protect Catherine for she knows nothing, protect Kurt who only suspects.

A shot, a loud, uncompromising crack rends the darkness. It must have been in the next street because that is where the screaming is coming from now. I know that scream well. It means the very guts are pouring from the wounded. I know because I used to hear it in the trenches. It will stop when it has gone on too long.

Here is the house. This is where they live. I hesitate at the very steps. Supposing I have the wrong number? I check it again and then again, afraid the darkness may mislead me. I push the papers through the letterbox and hold them there, afraid to let go. Fear, paralysing fear, as I feel someone take them from me, someone I did not hear but who heard me.

'Go, go tomorrow,' I say, whispering, almost whimpering.

'Thank you, Herr General.'

Terror. How can he know who I am? He cannot see me. The box-flap clicks ... and I wake on an unfamiliar bed in a modest room with a faint light behind the drawn curtains.

The next few seconds passed in a blur of confusion as I came from the past into the present where Wolfgang was pulling back the curtains and raising the blind. Outrage vied with awe as I looked at him.

'That was one hell of a trick. I'm not at all sure I appreciate being hypnotised against my will.'

'That, as any hypnotist will tell you, is quite impossible. You have to co-operate to make it work. However, you will be relieved to know I did no such thing. I am not a hypnotist.'

'No. That was something in a class of its own. You sent me into the past. I actually became my own father.'

He smiled. 'No. Nothing supernatural either. I merely assisted you to imagine what it must have been like. If you had really been there you would have known names and addresses. Did you? Was there any detail you could not have known, or rather not have imagined, unless you had actually been there?'

I was still simmering but realised he was right. The door of the house through which I had pushed the incriminating papers bore a resemblance to nothing more than the door of the house next to the pension up to which I had once walked by accident. I could not recall the number I had checked so earnestly, had not been aware of any precise form as far as the papers were concerned, could not have named the street I was in nor the name of those I was rescuing.

Even the fear was my own. My father would have been anxious but not frightened to the point of immobility. He, who had fought in the trenches and won medals, would not have crept along a street like a child trying to escape a nightmare. As I repressed a faint and surely absurd suspicion that he might have been ashamed of my feebleness, it struck me also that he, a Lutheran, would not have prayed as I had. My petitions to the deity had been unmistakably Catholic with their concept of offering up my own suffering in exchange for the alleviation of another's or as a contribution to my own salvation. Uncle Willi had always been scandalised by such ideas.

My smile had a bleak edge to it but it was enough to reassure Wolfgang that I no longer resented his experiment and I saw him relax.

'I suppose I should be grateful you didn't suggest I travel back in time and see if I could lust after my own mother.'

'I repeat, you haven't travelled anywhere except in your imagination.'

'Where did you learn to do that anyway?'

'It was the way I used to escape when my father was in one of his rages. Eventually I found I could even do it when he was beating me, although I realise that takes some believing. The pain afterwards was always real enough but at the time I just travelled elsewhere.'

I remembered how I used to marvel at his silence under punishment and believed him, yet I did not envy him his gift. I preferred to stay in the present, to be in control of both mind and imagination. It was in the same spirit that I had refused to try drugs at Oxford and had stopped in alarm the first and only time I had drunk too much. If others found me too staid or too serious I did not care. Rites of passage were not yet compulsory, I observed to one teasing friend.

I vowed that Wolfgang should never again exercise

such a power over me but I found the incident had left my own imagination in a heightened state and I wrote my examination papers with greater empathy for those whose exploits I was analysing or whose literature I was appreciating. I knew the quality of my work to be enhanced and nervously wondered if I might scrape a first.

When I was called before the examiners I believed I must be on the borderline of just such a degree but to my amazement found myself instead receiving their congratulations on the best papers submitted that year in my subject. They hoped I might take my studies further and asked if I had applied to read for a doctorate.

I had not. Although I was younger than German graduates I was older than British ones, and had assumed I would work upon leaving Oxford. I had made a few applications for positions in London but only in order to leave me with the option of continuing to base my life there, in reality expecting to return to Germany and to use the summer vacation to decide upon my future. I thought perhaps I might join the diplomatic service although all the posts I had applied for in Britain were within industry.

I left the interview with a spring in my step, knowing that it was indeed a tall, proud ship which would sail back into harbour at Ströbel-fields. I drove from my mind the awkwardness of explaining my behaviour in Paris, wondering instead whether I was right not to be considering further study, knowing that I was constrained not only by an unwillingness to rely yet again on the von Ströbel resources but much more by a conscious rebellion against the comparison with my father which my family would be certain to make if I looked set for a life in academia. Images of the two photographs haunted my sleep and I woke determined to be as unlike him as possible and that the course of my life should be different.

My belongings had accumulated vastly during my three years at Oxford and packing them up to be freighted back to Germany took the better part of a day, during which I was twice interrupted by friends bearing champagne and demanding to know how I intended celebrating my congratulatory first. The principal invited me to dine at High Table and my tutor spent an earnest half-hour exhorting me to read for a doctorate.

I began to waver, reasoning that deciding against a course of action merely because it was what my father might have done was to be as driven by him as to decide in favour of it. As I came from the Bodleian, where I had been returning books, and walked towards college I watched the sunlight bathing the tall spires and thought a life amidst such genial surroundings could hardly be undesirable. Many aspired to such a life and failed, yet it was being pressed on me, making me feel ungrateful and churlish in refusing it. I arrived back in my rooms resolved rather than resigned to spend the next three years immersed in the Punic Wars.

I threw myself into a chair and opened *The Times*, which I had bought that morning and not yet found an opportunity to read. I had picked it up carelessly and some inside pages fell onto the floor. I reached for them with a grunt of

241

annoyance and froze as my eye fell on the Court and Social page. The Earl and Countess of Bullchester had pleasure in announcing the engagement of their daughter Lady Arabella Bland to the Hon. Henry Horrabridge, younger son of Lord and Lady Horrabridge.

I read no further and decided that, after all, there was nothing to keep me in England for another three years.

thirteen

Recriminations

'Have you met anyone special yet?' my mother would invariably ask me whenever I returned to Ströbelfields and would, just as invariably, give a small sigh when I answered, 'No, not yet.' It was almost as if, being settled now herself, she was anxious for the same outcome for me.

In my last year at Ampleforth I had briefly fallen in love with Jack Marshall's elder sister and in my first term at Oxford with a girl from St Anne's. She had in turn been followed by Gillian from St Hilda's, who had been superseded by Alison from Lady Margaret Hall. Alison was tall, attractive and very ambitious academically.

'Pity a girl that good-looking should be such a bluestocking,' muttered Charles Emmett when he and Jack Marshall came to stay for a couple of days. I had not been intended to overhear the comment and kept my amusement to myself. A fortnight later Alison told me, very gently and with a guilty countenance, that she was breaking off the relationship and was writing to Jack. Jack also wrote in equally guilty terms, but I destroyed his letter and not even Charles's attempts at mediation were successful.

Alison was followed by Dido and Dido by Ginty, but it was Jessie, a country girl who loved dogs, horses and long walks in the rain, who, in my final year, made me forget Alison as we walked and rode together.

'So who is Arabella?' demanded Jessie with amused eyes when I had accidentally called her by that name.

'A girl I met years ago. She was only about fifteen and scared of lightning. In many ways she was like you.'

'Thanks. I am nineteen and not at all afraid of lightning.'

I quickly discovered there was precious little capable of frightening Jessie. She looked at me in disbelief when I suggested getting back to her college before the gates closed at midnight, telling me that she had worked out a climbing-in route within a week of arriving at Oxford. Undeterred by any donnish wrath she regularly failed to hand in essays on time and rarely attended lectures. She stayed at parties to all hours of the night and on many an occasion I had to leave before her and arrange for someone else to see her safely back.

Then, a couple of weeks before the Easter break, I was approaching her room in college when I heard her screaming. I raced to her door, throwing it open wildly and entering without knocking. Through the haze of cannabis I saw two other girls and a man. Jessie screamed again and I hastened to her.

'What on earth's the matter with her?' I asked one of the girls.

'Nothing,' answered the man. 'Just tripping.'

'Tripping?' The scepticism in my tone caused even the distraught Jessie to pause and stare at me. It was a look of confusion and non-recognition. A moment later she covered her eyes and wailed again.

'A bad trip,' said the man in a curious rather than concerned tone.

'She's hallucinating,' explained one of the girls worriedly.

'I'll get help.' I turned to go.

'Are you mad?' The other girl barred my way. 'Do you want to get her sent down?'

'Better that than LSD.' I pushed the girl aside but she caught up with me in the corridor.

'You can't do this to her. She'll be fine when it wears off. It's Matt's fault. He told her she would have beautiful, mystic visions.'

'While he of course sticks to something less dangerous? And you haven't had anything at all, have you?'

'No. I never do but they are grown-ups and must make their own choices. If you alert the authorities you will wreck her life for her in a way that one go at LSD won't. Come back with me and see her through it.'

'Surely half the college must have heard her screaming? Yet no one has come to see what the matter is. It's happened before, hasn't it? This is not the first time.'

'It's not your business. Leave it. This is just a bad one, that's all. No one will thank you for interfering.'

I shrugged and walked on. The girl fell back and I guessed the three of them would flee, leaving Jessie to suffer alone. I thought of Arabella and prayed it was a route she would never follow. As I entered the quad I saw one of Jessie's friends, a student in the same year called Elinor.

'If the others have gone, we had better see what we can do,' she said when I had explained the situation. Grateful for her calmness I returned with her, trying to steady Jessie while Elinor opened windows and looked round for incriminating evidence.

'Has she done this before?' I was conscious that I was asking for reassurance, that I already knew the answer and did not want to hear it.

'Yes. Jessie is the type to try most things. She is very innocent but yearns to be worldly and never seems to fear any consequences. Matt's always round here with the stuff.'

'Who is he?' I tried to make the enquiry sound casual.

'Matt Duffy. He's doing maths at Keble.'

When I saw Jessie two days later I did not tell her that I had written to her parents, naming Matt Duffy, merely that I would not be able to see so much of her in future as I needed to concentrate on my work. She wept only a little and I concluded that she had already begun to find me boring and altogether too lacking in adventurous spirit. My only consolation was a savage satisfaction when I read in the *Oxford Times* that Matthew James Duffy had been convicted of supplying drugs, including LSD and heroin. Heroin! I shuddered on Jessie's account, that one word doing more to convince me of the rightness of my actions than all those of the deeply grateful letter I had received from her parents.

Yet I felt guilty that I had somehow abandoned a vulnerable human being, although aware that none would resent that description more than Jessie herself. I told myself I should have waited longer before parting from her, that I should have confronted her squarely about the drugs or perhaps have been more subtle and gradually weaned her from her ghastly friends. I should have joined forces with Elinor to find distractions or more wholesome challenges.

Even when I saw Jessie entwined about a new boyfriend, the feeling that I had let her down persisted and I destroyed her parents' letter, believing it undeserved. On the few occasions on which we now crossed each other's paths she looked well and happy but I had never known her look otherwise and the guilt persisted, although with the passage of time it had become faint rather than insistent.

To my amazement I also began to feel some measure of responsibility towards Duffy. Of course he had to be stopped before his heroin killed somebody but I recognised that his life was now blighted by what I had done and I agonised over the alternatives that I might have considered. A letter to his principal? Should I have found out his address and written to *his* parents?

My confusion was augmented because I had never told anyone what I had done and therefore could not seek reassurance. I knew that the reason for my discretion was fear of being branded a sneak. It was a humiliating period of my life but I alone knew it to be so. Had I been at Ströbelfields I should have sought consolation from my mother and guidance from Uncle Willi. Absurdly I missed Omi.

Now, with the news of Arabella's engagement lying in the wastepaper basket, I acknowledged to myself that I had merely been playing for time, that even Alison and Jessie had somehow been unreal, that I had been waiting for Arabella to grow up so that I could claim her for my own but had somehow waited too long.

I called myself every kind of fool, informed my reflection in the bathroom mirror that Arabella would be most unlikely even to remember me, that I had not met her since that half-term holiday when I was sixteen, that she herself had written me three letters in a fortnight and then stopped and that I could have tried to renew the acquaintance at any time had I been remotely serious about doing so.

So why had I not taken that simple step? I demanded of myself in miserable fury. Why had I not sent even a Christmas card to her or at least added 'love to Arabella' on the one I dutifully sent to the Bullchesters for three Christmases or so after my visit? Why not a holiday postcard?

'Because you did not want to go back to that house again.' I supplied the answer to my own question aloud, momentarily disconcerted by the bitterness in my voice, by the consuming sense of loss. Surely I had not put off contacting Arabella because I could not face so many servants, so much formality? Or was it because I despised George and his buffoonish ways, yet recognised that he was the key to any further invitation?

At last I ran out of excuses and reluctantly confronted the real reason for my shrinking from a return visit to Leicestershire: I could not face Judy Margolis, the woman with the number on her forearm, the living reminder of the evil that had been Germany, which had commanded the service of my father and Uncle Willi.

So Hitler was to blame for my lost love. I tried to laugh and failed. Arabella, Arabella, Arabella.

'You don't look like someone who's just got a Congrat,' commented, Charles Emmett when he arrived to join me on the journey to Ströbelfields where he was to spend three weeks of the summer. 'You look more like a guy who's lost a fiver and found a shilling.'

He had just gained an upper second from Cambridge and was fairly pleased with himself. Jack Marshall, who had parted from Alison some months earlier and with whom I had been reconciled, was to meet us in Germany. His budget being too restricted to afford the air fare, he was sailing and hitch-hiking. Wolfgang Mueller was also to be of the party and I vaguely hoped that so large a gathering might deter my mother from any recriminations over Paris.

'I've lost that which is beyond the price of rubies, but never mind. Do you remember

George Bland?'

'George? Yes. He was a year above us at Ampleforth. His sister has just got engaged. It was in *The
Times*. I seem to remember he was as mad as a
ferret or, to put it in his terms, a most frightful ass.'

'That's him. I've been in love with his sister for
seven years.'

'Annabelle? Was that the name? Bad luck.'

'Arabella and, no, it is not bad luck. It was very
bad judgement.' I told him my sorry tale and
waited for his sympathy but instead was greeted
with disbelief.

'You mean you haven't seen her for seven years
and you fell in love on the basis of a single walk?
It isn't possible. Love has to feed on something.'

'Why should it not be possible? My stepfather
was in love with my mother from nineteen forty-
two to nineteen sixty-one and he didn't see her at
all after nineteen forty-four.'

Charles visibly groped for a reply. 'What about
all those other girls – Jilly and Ginnie and Alison?'

'Gillian and Ginty actually. None of that was
real. Not even Jessie, poor girl.'

'Well, if she meant that much to you, what was
to stop you contacting Arabella?'

'Nothing. That's the problem.'

His bemusement was so comical that I laughed
and turned the subject. Relieved, he began to
anticipate my triumphant return to Ströbelfields
and I did not have the heart to tell him that I
dreaded that too, that my laurels were wilting
with every mile that I drew closer to home. I did,
however, tell him about the disastrous visit to
France in May, describing both the storm of the

riots and my own lesser squalls.

He listened with gratifying suspense, but his verdict was much the same as Wolfgang's. 'You should have tried one of the others first. One of the younger ones who do not remember so well – your mother's baby brother, for instance. He cannot have any recollection of his brother who was killed or, for that matter, much recollection of the war. Even your grandmother might have been a better bet. After all, there are four new grandchildren.'

'My mother's baby brother may well have been carefully taught to hate all the people his relatives hate.' I began to hum the tune from *South Pacific* and Charles, smiling, sang the words, occasionally forgetting their sequence. I remembered sitting in a cinema during a half-term holiday to see the film for the first time, emerging pensive amidst my light-hearted friends.

On the aircraft, conscious that we had talked largely of my own affairs, I talked determinedly about Charles. He was entering the civil service, having passed the entrance examination with flying colours. There was a girl in his life, Deirdre, and I said he should have brought her to Ströbelfields, but he responded that she had spent a year at a German university as part of her course and wanted a change that summer. Jack had not replaced Alison so we looked like being an all-male group, but when we arrived it was to find that Otto had invited some friends, among them two sisters of nineteen and twenty.

I joined my mother and her family in the barn while the others stayed in the house. For meals we gathered together and the din of my half-sisters and brothers was augmented by that of Lotte's children when they came over with some of the other Pletzes. It was a vast party and I wondered how many Wolfgang would have drawn by the end of his visit.

Werner was missing from the Pletz party, as he was now working in Bonn. Ernst was present only briefly as he was enjoying the freedom of his first long vacation to travel in Europe. He was two years behind me at university because he had been caught by National Service, which had been reintroduced in Germany in 1956. Otto had just escaped and I had relied on my French nationality, but both Werner and Ernst had been obliged to spend time in the army.

As soon as I was alone with my mother and Kurt she berated me bitterly for going to Paris, reminding me of her vow, of her family's cruelty to her and of their rejection of me. At first I responded with restraint, telling her that I had taken no vow and that I could not let the Dessins interfere with my perfectly legitimate need to consult a document at the Sorbonne and that the study I had done there had contributed to my outstanding performance in the examinations.

I dreaded her next question but answered truthfully that yes, I had made contact with my grandfather. Then she began to shout at me and I heard my own voice rise in answer. Kurt protested but we ignored him until he began to struggle out of his wheelchair.

'I went in peace,' I said when we were calmer. 'The war ended in nineteen forty-five and this is nineteen sixty-eight. De Gaulle and Adenauer turned peace into co-operation and my generation must turn co-operation into unity.'

'I am not interested in politics.'

'I wasn't talking politics. I was talking of human beings living together.'

'So what part does rioting play in human beings living together?'

'I wasn't rioting. Can you see me rioting? I got caught up in the demo accidentally and escaped from it as soon as I could. And before you ask me, no, I did not give a Nazi salute. I was hailing a friend who was also trying to get out of the mêlée, not Hitler.'

'What about that silly hat?'

'I found it on the ground and put it on so that its owner might see it and claim it.'

My mother's mouth was tight with anger and sulkiness, but I continued to answer her questions quietly until she tried to extract from me a promise never to see any of her family again, which I vehemently refused, yielding neither to tears nor to recriminations. It was Kurt who put an end to the dispute and made it possible to join the others with some semblance of normality.

'Perhaps you *should* riot occasionally,' he muttered *sotto voce*.

A few hours later I found myself giving the same account to Uncle Willi as we sat in the library with the door closed. He heard me out, looking at me gravely, squashing down the tobacco in his pipe. From him I kept nothing, telling him how I had met Wolfgang Mueller on the way from England to France, how I had seen my grandfather's lecture advertised and, having decided not to go, had somehow found my way there. I repeated the conversation almost verbatim, having revisited it so often in my mind, and then went on to tell him how I had ended up in the middle of a riot.

'It is a pity about the photo,' he said eventually. 'Oddly your mother thinks she remembers the occasion when your father gave that salute, but there must have been many such instances. Vastly more important is the fact that you were in Paris at all and looking up your mother's family without warning us. I do not think it in the least matters that you were there – indeed, I might even say it was the right thing to do – but you should have told us. I might have then better prepared Catherine for what happened.'

'But for the photos you would not have known. By the way how did you see them?'

'I gave an interview to *Paris Soir* about Wanderer Bear. Clearly you did not see it but it was in the same issue and the paper was, of course, sent to me.'

So Wolfgang had been right. The article must have been positioned after the one containing the photographs and I had been too preoccupied to notice.

Uncle Willi reached in the pocket of the old check jacket he so often wore and, to Aunt Angelika's disgust, refused to discard, despite its frayed cuffs and leather-patched elbows, and withdrew a folded piece of paper, which he handed to me without further comment.

As I opened it I saw it was a letter, written in French and addressed to my mother. In it my grandfather said he was glad that his daughter had found happiness and that her marriage had been blessed with children but the words, even on paper, were so cold that it was not hard to discern that what he really meant was that she was lucky to have found someone willing to marry her at all, given the presence of an illegitimate child, even if it was a cripple with only half a leg.

Suppressing fury, I proceeded to the next paragraph, which stated that I had visited him recently in Paris and that while such curiosity on my part was understandable it was also profoundly unwelcome:

...What happened in the war was hard for all of us but we have learned to live with it and you have made a new life for yourself in another country. It is in nobody's interest to rake up the past and therefore I hope your son, who apparently still bears our name, will not cause any further distress by contacting any other member of the family...

The final paragraph was a formal expression of gratitude to 'the general's family' for having looked after her and me and the signature not Papa but Pierre Dessin.

I looked at Uncle Willi as I handed it back, hoping he had not seen my eyes dwell on the address and that the mental effort of committing it to my memory had not been visible.

'How did he know where to write?'

'Your mother wrote to him before leaving Provence and even if he had not kept that letter he could have asked your Aunt Marie. So, you see, that is why I say you should have warned us.

It was this letter, not the photos, which first told us you were in Paris, and it shocked your mother to the core. Just seeing his writing and his name after all these years was enough. According to Kurt, she all but fainted.'

'I'm sorry, but I really did not go there for that reason. I went because I needed to look something up in the Sorbonne.'

Even to my ears it sounded unconvincing. I remembered Caux and how I had become drawn to that window where I could see France if I looked to the left. No undergraduate needed to travel so far to look up so little and I was relieved when Uncle Willi, although looking sceptical, forbore to press me further, instead turning to my own reactions after that ill-fated interview with my grandfather. To forestall the inevitable judgement that I had started with the wrong member of my family, I offered that conclusion myself but I did not add that, now I had Pierre Dessin's address, I had every intention of approaching each of the others until satisfied for myself that none wanted to know me.

As if reading my thoughts, my uncle mentioned Aunt Marie. 'She could have sounded them out for you, told you if any was likely to be sympathetic and how to make contact. If you decide to take the matter any further do it through her and, for goodness' sake, warn either Kurt or me so that we can watch for any more irate missives from France.' Then, in an echo of my grandfather's thoughts and with resignation in his tone, he said, 'After all, we have always known this day would come and that you would want to find them, if only out of curiosity.'

There was a short silence before he smiled and added a sentiment, which would certainly never have been shared by either my mother or her father: 'Good luck, Klaus-Pierre, if it is more than curiosity which will send you back to France.'

I looked at him with gratitude but he had begun to talk about Wolfgang, expressing horror at his story. Yet, when my friend arrived, I sensed a wariness towards him, not merely in my mother, which of course I had fully expected, but in my uncle too. Perhaps memories lingered of the school bully or perhaps he found it difficult to believe that anyone could come from so appalling a background without unwelcome baggage, which might be out of place at Ströbelfields. Remembering the comparisons with Good King Wenceslas, I did not think the latter very likely but I knew that something was disturbing Uncle Willi.

The offer Wolfgang had received to join a firm of commercial artists had been withdrawn, doubtless because the personnel department had uncovered his unconventional past. He seemed resigned rather than resentful and when a group of us went to Lübeck he left us to the pleasures of the city while he exercised his artistic talents on its pavements.

There was more scope in Paris, he told me later, because of the tradition of boulevard cafés. Nevertheless, he seemed to have done well and said he would stay for a couple of days before rejoining us at Ströbelfields. I remembered how he had disappeared during our first night in Paris and wondered if he had a reason other than art to stay behind.

The others appeared genuinely regretful at the loss of his company, especially Hannelore, the younger of the two girls who had come with Otto's party. She was the first to greet him on his return and, when he said he could not join in a day ride which we had planned because he had never sat on a horse in his life, she at once volunteered to teach him during the course of their stay.

I watched her affection grow with a mixture of amusement and alarm but Wolfgang, with steady courtesy, refused to return it. I was so busy observing him and Hannelore that I wasn't at first aware that the older of the two girls, Alex, was showing an interest in me. She was good-looking and engaging but I felt no attraction and made a successful effort to avoid a picnic party which left in a convoy of three cars. Wolfgang and I had said we would follow on bicycles, but we both found mysterious punctures and took refuge in the kitchen where Aunt Angelika was baking and Uncle Willi had spread out different pictures of the Wanderer Bear for her to select the most appealing.

They lay on the large farmhouse table and he sat in a chair at its centre, first choosing this one and then another as suitable for the bear's latest adventures. Wolfgang and I stole some warm buns from Aunt Angelika's tray when her back was turned and then at once immersed ourselves in a study of the bears. Gleeful at having escaped Alex, the warm bun reminding me of the security I had known here as a child, conscious that I had returned with the highest honours from Oxford, I looked at Uncle Willi's bent head with affection.

Celebrity had come late to him and I knew he was tiring under its strain. His hair was now entirely white and sometimes his gait seemed that of an even older man. Until recently he had written and illustrated and promoted his books, but the multi-million-pound business which produced the toys and films was claiming increasing amounts of time and effort at an age when he wanted to do less rather than more. Otto was deputising for him more often in the wider world than he was at Ströbelfields learning the estate management he had found so uncongenial. I doubted he would ever return to medicine.

I pointed to a bear and Aunt Angelika, making *tch tch* noises over the missing buns, paused to agree with me. Wolfgang seemed immersed in the drawings, picking one up and taking it to the window to study it more closely, returning it and taking another. I was rather surprised when he chose one which I had thought the least promising and I saw Uncle Willi's reaction mirror my own.

'That one was destined for the wastepaper basket,' he said. Wolfgang asked him for a pencil and I went to fetch it, wondering what my friend was about to do. It took him but a few seconds and a few strokes of the pencil to turn the bear's expression into one which any sentimental being would have found irresistible. Then with a glance at Uncle Willi, who nodded his wonder and his permission, he pulled another picture towards him and, with similarly few changes, produced a wonderful comic effect, which caused amusement rather than delight, one to make a bear-weary adult roar with laughter.

There was a babble of appreciation. Until then I had thought my uncle's talent for drawing Wanderer Bear unique but now I knew that a much greater one existed and that the future might be more restful for him. Wolfgang was hired there and then. At the end of the break he departed for Cloppenburg, where the company's technical business was based.

Before he went I teased him about Hannelore and to my surprise he responded seriously, saying that he had liked her and if circumstances had been different would have wished to see her again, but that he had set his face against such attachments for life. I thought of the obvious explanation but as soon discarded it, thinking I had never seen a more unlikely homosexual, but the true reason was even harder to believe.

'I carry a bad seed,' he told me, and his expression was wholly without irony. 'It was in my father and my grandfather before him and it is in me. For all I know it might have been in Horst too. Well, it will die with me.'

'Rubbish,' I said with rude impatience. 'Your father was what poverty and Nazism made him. For that matter he probably had what we would now recognise as a mental problem, which might have been cured, and nobody could accuse you of being a bad man. Forget such lunacy. I never heard a less convincing reason for living like a monk.'

'I do not live like a monk.'

I remembered the night he had disappeared in Paris and the prolonged stay in Lübeck.

'That's not the answer,' I muttered. 'Not in the

long term.'

'They don't get pregnant. It's bad for their trade.'

I gave up but the conversation left me uneasy, my fears being less for his morals than for his sanity. Could he really believe such nonsense? I recalled how he had hypnotised me in Paris – for in spite of his denials I still thought of the experience as hypnotism – and shuddered, wondering what other dark arts he dabbled in and how he had come to discover what he madly described as a 'bad seed'.

I confided such fears to no one for Wolfgang had been the last of the young party to leave and I did not want to prejudice Uncle Willi against his new employee, especially when I recollected his earlier reserve. As for my uncle himself, there were other issues to be confronted.

'Tell me, Klaus-Pierre,' he said when we were once more just a few family members at the dinner table, 'if it is not too inconvenient a question, what do you intend to do with your life?'

fourteen

Laughter from Mount Olympus

It was Uncle Willi himself who suggested I should remain within the academic life, at least for the foreseeable future, saying that Wanderer Bear meant he had far more money than he knew what to do with and that there was nothing to stop me applying for the German civil service at a later stage, although he was not sure if I could do so while still holding French nationality. He would find out and I could then consider my options.

When I decided in favour of the Punic Wars he made a serious effort to persuade me to broaden my horizons by studying them somewhere other than Oxford, but as I had left the decision very late and Oxford had already expressed its willingness to take me, I somehow ended up there by default.

I went back to Corpus but had no sooner arrived than an urgent cable came telling me Aunt Marie was very ill. I telephoned my mother at once who asked me to go to Provence. I urged her to go herself, pointing out that Provence was not Paris, that it was only in respect of that city that she had taken her vow and that she knew Aunt Marie far better than I. Aunt Angelika would help with Kurt and the little ones, leaving my mother free to travel, whereas I was embroiled in the start of a new term, with a great many formalities to deal with.

A week later I was bound for Provence. In 1968 people did not travel around the continent as spontaneously as they do now. There was less airflight, it was far less common to hire cars and trains were fewer and slower. My tutors were unconvinced that I should depart on such an errand in honour of but a distant relation and it was in no very happy mood that I set out, unconsoled by the reflection that Otto, Kurt, Aunt Angelika, Uncle Willi and even the visiting Lotte had each urged on my mother that she, not

I, should go.

I found a taxi on alighting at Aix-en-Provence and was surprised by the butterflies in my stomach as we approached the village in which I had spent the first five years of my then tormented life. There were small changes: the baker's shop had been replaced by a boutique, the chemist's was painted in different colours, the school where Aunt Marie had taught had been enlarged and modernised, but otherwise it was as I remembered it, bringing gloomy recollections and none of the excitement or sentiment which often attends a return to a place lived in long ago.

The children, who were then just leaving the school, were more brightly clothed and laughed at the world from less pinched faces. I wondered how many of them were the children of the children who had made my life a hell. Some of the older ones might well now be married with school-aged offspring of their own, but probably not yet many. Did any of them remember the German brat?

The German brat had left in a chauffeur-driven car and was returning successful, I reminded myself as my reflections became tinged with bitterness.

We were at the gate now and I stared at it, marvelling at how small it was, remembering my fear when I had reached the top bar in my quest to climb over and join the English children who played next door, the great height which I then thought I faced now seeming negligible. As I pushed it open I glimpsed the back garden and I wondered if the sundial still stood in its centre and if any cat had curled up on it after we took

Macfidget away.

The door opened before I reached it and I saw a pale woman with a large apron.

'You must be Klaus-Pierre,' she said. 'I am Jeanette, Marie's friend. She is looking forward to seeing you. The operation went well but she is very weak and tires easily.'

I found Aunt Marie in the chair I remembered so well in the sitting room, which, like the gate, looked so much smaller than it appeared in my memory. She greeted me joyfully, seeing how the frightened child of five had become the scholarly man of twenty-three and I wondered that we had left the reunion so long.

After an hour of exchanging news, Jeanette came in and I took the hint, saying I would see Aunt Marie at supper, but she replied that she was going immediately to bed and would see me in the morning.

I helped her from her chair and watched worriedly as Jeanette assisted her towards the stairs. Presently there was a ring at the door and I opened it to find a nurse. It seemed there was little for me to do, so I told Jeanette I would go for a walk and rustle up my own supper in the kitchen. She gave me a spare key and I went out into the October evening, finding light only from the moon, stars and people's houses. I made my way round the house to the back garden where a beam from an upstairs window threw the sundial into relief. I could see the shape of the shrubberies into which I had plunged in a vain search for Mathilde's children. Lights shone from the house next door and I wondered who lived there now, thinking that a single old lady would not create so many lit rooms.

Eventually I turned and went through the front garden to the gate, the source of so much childhood terror. I smiled. Outside the Gate had proved pretty good territory and I forced from my mind any question of what might have happened if I had stayed. I wandered through the small village, past the church, past the tiny playground with its swings and slide still as I remembered them, past a man who said 'good evening' and called his Labrador to order, past the three darkened shops, past a horse that neighed as I approached, and with each step it was if I had laid a half-forgotten ghost to rest.

I stood against a hedge to allow a car to pass. It was an old Citroën full of noisy young people and heading in the direction of Aix. I thought of the young von Ströbels crowding into the Horsch, encouraged by a booming Otto, and grinned.

I wandered longer than I had intended and when I got back to the house the only visible light came from the hall. Aunt Marie must be asleep or perhaps, in pain, still trying to slip into slumber. I entered as quietly as possible and later took my shoes off before climbing the stairs. Automatically I turned towards my old room and was disconcerted to find it unprepared for me. Instead my mother's room, the larger of the two spare ones, was furnished with a turned-down bed, soap and towels.

I looked around curiously but there were no reminders here that she had occupied this space for six years. The photograph on the chest of drawers was of Aunt Marie as a child, flanked by her parents. The books on the bedside table were not the sort Catherine Dessin would have owned. The dressing gown in the wardrobe was of a Chinese design, startlingly loud, not the old, worn, dull red one I recalled my mother wearing.

The next day I looked around my old room with more success. Here were discarded books and toys which my mother had not found room to pack. My memories of them were but dim and it was the smell of my room rather than its contents which conjured up the past. Many other children would have stayed here since, including probably the offspring of my mother's siblings.

Aunt Marie herself was changed from a healthy, bustling woman with a zest for life into a thin, slow-moving invalid, but she still found pleasure in her piano and I recollected how she had played the organ in church and had taught a children's choir. I called out my choices to her from where I sat on the sofa and she played them without any musical scores, reproducing melodies stored in her memory, occasionally slowing down as she worked out the notes by ear.

After half an hour she was too tired to continue and slept until the middle of the afternoon. She did not even wake when the telephone shrilled in the hall and I answered it to hear my mother enquiring about her health. I replied truthfully that I was very uncertain. I had been told the operation had been successful but Aunt Marie was vastly weaker than I had expected. She had been diagnosed with cancer of the bowel and had lost what she cheerfully described as metres of intestine to the surgeon's knife. After a quick glance at my sleeping relative, I closed the sitting-room door, picked up the telephone again and whispered that I thought my mother should come at once if she wanted to be certain of seeing Aunt Marie before she died.

Later the telephone summoned me again and I picked it up to hear a familiar, precise voice ask for Aunt Marie. A coldness entered the pit of my stomach but I took some pleasure in saying, 'I am sorry, Grandfather. She is still asleep.'

There was a short silence during which I wondered if he would disown the relationship and tell me he was not my grandfather but instead he enquired after his cousin, pressing for more detail than I was able to give, and asking when I thought she would be awake. He acknowledged my efforts with a curt and probably reluctant thank you before requesting that she return his call whenever she was able. He made no enquiry after my mother or indeed me, and responded with brief and distant courtesy when I asked if all was well with him. He must have wanted to end the conversation at once but had the foresight to know that if he rang again it might be I who would answer. Perhaps it was for that very reason that he asked how long I would be staying.

I told him two or three days, mindful that I had made an unsatisfactory start to my term, and volunteered the information that I must return to Oxford where I was reading for a D.Phil. Before he could stop himself Professor Dessin asked what my subject was but when I told him the Punic Wars and that I had achieved a first-class degree the previous summer, he had regained sufficient control of himself merely to grunt a polite congratulation. Thus my second conversation with my grandfather ended as coldly if not as confrontationally as the first.

That evening Aunt Marie again went to bed early and when the nurse came I took the opportunity to press for the detail on her health which I had been unable to supply to Pierre Dessin. There was no reason why there should not be a full recovery, I was told, but Aunt Marie seemed unusually weak and for that reason was being watched carefully.

Indeed the following morning she did not get up at all and I whiled away the time wandering through the village, this time spotting the memorial stone, with the cross on its summit, which had eluded my memory altogether. I stood looking at it, reading the names of the men of the village who had given their lives in the last war, presumably fighting with the Free French. It seemed a small village to have produced thirty or forty such names. Six had a common surname and I winced at the thought that they might all be from one family.

I was aware of someone standing near and I turned to see a man of my grandfather's age looking not at the names but at me.

'It's good to see the young remembering.' His patois made it difficult for me to understand at first but I could guess what he was saying. On a visit to London I had seen Britons of this man's generation raise their hats on a bus when it passed the Cenotaph.

I muttered something sententious about freedom being too easy to take for granted, embarrassed by the German accent with which my grandfather had assured me I spoke my native French. If he noticed he did not react, instead nodding sagely and moving on.

I watched him as he walked away and then looked back at the names, understanding something of the feeling with which both I in my innocence and my mother in her defiance had been obliged to contend. I was about to turn away when someone else came to the memorial, this time a young woman, perhaps five years or so older than I. In her hand a small bunch of flowers glowed while around us in the road blew the coppery leaves of autumn. She laid the flowers at the foot of the memorial and murmured a short prayer.

I hesitated, feeling it rude to walk away but possibly ruder still to intrude on a private moment. While I debated what I should do she turned and smiled at me and pointed to one of the names: Gilles Aubin.

'My older brother,' she said. 'I never really knew him but I promised my mother I would bring the flowers here each year on the anniversary of his death for as long as I lived in the village.'

'Was he with the Free French?'

'No. He was living in Paris when the Germans came and eventually became involved with the Resistance. He was a doctor, more than twenty years older than me, so they left him alone after the invasion but in December nineteen forty-three they caught him and executed him. Before that they tortured him.'

'I'm sorry.'

'After the war the village decided to honour those who had died fighting with the Resistance alongside those who fought in arms. My mother was so proud. In the last years of her life I used to wheel her here every week to see his name.'

She looked at me and smiled. 'You are a stranger to the village?'

'Yes, though once I lived here. I am visiting Marie Ditte.'

'Marie Ditte! She used to teach me at school. I heard she was ill.'

'She is very ill. That's why I'm here but I'm leaving soon.'

'Where are you from?'

'Oxford in England,' I heard myself saying.

'Oh! I thought you had a slight accent.'

She could not have seen much of the world beyond her village, I thought with rueful gratitude. There can be little comparison between the way an Englishman and a German speaks French. Nevertheless I was uncomfortable.

'I'm Françoise Hardy, but no relation to the singer.'

I smiled and lied. 'I'm Pierre Dessin.'

'Dessin.' Françoise frowned in concentration. 'Dessin. Where have I heard that before?'

I tried to think of something to say to distract her from her search but then I saw memory dawn in her eyes and in the same instant those eyes darken.

'Of course! Marie Ditte had a young relative staying here after the war. She had had an affair with a German in Paris and fled here to avoid the

269

head-shaving or whatever other fate she deserved. It was terrible for my mother because the man this girl loved had been the very one who caught my brother and this young hussy used to turn up to mass as bold as brass and kneel next to my mother at communion.'

I waited quietly for the flow of vitriol to stop, for her to work out that if Aunt Marie's young relative was called Dessin then I must be related to her, as I was myself here visiting that same Marie Ditte. Perhaps, given enough time, she might remember that I had said I once lived here and might then work out the exact relationship, despite my smokescreen of Oxford and only the French half of my name. A part of me wanted to walk away from the situation but another part wanted to embarrass her, to defend my mother.

'Oh,' she said flatly but without a blush. 'You must be part of the same family.'

'The young woman you are talking about was called Catherine Dessin. She is my mother. My full name is Klaus-Pierre.'

I did not want to argue with her, here by her brother's memorial, with the flowers bright in the morning sunshine. I gave her a half-smile and turned to go and did not falter when I heard her murmur, 'What a bloody nerve!' sufficiently audibly for me to know she had meant me to hear.

Soon, I thought, her anger would ensure that the whole village knew I was back. Most, I reasoned, would not blame me just for being born, most would not have so close a connection with the activities of my father, most would be learning to forget. Yet I was glad my mother had not come, glad that all our urging had not prevailed, for I no longer believed that she simply hated France but rather that she understood how much France hated her, that guilt played a greater part in her bitterness than I had hitherto guessed.

As for my father, who had apparently spent his time in Paris rescuing Jews, the fall from the pedestal could hardly have been greater. If Françoise was to be believed then he had been the instrument of torture and execution of those whose only crime was patriotism. How much better was he than Wolfgang's father who had no education, wealth or loving upbringing to civilise him?

I longed to tackle Aunt Marie on the subject but she was patently too ill, although she seemed to be aware of some alteration in my demeanour because she twice asked if I was all right. That night Uncle Willi telephoned to tell me that my mother, Kurt and Franz were on their way, my mother having been so alarmed by my reports of Aunt Marie's health. Kurt, perhaps realising the hostility she might encounter, had insisted on accompanying her, while Uncle Willi and Aunt Angelika looked after the children.

'Catherine resisted that because it can be very difficult to manage the wheelchair through such a journey but Franz has to spend a month back in the world as part of his final decision to enter his Order so I suggested he went too. They should be there sometime late tomorrow.'

I groaned but could say little because the nurse was bustling about with Aunt Marie upstairs and helping her from bathroom to bedroom. From the landing they could hear the conversation. I listened to Uncle Willi as he told me that it would be quite impossible for Aunt Marie to cope with such an invasion in her house and that my mother remembered a farmhouse not far from the village which took in paying guests.

Could I please make some arrangements for their accommodation?

'Not in the village,' I answered in as neutral a tone as I could.

There was a pause at the other end of the line. 'Trouble?'

'A little.'

'Can you talk?'

'Not now.'

'There must be a public telephone in the village. Call me from it when you can and I will ring you straight back.'

'I often go for a stroll in the evenings.'

'I'll expect a call soon then.'

Aunt Marie called down to know if it was my mother on the line and I called back that she was coming to see her. I could only hope that the exclamation of delight with which she greeted the news sprang from a certainty that my mother's presence in the village would not rekindle old grievances rather than from an oblivion to their continued existence. Those who had known Catherine Dessin and had endured her being among them so long ago must surely not now be outraged that she visited a relative who might be dying.

My encounter with Françoise Hardy left me with little choice but to reject such reasoning. I gave Uncle Willi the gist of the conversation when

I spoke to him hater from the public telephone.

'Fate would appear to have played a nasty trick,' he said. 'A lot of men died for the Resistance but for a man from one small village in Provence to have run into your father's net is very bad luck indeed.'

'She said her brother was tortured and executed.'

'Your father would have collected intelligence and acted on it. He probably did organise this man's arrest. Indeed your mother told me that he once arrested her parents and sister but had somehow contrived for there to be no evidence against them and they all survived. After that matters would have passed out of his hands. Others would have decided whom to interrogate, whom to release and whom to execute.'

'He was a general. He must have had that power.'

'For most of his time in Paris, indeed until March nineteen forty-four, he was only a colonel, after which he was a very junior general. That makes him important but not God Almighty. Klaus would not have known how to torture a fly.'

'He would have known that others did.'

'Yes, but he did not belong to the Gestapo or the SS. He did what he could to help those unnecessarily in danger from the regime but he was fighting for Germany and he could hardly ignore the activities of the Resistance. Bluntly, I doubt if he would have lost any sleep because an agent of the enemy died. Nor do I think he should have done.'

I thought of the girl by the memorial. What had her brother done other than resist an invader?

'War is not a gentlemanly disagreement, Klaus-Pierre. It is always horrible. Your father's wife and Lotte's sister and brother died a most terrible death. Even if the bomb killed them outright they would have endured hours and hours of fear beforehand. The British carpet-bombed Dresden for two days. Grannies in their rocking chairs died and babies in their cots died and cats curled up to snooze died, not just fit adults, never mind just combatants. Many of them were burnt alive. In Hiroshima people are still dying from cancers caused by the bomb and in Nagasaki too. They were only children when those bombs fell, children as innocent as you were when you arrived at Ströbelfields. That's war.

'I do not know if you have ever read *All Quiet on the Western Front?* Your father and I did but the Nazis banned it, burnt God knows how many copies in Berlin. They banned it because it paints war as it is. As it was. As both Klaus von Ströbel and Harry Bullchester knew it and, indeed, as Pierre Dessin knew it. Young men killing each other, daily, hourly for no very good reason except that their rulers could not agree. So, no, your father did not fight a sanitised war.'

It was one of the longest speeches I had ever heard him make and I imagined Aunt Angelika rebuking him for the cost of the call. Despite my misgivings I grinned, but then brought us both back to the present.

'I suppose we must just play it by ear. How long is Mother to stay here?'

'She can't be there long because of the children. Four or five days perhaps.'

I decided to prolong my own stay to cope with whatever might arise and wrote a difficult letter to my college the following morning but it completely slipped my mind that I had told Pierre Dessin that I was only there a little while longer. If only I had remembered, if only we had spoken again in the interim.

I told Aunt Marie that I must find my mother, Kurt and Franz accommodation and she at once said they must all stay in her house. My mother and Kurt could sleep in the sitting room because Kurt would not be able to manage the stairs and Franz could have my old room. It wasn't much bigger than a monk's cell, she joked, and when I protested that it was far too much for her to cope with she sent me to an address just outside the village to ask for domestic help and also asked me to call on Jeanette to let her know what was happening. Jeanette was disapproving but knew it would be impossible to persuade Aunt Marie to take a different course of action.

They arrived the following evening and I found myself glad that it was already dark, hoping they might slip into the village and out again without being noticed. It was a futile hope and, I told myself as I set up a makeshift bed downstairs, based on illogical reasons. Françoise's reactions could not, after all these years, be typical. Franz was a monk and Kurt in a wheelchair. Who could hate them? At best we should be ignored, but as we had come to see none but Aunt Marie that would not matter.

On the morning after their arrival Aunt Marie was a little stronger, giving me my first serious hope of her long-term survival, but by the afternoon she was too tired to do other than sleep and the rest of us left the house to give her some peace. I hoped we would not meet Françoise but I had done so only on the one occasion and I brushed aside my fears until, the day passing without incident, I began to relax.

The next day we again left Aunt Marie alone for the afternoon, but this time I was aware of curious glances as we pushed the wheelchair. There was, I thought, nothing so odd about that, as it was not every day that a monk wheeled a disabled man through the sleepy village. On the third day of their visit I had begun to think that I had been over-cautious and that there was no longer any need for my presence, reasoning that I might as well return to Oxford, placate my supervisors and resume my normal life.

I mentioned this to Franz, who appeared to think it would cause no difficulty and indeed relieve the congestion in Aunt Marie's house. I left the others still on their afternoon walk and returned to the house to ring the railway and enquire about train times. As I turned the key in the front door I could hear the telephone ringing but by the time I reached it the caller had given up. Aunt Marie still slept deeply and had not heard it. Between asking about trains and checking flight times I went upstairs to use the bathroom and heard the telephone again ringing. Once more I was too late to pick up the receiver.

My travel enquiries settled, I went to rejoin the others but at the gate I thought I once more heard the telephone and turned back. At the door I dropped the key and lost a few seconds retrieving it from the plant pot into which it had fallen. This time the call ended when I was in the very act of lifting the receiver.

Even now I cannot believe our ill fortune. Three times Pierre Dessin rang and three times I was too late to answer him. It later transpired that he rang earlier that afternoon and indeed later as well but we were all out and Aunt Marie slept, drugged with painkillers. He tried once more during the evening but Aunt Marie had gone to bed, Kurt was helpless in his wheelchair with the makeshift bed between him and the hall, Franz was bathing and heard nothing, and I, wanting to hear a radio programme, had shut myself in the kitchen that I might not disturb Aunt Marie as she tried to sleep. I cannot blame my grandfather for taking alarm.

The ancient Romans believed that sometimes it was possible to hear the gods laughing from Mount Olympus. If so, then we should have heard them in Provence that night.

Pierre Dessin, his wife, his youngest daughter, Jeanne, and his son, Edouard, arrived on the doorstep the following afternoon just as I was packing the final items into my bag. They found a house full of Germans in which there was no room for Dessins and the first person my grandfather saw when she opened the door to him was the daughter he had disowned twenty-four years earlier, the source of the family's deepest shame and disappointment, the comforter of those who had killed his elder son, the one who had betrayed her family, her upbringing and her very country, the one who, by falling in love with an enemy, had for ever tainted them all with an act of treachery.

fifteen

Catherine Dessin

My mother's shocked exclamation reached me upstairs where I was packing. I ran down but my grandfather had turned away and I saw only a strange woman and a slightly embarrassed-looking young man, perhaps six or so years older than me. My mother had walked back into the house, leaving them on the step, and I raised a quizzical eyebrow at him.

'Edouard Dessin,' he explained with a nervous glance behind him and, following it, I saw a woman in earnest conversation with my grandfather.

'Klaus-Pierre Dessin. Aunt Marie is asleep but please come in.'

He nodded and turned to the older woman beside him. 'Your grandmother.' His tone was uncompromising, the sort of tone an adult uses to a child when demanding good behaviour.

I tried not to remember the four-year-old boy. *No, sorry, I am not your granny.*

She also nodded to me but immediately turned

to her son. 'I must just talk to your father. You go in.'

Neither of us went in. We stood on the doorstep and conversed in lower tones.

'I suppose I should call you Uncle Edouard,' I began, trying to lighten the situation.

'Not unless you want to drive my father completely mad. Hell. He rang all day yesterday and was worried when he could not get any reply. If nothing else it convinced him you had left. I don't think he knew anyone else was here at all, especially–'

'My mother?'

'Yes. Your mother. God knows what will happen now. I suppose you are both staying here?'

'There are four of us. My mother's husband, Kurt Kleist, and my cousin Franz von Ströbel.'

'Then we will have to find somewhere else if my father does not simply insist that we see Aunt Marie at once and then return immediately to Paris.'

'I was going to leave today but I do not think I can do so now. The others are going tomorrow and I will go then. There is a farmhouse just outside the village where you can probably find refuge for one night. I know Aunt Marie would like you to stay a while.'

'How is she?'

'Up and down but I think improving. The last thing she needs is a king-size family row. Tell me honestly, is it only your father or all of you who hate us?'

'Hate is a strong word. He simply cannot come to terms with what your mother did. I think my mother goes along with him for the sake of peace and quiet, but Annette is still bitter, having very active memories of Martin – you have heard of him? The one who died fighting with the Free French? – and of being arrested and interrogated. I think she was also embarrassed by other people's comments. Jeanne is different. She takes life as it comes, seizes the day as it were. As for me, I have only happy memories of Catherine and none at all of Martin.'

I was grateful for the frankness but felt a cold knot of apprehension as my grandmother began to walk back towards us.

'We are going,' she announced. 'We'll telephone Marie and arrange a time to visit.'

'We leave tomorrow,' I told her. 'By lunchtime we will all be gone.'

'Klaus-Pierre says there is a farmhouse where we can stay,' put in Edouard.

Then a weak, hopeful, invalid voice called from within. 'Pierre! Is that you? Come in. I'm afraid I am too feeble to come to the door.'

Edouard took his mother by the arm and propelled her firmly forward though she faced backwards, seeking her husband's reaction, I could hear Jeanne saying, 'Papa, we must.'

I stood aside to let Edouard and my grandmother enter the house and then walked to where Jeanne and my grandfather argued in the middle of the small drive.

'Grandfather, Aunt Marie is asking for you. We will leave shortly and return after you have gone.' I looked at Jeanne and she introduced herself.

Presently Edouard appeared again in the doorway to tell his father that Aunt Marie was becoming upset and they moved towards the house, one with reluctance, one with relief. The sitting room seemed very crowded, with insufficient chairs and an uncertain atmosphere, in which I discerned, with amusement, that the greatest awkwardness was that of Pierre Dessin towards Franz.

Men as clever as my grandfather did not practise religion from habit but from conviction and he was a devout Catholic whose instinctive reaction was to accord respect to those in holy orders, calling them 'brother'. He did not, however, feel the remotest fraternity with any von Ströbel and studiously tried to avoid addressing Franz by any name at all. My cousin's religious name, by which none of us had yet learned to call him, was Brother Blaise and that was how he had introduced himself to the influx of Dessins. Jeanne had responded with merely her Christian name and I had no idea whether she was married or not and whether I should call her madame or mademoiselle so I settled for Jeanne, although certain that the familiarity was an added irritation to her father. Eventually I glimpsed her left hand and saw an engagement ring but no wedding band. After ten minutes of stilted conversation I suggested that there were too many of us in the room and that my mother, Kurt, Brother Blaise and I should go for a walk.

I knew that Aunt Marie divined the real reason and hated causing her distress but the row which hovered in every glance between my mother and grandfather would have been more distressing still. When Edouard said it might be an idea to walk to the farmhouse to make enquiries about their accommodation and that he would join us, there was a perceptible pause while everyone waited for Pierre Dessin to object but he had begun to talk to Aunt Marie, that being the one way in which he could ignore everybody else in the room without causing anxiety to his sick cousin.

We set out in the desired direction, which took us past the memorial. Edouard glanced at it and at the small, now wilted, bunch of flowers at its foot, but he offered no comment. While I could speak to him without the inhibiting presence of his father I decided to tackle the issue head on.

'I am sorry my grandfather and my mother still feel as they do. They loved each other once and the war was a long time ago. There are four more, perfectly legitimate and very small, grandchildren in Germany. Kurt's parents are dead and it would be good for them to have a granny and granddad.'

'As I told you, Jeanne and I would agree with you and, I think, my mother might if she were prepared to risk a serious rift with my father, but Annette would not. For years I used to ask, "Where is Catherine?" and I was told she had been very bad and sent away. Just before Grandfather's funeral I was told about you as well and warned not to say hello. So I didn't but afterwards Jeanne wept and said what we had done to a tiny child was cruel and unChristian and I knew I agreed with her.

'That night she rowed very badly with my father, despite the family being in mourning. She kept saying, "Things have gone far enough. What about 'forgive us our trespasses as we forgive

282

those who have trespassed against us?" My father said there was no obligation to forgive the unrepentant and that your mother was still proud of her iniquitous ways.

'There were some relatives present, among them a man called Robert who said he had been very fond of your mother and would like to see her again. Unfortunately he is Annette's brother-in-law and she fairly screamed at him while her husband, Emile, tried to calm everyone down.

'So we are divided but Jeanne and I would love time with your mother to catch up and recall our childhood when we were all happy. I suppose we should have made some move ourselves but, of course, we have been too preoccupied with our own lives.'

For a while we talked of those lives. Jeanne was clever, had a degree from the Sorbonne and was engaged to a doctor. Edouard, inspired by tales of Martin, had spent five years in the French army and was now settled into civilian life as an accountant with a large company. I rehearsed my own history and Edouard thought that in any other circumstances my grandfather would have rejoiced in such academic prowess.

'None of us quite lived up to his expectations. Annette was awesomely bright but the war stopped her going to university and when it was over she decided she did not want to return to being a student. Jeanne has a very good degree but has always been more interested in living than in achieving. She did not want to settle either in marriage or a career and I think would not even now be marrying if she didn't think time was running out for having children. She has taught at missions in no fewer than three African countries, has been a ski instructor in the Alps and travelled all Europe. Nor did any of us specialise in English, which of course was his own subject, so to have a grandson at Oxford would have been a dream come true.'

'It is his loss, not Klaus-Pierre's.' Kurt spoke for the first time. My mother had lagged well behind us, feigning an interest in the war memorial, in reality giving the younger generation its opportunity to talk without inhibition. Franz had also been pushing Kurt at a slower pace than usual but at that moment had closed the gap between us, enabling them to hear what Edouard was saying.

Edouard looked round at him. 'My father said you were General von Ströbel's adjutant during the war?'

'Yes. I saw you when you were a small child. Catherine adored you. Whenever I had to deliver a message to your house and Catherine came to the door, there you would be behind her, peeping round and staring at my hat. Once I gave it to you to play with and you put it on but Catherine snatched it away because she was afraid your father would see. By the time we left you must have been about four or five.'

'Five and a big bit.'

Amid the laughter I thought of my own escapade with a hat. It inspired a question that I could not ask because my mother was catching up with us and was within earshot. We walked on to the farmhouse where, remembering Françoise and fearing that my German accent might

284

provoke ill-feeling, I left Edouard to go in and make the arrangements. He came out frowning.

'We have rooms for three nights but it was very odd. Madame seemed delighted with the custom until I gave her our names. I could swear that if I had said "Dessin" when I first went in she would have declared there to be no room.'

So Françoise had spread her poison and our arrival in the village was known along with our history. I gave them a censored explanation of my encounter with her.

Edouard shrugged. 'Aunt Marie is well thought of here and my parents were in the Resistance. I do not think it matters.'

As I turned from him I saw my mother's angry face but while I was trying to find the right words to defuse the situation she broke into a torrent of abuse against the proprietor and had to be persuaded not to enter the farmhouse and confront her directly. The walk back did little to help. We did not see Françoise but we passed two women who stopped to stare after us and I heard a muttered 'Dessin'. I understood somewhat better my grandfather's shame. It was not the name von Ströbel which my mother had caused to be hated but the name of her own family.

Without any spoken agreement to do so we walked straight past the gate on our return, prolonging the time the Dessins could have with Aunt Marie, but the air was colder than when we had set out and a slight drizzle was beginning. For want of any other shelter we turned into the church. I was mentally braced against a flood of unwelcome memories but none came. I had been too small when I had been rejected by the congregation, as the sinfully conceived child of a traitor, to retain any recollections of the building. The altar, lectern and pews were as unfamiliar as if I had never seen them.

Relieved, I glanced at my mother and, seeing the pain in her face, tried to find some excuse for returning immediately to the rain. Franz, oblivious to this particular episode in my life with Aunt Marie, was looking at the paintings and stained glass, while Kurt wheeled himself to where my mother stood and took her hand. I found my voice at last and observed that Aunt Marie tired easily and maybe it was time to return.

Edouard, who had noticed nothing odd, demurred, saying that we should give his parents time to leave without meeting us. My mother said she would wait in the porch but when I said I would like the air too she shook her head, signalling a wish to be alone. After twenty minutes I glanced out but could not see her. The rain had ceased and I felt no very great concern. Kurt was engrossed in a conversation with Edouard and the last thing I wanted at that moment was to interrupt any budding friendship between my mother's husband and her brother.

Franz wandered down the aisle towards me and asked where she had gone.

'Outside, probably to get away from memories. It's not raining any more.'

After another twenty minutes or so we began to amble back, expecting to find my mother on the way but we arrived back at the house without seeing her. Our approach must have been heard because as we reached the front door Pierre Dessin was coming through it. Our party went inside while the others walked to the gate. I went upstairs and, through the landing window, saw Jeanne closing it behind them.

I went into the bathroom and stood stock still. The sink was covered with hair, my mother's hair. Kurt's razor, clogged with soap and blonde strands, lay on top of it. I turned and ran downstairs, through the front door, along the drive, swearing when the catch of the gate accidentally caught. My heart was pounding.

Ahead of me I could see the Dessins turning a corner. I shouted but they disappeared from my sight. I ran with a speed I had not needed since I had played rugby at Ampleforth and caught up with them just as the war memorial came into sight. They scarcely heeded my arrival, their steps slowing almost to a standstill as they stared at the solitary figure by the stone. As we drew nearer my mother faced us, the defiance blazing from her eyes. Then, shaven head erect, she began to sing.

'Non, Je ne regrette rien'. My mother had a strong voice and the notes – angry, proud, nostalgic – seemed to fill the air. I stood, watching, until the last strain died away. Piaf herself could not have commanded a more astounded audience. Her protest completed, my mother left the memorial and passed between us, looking straight ahead. She did not look at her father or mother or at me, her son, or even at her husband who had wheeled himself in hot pursuit of Franz, as my cousin, alarmed by my sudden rush from the house, sped after me.

My mother's gaze fell only on a couple of passing villagers who had stopped in amazement to watch the spectacle and it was a glance not of embarrassment nor even of hatred but of a deep, heartfelt scorn. Mesmerised we watched her go and not even Pierre Dessin stirred until she was lost to our view. Only then did I look at the others. Jeanne and Edouard were white with shock while my grandmother silently wept, the tears pouring down her face. My grandfather tried to look both disapproving and dismissive but managed neither and, as they all moved away without speaking, his eyes were troubled and his mouth tight.

Franz was mopping his brow but it was on Kurt that my attention was fixed. His hands had become muddy from pushing the wheels of his chair and he was now cleaning them with a large, green-bordered, white handkerchief. It was a studied, thorough cleaning and Franz and I watched him, following every stroke of the cloth he plied between his fingers. It seemed a very long time before he neatly folded up the dirty rag, returned it to his pocket and at last looked up, not at us but straight ahead.

'We had better go home,' he said quietly.

'I'm sorry,' I said helplessly, reading his thoughts all too plainly, for I knew that what we had just heard was more than a statement of mere defiance designed to confound Pierre Dessin and disconcert the whispering villagers. It had been a hymn to a lost love, a proclamation clearer than words that it was a love which had never died and which still sustained the singer. *A haunted marriage.* I remembered Aunt Angelika's words and felt only pity for my stepfather. Today the ghost had walked.

Years later Franz was to tell me that shortly after their return to Ströbelfields he had passed one day through the Lutheran churchyard as he took a short cut to meet a friend and had seen my father's grave covered in blonde hair. It was, he told me unnecessarily, something which should never reach the ears of Kurt.

My mother, I thought, was still Catherine Dessin for all that she was called Frau Kleist and had four children of that name. I had become distant from her since being sent to school in England seven years before and had missed some of that transition which enables a young adult to perceive his mother as a human being rather than just a parent. Nevertheless, I thought I knew her fairly well, but the woman I knew was the mother of Klaus-Pierre Dessin, the wife of Kurt, the mistress the von Ströbels had brought home to the amusement of Walter Pletz and the scandalised disgust of others. I had never known Catherine Dessin.

'What was she like?' The question broke from me when Kurt and I were alone that evening. Aunt Marie, thoroughly exhausted from the day's events and to whom my mother herself had described the scene at the war memorial, had long since gone to bed. My mother was upstairs, lying down in my room, and Franz was visiting the local priest whom he had met when he had attended mass that morning. I reflected wryly that my quiet, gentle cousin must be thinking he had walked into a madhouse and was probably glad to escape.

Kurt looked at me for a moment or two in silence. 'She was very, very beautiful. The hair she cut off today was her greatest glory but even without it she would have turned heads and, of course, she was young and hopelessly innocent. In those early days Catherine Dessin didn't walk anywhere. She ran, she scampered, she all but jumped like a spring lamb. I think that was what fooled your father. He had taught the young for most of his life and he looked upon her as just another young person whose mind he could expand if they became friends but, by the time that scamper had turned into a womanly walk, he was well and truly enslaved.

'She was stubborn and headstrong and her father had no idea how to handle her but she was also genuinely in love. At first she merely thought she was in love but later became so in reality after your father returned from some home leave in Germany. She saw no reason to let a little thing like a world war get in the way.'

'But he was married.'

Kurt grimaced. 'Yes, and he always said he was going back to Ellie. At least he never deceived your mother on that score. I think both of them sheltered behind that resolution whenever their consciences told them they should end that which they should never have started.'

'What was my father like? Why did you salute him at the graveside?'

'He was a good man and a brave one. I should like to think I possessed only a tenth of his courage.'

'Can a good man seduce a teenager and leave

290

her with a child?'

'Seduce is not the right word for what happened. He was not so calculating. Your father was in the middle of it all before he knew himself and I am quite certain he would have been horrified had he known there was a child. Sometimes people do bad, uncharacteristic things and afterwards wonder at themselves. You ask me if a good man could do what he did, but could a bad man have put his life at risk helping Jews? He had to be seriously driven to do that and the only thing which could have been doing the driving must have been a moral imperative.'

I had heard the same arguments before, remembering Lord Bullchester telling me that a man could act in a way which would make him doubt whether he knew himself. The thought of Bullchester brought with it a stab of pain as a vision of Arabella rose in my mind. Here too Kurt might help and before I could have second thoughts I had poured out the story to him.

'You do not need to tell me that a man can carry a torch for a woman all his life but you knew this girl for just one weekend when she was only fifteen! Klaus-Pierre, one of the greatest survival skills that a man – or woman – can possess is to know when to let go and to do it convincingly. I am sure Willi would tell you that too.'

I was surprised by the reference to my uncle until I realised that Kurt was effectively telling me that it was not he but Uncle Willi who fulfilled the role of substitute father and that he hesitated to usurp his place by advising me in matters of importance. Then he went on to press

291

me on the virtues of consigning the irresolvable to the past.

'For instance, there is the issue of your father. I realise that today has been pretty extraordinary and that all our thoughts have been driven back to Paris but I suspect yours travel there more often than is wise. The question of whether your father was a good or a bad man is not going to be resolved by continually re-asking it. You know as much as you'll ever know, so stop agonising over it.

'People's lives can be destroyed by the past. I once knew a man, a long time ago, who argued with an official that his tax calculations were wrong by a couple of marks. The official would not give way and long after this chap was far too well off to worry about a couple of marks he pursued his claim, spending a fortune on litigation and driving his family to distraction. Pierre Dessin has rather more cause for a grudge but he too has been eaten up by it and so, sadly, has your mother, although her bitterness only surfaces when someone else brings up the subject. She never mentions her family otherwise.

'Your mother thinks she has let go of Klaus and, again, she rarely mentions him but, as you saw today, she has not thrown off the shackles of the past as successfully as she thought she had. You are Klaus-Pierre Dessin and that is how you must live and it is yourself you must know, not the younger versions of your parents. If you are wondering what all this has to do with Arabella then I must tell you that if her image stops you committing yourself to another woman you should let go of that too.'

I was taken aback by the emphatic tones in which he spoke as he ended by saying tritely but earnestly: 'Look forward not back. Return to Oxford and forge that way forward. Rejoice in what you have, including the goodwill of Jeanne and Edouard, and forget what you cannot have, including the goodwill of Professor Dessin. Take a leaf out of Wolfgang's book. He is an example, if ever I saw one, of rising above the past.'

'Not entirely.' I told him of Wolfgang's resolution never to marry and of his nocturnal ventures in Paris and Lübeck. We both found it a relief to talk upon a fresh subject and discussed Wolfgang with great determination until Franz returned.

The next day I left first and bade a regretful farewell to Aunt Marie to whom we had scarcely brought tranquillity in her hour of need. She squeezed my hand and said it was wonderful to see me again and how she hoped it would not be the last time. I was unsure how to interpret the words but I consciously set out to remember Kurt's and on my way to the station I turned my head away from the war memorial and refused to see if I could glimpse any Dessins as I passed the farmhouse.

I was Klaus-Pierre Dessin, scholar, not Klaus von Ströbel, soldier. I would probably never see again the grandfather who had been so cruel to both my mother and me but it was surely vastly more important that I had again seen Aunt Marie, whose unfailing kindness had seen us through those first five years of my life. It pained me to recall that I had thought so much about Pierre Dessin and Klaus von Ströbel and so little about Aunt Marie. Kurt was right when he had suggested that I had been governed by the wrong priorities and he was right about Arabella too. I knew nothing of the woman she had become but had measured every girl since against some estimate of her worth, which was in my imagination only. It was time to grow up.

I threw myself into the Punic Wars and soon placated the dons who had found my absence at the beginning of term so unsatisfactory. I made new friends and looked up some old ones and, in a declaration of independence, decided to spend my first Christmas away from Ströbelfields.

Elsa wrote in bitter protest:

It is bedlam here as usual. Your mother's children, Lotte's children and both Alessandra and Hedy are coming too with their screaming brats. I could even envy Franz his monastery and you stay all cosy and peaceful in Oxford, you rat. Have pity and come home for New Year.

I grinned and cabled that I would come after all. My mother later told me that Uncle Willi's face had lit up when Elsa read out the missive and I thought that I had not been so very grown-up to decide to stay in Oxford.

On the aircraft I wondered what my mother would look like. Presumably her hair would be just beginning to grow back and I wondered if she had bought a wig.

I slept throughout the second half of the

journey and dreamed fitfully of a shaven-headed girl being dragged by her father to a stone in the middle of Oxford. She briefly turned into Joan of Arc but then became Marlene Dietrich singing '*Je ne regrette rien*' which somehow became 'Where have all the flowers gone?' I woke from the confusion to find a Lufthansa stewardess asking me to fasten my seatbelt.

Otto met me at the airport. 'Thank God you have come. It's all chaos. The Pletzes are invading in force tomorrow and Alessandra's children are persecuting the twins. You'll see some more changes to the house. Father is spending quite a lot on it. He keeps saying he must leave every-thing in good order but he's only seventy and has years ahead yet. The farm is doing superbly well under my management with a bit of help from God who sent some good crops this year.'

I felt the tension drain from me as I began to laugh. 'My mother said you have a housekeeper now? She made her sound like Mrs Danvers.'

'Mrs Danvers?' Otto looked puzzled and I was again aware that we were living in different cul-tures.

'She's not bad really,' he was continuing. 'But she is not a housekeeper as such, just someone who helps every weekday, but it has made a mass-ive difference and particularly to Aunt Angelika. She isn't here over Christmas so you may not see her. Did anyone tell you Maria had died? She was the one who used to peel sacks of vegetables.'

I was briefly saddened but Otto was continuing with his news bulletin. 'Wolfgang Mueller has had a tough time of it in Cloppenburg. A prostitute was murdered and the police interviewed him.'

'My God!'

'Oh, that wasn't the problem. He had never known that particular girl but the fool had been going to the brothel where she worked and all known clients were taken in for questioning. Of course, it caused one hell of a stir in the firm because we are supposed to be a wholesome outfit producing stories for children. There was quite a demand for him to be sacked.'

'How did anyone there find out?'

'I don't know. Poor old Father was beside himself. Kurt says you had told him about Wolfgang's proclivities but it came as a terrible shock to the inventor of the Wanderer Bear, I can tell you.'

'You don't seem too bothered.'

'I am only bothered on my father's behalf. I do not see how the firm can answer for the morals of its employees.'

I felt a guilty anger. It was I who had introduced Wolfgang to Ströbelfields and, in my delight at his success with the Wanderer Bear drawings, had failed to warn my uncle of his darker side. In trying to help a friend I had failed in my greater duty. I groaned.

'Oh, it's all settled down again. After all, they haven't got a better artist and I don't know where they would find one. By the way, your mother is wearing a dark curly wig while her own hair grows again. She says she has always wondered what she would look like brunette.'

'What does she look like?'

'OK, but fair suits her better. Hedy is pregnant again.'

'I am beginning to lose count.'

'I already have. Shall we stop off for a drink before joining the mayhem?'

I agreed, and after he had drunk four times as much as I, he suggested I take over the driving. We arrived at Ströbelfields in a jovial frame of mind and I wondered how I could have contemplated staying in Oxford. The house being full, I was staying in the barn, which was lit with decorations and my bedroom was warm and welcoming. I put my luggage on the bed and turned to find the twins staring at me from the doorway.

Klaus, not having any von Ströbel blood, did not look in the least like his namesake and nor did Catherine in whom the Dessin darkness and plainness prevailed. My mother had been the odd one out in her family and her daughter looked more like my grandmother. Willi-Kurt soon joined the group at the door, hearing my voice and hoping for a present. He, like his elder brother, bore a strong resemblance to Kurt.

'Where's Bette?'

'In bed. She goes to bed before me,' announced Willi-Kurt proudly. 'She's only two.'

I smiled and went downstairs, piggybacking Willi-Kurt who squealed with delight.

Kurt said we were all expected in the house for dinner and that Alessandra's eldest would keep an eye on the younger children. My mother had already gone across. I asked how she was and he said none the worse for what had happened in France. To pass the time until we should follow her I began opening the small pile of Christmas cards on the table which Kurt had indicated were all mine.

From Jack Marshall's fell a Roneo-ed letter announcing his engagement. Charles Emmett had added a line to his saying he still had fond memories of the summer. The third card I opened was from Jeanne and Edouard. I held it out to Kurt.

'We guessed. The postmark says Paris.'

'Did Mother mind?'

'No. She said the younger generation must plot its own course.'

When I recollected how she had shouted at me for visiting the Sorbonne and indeed for setting foot in Paris at all and how she would never hear her family mentioned without a contemptuous response, a small flower of hope dared to blossom in my soul. The horrendous experiences and confrontations of our trip to Provence had not added up merely to a force for grievance. Out of it had come a small measure of peace.

I dared to stand the card on the sideboard and for the first time ever a greeting from my mother's siblings stood unchallenged among the other messages of seasonal goodwill. It was, of course, addressed only to me. They had not dared to hold out an olive branch to my mother and I guessed they were restrained not by any thoughts of their father's anger but by fear of my mother's.

Catherine Kleist was happy for her son to know them. Catherine Dessin had not forgiven.

sixteen

Mortality

In 1969 I did not return to Ströbelfields at all, not even at Christmas, and nor did I go to France again although I sent a holiday postcard to both Jeanne and Edouard in return for the birthday card they had sent to me in February. Indeed I do not remember anything but a thoroughly English life as that wild decade drew to its close.

I was content, my desire to effect reconciliation with my French relatives fully satisfied if only partially successful. Both Jeanne and Edouard had written to my mother and they were in touch as far as adult siblings separated by great distances were likely to be. I was reconciled to the continuing bitterness between my mother and her parents and hardly gave it a thought as it had no direct effect on any of our lives.

In the spring of that year I received a sharp reminder that I was not accepted in all quarters of British society. Both Charles Emmett and Jack Marshall were working in London and occasionally I went to the capital for a weekend or for an evening. Jack had a one-bedroomed flat in Chelsea and when I stayed with him I slept on the floor of his living room. He was an untidy fellow and I had difficulty finding a space for the sleeping bag.

'You should find somewhere bigger,' I complained.

'I can't afford it.'

I wondered what his fiancée made of the
conditions and for how long she would tolerate
living in them. Staying with Charles was easier.
He had a large two-bedroomed Victorian flat in
Clapham and rented out the second room. I slept
on his sofa, which was large, comfortable and, as
his flatmate was in the habit of retiring early,
nearly always available.

Charles and Jack were both part of the increasing trend towards buying property even when
young and single. In Germany renting was still
the norm and mortgages hard to obtain. Most
families, however, now lived without strangers as
the refugees had been absorbed and largely re-
settled. Germany was booming but Britain was
obsessed with inflation and Harold Wilson's management of the economy.

My own accommodation consisted of a research
student's rooms at Corpus. It was one advantage
of my foreign status for most of my fellow D.Phil
students lived out of college, which is what I knew
I would have to do the following year.

'You should join a club,' Charles Emmett advised me when I rose from a poor night on his
sofa. 'I could put you up for the Lansdown. It has
a fantastic pool.'

'In your case the Oxford and Cambridge might
be better,' said Jack later. 'I am sure you could
find someone to nominate you.'

'They're a stuffy lot,' countered Charles. 'They
don't admit women.'

'They do as associate members. But what about the Reform?'

I applied for membership of four London clubs and was rejected by each.

'It must be those old duffers who still think Germany is the enemy,' groaned Charles. 'When you live out of college you can give an Oxford rather than a German address. Call yourself Pierre Dessin on the form.'

'And be blackballed by someone still fighting the Hundred Years War? I don't think I'll bother.'

I did not bother and never did join a London club. The incident was hurtful but hardly serious and by the summer I had forgotten it. Charles and I had been intending to spend three weeks of the long vacation backpacking in Switzerland, Austria and Lichtenstein. He was now constrained by limitations to his annual leave while I could enjoy most of the long vacation and I left the exact dates to him, but that term he fell in love yet again and announced that instead he was spending the whole three weeks in Malta where the girl lived.

Jack was saving up his leave for his honeymoon so I contacted Wolfgang, although now with some wariness, only to find that another Wanderer Bear adventure was in the final stages of preparation and he had to be on hand to make any last-minute alterations to the drawings. Two or three of my Oxford friends said they would have been interested but had now made other arrangements. At first I thought I would return to Ströbelfields but on the spur of the moment decided instead to backpack around the British Isles alone.

It occurred to me that having lived in Britain for

nearly eight years I had seen precious little of it and that my academic existence gave me too little fresh air and exercise. At Christmas I had found it hard to keep up with Otto when we walked the estate together. A month of walking in the wilder parts of the kingdom could be nothing but beneficial and I began to draw up an itinerary. Scotland, Northumbria, Cumbria, I thought.

'The lakes are hell at this time of year,' objected Charles. 'Overrun with tourists. Why not just Scotland and a whole load of different islands? Skye has first-class walking and Orkney a lot of history.'

'The midges will be awful,' said Jack. 'But I'm green with envy. You perpetual students have a jammy life. Spare a thought for us slaving away in a hot and heaving London.'

A few weeks later I found myself on a ferry with the 'Skye Boat Song' for background music.

'I hope Bonny Prince Charlie and Flora MacDonald were better travellers than I am,' I observed to a fellow passenger as I stood by the rail. He moved hastily away but to my surprise I completed the entire journey with nothing more than a vague hint of nausea, which I probably would not have noticed at all if I had not been alert for it.

'One day they'll build a bridge,' the same man commented cheerfully as we disembarked.

I found a room in a small guest house in Flodigarry, finding the proprietor's accent incomprehensible, and was amused when she put our difficulties down to my own foreignness.

'Ye'll nae be here ower long if ye canna stay past Saturday.' She was rummaging among various leaflets and eventually produced one for the short-stay visitor.

'I'm really just going to do some walking. I need to blow the cobwebs away.'

She smiled. 'Aye, but mind ye in the hills.'

The warning, I discovered, was sound, as I misjudged my path on my descent from the Cuillins and spent two hours trying to see the road. It was no place to be marooned for the night. I arrived back at the guest house exhausted and dozed in a hot bath with a whisky on its edge. I was seriously out of condition, I thought, wondering if I was too old to take up rugby again.

Three days on the island did much to restore me and on the return journey I did not suffer at all, allowing me to hope that I might be growing out of seasickness. I took a week to travel through the north-west Highlands, walking the mountains, hitch-hiking the roads, and then spent more than the whole week had cost me on a ferry to the Orkneys. During the journey I studied a tourist brochure. The main attraction seemed to be Scapa Flow.

I knew all about Scapa Flow from Uncle Willi, who had of course fought and been taken prisoner at Jutland. It was from Scapa Flow that the British fleet had sailed to meet the Kaiser's for that great battle, after a visit to Scapa Flow that Kitchener had been killed on the *Hampshire* and to Scapa Flow that the German fleet had sailed to be interned after the Armistice. Then, in 1919, foreseeing that the peace would entail a surrender of the fleet, the German admiral, von Reuter, had scuttled it in front of the amazed eyes of parties of visiting schoolchildren. I had heard the story

303

often and was looking forward to seeing where it had all happened.

I found the site the following day and stared at the cold, unforgiving water, trying to imagine Uncle Willi in the sea at Jutland. Near to where I stood a man in boots and waterproofs was attending to a small boat from which he had been fishing. I wandered over and gave him a hand to pull it ashore.

'Thank you kindly.'

I looked at him. He was too weatherbeaten for me to guess his age. It might have been anything from fifty to seventy or beyond. His eyes were friendly and as he began to pull an old pipe from his pocket he asked me if I knew about Scapa Flow. I said I did, that my uncle had fought at Jutland but did not specify for which side.

'I was here the day it happened and saw it with my own eyes. A party of us had come along from school to see the German fleet and one moment all the ships were there and the next they were disappearing upside-down under the water.' He chuckled. 'Took them a long time to clear up the mess, laddie. They were still doing it when the next war came along. Can't help admiring that von Reuter chap, whatever they say about him.'

I smiled at him. 'But there are still half a dozen or so wrecks left?'

'Aye, about eight. There's diving parties if you want to see them closer.'

I had never learned to dive, indeed had never thought of it, and now rather regretted the omission. I shook my head but, working out that if he was at school in the First World War he had almost certainly been involved in the Second, I asked him if he had been in the Navy.

'Aye, the Merchant Navy, which I joined as a lad. Then it was the convoys in the war and then back home. I'd had enough by then and there was a lassie didnae want me away so much. There was work enough here if you weren't ower particular.'

I followed most of his story, my ears becoming attuned to the accent.

'Your uncle was in the German Navy, then?'

I remembered my own accent and gave a rueful smile. 'Yes. My father was killed in the Second World War and my uncle brought me up. He found himself in the sea at Jutland and has a wheeze to show for it till this day. Meanwhile my father was in the trenches and my other uncle flying with von Richthofen's circus.'

'They say it can't happen again with this EEC business but I'm not so sure. Reckon France and Germany get along like the devil and holy water, but your country's done well enough out of it.'

I had heard the sentiment too often and let it pass. Our economy was a constant source of grudging wonder and no one thought about the families divided by the Berlin Wall, the legacy of guilt which trailed in the wake of Nazism or the orphans who had grown up playing in the rubble.

Nevertheless I accepted an invitation to the old man's home that night and stayed in a tiny room which his children had once occupied. He and his wife fed me on freshly caught fish and afterwards insisted I had a 'wee dram', which I knew would give me a headache next day. The lavatory was outside and I washed in the kitchen sink.

They were living as their ancestors had lived, yet I saw signs of wealth on the island.

Contentment filled the atmosphere of that small, humble home and I left the next day feeling obscurely guilty. They had accepted pathetically little from me when I had insisted on paying and I had left a further sum under my pillow, which I was sure they would find patronising.

Returning to the mainland, I continued my exploration of Scotland until I stood on the shore at Lossiemouth and debated whether to return to Oxford immediately or to travel back along the east coast until I was within reach of the border. I decided on Oxford, being weary of the lifestyle of the past three weeks and, reaching Glasgow in easy stages, I then took a train to London.

I called Jack Marshall and offered him dinner, before wondering if any decent restaurant would admit me in my walking clothes. He took one look at me and we spent the evening at his flat with fish and chips, afterwards wandering along the waterfront at Chelsea Harbour, looking at the houseboats.

I returned to Oxford, refreshed and cheerful. I spent the next two days catching up with post-holiday tasks but on the third I met a girl whom I had once known through Jessie. I was coming from Blackwell's bookshop as she was about to turn into it.

'KP!' she exclaimed in delight. 'You're the first familiar face I've seen all vac.'

'Bev! What are you doing in Oxford? Surely you went down last term?'

'I got a first and they let me do a Master's.'

'Remind me which subject.'

'German. You've forgotten but you helped me with some Goethe once. I gather you distinguished yourself last year with a Congrat.'

I pulled a modest face and Bev laughed. She had been on the fringes of Jessie's circle of friends rather than an intimate and I knew her only slightly. Indeed she had always struck me as a rather immature girl, prone to giggles and silly observations, but there were few people around in the vacation whom I knew and I was willing enough to join her for coffee.

The coffee became a punt on the river, evening drinks at The Perch, dinner at the Tackley Hotel. I walked her back to St Anne's certain that I wanted to see her again.

'Klaus-Pierre,' she mused one Sunday morning when we leaned over Magdalen Bridge, looking down into the water and listening to the church bells pealing over Oxford. 'I suppose that's the equivalent of Nicholas Peter?'

'Sort of.'

From then on she called me Nicholas Peter, a silliness I hated and which caused me to grind my teeth with irritation, but my protests fell on deaf ears. If I was not to be called by my proper name I preferred KP. Occasionally she even called me Dessie, in an abbreviation of my surname, which was worse still.

'Why on earth can't you call me Klaus-Pierre?' I fumed.

'It is too much of a mouthful.'

'Nicholas Peter is longer.'

'Yes, but easier to say.'

I gave up, resolving to end the friendship, knowing that the resolution would not last five minutes.

Even now I am not certain what attracted me to Bev Burnett. She was passably attractive with curly chestnut hair, which she tied ludicrously in two childish bunches either side of her head. Apart from that she dressed modishly enough but was too plump to carry off the clothes really well. She was academically clever but had poor judgement and drove a Morris Minor, complete with split windscreen and wing indicators, so badly that I feared an accident every time I was rash enough to sit in the passenger seat. The car had no seat-belts and I surreptitiously clung on to the doorstrap for comfort.

Once, when we drove to see her parents in Hampshire, I insisted on taking the wheel.

'Fill it up with three-star,' I told the garage attendant when we called at a petrol station some ten miles into the journey, and I got out to look under the bonnet. The water in the battery was negligible, that in the tank dangerously low and the oil well below the minimum mark on the dip-stick. I raised my eyes to heaven.

'This is a great little car. You should look after it better.'

'You sound like my parents.' Bev turned to the petrol attendant. 'How much was all that?'

'Ninety-nine p for the petrol, Miss.'

'We need oil and distilled water as well,' I added hastily.

'It will make the sums complicated,' objected Bev.

Britain, preparing for decimalisation, was operating two currencies side by side. Bev still obstinately stuck to pounds, shillings and pence, and refused to deal with anything in the new currency over a pound. I began to lose patience.

'We cannot run this car without oil and water.' I was aware that I probably sounded more than ever like her parents and knew that most of my friends found me old-fashioned and far too sober. Bev was three years younger than me but at twenty-one had still a seventeen-year-old's approach to life.

She shrugged. 'Well, you do the sums then.'

I did, and we continued on our way. Bev chatted throughout the first half of the journey, then fell asleep. I was just appreciating the peace when the car slewed so violently that she woke up with a startled exclamation.

'Flat tyre,' I groaned as I managed to pull into a layby. Bev looked at me from large, hazel eyes.

'Poor Nicholas Peter. What will you do?'

'My name is Klaus-Pierre and this is your car. I shall change the wheel. Where do they keep the spares on these things?'

'In the boot, of course, but the spare is no good. It got a puncture last term.'

I stared at her in disbelief.

'Oh, don't look so cross. You know I am not as well organised as you. We can call the AA. We passed a phone box less than a mile ago.'

'You were asleep.'

'Yes, but I know it's there because I know this road like the back of my hand. It is after all the way home. I'll run back and phone them.'

I was ungracious enough to let her do it, wondering yet again what drew me so compellingly towards her. She was talented in nothing but her work, in which I had no doubt she would win the highest honours, but she spoke no other language than the one she was studying, played neither sport nor instrument, had a painfully bad singing voice, could not draw or even make clothes or cook. She had no interest in any hobby and preferred all her entertainment ready made. Her political opinions were vague and for somebody with a first-class honours degree she was remarkably ill read.

Although she accused me of being paternal I thought avuncular would have been a better description. I treated her like a somewhat mad goddaughter or favourite niece. Abruptly, standing by the Morris, watching for Bev's return, I remembered Kurt's description of my father's early attitude to Catherine Dessin. I was not in my forties, I was not married, I was not an enemy of her country, but in all other respects I was repeating history.

Impatiently I shook myself free of the thought and shaded my eyes with my hand as if that might miraculously produce a sighting of Bev but the road remained empty. After half an hour I walked in the direction she had taken and ten minutes later saw the red shape of the telephone box, but, as I approached it, I realised it was empty and closer inspection proved it to be out of order. Five minutes later, as I was walking back to the car, a Mini passed me and Bev waved from the window. I stared after the vehicle, which seemed impossibly crammed with people, and by the time I had arrived back at the Morris Bev was sitting on the verge while three young men changed the wheel.

'Isn't it wonderful?' cried Bev as I panted towards her. 'The phone didn't work so I knocked on the nearest door and they had a spare tyre in the garage. Tim used to own a Morris.'

'Who is Tim?'

'The one with ginger curls.'

Tim looked up, said hi, and returned to his nearly completed task. I stood by, feeling useless, until they had finished, before offering to pay for the tyre.

'There is no need,' said Bev hastily. 'We've already arranged that next time I am passing I will return this one.'

Tim looked pleased with the arrangement and I felt a stab of jealousy, which was not lessened by the diligence with which Bev proceeded to spend the afternoon acquiring two new tyres, one of which her father and I put on the car.

'We can drop off Tim's on the way back,' I suggested.

'Actually I was thinking of showing you a new way back. It's more scenic.'

I knew then that she wanted to return it alone and that she did not want to be encumbered with my presence when she next saw Tim. Jealousy coursed through me to be replaced by misery, yet still I did not know why I should be so in thrall to her, recognising that she had a power over me which not even Alison or Jessie had possessed, a power which, one cold November day, when we lay together on my sofa in front of the electric fire with the wind howling through the quad and

311

rattling the windows of Corpus, exploded in passion.

Even as I sought opportunity after opportunity to repeat the experience I liked her less, furious that her caresses should so often be accompanied by murmurs of 'darling Nicholas Peter', recognising that while I was a novice she had done this many times.

It was the end of the sixties but moral taboos, which were all but swept away in the seventies, still lingered. Too much licence on the part of women was still frowned upon and I frowned upon Bev, but I could not give her up.

My own morality stemmed less from my Catholic background than from my upbringing. I had been the product of wrongdoing and had suffered the consequences, so I approached relationships with a deep wariness, determined that no woman or child should, through any action of mine, live under the cloud which had so regularly emptied itself on my mother and me.

Bev, I knew, was not enslaved by me and would one day transfer her favours elsewhere. When, a few weeks before Christmas, I thought this about to happen, I countered by suggesting we go abroad for some winter sun during the vacation. She resisted sun but said she would like to try skiing. We departed to the Alps, where she decided she hated skiing on the very first day and spent the break flirting with a Cambridge student who had broken his ankle. I escorted his girlfriend to the slopes, knowing that he did not fear me but that I feared him.

'Give her up,' Charles Emmett risked advising

me when he came for a weekend during the following term.

'I can't,' was all I could reply.

'Who's the girl?' asked Otto cheerfully the term after when I telephoned to say I would not be returning to Ströbelfields that summer.

'But, Klausi, we haven't seen you for a year,' wailed my mother.

'How about coming to Germany with me this summer?' I suggested to Bev. 'You could get in a lot of practice with the language.'

When she demurred and said she wanted to use the summer to catch up on work and to be away only for two or three weeks, during which she wanted sun and swimming, I suggested Spain and we began to make arrangements for a lazy package holiday. It was with brochures under my arm that I set out to St Anne's one hot Sunday morning and found her in her room with a cup of coffee and a man who had all too obviously been there all night.

I left wordlessly and we did not speak again. To avoid the hammering insistence of my mind that I must see her again, that we could sort it all out, that it might have been a misunderstanding, I fled Oxford and spent a week in London with Charles Emmett, who must have been glad to see the back of his spiritless visitor. The first thing I saw when I entered my room in Oxford was an envelope with Bev's handwriting on it. I set down my case, picked it up and tore it repeatedly until it lay shredded in my wastepaper basket.

Once I saw her crossing the quad and I locked my door and did not answer her knocking. I threw myself into the Punic Wars, seeking to flee twentieth-century grief by contemplating that of Hannibal and Scipio. *Delenda est Carthago.* I wished love could be annihilated as easily as a city, that desire could simply be killed.

I was watching the rowing during Eights Week when a student from Balliol, whom I knew slightly because he had a girlfriend at St Anne's who was a friend of Bev's, mentioned to me that Bev was ill, that she had been sent home and that rumour was identifying glandular fever as the cause.

'Ghastly illness,' he concluded. 'A chap I knew at school actually died of it.'

I had never run across any case of glandular fever and knew nothing about the ailment but when I asked among my friends I found one who had suffered from it and two who knew others who had contracted it but had recovered. It was nasty, they told me, but very rarely fatal. I thought of sending Bev a get well card and even bought one, but I did not take it from the paper bag in which the shop assistant had handed it to me. It lay on my desk where it was soon submerged by the deliberations of the Roman Senate on the fate of Carthage.

Term had finished and I was preparing to move out of college and into a bedsit on the Banbury Road for my final two years, when a passing student, who also carried suitcases in the direction of the lodge, called out, 'Sorry about Bev. Terrible business.'

Ice poured into me as I stared after him and then ran to catch him up.

'Oh, God,' he whispered when I asked him

what had happened and then I knew before he told me. Among the letters I collected from my pigeon hole in the lodge was the announcement of the funeral.

I sat with my head in my hands while the sun dwindled from its midday strength to that of a weak sunset but it was only when I was packing up my desk and found the unopened get-well card that the dam of grief broke into tears and sobs.

Suddenly the childishly bunched hair became endearing not irritating, the immaturity charming not infuriating. I tried to think of Bev dead, a mere shell from which the life had drained. The funeral notice spoke of a crematorium and I thought of an urn of ashes but it was images of the living Bev which danced in my mind, of a girl walking across a quad in the summer sun with hope in her heart to knock upon a door and knock and knock.

It was with sadness not with resentment that I noted the huge number of young men attending the funeral of Beverley Elspeth Burnett. The very name seemed incongruous, conjuring up an image not of Bev but of Margery Bland of whom I had not thought in years, yet the name on the wreath did not seem incongruous as it lay among the others after the cremation and I found myself looking at an unfamiliar signature: 'Nicholas Peter'.

'Only twenty-two. Makes you conscious of your own mortality.' The snippet of conversation I had heard came from a man who looked about eighteen.

A woman, dumpy, middle-aged, red-eyed, stood beside me as we gazed at the floral tributes. She had been a neighbour of Bev and her family and it was from her that I learned the fatal illness to have been meningitis rather than glandular fever.

Kurt had been right. One must concentrate not on the past but on the present because you never knew how much of it you had left. My brain accepted I might die, as had Bev, young, un-fulfilled, the purpose of my life a mystery, but my heart did not believe it. I was very certain that I would die a grandfather and that life in between would be largely happy and successful, little knowing that hovering on the horizon, as if to punish my presumption, was a second and much greater reminder of mortality.

In response to protests from my mother I decided to spend six weeks of that summer at Ströbelfields.

'Thank God you've come,' said Otto when he met me at the airport. 'It's like a morgue. You are the only one coming this summer – even Lotte is off on holiday with Rudi and then has a Pletz family invasion to cope with so we won't see much even of her.'

I laughed. 'When you last picked me up at the airport you were complaining of chaos and bed-lam and too many children at Ströbelfields all at once.'

'Yes, and that was eighteen months ago. We were half-expecting you to come back engaged. What happened?'

'I found her with someone else and broke it off rather brutally. She died a couple of weeks ago.' The tears took me by surprise, causing me embarrassment rather than distress. Otto slowed the car to a halt. I did not look at him but stared through the windscreen, wanting Bev, wanting to see her run towards me, instead seeing her walking across the quad to knock on an unyielding door. I started as I felt Otto's hand on my shoulder.

'You poor old chap. Why ever didn't you tell us? What a thing to go through.'

This, I thought as guilt and grief overcame me and my shoulders shook under Otto's kindly arm, was how my mother must have felt when Klaus von Ströbel died, only it must have been worse because he had been killed in a strafing attack and she would have imagined him suffering appallingly. Bev too had suffered but in a warm bed surrounded by loving parents and attentive doctors. This was how Omi must have felt each time one of her sons died and when her grandchildren were bombed to nothingness at Dresden. None of it diminished my own misery or convinced me that there was any grief greater than mine at that moment.

I recovered and sniffed a rueful apology to Otto, who looked at me gravely.

'I'm OK,' I told him. 'Let's go.'

He turned the ignition key and started the car but he could not stop himself throwing me worried glances until I managed to distract him with family talk and anecdotes from Oxford. He told me I would see a big difference in the Kleist children.

'They've grown at an immense rate. Father has got a lot older. It worries Aunt Angelika although I don't know what she expects, given that he is seventy-two and still actively involved with that damn bear.'

'That damn bear saved Ströbelfields or at any rate strengthened it to the point where survival became certain. But surely he can't do it for ever and a day?'

'So we keep telling him. Anyway there are some big changes coming. Perhaps I should have let them tell you themselves but your mother and Kurt are moving to Cloppenburg. He has been expanding his Russian translation business and is going to work for himself, but still do some bits and pieces for Wanderer Bear. They have found a large ground-floor apartment and Father is adapting the bathroom as a housewarming present.'

I was unsurprised, having subconsciously expected Kurt to take my mother away from daily reminders of Klaus von Ströbel since the drama in Provence.

'We shall always keep your room for you here,' Uncle Willi told me. 'The apartment would not be large enough to house you permanently but, of course, you will be able to camp there for Christmas or the summer holiday – what do you call it? I always forget.'

'The long vac.' I was disconcerted and answered him distractedly. It had not occurred to me that I should be included in the move.

He read my thoughts. 'You know that we will be jealous and still expect you here as often as possible? As I say, your room here will still be your base when you are in Germany, but your mother will want you with her whenever she can get you.'

'This is my home, Uncle Willi, and you have

been as good as my father. I may be called Dessin but in every other way I am a von Ströbel. My mother has a husband and a family of young children, and I am building a life for myself in England. I do not want to uproot to Cloppenburg.'

He smiled. 'I am not suggesting you uproot, but you must surely visit your mother?'

'Of course. But there it will be visiting. Here it will be coming home.'

'I would not want it otherwise.' My mother had come into the library unseen and ran to embrace me, the tightness with which she held me proof that Otto had told her about Bev. 'Ströbelfields has been your home since you were five.'

And if I stay here, a bit of you stays as well. You will not altogether leave. The thought struck me with such force that for a moment I could not be sure I had not uttered the words aloud.

That night I found the courage to ask her why she had insisted I keep the name Dessin.

'Because your grandfather would have wanted you to change it,' she replied. 'To leave his name unstained with illegitimacy or, worse still, German blood. I was determined you should always know that you were both French and German and who your families were.'

So it had been in hatred not in hope, I thought sadly.

'I am pleased you still bear the name of Dessin,' my grandfather had said to me with formal politeness. Until that moment I had believed that the name must form a bond between us, because I was a Dessin, because I bore his name. My mother,

however, had seen the name merely as a protest, as an act of defiance, and it must have been in the same spirit that she had called me Pierre.

By Christmas the barn was empty and my mother and stepfather established in Cloppenburg. By then Otto, who had given up any idea of returning to medicine and looked set to be running the estate for life, had persuaded Uncle Willi to hand over all the remaining executive responsibilities for Wanderer Bear and to content himself with owning the company and making guest appearances in promotions.

Otto himself was courting and when I arrived at Ströbelfields for New Year I found only Uncle Willi and Aunt Angelika at home. The house was strangely silent and I hoped that Otto would marry soon and fill it once more with the sound of a new generation.

seventeen

Father Tessier Remembers

By the autumn of 1971 I was lecturing at Heidelberg, having been offered similar posts in three English universities, and had applied for German nationality. The two decisions seemed to me to confirm my identity. I was French-born and had felt at home in England, but I was a German. It must have been about this time that I also began to think about changing my surname but I hesitated, recognising that to do so would not merely give me the same name as Uncle Willi but also as my father, and I was not yet reconciled to the role he had played in bringing me into the world.

I had not been back to France since the disastrous trip to Provence but Aunt Marie had recovered from her illness and Jeanne and Edouard continued sending Christmas cards to the sister their parents still disowned. Uncle Willi grew visibly stronger, no longer worried by the day-to-day complexities of Wanderer Bear, and spent much of his retirement walking through the woods and fields of Ströbelfields, occasionally irritating Otto with his views on the running of the estate.

Otto himself was now engaged to Anna, a distant relation of the von Forstners who used to come to Sunday lunch when I was a child but whose estate had not survived the land tax and the earlier years of the German post-war economy. They had moved to Bavaria, where they were moderately prosperous. I had met Anna during the summer and liked her, her quiet good sense a perfect foil to Otto's energy and enthusiasm.

My mother and Kurt were happy in Cloppenburg, where Wolfgang Mueller still drew the Wanderer Bear for his living. Life seemed settled, predictable and, on the whole, congenial. There was for me a new dimension, a subtly relaxing one, which at first I noticed only vaguely but which now crystallised in my consciousness: I was no longer actively aware of being German, no longer mentally braced to repel prejudice, to disown Hitler, to defend my family's role in a war it had hated.

When the future of the EEC was discussed it was not in terms of whether it was a new mechanism to afford West Germany the hegemony which two world wars had denied her. When people looked back to Nazism it was with a shared shame and burden. I was not the victim of hate which I had been in France nor of uncertainty which I had been in England. I had nothing to defend because there was no one to cast stones. Here, in an academic environment, my French surname caused not the merest twitch of an eyebrow.

I missed Oxford but I had no close to ties to anyone in England to make the parting difficult. Charles Emmett and Jack Marshall were both married and we had been seeing each other only rarely and then seemingly with increasingly difficult feats of organisation. The friends I had made at university had nearly all left and the few who had stayed on to take their studies to higher planes were dispersing too. Leaving seemed natural. No one had replaced Bev.

From the lofty vantage of my twenty-six years I enjoyed the antics of the students. The men had long hair and wore strings of beads while the girls dressed in swirls of bright colour, which they called psychedelic, or in skirts so short that I found it difficult to look at them when lecturing and keep what the monks who taught me at Ampleforth called 'custody of the eyes'. Sometimes I recognised that I was too distant, had grown middle-aged before my time, had too serious an approach to life, but I had long accepted that I was Franz not Otto and was reconciled to my old-fashioned bookishness. Perhaps, if I had spent more time at Ströbelfields and less away in England, my mother might have laughed at me and urged me to more worldly ways.

Once, when he did not know I was approaching, I heard Uncle Willi tell Walter Pletz that I had inherited all my father's brains but had not half his ease in the world, to which Walter had replied, with his usual good-natured boom, that perhaps it was a good thing. Yet, I thought, I had learned earlier than most the extent of the world's prejudices, hatreds and fears, and Uncle Willi had ensured that I learned to handle them alone at the earliest opportunity.

In that Christmas term of 1971 I was learning the ways of Heidelberg and assuming that the course of my life was set. I was also seeing more of Elsa, who was temporarily working in Mannheim in order not to be parted from her love of the moment whom we all expected her to marry in due course.

'The students have such fun,' she said wistfully on one visit. 'In a year's time I shall be thirty and will have to hurry up if I want children.'

'People have children at forty.'

'Yes, but after thirty they classify you as elderly in the gynaecology department. Did you know that?'

I smiled. 'You can't complain. You loved Switzerland.'

'I'm not complaining but I would like to see more of the world. You were a fool not to go off travelling when you had that gap after Ampleforth – I still can't say that word after all these years.

English is the most awful language. Do you know I've never even been to Paris or London? Uncle Willi is always reminding me that I spent too long in Switzerland and that I should have gone off to Italy or Spain to complete my education. I suppose he is right. Anyway, I am determined to go to both Paris and London before I marry. Will you come with me?'

'Why can't Hans take you?'

Elsa pulled a face. 'It is all work, work, work with him. He says he must keep his nose to the grindstone until he has made an impression in this new job.'

'Well, ask Otto. He would probably welcome the chance to get away for a break.'

'This time last year he might but now he cannot be separated from Anna for five minutes and, before you say, "Why not ask Anna too?" it's because they are so lovey dovey together it embarrasses me. You would have thought Otto would be the last to bill and coo.'

I laughed and said that we could go in the Christmas holidays between the end of term at Heidelberg and the festive season at Ströbelfields. I tried to steer her towards London but she strongly preferred Paris.

'I suppose there is no reason why not,' I conceded. 'I had two spectacularly bad visits to France in nineteen sixty-eight. In the first I got caught up in the beginning of the riots and disgraced the family by appearing in the papers and then made a hopelessly bungled attempt to make the acquaintance of my grandfather who told me to go to hell, or words to that effect. A few months later I was back in Provence and our family and theirs met by accident. It was like World War Three.'

I thought of that lonely, shaven-headed figure, defiant by the war memorial, singing '*Je ne regrette rien*', my own mother ruined by passion, hatred and vengeance.

Elsa nodded. 'I've heard all about it. At least your mother's hair is back to normal.'

I was not sure what that had to do with the conversation until she added, 'Time heals anything if you give it a chance.'

At least the prospect of a return to France held no terrors for me. I had long since taken Kurt's advice and left the past alone. I thought it probably held few temptations as well – I had not the slightest desire to contact Pierre Dessin or his wife, although I would, of course, look up Jeanne and Edouard.

Elsa was looking at me. 'You don't really mind, do you?'

I shook my head. 'My stepfather once gave me a very long, but very pertinent, lecture on being myself rather than being merely the product of the past and its players. He was right and I have made a conscious effort to follow his advice. So yes, I will go with you to Paris but I think you must find someone else for London because I do not have limitless time. This year is important if I want to stay in Heidelberg; I must produce some original research or at any rate commence it.'

'You know your father once taught here? He specialised in Scottish history. I bet the library has lots of his learned tomes.'

'Probably no more than in the library at Ströbelfields and I expect it is all in the archives. His stuff will be old hat by now.'

'Father says we've never had a classicist in the family before unless you count someone called Rudolfus who offended the monks with some Latin translation in the fifteenth century.'

I laughed. 'Perhaps that was the dark beginning of the family's Lutheran tendency.'

Elsa wandered over to the window. 'There's a man there with hair to his waist. Are they very rebellious here?'

'Not as much as in France or Britain a few years ago. Actually when I left Oxford they were becoming pretty right-wing.'

'Of course, they have a right-wing government now, don't they?'

'They have a Conservative one but Edward Heath is not what we would understand by right-wing. He is very keen on Europe and the EEC.'

'So am I, if it stops another war.'

'If you are worried about another war look to the East.'

'Russia? No, the Americans will never let them get the upper hand in the arms race. Starting a war between those two would be Armageddon. There's a girl there in an ankle-length dress.'

'It's all the rage in England. They call it the maxi. I've seen it round here quite a bit too.'

'I know. I've taken a risk and bought an ankle-length coat for winter. So much warmer. Our ancestors were cleverer than we often think.'

It was in that long, black, fur-collared coat that Elsa accompanied me to Paris. We spent three days sight-seeing, gazing at the Eiffel Tower, climbing Notre Dame, visiting the Louvre, taking a boat ride along the Seine on a cold, blustery day. I noticed heads turn and eyes follow Elsa and realised that my tomboy cousin had grown into a beautiful woman. On the fourth day I lunched with my aunt and uncle who produced presents for me and my mother. Elsa had foreseen this and I had purchased gifts in Heidelberg before we left.

Jeanne was not accompanied by her husband but Edouard had brought a girlfriend and it was a relaxed, convivial occasion. I noticed the small bulge beneath Jeanne's peasant-style jersey and congratulated her. My mother would have at least one nephew or niece who would not be taught to disown her.

I made a formal enquiry about their parents' health.

'They are both fine,' said Jeanne, 'but Papa is utterly unthawed. We haven't told him about today because it wouldn't be worth the row. How is Brother Blaise?'

'Well, but much missed by us all. I haven't seen him since that awful business in Provence but Uncle Willi has visited him once in that time.'

'I admire anyone who can give it all up,' said Edouard's girlfriend, throwing him a glance of meaning, which she must have supposed hidden but which was obvious to all of us.

Elsa joined us for coffee, encumbered with much shopping. The following day was a Sunday and she said she wanted to do nothing more than have an easy day so, after I came out of mass, I decided to stroll through Paris, heading away from the city centre and towards those parts where there were fewer shops but more houses and apartment blocks. I walked past schools and churches and children playing. It was a crisp, chilly day with a weak sun and everywhere was evidence of preparations for Christmas. I noticed a street sign on my left. Rue de Varenne. I glanced at the road as I passed, noticing a large, unlit school with a huge crucifix over its entrance. It must have been a convent school but I refused to explore further. There must be many convents in Paris and, even if this were the one my mother had attended, it could have no relevance to me now.

At the point where I decided it was time to turn round and make my way back to Elsa there was a Catholic church and I decided to go inside to rest and warm up.

I ascended the short flight of steps, pushed at the large wooden door and entered cautiously in case there was a mass in progress. Finding there was not, I wandered along the side of the pews, looking at the stained glass, the carvings of the Stations of the Cross and the statues. Halfway along was a small side chapel in which candles blazed. The previous month had been that of the Holy Souls in which Catholics prayed for the souls of the dead and especially for those of friends and relatives. The book in which such remembrances were inscribed lay on a small table, closed now but not yet put away.

I opened it idly and turned the pages with no real objective but to while away some time before starting the walk back into the city centre. My eyes were at once fixed on an entry near the beginning of the month: Martin Dessin. The petitioner was Pierre Dessin and immediately below his name was an identical entry by Margot Dessin. Once I might have stared at the names hungrily, knowing that in them were the seeds of my own past but now my only emotion was a vague curiosity as I looked at them, only momentarily arrested, before resuming my page-turning.

Some six pages further on my attention was caught again and this time held. Paul Blanc remembered in his prayers Klaus von Ströbel. So did Isabelle Blanc. Amazed, I stared at the writing, certain that my eyes misgave me. At the foot of the same page Edouard Dessin had entered the name of his brother. I wondered if he had noticed with whom he shared a page, if my grandfather had seen the entry some ten or so above his son's.

This then must be the church where I had been rejected all those years ago at my great grandfather's funeral. I had not seen it since I was four and then my attention had been wholly absorbed by the players rather than the scenery, so it was little wonder I had not recognised it. A rustle behind me caused me to turn and I saw an elderly priest watching me.

'We have to close the church, my son. Sadly it is no longer safe to leave it open all the time.'

He must be wanting his Sunday lunch and I was holding him up but I was driven by the startling coincidence of my find and heard myself saying, 'Sorry, Father. I did not mean to delay you but there is an amazing entry in this book.'

He moved to look where I pointed and then gave me a sharp glance, in which I saw curiosity become comprehension. This time there was no need to ask why. I had a German accent and looked like Klaus von Ströbel. It was no very great mystery.

'Did you know Klaus von Ströbel, Father?'

'I came to know him very well, at least as well as a priest can know an enemy soldier with whom he spent a great deal of time conspiring. You are Klaus-Pierre Dessin?'

'Yes. I came to this church once many years ago.'

'I know. I have been the priest here for forty years. My name is Father Tessier. I knew your mother well. How is she?'

'Well and happy. She married my father's adjutant, Kurt Kleist, and has four children.'

'I'm glad for her. It was a bad business. I must lock the church now but why not join me for lunch at the presbytery?'

'May I ring my cousin from there? She is expecting me back before lunch.'

'Of course.' He looked again at the book. 'Monsieur Blanc remembers faithfully every year and I expect there are many others who do so more privately. Your father saved scores of lives, including my own brother-in-law's.'

'Didn't the Church regard him as a heretic and an adulterer?'

'He was both,' said the priest uncompromisingly. 'And he was also an enemy oppressor. He took life as well as gave it.'

Your father did not fight a sanitised war. I remembered Uncle Willi's words as I followed Father Tessier down the aisle towards the door, noting his limp and his somewhat elderly gait.

Here, I thought, at last was the key to my understanding of Klaus von Ströbel, of my mother's lawless love, of my very being.

The presbytery was warm, its atmosphere one of perpetual welcome, its furniture old and worn but comfortable. A middle-aged woman busied herself about the table, seemingly unperturbed by the unexpected addition, announced all to be ready and asked the priest if he would need anything more. When she had gone Father Tessier said grace and we sat down to a meal of roast lamb. Such fare had been a staple of Sunday lunches in England but here there was no mint sauce nor redcurrant jelly and somehow the meat tasted quite different. I realised that, since the age of five, I had sampled very little home cooking in France.

To my surprise and discomfort he began to press me on my Catholicism. Did I keep the faith? Had my mother kept the faith? I replied truthfully that I went most Sundays to mass but beyond that practised little, that my mother indeed remained loyal to the Church and was bringing up her children accordingly, although Kurt was a Lutheran. I told him of Ampleforth and he expressed admiration for Basil Hume.

As we reached the cheese he steered the conversation towards the changes in the Catholic Church, the second Vatican council and Pope Paul VI. It was not until we were settled in armchairs with the coffee I had helped him brew that he finally turned to the subject which had brought me to the presbytery.

'Both your parents have sat in that armchair at one time or another, both defiant of God's laws, both brave in their different ways, but your mother was a member of my flock and I heard her confessions and therefore I must speak no more of her because I am bound by the seal. Your father, on the other hand, was not a Catholic and never visited me in any spiritual capacity. He was a proud and decisive man who, when he had decided on a course of action, was, I imagine, not likely to ask anyone else for reassurance. Certainly he never found it necessary to apologise for the highly successful war he waged here on the Resistance or to explain why he played at dice with his own life by helping Jews to escape the clutches of the authorities.'

Father Tessier paused and I waited, conscious of some revelation in the shadows behind his words.

'Yet there came a moment, a couple of months before they were all driven out, when he sat where you are now and actually asked me if it could ever be possible, in the sight of God, for a man to love two women. Of course, I reminded him of the sanctity of his marriage vows and he just smiled and said no more. I tell you that because I want you to know that he really did love your mother and that she loved him. It was not simply lust on his part and a schoolgirl crush on your mother's. That does not make what happened right, of course.'

'Do you know my grandfather?'

'Yes, but I am his priest also and cannot discuss him with you. Both he and your father were exceptionally brave men. You will know of course that he played a large part in the Resistance?'

'Yes, and also that my father arrested him along with other members of my mother's family but made sure there was unlikely to be any evidence against them. If that is so then my father saved my grandfather's life.'

'Yes, but meanwhile he had ruined your grandfather's favourite daughter and, believe me, Klaus-Pierre, it *was* ruin. She was a Catholic girl from a highly respectable family and very young. He left her without reputation and with an illegitimate child. In nineteen forty-four that would have been quite enough for any woman to face even if the man in question had not been an enemy of France. And what was his excuse? That he could not help himself! That was what he said whenever I challenged him.'

I thought of Bev and my unwilling thraldom. Yet to a man who had vowed celibacy for a lifetime it seemed a weak answer and I was silent.

'Nevertheless there are many people alive today who would not be but for him, people who would have suffered horribly in Auschwitz for no crime other than being born into Jewish families. Paul Blanc was one of those men, his mother Jewish and his father a Catholic. So was my brother-in-law. Some of those he rescued have since had children and those also owe their existence to Klaus von Ströbel.'

I smiled. 'So do I.'

I watched the amusement enter his eyes. 'Yes, which is your mother's answer to her critics. He didn't save all those people without huge risk to himself and possibly also to his family in Germany. Once when I asked him why he did it he gave me the same answer as he did when I confronted him with his sins regarding Catherine Dessin: "I cannot help doing it, Father." I can see him now, laughing as he said it.'

I thought of Wolfgang Mueller's experiment with my imagination. 'Was he afraid?'

'He must have been. Who would not be? Yet his main anxiety was that your mother must never find out. He was terrified for her safety for all that he acted so calmly. I alone knew the extent of what he was doing because it was I who often alerted potential victims and passed on travel warrants and other documents. He needed somebody who could move about a great deal, visiting and being visited, and who better than a priest?'

'My father's wife and two of his children died at Dresden. If he had lived and returned to marry my mother, do you suppose my grandfather would have forgiven him?'

'I think your grandfather is still bitter over the death of his son who died fighting with the Free French. That, I suppose, would not have changed. Still, I know of one such case, although in that instance there was no child and the soldier in question was young and unmarried. The girl was pilloried badly after the Liberation but a year later the young man made contact and they eventually married. The families seem to get on. That, however, was rare. On the whole the men disappeared and left the girls to their fate.'

'It was a long time ago. My stepfather told me to look to the future and that is what I shall do. I cannot change what my father did nor how my grandfather thinks of him, nor, for that matter, what he thinks of me, but I shall always be grateful for this conversation, Father. You were a priest, a Frenchman, someone who had to pick up the pieces of oppression and iniquity, yet in the midst of that you made friends with one of the enemy and together saved a small part of mankind. There is a parable there somewhere.'

'Klaus-Pierre, I did not simply admire your father. I *liked* him. Even when I was angry with him on your mother's account I liked him. Even when he was unmistakably the enemy and doing his duty here as a German officer, I could not dislike him, and that had nothing to do with my own duty as a priest. He was good and kind and had a sense of humour. I suppose you could say he was a civilised man in what was then a pretty uncivilised world, but for what he did to your mother there was no excuse.'

'He loved her.'

'And she him, but he was married with young children and God could never bless what they were doing. Yet He is merciful and I am glad that her suffering is over, that good has come from it, that she is happy now and that you have been a blessing both to her and to your father's family.'

It sounded like a sermon and I half-expected him to ask me to join him in prayer, but instead he rose and held out his hand. A few minutes later I was thanking him on the doorstep of the presbytery, but I had meant it when I had told him I would always be grateful for our talk. *I liked him*. It was not a bad epitaph.

'Did you help with the washing-up?' asked Elsa when I recounted my morning's adventures.

I threw a paperback book at her, which she caught as deftly as those I had hurled in childhood.

'Will you see Monsieur Blanc?'

'No. The past is the past. Kurt was right when he said I travelled there too often. Let us live, *mea Caterina*, and let us love and care not what the crabbed old priests say.'

'What?'

'Catullus, or rather a serious misquoting of Catullus. I bet that is exactly what my father said to my mother when the likes of Father Tessier were pontificating about illicit love, although I am probably being unfair because he is a very kind priest and I suspect he tried to make things as smooth as he could for her in an impossible situation.'

'I doubt if Uncle Klaus ever said anything so abandoned. Aunt Angelika always says that he and my father were old men before their time. She puts it down to the First World War when they went straight from school into the fighting. Thank God we grew up without all that. Just imagine if Franz and Otto had been learning irregular verbs one day and killing the next, or the Pletz brothers had died before twenty. It's a miracle our parents stayed sane. Anyway, never mind wars. What are we doing with the rest of the day?'

'Versailles?'

'Haven't we left it a bit late? I think that is one for next time we come.'

For Elsa the return visit and Versailles came quickly, as Hans took her to Paris for their honeymoon, but it was to be five years before I returned. I did, however, visit England briefly the following year. Both Charles Emmett and Jack Marshall were progressing in their careers and Jack had moved his family to a small house in Surrey from which he commuted to London. He complained bitterly about the trains and the strikes.

Otto married and Anna began to take on some of the work previously done by Aunt Angelika at Ströbelfields. I settled down in Heidelberg, occasionally visiting my mother or Uncle Willi, but otherwise content with the university and my growing academic reputation. I spent the summer of 1973 in Rome, gathering material for a book on the Ara Pacis.

'Rome is the right place to be,' grumbled Charles Emmett to me in one letter. 'The unions here are hell.'

The winter of that year saw Jack Marshall take up the same refrain, as the miners' strike drove Britain into a three-day week. He painted a dramatic picture of working in the dark and the imminence of petrol rationing, but I was too immersed in the Ara Pacis to pay much attention to what was happening in another country and not even the change of government there the following year made much impact on me. England, once so central to my life, was now of only peripheral interest.

I responded, therefore, merely with a grunt of thanks when one of my senior colleagues, who had just returned from a week at Cambridge as a visiting lecturer, looked into my room and tossed me an English newspaper, but two hours later I emerged, exhausted, from a close study of an inscription involving a magnifying glass in the dying light and realised that I was too tired to make further progress that day.

I stood up and switched on the light, passing the newspaper as I did so. I vaguely thought of returning to the inscription now that it was better illuminated but instead sank into my easy chair and picked up the *Daily Telegraph*. The rest of the world was worried about oil, Watergate and Solzhenitsyn but Britain's preoccupation appeared to be the sale of a large mansion owned by an old aristocratic family which was facing unpayable death duties. Pages were devoted to Mentmore, the family history, inheritance tax and the preservation of historic buildings and, although I began interested, the relentless coverage soon had me turning the pages in search of other news.

The last page devoted to Mentmore offered a series of photographs of other unfortunates who had resorted to the sale of valuable assets in order to meet the ruinous expense of their estates, who had given up and handed over to the National Trust or who were predicting disaster when the present incumbent died. My attention was at once arrested by a picture of Harry Bullchester and his family.

I stared intrigued. George was there, already portly in his early thirties. Hugh, his elder brother, looked in better shape and the last thirteen years had been kind to Margery who appeared to look at the world less crossly but, however hard I tried to pretend otherwise, my eyes were drawn irresistibly to Arabella, to that open, laughing, carefree face and the hair which seemed to be blowing in the wind, although the photograph had been taken indoors. Under her arm was a small terrier, Marmaduke's successor.

The short paragraph underneath told how the family had sold a Rembrandt to make ends meet and how Hugh would almost certainly have to sell the estate when Lord Bullchester died.

'Fairyland,' I said aloud, remembering the opulence and my teenage awkwardness. 'I can't believe you lasted as long as you did.'

Something was tugging at my mind. I looked again at the photograph and its caption. Margery had married somebody called Teston and two of the children seated on the ground in front of the adults bore the same name, but Arabella was identified as Lady Arabella Bland.

She's not married. For a moment I was not sure if I had spoken the thought and then I did so, several times over, my voice rising in exaltation as I jumped from my chair. Arabella was, miraculously, at the age of twenty-eight, still free.

I told myself I was a fool and had better get back to the Ara Pacis. I threw away the newspaper and retrieved it from the wastepaper basket ten seconds later, I reasoned with my wild imagination, I drank a toast, I had to force a sober pace from myself as I returned to my lodgings where I cut out the photograph with trembling hands. I told myself I was behaving like a teenager with a crush, that if I met Arabella now she would be a stranger, that the girl I had known might have

339

matured into a very different adult, that if someone else were acting in such a fashion I would call him a fool.

Next day I wrote to Lord Bullchester, saying I had seen the article and was sorry the family was under such pressure, knowing I lied. I said I was following in my father's footsteps and was a very junior lecturer at Heidelberg and gave him such family news as I thought might interest him. No lover could have waited for a reply to a proposal with as much suspense as I waited for a reply to that letter.

It was three weeks before it came, three weeks in which I rushed to the post each day, three weeks in which I returned each evening, hoping to see a letter on the small table in the hall. When my landlady called me to supper I hoped only that she would hand me an envelope, telling me she had picked it up and carelessly mislaid it. When my students embarked on answers to my questions, I thought of a walk in a storm with a girl clinging to my arm in fear and sometimes had scarcely wrenched my attention back by the time the answer was finished, unable to praise or criticise because I had heard not a word of it.

When the letter did arrive I left it on my desk, unopened all day, before tearing the envelope apart and reading without any comprehension so eager was I to reach the only part of it which mattered.

Lord Bullchester thought it very kind of me to write. It was remiss of him not to have done so before now and indeed he and George sometimes wondered what had happened to me and how life was treating me. Damn George, I muttered impatiently. What did I care for George's thoughts? Lady Bullchester was in good health and there were now nine grandchildren for her to dote on, as all but one of their children had married.

Perhaps I remembered Arabella? I once rescued her from a bad thunderstorm. She sent her regards. Regards? The word sounded cold, formal, discouraging. She, poor soul, had been through an appalling time, having been engaged to a very pleasant young man whom all the family adored and then having to watch while he died of cancer: *'Such a cruel disease ... terrible to die so young ... had stayed optimistic ... wedding twice postponed ... his poor parents ... only child ... only recently that Arabella seems to have got over it ... wonderful daughter...'*

Then came the line, which, during the last three weeks I had read a score of times in my imagination: *'If ever you are in Britain we would love to see you.'*

eighteen

Two for Sorrow

'Oh, go away!'

I turned sharply, alarmed by the anguish in Arabella's voice, and saw her staring at two magpies which had flown into the field through which we walked. I had been a little ahead of her because there was a gate to be opened and a previous walk had revealed it to be a particularly difficult one.

'What's the matter? Are they after something?' I looked in vain for the cause of her distress.

'No, but there are two of them. I hate two magpies.'

I was baffled, taken aback by the insistence in her voice.

'It's an old saying we have in this country. One for joy, two for sorrow. I used to laugh at it but there were two magpies on the Great Lawn when Henry died.'

For the first time in years I remembered the large black birds which had flapped through the heavens at moments of particular anguish in my childhood. I went to Arabella and hugged her but she remained inconsolable, unwillingly looking back at the birds, undistracted from them even by the effort of mastering the gate. We would have saved ourselves the trouble and climbed it but for Arabella's having pulled a calf muscle, which meant jumping down would have been unduly painful.

'Don't look at them,' I said, abandoning any attempt at reasoning.

She turned back to me and smiled but her eyes were tormented. I was about to urge her forwards when a rhyme formed itself in my mind, something I had heard years ago, perhaps only once, when English was still an awkward language for me.

One for sorrow, two for joy, three for a girl, four for a boy. Unthinking, wanting only to relieve her fear and misery, I exclaimed in delight and recited the old superstition.

'Two for joy!' I looked in the direction of the birds but only one remained. Groaning inwardly, I turned back to Arabella but she had been looking resolutely away and had not noticed.

'Not you as well! How can everyone be so blind? I told you there were *two* magpies on the lawn when Henry died, not one. It's two for sorrow.'

This time I had the sense not to argue, seeking instead to distract her with aspects of the countryside and the antics of Scooter, a terrier of the same breed as the late Marmaduke, pleased that the shadow soon lifted from her face.

It was the summer of 1975. I had repressed the instinct to accept Lord Bullchester's invitation immediately, judging it insensitive, but had written at once to Arabella. It had been my intention to visit at Easter but the family was in mourning for a close relative. The disappointment which filled Arabella's letter caused the hope to hammer painfully in my heart, even though my journey had been postponed.

'Good luck, but be careful,' had been Otto's advice. 'You haven't met her since she was fifteen. She may not be the same.'

'You were only sixteen,' warned my mother. 'You will both have changed a great deal in that time.'

'There is a difference between a girl and a boy and a man and a woman and this woman has been through hell,' pointed out Uncle Willi.

'Don't take any notice of them,' advised Lotte.

'They tried to stop me marrying Rudi and they were wrong.'

The summer of 1975 also saw an outbreak of celebrations as Europe celebrated the thirtieth anniversary of peace. There was the usual argument as to whether it was appropriate for Germans to take part and a vague air of embarrassment attended the watching of news bulletins when we were gathered together.

'Thirty years!' exclaimed Arabella as if it were a hundred. 'And, just think, your father and mine were in the First World War as well.'

So was Pierre Dessin, I thought, but he had come through unscathed. Only the Second World War appeared to have scarred him with hatred. To fight in the hell of the trenches was as nothing compared to losing his eldest child. Certainly he would never take part in any celebrations which included Germans.

At the end of the first week of my stay Judy Margolis came to lunch. We greeted each other enthusiastically but an image of our last farewell rose in my mind and, from the expression in her eyes, I thought her own memory similarly engaged. The intervening thirteen years had not been kind to her and she had aged more visibly than Arabella's parents. The sun beat down with almost tropical force but she alone among the ladies wore a long-sleeved blouse. I tried not to think about the reason, about the arm beneath the sleeve with its number, its reminder of iniquity. Did she cover it for herself or for me?

In the second week I invited Arabella to Ströbelfields and she said she would come the following

Easter, because Christmas was for families. In the third week I returned to Heidelberg uncertain whether I had been right not to propose but very certain that I was in love and that it was returned. The Ara Pacis competed unequally with my memories of the visit and a few weeks later I found myself back in England with Arabella running to meet me at the station.

'Must you go back?' she wept as term loomed.

'Yes, but you could come with me and see Heidelberg. My landlady has a spare room. The only problem is that I shall be working.'

'I'll ask Daddy.'

I stared at her in disbelief. She was twenty-nine.

'He relies on me to help run this place. As you will have noticed, it isn't like it used to be.'

I could hardly have helped noticing. There must have been fewer than half the number of servants who had so confused me on my first visit. I performed my own packing and unpacking, members of the family poured and handed round drinks, weeds were visible in some of the flowerbeds and I was met at the station by Lord Bullchester himself. It was still a far cry from Ströbelfields and I wondered if Lady Bullchester would ever spend as much time organising meals and clearing up as did Aunt Angelika. I thought of my mother dusting, of Otto lugging wood, of Elsa ironing, of the arguments among us when, as children, we disputed whose turn it was to wash up and whose to dry.

I was unsurprised when Lord Bullchester said he could not spare her. I knew that he did not want Lady Arabella Bland compromising her name by taking a room in a lodging house occupied by her boyfriend. I was angry with myself for not having suggested a hotel and that another member of the family accompany her, but when I put this to her she shook her head.

'He is very protective. He thinks I am not yet over Henry and that we are moving too fast. Mother disagrees but says I must not worry him.'

'It is nineteen seventy-five.'

'I know, but he has been such a brick. He would probably feel happier if it was Ströbelfields rather than Heidelberg.'

I gave up but not before I had extracted a promise that she would let nothing stand in the way of her visit at Easter. The months which stretched between seemed unbearably long but I returned to Germany hugging myself on hope.

I spent the whole of the Christmas holiday at Ströbelfields because my mother and Kurt were also there throughout the festivities, as were Hedy and her family and Elsa and Hans. I was relieved that Alessandra was not among the family gathering, for her attitude towards my mother had never thawed and she remained offhand with me. The Pletzes arrived the day after Christmas and the children played deafeningly in the barn.

Otto suggested a walk and he, Ernst Pletz, Elsa and I set off through the snow. We wandered to the lake and tested the ice with our toes, finding it thin and treacherous. The others began recalling how Elsa had fallen in but I could see only a vision of Arabella skating here, dancing as gracefully and confidently as had Elsa before her immersion. Ahead of us ran the Pletz dogs but I saw only Scooter.

'What are you dreaming about?' demanded Ernst.

Elsa and Otto exchanged grins.

Elsa was still grinning as she and Hans waved goodbye at the beginning of January. I watched their car winding slowly away in the distance closely followed by Hedy's. My mother and Kurt left two days later and Ströbelfields was once more childless. Uncle Will retreated to his library, Aunt Angelika said we would have to be content with cold meals for two days and Otto and Anna announced their intention to go to a party ten miles away, stay overnight and return the next morning. They invited me to join them but I did not know the hosts and preferred to spend time with Uncle Willi.

The snow was falling harder when, early that evening, Otto and Anna prepared to leave. I emerged from the warmth and light of the stables into the cold air to hear Uncle Willi urging Otto to drive carefully and Aunt Angelika advising Anna to wrap up well. Holding a bucket of horse feed in one hand, I waved to them with the other, calling out that I hoped they enjoyed the party, joking with Otto that he should not drink too much, complimenting Anna on her new dress.

We watched the tail lights of the car dwindle into the distance before I returned to the stables and the others to the house. Otto had recently acquired a new horse, a large bay mare, strong but nervous, still uncertain of the other horses and of the dogs which ran round her feet whenever Otto rode her. My other tasks completed, I spent a few minutes with the animal, rubbing her nose and talking to her, telling her it wasn't a bad life for a horse in the von Ströbel household.

I switched off the stable lights, checked the bolts on the door of each stall and went out into the yard, only to start back as two large, black crows suddenly flapped down immediately in front of me, intent on some bread which I had dropped on my way from the house to the stables. A sudden shaft of unease entered me and I looked at the birds with loathing. Two for sorrow.

I shouted at them and they flapped away, cawing in protest, while I turned my irritation on myself. I had never been a superstitious mortal and even if I had been it was, according to the rhyme, two for joy so I should be pleased not fearful. The fear however remained, at intervals unsettling me with its formless threat, and I was quite disproportionately relieved when Otto and Anna safely returned the next day.

At the end of that week I too left, leaning out of the train window, telling them that I would see them at Easter when all my happiness came from knowing that it was Arabella I would see.

Six weeks later I was back at Ströbelfields. Uncle Willi was seriously ill, his already weakened lungs full of pneumonia. As I looked at him, alternately shivering and feverish in his hospital bed, I prepared for the worst but he rallied and returned home, where he refused to stay in bed but was too enervated to leave his library in which he sat all day, his meals brought by a grey-faced Aunt

Angelika. Nevertheless there were signs of a slow recovery and I judged it safe to return to the university, delaying my departure by two days when I learned that Wolfgang was coming from Cloppenburg with drawings of the Wanderer Bear's latest travels.

'Surely it's too soon for Uncle Willi to be working,' I protested to Otto.

'Oh, it isn't really work these days. They let him see the stuff on a for-your-information basis. After all he still writes most of the stories and the Bear keeps him amused.'

I had not seen Wolfgang since he had first come to Ströbelfields and was curious to see whether he had changed after years of well-paid employment. His hair was now short and conventionally cut and he had put on some weight but otherwise he was the Wolfgang I had met on the channel ferry.

'Do you still do hypnosis?' I teased.

'It was *not* hypnosis,' he insisted.

I could not ask about his other activity other than obliquely when I told him about Arabella and said I hoped his fortune would be as good.

He shook his head. 'No. I meant what I told you when I said the line stops with me.'

'Your sister?'

'Cannot have children.'

'I'm sorry.'

'I am not at all sorry.'

It would have been useless to press him. I shrugged and he began asking me about Arabella and whether I had been to London or Paris in the last couple of years. He had been to Norway the previous year and was as unenthusiastic about the

349

people as he was enthusiastic about their fjords.

'They don't like Germans. Thirty years of peace have passed them by.'

'They went through rather a lot. We thought they might be good candidates for producing the master race and–'

'*We* thought nothing of the damned sort. We were still in our cots when the war ended.'

'Perhaps they think *we* bear a bad seed. If you can think that about your family then the world can think it about a nation which has caused two wars and slaughtered millions in the twentieth century. It is about as logical, which is to say not logical at all.'

'That is quite different,' snapped Wolfgang, but he could not tell me how.

I did not see him much after that because he was closeted in the library with Uncle Willi for most of the day. When they emerged my uncle looked vastly better and I thought that if Wolfgang's drawings had been so instrumental in cheering him up then we should all see them after supper, but before he went to bed Uncle Willi called me into the library, thanked me for interrupting my term to look after him, offered to reimburse my fares and then asked me if Wolfgang had ever tried to hypnotise me.

I nodded, the truth slowly dawning. 'Yes, and very effective it was too, but he insists it is not hypnosis.'

'Whatever it is, it is pretty powerful. He asked me to lie back in my chair and imagine myself well and now indeed I feel a great deal better, even if I am still wheezing and coughing. I am half-inclined to ask him to stay and do that every day but I do not like people playing tricks with my mind, so perhaps I prefer to get better naturally. I shall still get up late tomorrow, so if I do not see you, have a good term and see you at Easter. We are all dying to meet Arabella.'

'Let us know when to expect you and Arabella.' Aunt Angelika echoed the sentiment next morning. 'Otto will be here in a moment to run you to the station. He is out on that wretched horse, a bad buy if ever there was one.'

The horse in question was the bay mare, still a terrified and unpredictable animal who shied at the smallest rustle in a hedge. So far, Otto's kindness and equestrian skill had been employed to no avail, but he refused to concede defeat.

'In a year's time it will be the most docile horse in all Germany,' he had predicted cheerfully.

Going outside to help Wolfgang load the drawings into his car, a second-hand Jaguar which I coveted the moment I set eyes on it, I saw Otto riding along the verge of the drive, still beyond the lake. The mare was at full gallop, its rider conscious of my train.

'Go carefully past that brute,' I cautioned Wolfgang. 'It's not exactly house-trained.'

He nodded and sat in the car, waving to me and Aunt Angelika. I saw him slow down to a crawl as he drew near Otto but the horse began rearing and plunging. For a moment it seemed Otto had mastered it but, as we watched, Otto was thrown, to land on his back on top of Wolfgang's car before sliding off, seemingly in slow motion, head first into the road. For the first time in my life I heard Aunt Angelika scream.

'Get an ambulance,' I yelled over my shoulder as I raced towards the scene.

Otto was lying in the stillness of death, his neck broken. The mare had already passed me, careering back towards the stables, her bridle trailing, her nostrils flaring, her eyes distended with fright. Wolfgang rose from his knees beside Otto and we stared at each other across the body.

Then I saw his eyes look past me and, turning, I saw Aunt Angelika and Anna running towards us. I moved to intercept them, to give them some warning, to prevent them seeing Otto before they knew he was dead. My aunt slowed down, her eyes pleading for reassurance, but Anna evaded my outstretched arm, flinging herself down beside Otto, calling him, sobbing.

I nodded as Aunt Angelika's eyes asked a question to which she already knew the answer. She knelt down beside Anna, her own body shaking convulsively, her hand on Otto's cheek. She spoke only once and then it was to mention neither her own grief or Anna's.

'My God,' she breathed. 'This will probably kill Willi.'

I stood looking down at Otto, now covered by Wolfgang's coat, wondering how the life could be so suddenly gone, how the wild energy that had been my cousin could so suddenly dissolve into nothingness. It could not be possible that we would never hear that booming laugh, that cheerful banter again. Otto just *was*. He couldn't *not be*. He could not just *end*. If I looked up the mirage would disappear and Otto would be riding towards me. I looked up and saw the woods and fields of the estate – empty, empty of Otto.

Aunt Angelika was trying to calm and comfort a near-hysterical Anna as I came back to reality. I looked back at the house but no one came from it. Uncle Willi must still be asleep, oblivious to death and anguish, to the morning sun which failed to warm us, to loss and grief.

'The ambulance will be here soon,' said Wolfgang, knowing that it still had miles to cover. 'We should get Anna back to the house.'

Anna protested and would not go, would not leave her husband's body. Later it was a shock when one of the ambulancemen asked me, out of her hearing, if I thought the widow needed treatment. Widow! Anna was thirty-three.

Aunt Angelika told Uncle Willi, who did not appear for the rest of the day, seeing only the doctor and the pastor who called in the afternoon. Wolfgang, assured there was nothing he could do, had by then left. Lotte joined us while the doctor was still with Uncle Willi and together we set about contacting the others. I left Alessandra, who was in Tokyo, to Lotte while I telephoned first Franz's monastery and then Elsa. I used the house telephone while Lotte used the business line we had installed for Wanderer Bear. Aunt Angelika went to the barn to use the other phone, which we had not disconnected when my mother and Kurt left.

'Hedy is in a terrible state,' my aunt reported later. 'She was very close to Otto. It must be unbearable to lose a twin, much worse than for the rest of them.'

'Alessandra says Franz should get out of his monastery and look after Uncle Willi and Ströbelfields,' said Lotte when she had finally been connected to Tokyo. 'She's flying back tomorrow if she can.'

'Elsa was quite brave,' I told them. 'Should someone be checking on Uncle Willi?'

Aunt Angelika shook her head. 'The doctor gave him sedatives and said let him sleep. Lotte, you should go home now. There is nothing more any of us can do tonight.'

'Your cousin?' said a sceptical professor the following morning when I rang to ask if my teaching commitments could be covered until after the funeral. 'Dessin, this is the middle of term. Of course, if it was a very close relative–'

'He was my brother in all but name. We were brought up together.'

'Very well, but it is most irregular.'

I half-expected Alessandra to use the same words when she found it was I and not Uncle Willi or Aunt Angelika who was managing the funeral arrangements. My uncle was not yet well enough and Aunt Angelika had her hands full attending to him, Anna and the family, whose members were now arriving daily.

Anna chose the hymns and left everything else to me, wanting only to grieve and be left alone. It was I who dealt with undertakers, sent out notices, talked to the pastor and handled queries. Lotte looked in occasionally to help and took over the arrangements for the reception, but when the day came we found ourselves, mere cousins, sitting behind the massed ranks of the siblings and their

354

families. I remembered Omi's funeral and how my mother and I had sat behind the rest, behind the *legitimate* family.

I looked at the coffin with a sadness that even now was tinged with disbelief. It had happened too quickly to be real.

Walter Pletz put his hand on my shoulder as I was passing round sandwiches at the reception, 'You've been a tower of strength to them.'

'Lotte's been pretty handy too.'

He smiled. 'She's a good girl. It's been grim. The worst thing that can happen to a man is to have to bury his son. It can't have helped that Willi was so ill.'

Uncle Willi himself said much the same thing when I once again said goodbye to him in the library. Was it really only a week ago that I had stood here and talked about bringing Arabella home for Easter? Only a week since Wolfgang had been showing him the Wanderer Bear drawings? Only a week since Otto had been filling the house with his presence?

Anna had gone home with her parents after the funeral and I was glad she was not there when the mare was taken away. Walter Pletz had found it a good home but I could not bring myself to pat it or look at it and it was a couple of farm-hands who coaxed it into the horsebox while the rest of us stayed indoors.

As Aunt Angelika drove me to the station I stared straight ahead, not wanting to see the lines in her face made harsh by the merciless northern light or the eyes still red from the sporadic weeping which often caught her unawares and which, while it lasted, caused her to shake uncontrollably. We had always taken her strength for granted, assuming that her determination and independence would carry her through any turmoil of body or soul, and all our eyes had been turned in Uncle Willi's direction as we sought anxiously for the slightest sign of a worsening of his precarious health.

We were dispersing now back to our own lives without having solved the very practical but urgent question of who was to take over Otto's role and run Ströbelfields. Alessandra had continued to insist it was Franz's duty but I could not see why it should be less necessary for him to pursue his chosen path than for the rest of us. There was some talk of my mother and Kurt returning but I did not think my stepfather would relish a return to the von Ströbel shadow. In Cloppenburg he was the undisputed master of his own house, here he was but a pale substitute for my father.

Three weeks before the Easter holiday, when my head and heart were full of Arabella, Uncle Willi telephoned to ask if I had a spare weekend in which to visit Ströbelfields, offering me a helicopter to save the long train journey north. Amazed, I watched as the estate came into view below me, identifying its features, appreciating its scale afresh. We came down in a field below the lake and saw farmhands and their children gathered to see the spectacle.

'They'll get covered with dirt if they stand that close,' warned the pilot. 'Haven't they seen a chopper before?'

'Not landing here. I've lived here since I was five and this is a first.'

He smiled and, when I was on my way to the house, I looked back to see him lifting a child inside to explore his wonderful machine. The generation which took moon travel in its stride could yet marvel at a helicopter.

Aunt Angelika was looking much better and had recovered some of her old brusqueness. Uncle Willi was still weak and wheezed heavily but his spirits were showing some sign of at least outward recovery. I asked after Anna and he said she was still with her parents.

'She is still considering what to do but on one point she is very clear: she has not the slightest wish to come back and make her life here, where the only real attraction was Otto. The burden of running this place is one she does not want and, when she is ready for it, she will return to her former career. Although it must be the last thing on her mind, I have no doubt she will re-marry and forge a life for herself in which the rest of us are but distant memories and, in time, even Otto will be one of those.'

I made some facile comment about time and healing. Uncle Willi began to cram tobacco into his favourite pipe and I winced, listening to the rasp of his lungs. As if reading my thoughts he smiled and tapped the pipe affectionately.

'They told me to give this up years ago but I've passed my three score and ten years which the Bible tells us is man's allotted lifespan and I'm still here, but I won't be here for ever and that's why we should talk. I need to settle the future of

357

Ströbelfields now that Otto has gone.'

He stumbled slightly over the last words and I waited uncertainly.

'My brothers are dead and your Aunt Angelika is getting on. It is time to hand on to the next generation but Franz has renounced all worldly concerns and Otto is dead. That leaves you.'

I looked at him, nonplussed, finding nothing to say. Eventually I managed a single word: 'Alessandra?'

'Will strongly disapprove but she, of course, was offered the chance to take over the reins herself. In this day and age it does not have to be a man, even though that would mean losing the von Ströbel name, but she refused and I can't say I blame her. She travels the world with a diplomat husband, who is ambitious and devoted to his career, and this is not a job that can be done from a distance so in effect she would be choosing between him and Ströbelfields. She has chosen him and rightly so.'

'What about the others?'

'Hedy's husband is also unwilling to embark on such a change and, anyway, Hedy herself has grown to prefer metropolitan ways to rural ones. She had two elder brothers and never expected to inherit the estate so she went off and built her own life as I wanted her to do. Elsa is different. Apart from you she was the last to leave and, because she has been late in marrying, has come back often. I think she would have liked to bring a family up here but Hans is understandably frightened by the number of estates which have gone down. Few survived the war and fewer still the age of equality. He fears failure more than most. Eventually they said no.'

Eventually? Otto had been dead only a matter of weeks and yet the issue of his successor appeared to have been settled with almost indecent haste. There could be only one reason for such urgency and I looked at Uncle Willi with a sinking heart.

'That left Lotte. As Klaus's daughter she had a very clear claim and there might have been some sense in joining the two estates but Rudi thinks the one he will inherit is problem enough and Walter Pletz agrees. They have hung on by their fingernails and, but for the Wanderer Bear, we might have been in the same state. We did consider Walter's leaving his to Werner or Ernst and then Rudi taking over ours, but Rudi and Lotte have put a huge amount of effort into saving the Pletz estate and prefer to follow through the fruits of their labours.'

'Uncle Willi, you haven't had all these discussions in the course of three weeks?'

'No. Before Anna was on the scene all our eggs were in the Otto basket and I thought it wise to have a back-up strategy in case for any reason he couldn't or wouldn't carry on. He wasn't keen to take over when Franz announced his intentions to withdraw from the world. So I sounded everyone out then and thought Elsa would probably fulfil the role if she had to. There was no Hans at that time. When Otto died I simply asked them all if they had changed their minds and they had not.'

'Do they know you are offering it to me?'

'Yes.'

'And they don't mind?'

'With the exception of Alessandra they consider it entirely natural – you all grew up together. Alessandra was very fond of Aunt Ellie and never really forgave your mother. She would have felt the same way had Klaus survived Ellie and married his Catherine. But she had her own chance and refused. There are more distant relations in Switzerland but nobody else here would seriously put their claims before yours. You are Klaus's son.'

'I am his illegitimate son.'

'Some very old families started life that way. I think you will find that Lord Bullchester owes his ancestry to some extramarital dalliance on the part of Charles the Second.'

'How on earth do you know?'

'I was clearing out some papers the other day and found a letter from your father describing the Bullchester household. I have kept it for you in case you find it amusing. Clearly they are not remotely bothered by the circumstances of your birth or they would not encourage your courtship of their daughter.'

'I always thought they were more likely to worry because I was a German.'

'Unlikely. The British royal family has German blood. If Arabella wants to marry you I think she will not mind being Arabella von Ströbel and living in Germany.'

'Not Arabella Dessin? I'll have to change my name?'

'You do not *have* to, but if you agree to take on

Ströbelfields I would be grateful if you did. It is, after all, because you are Klaus's son that you are succeeding to the family possessions. It will be, I am afraid, mainly possessions – land, buildings, farms. I must leave most of the money to your cousins and half-sister. At least Arabella will not be new to the problem.'

I could manage only a ghost of a smile. 'I am half-French and Arabella is all English. Our children will be German only in fractions.'

'What of it? Alessandra is spelled that way because her grandmother was Italian. Your children will be called von Ströbel and grow up in Germany and will probably marry Germans so the wheel may turn full circle. Now, put me out of my suspense and tell me you agree.'

'Klaus-Pierre von Ströbel. K-P v S. Even the initials sound a mouthful. Uncle Willi, I don't know what to say.'

'Say yes.'

'Yes.'

'Without even consulting Arabella? You are not what they call modern man.'

I looked at him. *Sorting out the succession. Clearing out his papers.*

'How long have they given you?'

His expression did not alter. 'Six months, so for heaven's sake, hurry up and propose to the girl so that I can get to the wedding.'

nineteen

From Death to Birth

My mother sat in the front pew flanked by Elsa and Lotte when I married Arabella that June. In the event, Uncle Willi was too ill to travel to England and Aunt Angelika would not leave him. Kurt had stayed behind to look after the younger children, saying that my mother would have plenty to do without having to worry about him and his wheelchair. Jeanne and Edouard had sent generous presents but both found it impossible to leave France for the wedding itself.

Ernst and Werner Pletz had made the journey and Charles Emmett, along with Jack Marshall, had come complete with their families. Two of Lotte's children and the Kleist twins were in the long train of bridesmaids and pageboys which followed Arabella up the aisle in descending order of height.

Everyone else was there by invitation from the Bullchesters and the large church was packed with their family and friends.

'Half Debrett's must be here,' muttered Charles who was my best man. In my imagination it had always been Otto who stood beside me as we waited for my bride, Otto who calmed my nerves with his humour, Otto who made a funny speech in uncertain English.

'The other half will be at the reception,' I whispered.

He smiled. 'This may well be one of the last of these great weddings. Look well on it for you may never see its like again.'

The same theme was common to the press coverage which followed. The event took up two pages in *'Jennifer's Diary'* in *Harpers and Queen*, and only fractionally less in the *Tatler*. To my amazement it also featured prominently in the inside pages of the newspapers where I was described as the nephew of Willi von Ströbel, the inventor of the Wanderer Bear and where the details of my parentage were politely overlooked, despite the photographs of my mother looking beautiful and radiant.

We were in Casablanca on our honeymoon when the less fastidious papers released the lurid details to the world. Lady Arabella Bland, younger daughter of the Earl of Bullchester, had been consoled, following the tragic death of her fiancé, by the illegitimate son of a German general and a French teenage collaborator. The recent marriage had been attended by dukes and even minor royalty such was the standing of Lord and Lady Bullchester, who refused to comment.

Henry, the papers claimed, was distantly connected to royalty and the match had been widely welcomed but Lady Arabella had been devastated by his death, *of which this upstart adventurer took full advantage.* The words were in my imagination only but the implication was clear enough without them. There were pictures of my mother taken at the wedding and, in the absence of any

363

from her youth, also of the family home in Paris where she grew up and where her parents still lived.

'My grandfather must be apoplectic,' I told Arabella as we looked at the paper, now three days out of date and which we had found on sale in a large international hotel, having been alerted by a call from Lord Bullchester. 'He thought he had got rid of the scandal when he disowned my mother.'

'It's all rot,' protested Arabella. 'Henry connected to royalty indeed! He was the twentieth cousin about fifty-five times removed of an in-law of someone who had married a cousin of a minor royal.'

I grinned at the outraged exaggeration. 'My mother was twenty when I was born, not a teenager, my father was not an enthusiastic Nazi who sent Jews to Auschwitz and I most certainly did not grow up in servanted splendour at Ströbelfields in a rich family untouched by the war. No family in all Germany was untouched by the war and Ströbelfields was surviving by the skin of its teeth.'

'I suppose we're lucky they haven't tracked us down. Thank heaven we didn't broadcast the whereabouts of the honeymoon. Given this paper is three days old, it will have blown over by now. I wish I could publish the scandalous lives of the editors' families. I'm so sorry. I'm afraid the British press loves scandal and it's just obsessed by aristocratic ones.'

'Ditto the German press, not that there is much aristocracy left for it to write about, but Uncle Willi is famous because of the Wanderer Bear and

364

if it is all over the British press then the scandal will have reached Germany by now.'

'It's all quite friendly here,' Kurt reassured me when I rang. 'We don't tend to dwelt on what we did in Paris and it is regarded as heart-warming that a nephew of the Wanderer Bear inventor has married in such fairytale surroundings. There is a rather endearing cartoon of a wedding between a Wanderer Bear and a beautiful bear princess which we have cut out for you.'

'Are you sure?'

'Yes and, anyway, it is now well known that your uncle is very ill and it wouldn't do circulation figures any good to be seen as having killed that nice Uncle Willi who writes all those wonderful stories for children. I promise you there is no pressure here or at Ströbelfields so enjoy your honeymoon and stop worrying.'

We took his advice but on our return I rang Jeanne.

'It was pretty ghastly while it lasted. There were English journalists everywhere, at my parents' house and even at our old convent school. They tracked down Annette who said some very harsh things but the rest of us, including Papa, maintained a dignified silence. They actually dared to try it on with Father Tessier and got short shrift. Then it just suddenly went quiet again. How is Arabella taking it?'

'Philosophically. She is tough beneath that vulnerable exterior, but she feels, quite unreasonably, responsible, saying that if she hadn't been the daughter of an earl this would never have happened and that perhaps we should have had a quiet, private wedding instead of that extravaganza and, believe me, it *was* an extravaganza. It was enough to make "The Field of the Cloth of Gold" look like a paupers' affair. No wonder they resort to selling Rembrandts.'

Jeanne laughed and I asked after her family. They were, she told me, all well but her father was slowing down a little with age.

Two weeks later Pierre Dessin died peacefully in his sleep, unforgiving and in turn unforgiven. He would have been eighty the following month. I wrote to Jeanne and also to Edouard and, in my letter to him, I enclosed one to be passed on to my grandmother if he thought it right to do so, stressing that I would understand if he thought it unwise. He replied that he thought it too soon.

Shortly afterwards Uncle Willi became bedridden. My cousins came to Ströbelfields, knowing they were seeing their father for the last time, as did the entire Pletz family. Walter spent hours with him and I could hear his booming laugh and my uncle's wheezing response but when he came downstairs it was with a taut, unhappy face. For the next seven weeks he came each day and left with the same expression.

Franz came from his monastery and stayed three days. As I drove him to the station he asked me to stop at the place where Otto had died. We paused while he prayed and I joined him in the Catholic prayer for the dead: *'And let perpetual light shine upon him. May he rest in peace, Amen.'*

'So much has changed,' Franz said sadly as we resumed our journey. 'Thank you for taking on Ströbelfields. I do not know what would have happened if you had not come into our lives.'

'I am very sure about what would have happened to me if I had not come here and I shudder merely to think of it. The thanks are entirely mine.'

'On the contrary you were a gift from the very start. Omi had been desperately cut up by the loss of Willi-Lothar who was her favourite grandson. If Otto and I had not been so much older we would have been bitterly jealous, but along you came, looking exactly like him and roughly the same age as he was when he died. She adored you.'

'And I her. I wonder if my other granny will ever want to know me.'

'Time heals.'

'Time also runs out.'

'You made your own act of peace. Others must respond how they will. You have gained Jeanne and whatshisname.'

'Edouard. Yes, but I made an even greater act of peace in Paris. I made peace with my father, thanks to a coincidence in which I found that Frenchmen were praying for his soul and that a priest remembered him with affection. He used his life to save other lives and that is more than I can say for myself. I learned to stop judging him.'

'Coincidence is a term we use when we are embarrassed to acknowledge the power of God in our lives. If we trust Him He is merciful and just.' Brother Blaise's voice was as stern as I had ever heard it.

'If You are merciful and just, then it is time to take Uncle Willi,' I told the Deity as I sat by the old man's bedside and watched him sleeping. He was propped against three pillows, his Jutland-damaged lungs so weakened by his illness that he could no longer sleep lying down. He lived only to suffer but even as I said the words I knew I did not mean them. I wanted him always to be there.

I began to whisper the prayer for the dying. *'Go forth, O Christian Soul, in the name of the Father who created thee—'*

'Papist mumbo-jumbo.' His eyes had opened and he was looking at me with amusement.

I smiled back but it occurred to me that perhaps he was not enthusiastic about the prospect of Ströbelfields passing to a Catholic line. I had asked him about illegitimacy and foreignness and he had said they were irrelevant, but neither of us had mentioned religion, I because I had not thought of it, he, perhaps, because he could not be both polite and truthful. I remembered the conversation between him and Walter Pletz which, so many years ago, I had overhead as I passed the library. There had been no effective ecumenical movement then and now it was a different world but prejudices could linger through even the greatest social changes, as I knew to my cost, and I suspected that, despite his teasing tone, I was encountering one now.

Uncle Willi was following a different train of thought. 'Remember that nothing lasts for ever. If Ströbelfields does not survive, don't blame yourself. In many ways Walter and I are from a vanished world.'

'Born in the last century,' I reminded him, and was rewarded by a smile. 'If it has survived all the upheaval of the last sixty years it should be good for at least another sixty.'

I remembered how he had made Otto give up medicine to come and run the estate and wondered if he blamed himself, if he reasoned that Otto might be alive now had he been allowed to pursue his own choice of life, if that was why he was telling me that the von Ströbel possessions were, after all, expendable.

Suddenly there was urgency in his voice. 'Let it always be a haven for any of us in distress. When my wife was ill, in the war, we came and lived here. Gerhardt would have been looked after here all his life. If Franz should ever leave his monastery he will have nothing. Not a *pfennig*. Make sure this is a refuge for him or any of them.'

I promised him and squeezed his hand. He had given a refuge to a small, persecuted child and that child would certainly not turn others away, not even proud, cold Alessandra.

'Ask Geli to look in,' he said when I rose to go.

Aunt Angelika came and was with him when he died.

In the week which followed I was reminded in a dozen small, careless, hurtful ways that although I was master of Ströbelfields I had not been Uncle Willi's son. His children arrived and made the arrangements for his funeral, discussed which hymns he would have chosen, divided the purely personal and sentimental of his possessions among themselves and fussed over Aunt Angelika who suddenly no longer seemed the formidable figure who had dominated our childhoods.

'His niece,' I heard Lotte say in response to one telephone caller. She rolled her eyes and called Alessandra.

'Wanderer Bear,' she enlightened me as she handed the receiver to her cousin. 'They wanted to speak to "a member of the family" about a "fitting tribute" but a mere niece won't do.'

'Don't,' I said. 'They can't know that we think of him as a father. In the absence of a widow, it's natural enough to ask for a son or daughter.'

'I wonder if it would have been like this if he had adopted us instead of just bringing us up. Talking of widows, Anna is coming to the funeral. I should like to know how she is coping.'

'She sounded well when she rang up,' said Elsa who had joined us in time to hear Lotte's query. 'Klaus-Pierre, Wanderer Bear is sending a coachload. Can we manage them all?'

So she had heard the rest of our conversation as well. From then on she and Hedy made a point of including Lotte and me in discussions. Franz arrived the day before the funeral and I realised that he had been consulted as little as we had. Alessandra had sorted out a small pile of photographs and religious books for him, which, mindful of monastic restrictions, he diminished by half.

'What about the family Bible?' offered Alessandra.

'It stays where it has always been, here at Ströbelfields.' Franz's tone brooked no argument.

I thought of the family tree folded away inside it, the one which had made no mention of my existence but to which I must now somehow add myself and Arabella if a continuous record were to be maintained. I half-expected Alessandra to lay claim to it in order to prevent such pollution but they all left the library alone, as if recognising that it was as much a part of Ströbelfields as the bricks and mortar. I could not yet bear to go there, could not face its emptiness.

When I at last did so I was shocked to find all the windows open, combating the stale smell of pipe tobacco about which Aunt Angelika so often bitterly complained. I longed for that familiar smell and when I noticed it in one of my uncle's old jackets I spirited the garment away to my own room and put it at the back of the wardrobe.

Walter gave the funeral address, looking every bit as solemn as when he had stood with Uncle Willi by my father's new grave. The choice of 'Jesu, Joy of Man's Desiring' as the music to which the coffin was carried from the church reinforced the memory as the man, who had been the only father I had known, was laid to rest between my real father and Otto.

Wolfgang had come on the coach from Wanderer Bear. I supposed there must be a great deal of uncertainty about the future for all the employees but it was hardly the occasion for them to raise it and I could not broach the matter myself because Uncle Willi's interest in the Wanderer Bear company was left to his children and I did not know their plans, indeed was quite certain they had not yet thought about the matter.

'Oh, Wanderer Bear will go on,' Arabella said when I mentioned the awkwardness to her later. 'Somebody else may write the stories but even if our Bear never has another adventure, there is still a nice little industry there. Think of Winnie the Pooh or Rupert or Paddington. Disney films, pantos, soft toys, television adaptations. It'll last for ever and a day. Anyway that is not our worry but making Ströbelfields work is.'

Between us we had little enough experience. Unlike Otto I had no extensive training in estate management and I had spent too many years away to have absorbed much of what he was doing. The lowliest estate worker almost certainly knew more than I did. I had been obliged to give a term's notice to Heidelberg and I had been preoccupied with the arrangements for my own wedding, which was prepared with great haste to accommodate Uncle Willi's wish to see me married in his lifetime.

Arabella had helped her father with his estate but it was run on a different scale and with a different philosophy. We had no convenient Rembrandt hanging on the wall.

Walter was helpful, as were Rudi and Lotte, but their lands were only a quarter the size of ours. It was Ernst who suggested letting out the barn as a holiday home for the increasing numbers of people who liked to walk through woods and fields in the crisp northern air and advertising it internationally, making play of its connection with Wanderer Bear and setting up a small museum of the Bear's history.

The barn was only twenty metres from the house and I at first demurred but Aunt Angelika talked about how her father had told his sons that they had a choice between pride and survival and I reluctantly agreed. Within six months the museum was formed and two months after that it seemed as if every school in Germany was book-ing visits. The barn took longer to become a success as a holiday home but a television company from the south ran a feature on it and suddenly we had more requests than we could meet. Elsa, on a visit, suggested adding riding holidays and we expanded the stables.

Nevertheless, we had to sell some land but, as Walter pointed out, there were now those who could afford to buy it. Arabella took courses in cordon bleu cookery and I suggested we offer a gourmet dinner as part of the holiday home package but she shook her head.

'No. I shan't have time. I am learning to cook because I did not learn at home but it is to feed you and our family not the holiday visitors. I think you will find this recipe has worked rather well. I shall try it on Rudi and Lotte next time they visit.'

'I wish Walter would come more often. He was always here in the old days but now he appears to leave it to our generation to do the visiting. I'm sure Aunt Angelika misses him.'

'They should have married. Walter has been a widower for long enough. I suppose it is too late now. He must be nearly eighty.'

'I do not think either of them wanted it. Walter came here to see my uncle because they were friends from boyhood, not because he wanted to court his sister.'

'I only got about half of that. You are speaking much too fast.'

I repeated my observation slowly. Arabella had O level French and German and spoke neither language with the smallest competence. Used to the linguistic proficiency of the von Ströbel clan, this had at first disconcerted me but since our marriage I had insisted we spoke German on alternate days. Arabella was a willing but slow pupil and when we had visitors those who could frequently switched to English to ease the flow of conversation. Neither Jack Marshall nor Charles Emmett spoke anything other than their native tongue, assuming that wherever they travelled they would always find someone competent in it. It was an attitude which never failed to surprise me each time I encountered it.

Lotte's eldest son, Willi-Klaus, would always space his words out with exaggerated clarity, being vastly amused that Arabella could understand so little of what he said. His cousin, Ernst, one of Werner's children, would do the opposite and deliberately speed up so that she could not understand him. My wife took it all in good part and was hugely popular with the burgeoning Pletz clan.

I was so used to her inexact German that at first I did not focus on what she had said, ignoring the clumsily constructed future tense, assuming that she had meant she had no time to cook for holiday visitors. She look disappointed and I wondered why.

'Is something the matter?'

'I thought you might ask me why I shan't have time.'

I blinked and then held out my arms.

'It's quite certain. I saw the doctor this morning.'

'You said you were going shopping,' I accused her.

'Of course. It might have been a false alarm.

Anyway I did go shopping – for baby clothes.'

I laid my hand on her stomach and she laughed at me. 'You won't feel anything for ages.'

By the evening we were discussing names. Harry Bullchester was showing signs of senile dementia, forgetful, repeating himself, often disorientated in the home he had known from birth, and Arabella was keen to name a child for him while he might still be capable of appreciating it.

'Harry is short for Henry but I rather like it in its own right.' Yet if she chose Henry she could commemorate also her dead fiancé and I wondered if she feared to suggest the name for that reason, if she was too careful of my feelings.

'Then we must take a name from your family for his middle name,' she said.

'It might be a girl but if it is a boy then Harry or Henry must be his middle name. He must have a German first name and the same for any siblings.'

Arabella looked at me in surprise and I myself was somewhat taken aback by the almost angry emphasis in my tone.

'They must have a clear national identity,' I went on more gently. 'I never knew what I was. Klaus-Pierre was bad enough but I was called Dessin while growing up among von Ströbels. I thought of myself as German but the law said I was French. When I was in England I seemed one day French and one day German, depending on whether people reacted to my surname or to my accent. Of course it didn't help that there had just been a war but we do not know what the future holds and even though we are now all part of one supposedly united European Community, I want my children to know they are Germans. They can have English, French, Russian or Chinese middle names but their first names must be German. If they grow up to prefer England or indeed France that will be entirely up to them, but at least they won't have grown up in a muddle.'

'I think Klaus-Pierre was a pretty heroic gesture from your mother, given what you have told me about her father.'

'It was nothing of the sort. She didn't mean it to be an olive branch – she meant to rub his nose in it and she certainly succeeded. I still sometimes think about that crazy meeting in Paris when I told him my name was Dessin. I keep thinking there was some trick I missed, something I could have said to win him over.'

'At least our children won't go through that. So what shall we call him? Klaus? Willi? Otto? And if it's a girl? Lotte? Elsa? Angelika? Or shall we just find one we like and nothing to do with the family?'

It was not a question which needed an immediate answer and I was disconcerted when Arabella took to referring to the baby as Cecil. It was, she explained, what the Blands always called their babies before birth because it was considered 'so much nicer than it' and, being a name for either sex, made no presumption as to boy or girl. I retorted that I knew no female Cecils and that whatever middle names we chose Cecil would certainly never be among them.

'Of course not. That's the whole idea. No Bland has ever been called Cecil,' replied Arabella and I gave up.

In November 1977 President Sadat of Egypt was in Israel addressing the Knesset in one of the most startling acts of peace in my lifetime and I was pacing a cream-walled hospital corridor, waiting to be told of my child's birth. It was now widely accepted for men to be present to see their children born but Arabella had reacted with horror to my tentative suggestion. Her mother could not leave her rapidly declining father and, of all people, Margery was with her in the delivery ward. In between bouts of anxiety I went in to the day room to watch the coverage of Sadat's speech on television, seeing in it an omen. Our child would grow up in a peaceful world, even if at that moment I had all manner of decidedly peaceless thoughts about Margery seeing the baby before I did.

Otto Henry Edouard came into our lives an hour after the coverage had dissolved into a regular comedy programme in which I had no interest but which seemed to be claiming the rapt attention of others in the day room. In that hour excitement and anxiety had battled for supremacy in my mind and fear for Arabella was just beginning to win when Margery emerged to tell me I had a son and that my wife was exhausted but very happy.

'Perfect in every respect,' pronounced the obstetrician of Otto.

It seemed a fair summary of my life at that time. I was thirty-two, secure, happily married, a proud father of a healthy child. Outside the Gate had proved not to be such a bad place. I was almost afraid to acknowledge my happiness to myself, believing that merely to do so would persuade some malign force to snatch it all away from me. Arabella had no such inhibition.

'There cannot be many people as happy as we are, Klaus-Pierre,' she whispered as we looked at a sleeping Otto.

Later, when she had slipped away on some errand for the baby and he had woken and was looking at me with eyes that did not yet distinguish between the humans who stared at him, I vowed that no ill should ever befall him, that I should protect him against any threat, that no living being should hurt him. This, I realised, must have been how my mother felt about me when I lay newborn and innocent of my shameful origins, surrounded by hostile forces, a focus for vengeance and hatred.

For five years she had failed. How would I feel if I failed Otto? If not all my love and devotion, not all my physical strength nor any amount of valour could stave off harm to him? For a moment I entered into Catherine Dessin's soul, more completely than if Wolfgang had hypnotised me, and glimpsed its torment.

I had not seen Wolfgang since Uncle Willi's funeral. He still designed Wanderer Bears and now that the stories had come to an end his work was largely to be found in toys and on cards, jigsaws and posters. A range of Wanderer Bear mugs and plates had been produced for the coming Christmas and featured in children's shops across the world.

I made a vague promise to myself to contact him during the following year. Absorbed by Arabella and Ströbelfields, I had neglected even friends such as Jack Marshall and Charles Emmett but now I was trying to decide which of the two I should invite to be godfather to Otto. Margery was to be one of the godmothers but when I suggested Elsa as the other the priest demurred. He was of the old school, rather resented some of the changes in the Catholic Church and, although it was now permitted to appoint godparents from other Christian denominations, it was not acceptable to him.

'Go to another church,' advocated an outraged Arabella.

'Appoint a Catholic proxy in Elsa's place,' said Aunt Angelika. 'Then Elsa can still be the real godmother.'

It was an elegant compromise but I did not feel like compromising. I wrote to Franz who wrote to the priest who offered his own compromise by leaving the baptism to a younger colleague who had no objections to Protestants around his font. I remembered my years in Britain and the problems of Northern Ireland. There was some chap over there who was always yelling about the Pope being the anti-Christ, carrying on his crusade in Parliament itself. What was his name? Parsley? Paynesley? I could not recall.

'Paisley,' Arabella reminded me. 'But I would take a very large bet with you that the time will come when the likes of him and that priest of yours join forces against secularism. There is nothing like a common enemy to promote unity.

Anwar, get down!'

Anwar was a dog which had strayed into Ströbelfields while Arabella and I were at the hospital. A farmhand had taken pity on it, although it was a mongrel and no use as a working dog. He had brought it with him one day when visiting the house and it made instant friends with Scooter. Thereafter, no matter how often he took it to the farm, it made its way back to the main house and in the end Arabella and Aunt Angelika decided it could stay. It was a rusty brown in colour and the farmhand had called it Brownie but I demanded greater originality and, remembering how I had employed my time at the hospital while waiting for news of Otto's birth, I named it Anwar.

'Well, it's easier to say than Menachem,' agreed Arabella.

I became more attached to Anwar than to any dog since Hermann but one day I came back and found a small black-and-white kitten curled up on the upright chair which Omi used to sit on when easier chairs began to prove too difficult to rise from. Since Macfidget there had been other cats at Ströbelfields but I had never bonded with one, being too much away.

'I'm calling it Mitten,' Arabella told me. 'Because it has four white paws. There's a song about Mitten the Kitten.'

'There may well be, but in German mitten means middle. I cannot go around calling "middle!".

Arabella looked disappointed and, to give her time to think, I began to run my fingers through the small creature's fur. It responded with a puny but needle-sharp bite.

'Ouch! You little devil!' I protested in German and thereafter the animal was known as Teufel, the German for devil. I wondered what Franz would make of it.

And so, I settled to an industrious, happy life, complete with wife, child, dog and cat. Life's winds blew fair and my ship was sturdy.

The first squall came in March of the following year when Elsa had a second miscarriage. She had taken the first in her stride but the second was a bitter blow. On a visit to Ströbelfields that Easter she was quiet and uncharacteristically subdued. Arabella and I felt guilty for having Otto.

The second squall came only days after she returned home when my mother's youngest child, Bette, was knocked down by a car. Her life was never in danger but she had broken a large number of bones and my mother and Kurt spent long days at the hospital, from time to time telephoning us with news.

No sooner had a heavily bandaged Bette been discharged with her limbs in plaster than the squalls became storms. In June Harry Bull-chester died and the three of us went to England for the funeral to find Lady Bullchester broken with the strain of the mental illness which had bedevilled his last year, the family home having to be sold to pay death duties and Margery diagnosed a day earlier with breast cancer. Arabella stayed on to help her mother and I returned to Germany without either her or Otto.

The house seemed empty and I felt my life was

suspended as I waited for their return. One morning it seemed emptier than usual and I realised that Aunt Angelika had disappeared. It was her habit to call out to me, if I was in the house, when she left for any reason so I had no cause to expect a long absence but by lunchtime there was no sign of her and I felt the first stirrings of unease. Her car was in the yard so I thought perhaps she had walked down to the farm. At sixty she had the energy of many half her age and I rang the estate office more out of curiosity than any real worry. No, I was assured, Fräulein von Ströbel had not been there at all that day.

The unease swelled. I began calling her but to no avail. I searched the house fruitlessly and then began on the grounds. I found her in the vegetable shed, sitting slumped on the chair old Maria had used when she scraped carrots and told me tales of past glories. She looked at me, seeming not to know me and her speech, when it came, was slurred.

'A stroke,' I told first Arabella and then my cousins in turn.

'A mild stroke,' I encouraged them next day. 'They say she'll be fine.'

'How much more?' wept Arabella.

'Take Arabella home,' George's bluff tones bellowed at me along the telephone wires. 'She's wearing herself out here and there is nothing she can do.'

Arabella arrived back, exhausted, her face drained of its normal liveliness. She patted Anwar only absentmindedly while I held Otto, hungrily noting each small change since I had last seen him. Nothing, I thought, could really hurt us while he was at home and from then on our lives slowly returned to normal. Aunt Angelika made a full recovery and went to spend a month's convalescence with one of her cousins in Switzerland. Margery had a successful operation and Lady Bullchester began the much longer process of a return to health. The sale of the estate would also be a long, slow process, especially as Hugh was trying to rescue it by some deal with the National Trust, but as long as everyone was healthy I was unbothered by the inevitable and only thankful that Arabella was no longer caught up in all the turmoil.

'I can't believe we'll ever have a worse patch than that one,' said Arabella as we at last dared to believe ourselves once more tranquil and content, our anxieties a quiet background hum rather than an insistent shout demanding immediate response.

Neither of us could have known as we celebrated the confirmation of Arabella's second pregnancy that Wolfgang Mueller was about to be at the epicentre of a storm, the darkness of which engulfed us, as the past rose in evil triumph over both present and future.

twenty

A Pitiless Destiny

It needed only a fine, crisp, autumn morning at Ströbelfields to convince me that man could experience heaven before he died. On such days I wondered that Otto could have wanted to forsake it all for the clamour of a city or that I had been prepared to bury myself in manuscripts at Heidelberg. How could Franz prefer the cloisters to the woods, the lake, the rolling meadows on which the first frosts were dissolving in the morning sun? No wonder so many generations had been so intent on preserving this world for their successors. I vowed that I myself would preserve it for little Otto.

In theory I walked now to observe the state of the farm, to check for broken fences, signs of pest, growth of trees, husbandry of hedges. In reality I walked to savour the unpolluted air, the quiet contentment of the animals, the rustle of small wildlife amidst the whispering of the woods. Often I would stand gazing at the lake, watching its calm surface gently rippled by the life which pulsed below.

I paused to speak to Gunther, a farmhand who occasionally helped us with the expanded stables. He talked about the placidity of a new pony he had seen for sale but as he talked he worked, hauling dead branches from the tangle of a broken tree. I helped with a particularly difficult bit while Gunther passed uncomplimentary remarks about the sawing party which had been working there the day before. We pulled the branch clear together and, for a moment, our hands rested side by side on the wood.

From the moment I had arrived at Ströbelfields I had been aware that everybody was engaged in hard physical work. As a child I had trailed behind Otto, proudly carrying two small logs, while he lifted a huge burden. It was Franz who showed me how to ply the saddle soap when cleaning tack. My mother pulled up the vegetables which Maria would prepare. Aunt Angelika would be red-armed and elbow-deep in washing in the days before machines released women from such labour. We cleaned our own rooms and polished our own floors. Uncle Willi wheezed as we harvested.

Yet my hands were smooth, clean-nailed, unblistered and I did not think I could ever recall them being otherwise. Gunther's were weathered and work-swollen and I felt a small arrow of guilt. Perhaps we thought we worked but it was others who actually did so.

A few moments later I had resumed my stroll, but now it became more arduous as I went deeper into the woods. It must have been around here that Old Joachim used to live occasionally. I remembered Elsa telling me about the tramp when I had first arrived and I had heard his name at intervals after that but no one had mentioned him for years. Had he died? Or did he just come no more? I must remember to ask Aunt Angelika.

It was a good place for a wanderer to rest. The trees met thickly overhead and a man could keep dry. It was said he trapped rabbits and got his water from a nearby stream. In winter he disappeared with the money he had earned from occasional work on the farm and then in spring he came again.

'Old Joachim has arrived,' Uncle Willi would tell Aunt Angelika.

I walked on, startling a fox, causing the birds to gabble warnings high above me. I watched a large beetle crawl slowly away just centimetres from my foot. Emerging, I turned towards the drive and walked on its verge rather than its tarmac back to the house. Once this long, winding road had been little more than a dirt track, uneven, broken, full of holes. The cars would bump along at a snail's pace and the horses stumble. One of the earliest uses of the money from the Wanderer Bear was the laying of the tarmac.

I stood and gazed at the house as it came into view. What would it look like now had Uncle Willi not been invited back to emergency teaching in the village school? There would have been no Wanderer Bear, no sudden pot of gold. Would we even still be here among the dilapidations or would the family have been forced out and Ströbelfields made into a school or an old folks home or a shelter for the war disabled?

I made my way along the verge. These days I could pass the place where Otto had died without active grief, often without even noticing, just as the barn, metamorphosed into first a home for my mother and Kurt and then into a holiday home, no longer provoked in Aunt Angelika memories of those earlier tragedies, of finding her handicapped brother hanged.

Today, however, I was in reflective mood and I did stop as I reached the scene of my cousin's death but only fleetingly did the horror replay itself in my mind, which was instead focused on the train of events that had led to my ownership of Ströbelfields. If my grandparents had forgiven my mother and had taken her back, I would have grown up in Paris where I would have encountered prejudice and disapproval but perhaps not the cruel and concentrated persecution which had blotted out all gentler feeling in that small village. I would have grown up French, part of the injured not the injuring nation.

If my mother had been more self-sufficient, had left Provence and started again somewhere else in France, calling me Pierre rather than Klaus-Pierre then there would have been no tales of persecution for Bette to relay to Kurt at that chance meeting, which brought Angelika von Ströbel to my rescue. If Ellie and my father's children had lived no such rescue could have been possible.

But these things had not happened and I had been rescued, bringing my religion with me. Of course, Franz might have encountered Catholicism at any time, could have become first a convert and then a monk without any unwitting help from me. Yet from my mother's bad cold and Franz's chance presence in the house that Sunday had started his path to Rome and mine to his place as heir.

If Otto had married sooner, had children to

inherit his right to Ströbelfields, had chosen a different horse to ride that morning, or if I had chosen a different train and he had no need to hurry...

For a moment my thoughts were submerged by memories of that terrible accident, seeing again Wolfgang's car slowing to a crawl, the maddened horse, the body sliding from the roof of the car. Then I returned to my *if* game. If the girls had not all husbands with demanding careers and no interest in giving them up, if the Pletzes had thought combining the two estates the answer to their own problems then I would now be a lecturer at Heidelberg, trying to enthuse young minds with the glories that were Rome and Greece. Instead my work on the Ara Pacis had never been completed. It seemed a shame to have wasted so much effort and I wondered if I might perhaps find time to finish it, stocking the library with volumes on the classics.

I was drawing near to the house now and saw Arabella coming from it. She waved and disappeared into the barn, emerging just as I reached the kitchen door. We went in to see Otto beaming at us from his high chair.

'Heaven,' I told Arabella. 'Heaven on earth.'

'You mean your son's smile? You should have been here earlier when he hurled his breakfast at Aunt Angelika. If this is heaven there are no angels. Elevenses?'

Arabella spoke the last word in English. There is only a clumsy German equivalent.

'I feel ready for lunch after that walk.'

'It's too early. What about brunch?'

Again she finished a German sentence with a single word in English. I smiled. We spoke to Otto in three languages and I wondered how easily he would come to distinguish them. I spoke French least often because Arabella was as unlikely as Otto to understand. For the first time in a long while I recalled how, in my infancy, I had thought of German as a special secret language spoken only by my mother and myself.

I was about to tell Arabella the story when she forestalled me by saying that there had been two telephone messages while I had been out. Lotte would not be able to come for supper as arranged because Walter had had a fall during the night. Nothing was broken but he was bruised and shaken and he would not be able to keep an eye on the younger children while the older ones were themselves away on a school trip.

'He's getting on. He can't be that much younger than Uncle Willi was.'

'He certainly never seems that old. The other message was from Christoph Steiner.'

I frowned in an effort of memory but could not place the name.

'He's the big panjandrum at Wanderer Bear.'

'Of course! He took over last year and I have never met him. What does Wanderer Bear want with us? Uncle Will left everything remotely connected with it to my cousins and Lotte.'

I telephoned later that morning and was put through to Steiner immediately. Throughout the pleasantries which followed I was relaxed and cheerful, the mood of my walk sustained, my time unpressured, my mind unperturbed by any premonitions of catastrophe, until I began to notice that somewhere in the conversation there was a discordant note, unheard but ruining the harmony nonetheless. I realised that he was a busy man and did not wander through a country estate for a living so I eventually ceased to ask after Wanderer Bear and to reminisce about Uncle Willi and waited for him to explain why he had called. He responded in what Charles Emmett had been wont to describe as 'ha-hum mode'.

'Er... It is a little awkward, Herr von Ströbel. We were wondering, I mean, is it possible, if by any chance...'

A small sliver of ice slipped along my stomach. He might have been betraying the embarrassment of a man about to ask a favour, but my every instinct told me instead to expect bad news.

'Has Wolfgang Mueller been in touch with you?'

The ice stabbed sharply. Surely I had been waiting for this moment ever since I had met Wolfgang Mueller on the ferry, had been subconsciously expecting something evil without having the faintest notion as to the form it would take? Wolfgang, with his battered past and his hypnotism and his talk of bad seed, was not normal. *Not normal.*

The thought crystallised even as I mentally shook myself. What had Christoph Steiner said to merit such extravagant thoughts?

'He has not been to work all week. He hasn't answered the telephone and today we persuaded the police to break in. Herr Mueller is normally such a reliable employee and has not had even a day's sick leave in all his time with us. Naturally we were very worried, especially as he lives alone and there was no family we could ask. The police were reluctant, of course, but in the end they agreed.'

You too are reluctant, I thought, reluctant to come to the point. And you are, for heaven's sake, the managing director, not the director of personnel, not just a worried colleague, but the managing director. Why is the managing director phoning me because a middle-ranking employee is absent for a week?

'No. I haven't heard from him since my uncle's funeral, well, apart from the usual Christmas card, that is.'

'I am afraid the police made a rather terrible discovery when they did break in. A ... a woman's body.'

My mind denied his words. He had not said them. Presently he would say something else, something quite different, which would make me realise I had just imagined what I thought I had heard. Then my own words tolled the death of so vain a hope.

'A prostitute?'

'They think so but of course it is far too soon to say. They will have to make a proper identification.'

Neither of us could say the word that lurked menacingly in the shadows of our thoughts. *Murder.*

'They need to ascertain how she died,' prevaricated Steiner.

No, they don't, mocked a voice from the same shadows, a voice that was Wolfgang's. *They know now. Sorry, Klaus-Pierre.*

I uttered the word, or rather its euphemism.

'The death is suspect?'

'Yes. They won't say more publicly but privately they tell me she was strangled. They are treating it as murder.'

The word hung in the air, demanding to be denied, undeniable.

'I expect they will be in touch and it will all be public tomorrow. I wanted you to know in advance.'

'You have told my cousins?'

There was a short silence. 'We have several calls out...'

They had come to me first because somebody there remembered that it was I who had introduced Wolfgang to the company, that to my cousins and Lotte he was just a name, no more significant than any other on a long roll of managers, artists, salesmen and secretaries.

The police called an hour later. No, I told them, I had not had any contact from Herr Mueller for some time. Indeed, we had not often been in touch in recent years. Yes, I had known Herr Mueller as a young artist. Yes, I could tell them about his background. No, nothing had ever led me to believe him violent in his adult life. No, I knew of no particular friends. Yes, he probably was a loner, although that was when I had known him years ago. Yes, he did consort with prostitutes. Yes, quite often, as far as I knew but my knowledge might be outdated. Reason for murder? Yes, she was probably expecting his child.

No, said the same policeman the following day. The postmortem showed no sign of pregnancy. They would like to interview me. Would tomorrow be convenient? I thought it did not much matter whether it was convenient or not, they would come anyway. In the morning I listened to the sounds of Arabella's morning sickness, feeling nauseous myself.

Two detectives arrived at lunchtime and I answered them without prevarication, telling them all I knew but again saying that the only reason I could imagine Wolfgang inflicting violence would be to prevent propagation of his line. I could see they thought me mad but they had not heard Wolfgang talking in that coolly convinced tone about a bad seed.

'He knows this area well?'

'He hasn't lived here since he was ten or so.'

'But he knew it then?'

'I suppose he must have explored it as we all did as children.'

'Has he been back here for holidays?'

'No.' The ice was back. 'Why?'

'We think he was heading this way, sir.'

'Surely, if he had a week, he would have left the country?'

'His passport was still in the apartment, sir. He could not have known that he would have so long and probably fled in panic. These girls normally have ... er ... colleagues who raise the alarm. It appears this one operated solo but he might not have known that.'

'Why do you think he is coming here?'

'A woman who works in the same company has been on compassionate leave about ten miles away – her mother is dying. She saw him, she says, being dropped off by a lorry, as if he had been hitch-hiking, just outside the village. Of course, now that it's in all the papers, we'll get a lot of reported sightings but this one sounds serious.'

Clearly it was sufficiently serious for the police to turn out in force and deploy themselves throughout the policies of Ströbelfields later on that day. Lotte rang in fury when the Pletz domain was similarly invaded. I had just replaced the receiver when Elsa called.

'This could do pretty serious damage to Wanderer Bear. This is the man who drew all those endearing pictures and the media are having a field day. The newspapers will follow tomorrow. I hope it doesn't break the company.' My cousin sounded strained and unhappy.

'The press are fairly swarming outside Wolfgang's old house. The present occupants have called the police twice,' reported Lotte.

'They've been bothering the school,' Aunt Angelika protested when she came back from the village. 'I could cheerfully do a murder of my own.'

'There's a policeman hiding in our barn,' an excited small Walter told his father.

'The hell he is!' swore Rudi to his son's delight and Lotte's dismay.

'I keep telling him not to say "hell" and then Rudi sets that sort of example,' she complained to me later.

It was Walter senior, recovered from his fall, who mentioned Old Joachim's hiding place.

'I don't think so. I was there only a couple of days ago and there was no sign of any occupation,' I said thoughtfully. 'Anyway, they must have combed every inch of this estate by now.'

'And ours, but they haven't gone away, have they? They are still here and that can only mean they are expecting him. I even found one hiding in my pigsty when I went to muck out the occupants.'

'Are you sure you're well enough to be doing that sort of thing?'

'There's no choice but to do it. Lotte is expecting yet again. I would have thought the novelty would have worn off by now.'

I grinned. I suspected that the death of Uncle Willi had left a gap in his life and he was finding jobs on the farm to while away his time and keep his mind from the future. I feared the future too.

'They won't take him alive,' I told Arabella. 'He is terrified of the police. My God! Whatever's that?'

'Dogs,' said Arabella. 'Tracker dogs, possibly even bloodhounds. Surely they should have asked us?'

Teufel rushed in and sped upstairs but Anwar's ears pricked up and he looked ready to challenge the baying beasts whose noise reached us from somewhere below the lake. I shut him firmly in the kitchen and, outraged, went outside, almost bumping into the detective who had first interviewed me.

'I have livestock on the farm.' My voice was shaking but on Wolfgang's account, not the animals'. I had a horrible suspicion that he knew it.

'I'm sorry, sir. The dogs are very well controlled. We need to make a thorough search. We have every reason to believe he is here somewhere and it *is* a murder.'

'And it *is* my property.' I returned inside, slamming the door with furious force, before it occurred to me that he must have come to the house to speak to me. But if that were so, then he must have changed his mind because he had disappeared when, ten minutes later, I was in the yard, resuming the normal routine of my day, waiting for the blacksmith.

The holidaying occupants of the barn, a couple of about sixty and their two grown-up children, were at the windows, staring at the scene and calling each other's attention to the goings-on. The blacksmith told me that his car had been searched and Arabella said someone she knew in England had a clever machine which took telephone messages and that we could put the press off if we had one. Meanwhile we ignored the telephone's summons.

Suddenly Wolfgang was reported to have been seen in Berlin and the noise and fury drained from our lives. A week later it was possible to pick up the newspapers without seeing any mention of the dark secret of Wanderer Bear but pre-Christmas orders were badly down and my cousins conferred, according to Lotte, in a spirit of gloomy foreboding.

Then, one morning in late October, I found myself making up a pack of sandwiches and a thermos of hot coffee and heading into the woods, bound unerringly for Old Joachim's hiding place, which usually I found about once a year by accident. Wolfgang was sitting in the middle of it, looking in my direction as if expecting me.

I was exasperated rather than surprised and I

handed him the refreshments with resignation.

He looked remarkably well for a man on the run and reasonably clean, but his face had a pinched look and he fell on the food.

'How did you do that?'

'Do what?'

'You know what. Make me come to you.' I heard the irritation in my tone as I sat down on the ground opposite him but there was nothing but amusement in his.

'So you still think I have dark powers. I do not. I have no doubt I was somewhere in the back of your mind and you suddenly thought of Old Joachim's lair and decided to see if I was here and naturally, because you are a good Catholic and liberal to the poor, you brought me sustenance.'

I watched him as he poured coffee from the flask with untrembling hand. He smiled.

'In fact I thought you might have been here before now.'

I was not to be deflected. 'You were looking in my direction. You were expecting me.'

'For pity's sake! Of course I was looking in your direction. You were crashing through the wood like an elephant.'

'I could have been anyone.'

'Certainly. Any *one*. The sounds were unmistakably of one man. I could deal with one man if he threatened me but I knew I would not have to because you swore just now and it could have been no voice but yours.'

I remembered tripping and saving myself and thinking no more of it, so intent had I been on my objective, but, yes, I had sworn. He watched me working it out.

'So, you see, no mystery, just as there was no hypnotism all those years ago.'

'You are supposed to be in Berlin.'

'Indeed. That is very convenient. I haven't been there for years. Nasty place.'

'Wolfgang, there is one hell of a manhunt and it could switch back here any time. Tell me what happened.'

He had finished the food and I wished I had brought some more.

'I think it will not come back with the same intensity. She was a woman I used to go with years ago and then suddenly she appeared again. She told me she had been selling her services to a businessman who eventually installed her as his mistress and showered her with gifts and money but forbade her to work. I think it was all lies and that she had probably been in prison but I pretended to believe it.

'Anyway I began going to her occasionally and then quite a lot until I realised it was not just work to her. She was becoming attached. Damn stupid of her, of course, and bad for her trade. I stopped using her.'

Moral anarchy, I thought, the triumph of the animal over the human being, of coarse satisfaction over intellect and emotion, of lust over tenderness. He spoke as if describing a harmless hobby.

'Then one day she turned up on my doorstep and told me she was pregnant. When I asked how she could be so sure it was mine she said she had not been with anyone else for months, that she did not want anyone but me. This time I did believe her although I wondered how she had been living if I was the only customer. I offered her money for an abortion but she said she wanted to keep it because it was mine, that if she couldn't have me she would at least have my child. She kept saying she hoped it would be a boy and look like me. I am afraid I don't remember much more.'

'Wolfgang, you *murdered* her.'

'Yes, I meant I can't remember doing it. I can't remember much at all, not until I was packing my bag. It never occurred to me to dispose of the body like they do in detective stories but now I wonder if I shouldn't at least have tried.'

I looked at him in disbelief. 'You mean you would have gone back to work and drawing bloody Wanderer Bears and just carried on as usual?'

'If I had been certain of getting away with it, but one can never be certain.'

'Wolfgang, we're talking *murder*. Not theft, not fraud not even violent wounding. Murder. You killed this woman. *Killed* her.'

'She was about to bring a monster into the world.'

'Oh, not that nonsense again. She wasn't even pregnant.'

He stared at me, absorbing my words, believing them. Then he began to laugh, helpless, bitter, ironic laughter that seemed to fill the wood. 'The other one wasn't either. I don't learn very fast.'

'The other one?'

'Yes. You must have heard about it. They actually picked me up and interviewed me. It gave

Wanderer Bear a real fright.'

'But Otto said you were not one of her clients.'

'Not then. I had been a couple of months earlier before she joined that particular establishment. She was very discreet. She was about the baby too. Said she would never tell anyone who the father was but that she fancied a nice little room somewhere and that now the authorities would have to took after her or perhaps some charity. I don't remember much about that one either except sitting in my own apartment, deciding I might just be lucky. No one had seen me go in or out. There was the other girl to confirm that I was her client, not the dead girl's. I had been wearing gloves. The big danger was a blood test on the baby. I knew nothing about tests on foetuses but if they wanted my blood they would have to ask for it and that would give me warning. They never did and there was no mention of any pregnancy in the press reports nor in the gossip of other girls.'

'But surely they went back into her past and checked out her contacts from those days?'

'I do not know what they did except that they did not come back to me. I suppose they bungled it.'

'Wolfgang, listen. Come back to the house and I'll get you the best doctors in the country. They won't put you in prison. You're sick. You need help.'

'You mean I am mad.'

He was certainly mad, I thought, as mad as an outwardly sane man can be. I was alone in the wood with a madman.

He guessed my thoughts and smiled. 'I told you before, Muellers are bad, not mad. Those women should not have died.'

'Come back with me. It's getting dark.'

'Stop babbling. It's not yet noon.'

'Come back. You need help. You can't live in a wood for ever.'

'I don't intend to, especially now that you have seen me. Leave me now but if you have any goodwill left towards me don't phone the police for half an hour after you get back.'

'Life on the run will be bloody awful. Get help now. Come on.'

I had risen to my feet and was walking towards him where he sat on the ground. He shook his head. I grasped his arm and tried to pull him to his feet. A hot pain shot through my shoulder and I found myself on my back, looking up into his face as he knelt on my stomach. It was an older face than the one which had sneered within inches of my own almost a quarter of a century ago, but the eyes were seemingly the same, glittering with hatred, gloating with dominance.

I had the sense to lie still. It used to please him when he felt my feeble struggles. Then suddenly he was gone. This time there had been no Uncle Willi to pull him off. I sat up and looked for him but he had disappeared. I listened but there was no sound of a retreat through the woods. He must be hiding somewhere, watching me. I got to my feet cautiously, feeling my injured shoulder, half-expecting another attack, uncertain from which direction it might come.

I leant weakly against a tree and spoke into the

seemingly empty space, raising my voice.

'Wolfgang, listen to me. I'm going now and I won't ring the police for half an hour after I get back. But if you change your mind, just come to the house. Remember, we're friends. I'll get you all the help you need.'

Even now the memory of that wild dash through the wood has the power to cover me in cold sweat, to come to me as a nightmare, to cause me to pause in some routine activity and look towards the wood as I recollect each small sound at which I jumped and looked behind me, certain he was following. I ran, tripped, fell, picked myself up, ran, tripped, fell. Brambles tore my clothes and my flesh and I scarcely noticed. I would have bellowed for help but I had no breath to do so, enough sense to know that no one could hear me and enough fear to know that he alone could hear and might be provoked to attack. When I emerged from the wood, gasping for breath, I saw Gunther in the distance, out of range of any call but a reassuring sight none-theless. I hastened towards him.

Every few paces I glanced fearfully over my shoulder. Did Wolfgang watch that flight from the woods? If so was he amused at the fear he still inspired, or saddened as he watched one of his few real friends turn his back and flee? Or per-haps he merely sat down again in Old Joachim's den and listened to the sounds of my ignominious retreat growing fainter. Almost certainly he did not. He must have left the wood with as much speed as I but in a different direction because they never found him.

Arabella listened incredulously as I told her we must wait half an hour and twice I seized the telephone from her while she protested in outrage and incomprehension, crying that Wolfgang was dangerous and every minute counted. When the police came I told them honestly that I had delayed my report by thirty minutes because that had been the price of my life. I was not sure whether I believed it myself but they looked at me with pity rather than anger and indeed I must have been a sorry spectacle, still covered in drying blood and wearing nothing that was not ripped and ruined. Arabella was worried less by my petty injuries than by my shaking, which was at first continuous and then returned in spasms.

I had been a coward but I knew I could never have won in any fight with him. He was stronger, faster and not handicapped by scruples or pity. Yet I shook not from contemplation of my escape but from the shock of learning what he was. It appalled me that I half-hoped he got away, but I remembered too keenly a small, beaten boy who had the courage to try to protect his even smaller brother. I thought of the baby shaken in her cot, the cowering mother, the devotion to evil which displayed a swastika in contravention of the law, the Nazi songs, the yearning for a lost power, the poverty and a child who bullied others as mercilessly as his father bullied him.

Arabella had no such memories to palliate her condemnation and she wanted him caught with all her heart. For days we expected news of that capture but the days became weeks and all was silent. The police disappeared and the only dogs which barked in the woods were our own.

'You must not go in the wood again until they have caught him. It's happened before. We all thought they had crawled over every last inch and that he must be miles away but somehow he gave them the slip. If he can do it once then he can do it again.'

I promised instead that I would go into the wood only if accompanied by the dogs. It was somehow more respectable than admitting that I would not dream of going there, except in a party of strong men, for as long as Wolfgang remained at large.

At Christmas I restricted the visiting children from playing in the wood and was greeted with a chorus of protest, which dissolved only when I said I had found a new place to toboggan. Generations of von Ströbels had run free and the sudden imposition of supervision surprised my cousins. I wondered if Wolfgang watched the children from the woods, saw the lights of the Christmas trees, heard the sounds of normality in which he no longer had any place and I pitied him, but when I thought of the dead women, one in love with him and one fantasising about the new life his child would bring, I hated him and wondered how I had been so easily deceived.

In early January, when the annual family gatherings were over, the only childish sound in the house Otto's, and Arabella and I again discussing names for a forthcoming baby, the lake was frozen over. I pulled back the curtains on a clear, cold morning and saw Wolfgang walking across it.

I recognised him despite the distance and he

seemed to be gazing in my direction, perhaps alerted by the movement of the curtains. Then I looked beyond and saw the police fanning out from the wood.

I opened my mouth to shout a futile warning which he could not have heard and did not need. He knew the peril of the ice, knew it was too thin. So I kept silent instead and watched the scene I could see but not hear. The policemen must have shouted, in warning, in triumph, in demand, but the window was closed and the wind in the wrong direction and they were too far away for me to hear. Wolfgang stopped suddenly, still looking at me, not so much as glancing at the pursuit which was now racing for the lake. I saw him stagger slightly as the ice broke and then he was gone. I knew he was not struggling to escape the icy water, that he probably swam under the ice, away from the light and air, towards darkness and death.

I stood and watched as the police roped one of their number and he moved warily over the ice. Then I turned to tell Arabella what was happening but she was asleep and somehow it seemed pointless to wake her. Instead I shaved, showered and dressed as if for a normal day and when I arrived downstairs it was to find Aunt Angelika serving hot drinks to the policemen.

Throughout the day the sound of ice being forcibly broken split the countryside air. I kept the estate workers at their normal tasks and there were no holiday-makers in the barn, but towards the end of the day a small contingent of pressmen arrived at the lake. The following morning police frogmen began their work but without success and I was told the lake must be dragged.

Wolfgang's body was eventually pulled from the water along with a farm implement from the last century and a great deal of slime.

A Lutheran pastor, a detective and I were the only ones at the funeral and only one of us mourned. Neither Wanderer Bear, for whom he had worked so long, nor the sister he had tried to protect from his brutal father sent flowers or a wreath. I do not know whether he was mad or bad but his unhappy life was in many ways an indictment of that terrible regime which had dominated my country as was the much greater suffering of Judy Margolis. She and so many others had emerged still good and kind, their bodies wrecked, their minds tormented, their terrible memories ineradicable, but their souls unsullied. Wolfgang Mueller, who had been tried in a much lesser heat, had proved a much lesser mortal but only God could judge him. Unlike Arabella, I could not bring myself to do so.

twenty-one

The Ghosts of Ströbelfields

I was alone at Ströbelfields for the first time I could remember, but the house had that expectant air which always preceded an influx of visitors. I glanced at my watch. They were due in an hour. Arabella had been in England visiting her family with Otto and two-month-old Willi and would be returning later that day after the guests, who were being met by Aunt Angelika at the station, had arrived.

Aunt Angelika had already left and it was a silent house without the cries of the baby and the experimental babble of Otto. Contemplating their return, I felt as excited as a child before Christmas.

I walked through the house and towards the stairs, intending to check that all was in order in the guest bedrooms. I should not have dared to do this if Aunt Angelika had been there; she would have told me that she had been getting the house ready for visitors since before I was born. I was the undisputed owner of Ströbelfields and a married man with a family of my own but I noted, sometimes with irritation but usually with amusement, how often we deferred to Aunt Angelika. Arabella, happy and confident, seemed unbothered.

I remembered Aunt Angelika as she was when I first knew her, or at least as she was when I first came to Ströbelfields. She had come to France to offer a refuge to my mother and myself. We had few visitors to the small house in Provence and none who spoke to me in German, yet my memories of that dramatic arrival had faded with the years.

I remembered every turn of her countenance when Elsa or I was the subject of her displeasure, the sudden advent of brown-rimmed spectacles which she had needed so much earlier and which she wore only to study the accounts, her red-rimmed eyes when Omi died. I could hear her too, calling us to meals, telling Uncle Willi to slow down, joking with Walter Pletz. She had kept Ströbelfields going during the war. She had preserved it for the next generation, for me.

I paused at the top of the stairs and looked down at the hall, as once I had crept from my bedroom and peered through the bannisters and it was as if I could see them all again.

Otto, dear Otto, was playing Offenbach, thumping the piano keys, missing notes in his enthusiasm, but it was a grown-up Otto I could see now, the man who had died, not the boy full of Christmas enthusiasm.

On the chair by the wall sat Omi, frail, much older than she had been that Christmas. Uncle Willi stood with his brothers. That was odd because neither of them had been alive when I came to Ströbelfields. He was filling his pipe and smiling at a scene which should have contained his children but, unlike that far-off evening, did not. Beside him stood a man I had never seen in life, a middle-aged child lost in a world he did not understand but happy when his brothers were with him. Then, beside him... I looked, trying not to blink, afraid he might disappear. He wore the expression that had peered at me from the photograph in my mother's room, that portrait which I had not seen since her marriage to Kurt. His general's uniform was immaculate, the red collar glowing. It would not have looked like that when he died. As I gazed it seemed they were all smiling at me, affectionately, perhaps wistfully, as if to say they were happy it had turned out this way.

I came out of my reverie with a jolt. *The ghosts of Ströbelfields smile kindly on their successors.* Aunt Angelika's words came to me so vividly that I thought I heard them rather than merely remembering.

I looked down into the empty hall. I had not seen ghosts even though no living person had been among those I pictured. If I had seen ghosts there would have been others, a fourth brother, a grandfather I had never known. I had seen only those who had played a major role in my destiny and I had seen them only as I knew them from life or from pictures. They came not from any spirit world but from my imagination, just as once, in that same imagination, I had briefly become my father as he walked the dark streets of Paris on an errand of great danger and greater mercy.

Yet I was glad I had seen them, believing that had they been spectres they would have looked on me in the same way. I glanced towards my old room, the one I had occupied in childhood, but no small boy peeped out to be frightened by a large, black dog. That child had become a man as surely as the living had become the dead.

I carried out my tour of guest rooms, wondering if solitude could drive a man mad in less than two hours, which was all the time Aunt Angelika had been gone. Yet, perhaps, today I could be forgiven for looking back as well as forwards.

Anwar trotted beside me as I made my way downstairs. I began to look at my watch every five minutes, unable to settle to any activity until I heard the sound of a car engine, made faint by distance. It drew nearer and I went out into the yard to watch the BMW's progress, to see it grow larger as it approached, its outlines more sharply defined. It was level with the lake and Aunt Angelika's features would soon be distinguishable.

The car purred into the yard and they began to get out, Aunt Angelika saying something about the train being early. Edouard looked curiously about him and then opened the rear door. She got out slowly, stiffly, feeble now with age, her face gentle beneath the white hair, and stood supporting herself on her son's arm.

'Granny!' I hastened towards her and this time she took me in her arms.

epilogue

Berlin 1989

I start, uncertain if I have cried 'Granny!' aloud, but no one seems to be startled. I force myself back to the present but I catch Kurt's eye and he smiles. Perhaps we have all been remembering.

'Maybe we should make an effort and go out there,' says my mother.

Kurt replies that it is a good idea and that he will remain here in case any of the others comes back and wonders where we are. We agree a time by which he should expect our return and then go down the stairs and out into the street but cannot see any of our own young.

'When this was being built I remember watching two girls on the other side who were looking out of their window. They were teenagers and so they must be in their forties now. I wonder what happened to them.'

'I imagine the same as happened to everybody else. They probably married and had children or stayed single and worked.'

'I hope neither of them fell in love with a border guard. If so people will be very cruel now.'

I put my arm around her. 'This is different. It lasted twenty-eight years not six and people got used to it. Anyway, border guards tried escaping and occasionally died in the attempt. I suppose there might be the odd angry relative of someone who died crossing the wall but they cannot know who killed their loved ones. They will all claim to have fired in the air and no one will follow that up too closely.'

My mother looks unconvinced, her handsome face strained. 'But there were the officials, those who imposed the regime.'

There is a short silence while we think of communism, of oppression and the KGB knocking on the door at dawn, of the courage of dissidents like Sakharov and Solzhenitsyn, of poverty and political uniformity, of Trabants and tenement blocks, of the Prague uprising and Russian tanks.

I shake my head. 'It will be about hope not vengeance. It is different.'

'Kurt is right. Soon there will be a new enemy. Yesterday the Soviet regime, tomorrow something else. Freedom is always challenged. A world in which we can go where we like and think what we like and love whom we like is as far away now as when I was a girl scandalising half Paris.'

'We live in a free country for which we should thank God every day and now so will those poor devils on the other side of that bloody wall, or what was the wall. A united Germany!'

I speak confidently enough but I recall so many conversations from my past in other countries. A united Germany, strong, confident, its size once more dominating Europe on the map will not be welcome to everyone. We will have to go on earning trust, living down a brutal reputation, reassuring the rest of the world that we are not as we were.

The generation of Pierre Dessin is passing but hatred can be handed down like an heirloom. What, I wonder, has Annette taught her children? What does she think of Germany and France together dominating the European Union? Do her grandchildren proudly display their German homework?

I look at the crowds and grin. These are not just Germans. People have poured into Berlin, especially the young. An old woman walks timidly along the pavement.

'Are you all right?' I ask.

'I may be,' she replies cryptically and I wait. 'Somewhere here in the East I have a grandson. I should like to trace him before I die.'

'He will trace you,' I assure her, this time very confident.

My mother talks to her for a while and she tells us the tales she has heard of East Germany, tales which will, I know, become familiar over the coming weeks from the sufferers themselves. I glimpse Ernst and wave but he is too busy exuberantly embracing a girl. There is no sign of Willi-Klaus.

'My nephews have disappeared,' I mutter. My cousins' children are not, of course, my nephews but they have called me Uncle Klaus-Pierre all their lives and it is how I think of them. Alessandra's have always called me Monsieur Dessin and I suppose now would call me Herr von Ströbel but I never see them. 'And where is Bette?'

'Oh, my daughter will come when it suits her. Shall we go back?'

We turn again and go back to Kurt. He has wheeled himself away from the window.

'It is quite a moment,' I say. 'How lucky we should be here.'

We are here because we came to the wedding of one of Hedy's sons to a girl from Berlin. Most of our number had gone back before the drama started but another of Hedy's sons had stayed on because he wanted to see more of Berlin and two of Lotte's children joined him, as did my mother's Bette. I had wanted to go back with Arabella but Bette persuaded her mother and Kurt to stay for two more days and I remained too in order to escort them back home to Cloppenburg. My mother hates managing the wheelchair alone, although I think Kurt would quite cheerfully risk travelling solo without either of us.

I am glad now that I did not go back and only wished Arabella and the boys had stayed. It would have been a wonderful memory for them in years to come but it happened so suddenly, so unexpectedly. None of us has seen a liberation before. My mother had kept well out of the way when Europe was celebrating the last one.

'After this, I can believe anything,' says Kurt. 'I think there must be hope even for the Middle East.'

I mention the Ayatollah and the *fatwa* published against Salman Rushdie earlier this year. Perhaps this is the new enemy.

'There is still China,' observes my mother. 'Remember Tiananmen Square.'

And so we look gloomily for strife while the young roar with happiness and the world watches rejoicing.

Arabella rings at six just when we are debating whether to go ahead with arranging supper or whether to wait for the others.

'Jack Marshall rang this afternoon. The baby has arrived and he wants you to be godfather. Jeanne rang yesterday to say her eldest daughter is coming to spend a year in Germany as part of her university course and she wonders if she can come and stay here occasionally. I said of course she could...'

I smile. The young may be making a lot of noise out there but our generation is trying pretty hard too.

The publishers hope that this book has given you enjoyable reading. Large Print Books are especially designed to be as easy to see and hold as possible. If you wish a complete list of our books please ask at your local library or write directly to:

Magna Large Print Books
Magna House, Long Preston,
Skipton, North Yorkshire.
BD23 4ND

This Large Print Book for the partially sighted, who cannot read normal print, is published under the auspices of

THE ULVERSCROFT FOUNDATION